I0557485

PAPERBACK VERSION
ISBN-13: 978-1634430067
ISBN-10: 1634430069
BIASC: FICTION/URBAN

Published by EducatedThugPublications
Cover Art: AMB BRANDING AND DESIGN

TO ORDER ADDITIONAL COPIES OR OTHER WORKER CONTACT
Facebook: King Chuck. Instagram: @kingchuck6925 or @educatedthugpub
www.EducatedThug-Publications.com

Today's emissaries are potentially tomorrows enemies, and if one is to survive, he must be able to run Hot and Cold and be genuine in both! He must be decisive at all times and indifferent when necessary.
Trust No One: Tony Mills

-Introduction-

It's June 10th, 1990. And the heat advisory in Columbus, Ohio had advised the city to stay in doors. Joan Mills took heed to the advisory as she relaxed under the cool air from her newly purchased air conditioner. She layed stretched out on her queen size bed awaiting her favorite soap opera, "The Young and the Restless". She never missed an episode. She could tell you what was going to happen before the scene played out. She mumbled under her breath as her grandsons arguing grew louder than the theme music to her soaps. Then her super woman senses kicked in and she sensed her front door being held open. While the cool air from her air conditioner seeped outside. "I know them hard headed boys aint holding my door open passing air out to the whole dang on neighborhood' She said to herself, before letting her thoughts roar through the house. "Tony! Jimmy!!" Ya'll better stop all that yelling in this house! And shut that door! I aint got no money to be supplying the whole dog on neighborhood with air, don't make me come down there!". Tony, being quick on his toes, ended the dispute with his younger brother by compromise. "Jim, you cant roll wit me this time, but if you be cool, I'm ah bring you a big bag of candy back, iight" Tony said, playing on his younger brothers weakness for sweetness. "Iight man, I want Johnny Apple Seeds, and Lemon Heads, and Now Laters and…" Before Jimmy could go any further. Tony cut him off. "Iight iight I got you lil Bra" He said, before closing his grandmother's door, and sprinting off her porch.

Tony is ten years young, and his baby brother is six. Although Jimmy is four years younger, Tony doesn't mind him tagging along at times, but there was some places

Jimmy just couldn't go, and today he was headed to one of those places. Tony was in a rush to go stand on the block with Buckshot and the rest of the hustlers. Buckshot is like an older brother to Tony and Jimmy. He helped their grandmother take care of them while their Mother and Father were doing stretches behind bars. Tony and Jimmy's Father, "The Notorious Tony Keys" taught Buckshot everything he knew, and together with the boys Mother "Torry Mills" they raised Buckshot from the young age of eight until his late teens. Tony Keys was now serving a Life Sentence in the State Pen. While Torry was serving a 20 year sentence in a Federal Facility. Tony Mills had his father's first name, though he was a spitting image of his mother, and carried her last name. Jimmy on the other hand was a replica of their father, and wore his last mane proudly. Torry's mother loved her grand children. And did here best to raise the boys right. Yet every single mother knows how difficult it can be for a single woman to raise two boys on her own. This fact, along with her low income and ghetto housing made Buckshot's assistance heaven sent.

As Tony walked up Mound Street. He ran into his three closest friends. Fella, Peko, and Shawn Shawn. Shawn Shawn stood on the pegs, as he rode on the back of his brother Peko's bike. "What up Mills" Fella said as he pulled his bike to the curb. Noone called him Tony, everyone called him Mills or T.Money, thanks to Buckshot. "Shit, What up Wit ya'll" Mills said. They all looked at the new bikes before replying "Same ole shit" With a big smile on each of their face. "Where you headed Mills" his chubby friend Fella inquired. "I'm bout to go holler at my big bro" Mills answered, referring to Buckshot. "Man they got Buck hemmed up around the corner" Peko added. "Who got Buck hemmed up" Mills asked curiously. "Five-O" Fella blurted out. Aggressively referring to the Cops. Mills climbed onto the pegs on the back of Fella's bike and said. "Hurry up man lets go". As soon as they reached the scene, Mills hopped off the bike and stared at Buck who sat handcuffed in the back of a Cop car, while his girlfriend Mek was stretched out on the hood of another cruiser being frisked by a female Officer.

The block was packed. Dope fiends, Hustlers, and Noisy bystanders stood around watching the episode, as the Cops searched the grass looking for the package they saw Buck throw. Once Buck and Mills made eye contact. Buck used his head to point to the bag the Cops were looking for. He made plenty of facial gestures, while quietly mouthing the words "get the bag". Mills looked around searching for what ever it was Buck wanted him to see. He spotted the brown paper bag, and glanced up at Buck, then back to the bag, then back to Buck. Buck nodded his head letting Mills know he was on the Right track. His heart beat raced as the Cops moved closer to his package. "I gotta get that bag" Mills said to his friends. "What bag" Fella inquired. "That bag" Mills said while using his own eye's to lead his friends eyes to the brown paper bag. "How you plan on getting that?" Peko asked. "I don't know yet, but I gotta get it, or they gone take my big bro to jail" Mills said. He looked at Buck and the look on Bucks face told Mills how serious the situation was. Buck motioned to the bag with his eyes. Mills looked at the bag one more time before generating a plan. He looked at the football in the yard behind him, and the plan came to life. He grabbed the football and turned to his friends "Look ya'll This is what we gonna do, ya'll throw the football over there in the grass where the police is at, then ya'll run over there, dive on the football as if the police isn't even there, the police will direct their attention on ya'll, and as soon as they do that, I'm grab the bag and get gone" They all gave Mills a look that said His plan sounded stupid. As usual. Fella

voiced his opinion. "Maaannn, that's just stupid, that plan will never work" He said,

"stop trippin Fells, Is you wit me or what" Mills asked seriously "I'm always wit you bro,

but your plan still sounds stupid" Fella replied. Mills just shook his head, as if to say

"Whatever" and shoved the ball into Fella's hands. "Lets do this man" Mills said before

taking off across the street. Fella slung the ball over the cars and it landed in the field

where the officers did their search. Fella dove on the ball, Peko dove on him , and Shawn

Shawn dove on Peko. The Cops instantly became furious, as the kids rolled around in the

grass, laughing and playing as if the Cops didn't exist. "Hey! Hey! Hey! Don't you see a

search going on over here? Get The Hell Out Of The Grass!!" the officers yelled. While

he and his two partners focused on the playing children, Mills swooped in. He grabbed

the bag stuffed it under his shirt, and quickly walked off. The Cops were only distracted

for a split second, but that was all Mills needed. Once he bent the corner, he ran full

speed all the way home. Buck rocked back and forth in the back of the cruiser while

laughing. "That's my lil Nigga" he said to himself. Everyone out that day peeped the

move. They acknowledged Mills courage and loyalty to Buckshot and knew the

youngster would one day be a force to be reckoned with. The only ones who missed his

demonstration were the distracted Cops. The young Hustler's dapped it up with each

other while laughing at the Cops stupidity. While the Dope Fiends, and on lookers stood

in awe, fascinated by the youngsters trick. Little did they know, the youngster had a lot

more tricks in his playbook.

Torry Mills, born 1960, was the second youngest child in her home. She was accompanied by four siblings. 2 older brothers, 1 older sister, and a brother just a year beneath her. They were all raised in one of the toughest neighborhoods Columbus, Ohio had to offer. East Main Street. The mother of prostitution, drugs, and violence. At the age of 15, Torry was not only one of the most beautiful females to walk the mean streets of East Main, she was also one of the toughest. The Mills were a highly respected family throughout the Ghetto's of Columbus, Ohio. Especially the Ghetto's of East Main. If it wasn't for Tony Keys, Torry's older brothers Lonny and Donny would have the neighborhood on lockdown. Tony Keys was a smooth, but ruthless young Hustler. His hustle varied from Robberies, B-N-E's, carjacking, selling Erb, to gambling. As treacherous as he was with his pistol. He was just as frightening with his hands. Tony Keys not only believed he was the roughest, toughest, and most dangerous man to walk the Earth, he also believed he was GOD's gift to women. He often said, "There was not a lame he couldn't game, A Gang he couldn't Maime, nor a Dame he couldn't train. Like Muhammad Ali, He was A baaaddd Man. Luckily for Torry's brothers, they were down with Tony Keys, so they never had to feel his wrath. Keys hung out on East Main, but he lived on Long Street, which was also one of the reputable Ghetto's on Columbus East side. Truthfully, Keys hung out where ever he pleased, and no one questioned his position. It was known everywhere, Tony Keys is a Certified Gangster! Keys life differed from the rest of his family. His mother, father, and siblings were all devout Christians. How Keys turned out so evil, no one knew, but ever since the age of ten, the streets have been his home.

It's the middle of the summer in 1975, and Keys, along with Lonny, Donny and a few more of his soldiers are posted in front of Main Street Market, discussing a robbery Keys had planned for later that night . as Keys explained the layout of the lick to his crew. He noticed a couple of females gravitating towards them. "Who is this fine thang strutting our way? Damn, she's a sight for sore eyes" Keys said smoothly. Heads rolled as the rest of the crew turned to get a look at the Hotties. Lonny and Donny's jaws tightened when they saw who the showstoppers were. "Torry get yo fast ass off the strip!!" Lonny ordered like the protective older brother he was. "I'm just going to the store, Dang!" Torry snapped while rolling her eyes. "Why you have to come all the way to this store wit yo fast ass" Donny added. "First of all, your only a year older than me, so you cant tell me nothing, cause you aint grown neither" Torry replied with sass. "Well I am, Now get in the store and get what you came to get, and get off the strip" Lonny ordered, throwing his Eighteen years of Age and Man of the House rank around. Lonny looked at his other sister who accompanied Torry. Although she was only a year younger than him, he scolded her as well. "Terry yo ass know better than to have Torry on the strip. Don't make coming to this store a habit", "okay Big Brother you don't have to yell" Terry said while rolling her eyes, as she and Torry walked through the crowd of young men. Keys sized Torry up. Then lustfully stared into her eyes. Keys was smooth, and although he didn't say anything. Torry heard him loud and clear. She and Terry nudged one another with their elbows, as Keys admired Torry's beauty. Once they were out of the guys sight, they burst into laughter. "Got Damn Lon! How old is ya lil sister?" Keys asked while rubbing his hands together. "Fifteen, and way to young for you" Lonny replied firmly. "Whoa! Tone it down a little Main Man, I don't mean no disrespect, but

I'm only seventeen, so technically she's not to young for me" Keys shot back, now feeling a little offended. "C'mon Keys, lets drop this subject, your way to fast for my little sister, she aint giving up no skins, and she's off limits to brothers of our kind, bottom line, ya dig?" Lonny knew Keys was becoming angry by the way he screwed up his face, but he'd swim in those waters for his baby sister. "I'm offended, I mean I'm truly offended by the way you view me as some pussy hungry heathen. I thought we was pals" Keys replied with a smirk on his face. He'd back off right now, because he didn't want Lonny's mind on anything but the lick he had setup for tonight. But Torry would be his and he didn't care how Lonny felt about it.

A few days later his opportunity presented itself. While hanging out on the corner with a few Pimps and small time hustlers, He spotted Torry walking up Mound Street with her sister and younger brother Mike. Mike looked up to Keys, and Keys used that idolization to his advantage. "AYE! Money Mike" Keys yelled from a distance. Instantly Mike knew who it was that was calling for him. Keys was the only person that called him Money Mike. In fact, it was Keys that gave him the name. Mike left his sisters standing a few yards away. While he jogged over to the stoop Keys sat on. After tilting his bottle of Old English in the air, taking a few puffs from his cigarette, and flicking it to the ground, he greeted Mike with some dap. "Whats happenin main man, Whats new and exciting" Keys said. Mike smiled from ear to ear. "Not a whole lot whats up with you Keys?". Nobody called him Tony except for his mother. He didn't even allow his father to call him Tony. Not that he didn't respect his father, because he respected both of his parents. He just didn't like being referred to by what he labeled a Womans Handle. He was named after his mother, so that was something special that only they shared. "Whats your sister's name" Keys asked. "which one" Mike inquired. Keys pointed at Torry. " Her right there" "Oh, That's Torry" Mike said un enthusiastically. "Tell her I would like to take her out sometime" Keys said more demandingly, than asking a favor. "You can tell her yourself man" Mike said before yelling Torry's name. And waving her over to where he and Keys stood. Torry and Terry mumbled words to one another as they sashayed over. "I told you Keys like you girl" Terry, I aint playing with you" Torry whispered as they got closer. "Tee, this is Keys, Keys this is my sister Torry" Mike said. "How you doin beautiful" Keys greeted. "I'm Fine" Torry replied, shyly standing in front of him. Keys smiled before turning up his charm. "Any man wit eyes can see that, tell me something I don't know". "Huh" Torry replied with a confused look on her face. "I asked, How are you doing? And you said you were fine, any man with eyes can see how fine you are, so I asked you to tell me something I don't know" Keys explained. Torry smiled after catching on to his compliment. "Your name is Tony Keys, right?" Torry asked, "the one and only, but my friends just call me Keys" He said proudly. "Well I guess that means I'll be calling you Tony, since I don't know if were friends or not yet" Torry said with sass. Keys chuckled, her sassiness turned him on. "Well actually I was hoping we could be more than friends" He said while staring her down with sincere eyes.

Keys knew he had her where he wanted her. The look in her eyes, along with the shifting of her weight from one foot to the other told him he had her hot. "Tony don't you have enough "GIRL" friends already?" Torry emphasized the word girl. Keys laughed. The fact that she insisted on calling him Tony kind of tickled him. Usually being called Tony would have offended him, and probably got the person calling him that a beat-down, but for some reason, Torry's use of the name amused him. "Actually I don't have any "GIRL" friends, I have a few female associates, but I've yet to meet one special enough to label my lady, until today that is, or at least that is what I'm hoping. I wanna spend some time with you, getting to know you, becoming your friend, while giving our friendship a chance to grow into something more. How about we start off with a phone number?" Keys said. He liked a woman with a little defiance. It gave him a chance to showcase his manhood, while earning the respect he desired and demanded. He loved to bedazzle women with his slick talk. He felt that in the streets, you either peeped game, or you got gamed, because the game was either in you, or on you. Torry gave in to Keys allure. But walked off feeling proud of herself for handling the infamous lady killer as well as she did. Keys didn't waste anytime using her phone number. He gave her a call that same night, offering to take her out to lunch the following day, but to his surprise, she declined. She learned that making men wait for things like dates, alone time, and first kisses is a for sure way to find out if a man is really in to her, or just trying to get into her pants. She made Keys wait a full three weeks before going out on a date with him. Keys didn't mind the waiting game. He enjoyed chasing her. He called her every night, talking to her about things like her favorite color, food, type of music, and etcetera. Game recognized game on Keys behalf, so he used this time to gain her trust.

By the time school was back in session, Keys had won Torry over. They were officially an item, and Keys didn't care who disliked it. Lonny and Donny separated themselves from Keys after a heated argument over his involvement with their sister. Weapons were drawn behind the confrontation, but Keys knew that if he hurt Torry's brothers he could kiss their relationship good-bye, so he controlled his temper as best as he could. Had it been anyone else, Keys would of left them in a puddle of blood. Lonny tried preventing Torry from seeing Keys, but her feelings for him were uncontrollable. Keys had robbed her of her young heart, mind, and soul. The only thing she was yet to give him was her virginity. Not only did Keys now have a woman he adored, but he also had money coming in, in abundance, and that had him feeling larger than life.

Some guys from New York City migrated to Columbus with hopes of finding a gold mine, quickly setting their sights on Main Street's mean strip. Once Keys got wind of the out of towners making major dough on his strip he muscled his way in on their heroine and cocaine operation. Power and Respect already had Keys with an "I don't give a Fuck Attitude", add money and a Bad Bitch to that equation, and you could easily understand why Keys was living on Cloud Nine.

Keys pulled his Impalla to the curb in front of Torry's High School and killed the music so he could finish schooling his young Homie Buckshot to the ways of the world in which they both lived. Buckshot was only 8 years young, and Keys was more of a father figure to the youngster than a Big Homie. On the strip, Buckshot was known as a "Runner": meaning he got paid by the Pimps, Hookers and Hustlers to make runs to the store and local Church's Chicken in the hood. After continuously running into the manchild on the strip. Keys became fond of the youngster. He began spending time with the youngster, putting him up on game, taking him out to eat, and making sure he got home safely. Buckshot, like a stray dog when it gets fed, always found his way back to his feeder. As Keys started recognizing more and more of himself in the youngster, he started spending more and more time with him. Buckshot is a survivor, and as dangerous as the strip is. It was the place he was most comfortable, just like Key's was at his age. Keys gave him the name Buckshot, because he one day led Keys into an alley, where he retrieved a shotgun loaded with Buckshots from the side of a dumpster. He asked Keys to hold the shotgun for him because he might need it for the Pimp who beat on his prostituting mother in front of him. Keys took the shotgun and stored it at the house with the rest of his arsenal. Then he tracked down the Pimp and beat him mercilessly. From that day on, Keys called the youngster Buckshot Shorty. That was also the day Keys took Buckshot in. he cared for him like a son, but tutored him in the game like a younger brother or star pupil.

Keys cut his lesson short as Torry approached the car. He hopped out so he could open the door for her. Buckshot already knew the deal, so he climbed over the front seat landing in the back of the ride, as the couple locked lips. "How yo day been baby?" Keys asked. "Okay I guess, considering I've been getting dirty looks from yo hoochies all day" Torry answered with a hint of an attitude. Keys didn't respond. He guided her into the front seat, safely shut the door behind her, and made his way around the car to the driver seat. Once inside the car, he braced himself for what he knew was coming. "Tony! Don't act like you aint hearing me!" Torry said with mad attitude. "I hear you, and I heard you baby, but I don't care nothing about no looks you been getting from some silly ass dames, and you shouldn't either, because everybody know who Tony Keys belong too, I love you, I'm your man, so fuck them silly ass broads, IIGHT!" and I don't wanna discuss this no more with Buckshot in the car. He already hears enough arguing from his momma and all the chumps she brings home!". "What ever Tony" Torry said, then turned her attention on Buckshot. "Hi Buckshot" She said. "Sup" He responded with a slight nod of the head. Torry knew Keys was having sex with other women, because he was'nt the type of man to be sexless for months. She was'nt stupid and Keys knew it. But he took such good care of her that she let a lot of things slide. He took such good care of her that her mother no longer had too. He was truly in love with Torry, and he had no problem waiting until she was ready to have sex, but that didn't mean he wouldn't have sex with other girls while he waited. Truthfully, Keys knew that he'd have sex with more than one woman, even if he and Torry were having sex. This was a part of him that would never change. But he loved Torry to much to admit it to her. So he made sure that all his affairs were kept on the down low, and that every woman he slept with knew that he had a woman, and that he was'nt leaving her for anyone nor anything.

One day while in school, one of Keys flings couldn't take seeing Torry floss Keys jewelry, or sporting all the latest designer gear any longer. She felt that because she was having sex with Keys, she should be the one receiving gifts. Maria was a couple years older than Torry. She was the "It" Junior. While Torry was the smoking hot freshman that was stealing her shine. Maria was also the head of a popular female gang called M.S.Q. ("Main Street Queens"). They didn't just shake up things at school, they shook grounds around the neighborhood, and at every teen club as well. Maria was a pretty girl of Spanish decent, but after a few fights around the neighborhood she quickly became known as a female scrapper. Although Maria was a scrapper, she had sadly mistaken Torry's humble demeanor, and pretty face for weakness. She approached Torry in the hallway, as Torry carried a conversation filled with laughter with her older sister. She tapped Torry on the shoulder as the rest of the Queens formed a circle around Torry and her sister. When Torry turned to face Maria, Maria didn't waste any time with small talk. "I advise you to leave Keys alone bitch! Before I _ _ _" she never had a chance to finish her threat. Torry dropped her books, and sprang into action. Her punches landed with accuracy, dropping Maria to the floor. She straddled Maria like a horse and dropped bombs on her face. "Bitch! Don't you ever call me out my name and don't you ever approach me about my man, Bitch! Bitch! Bitch!" She yelled out with each blow that landed. As the Queens moved in to assist their leader, Mike and Donny burst through the crowd that had emerged. "I wish one of you sluts would try to jump my sister!" Donny said with authority. Terry, not being a fighter was elated to see her brothers' show up. She began to cheer her little sister on "Get that bitch Tee" she screamed while pounding her fist into her own hand. Torry was suspended from school for fighting, and from that day on she stayed in a scuffle or verbal battle with one of Keys flings.

Now rolling with Keys as he made a few pick-ups and drop-offs, Torry sat quietly while Keys schooled her to the game, and what a Hustler expected out of his wife. School was always in session when her and Keys were alone. He wanted the two of them to be on the same page at all times. He felt he had finally found his queen, and he wanted their bond and love to be as strong as an impenetrable force field.

The Couple was now on their way to see one of Keys most unreliable workers. Keys hated dealing with Pete because Pete always had a story to tell about why his money was short, or why he needed more time to get rid of his package. Keys only dealt with Pete on the strength that he was one of his oldest partners. But Keys didn't believe in friendships when it came to doing business. So Pete was on his last leg. Keys didn't care how long they had known each other. He warned Pete that if he played with his money again he would kill him, and he meant every word of it. "Tee I always want you to remember this, and I'm telling you this because I know how important family is to you. Everybody that shares the same blood as you is not your family, they're your relatives, meaning that ya'll are related by blood. Although these are the closest relatives you have, that doesn't make them your family. Your family are those who share a special bond with you. Those you can always depend on, those that are loyal to you and always have your best interest in mind. Never mistake a Relative for Family, especially when doing business, because they'll be the first ones to fuck you simply because they believe that their punishment wont be severe. And never let a mutha fucka play you like you aint hip to game, cause "the game" is either in you, or on you, there is no in-between, you hear me?" Keys said while giving Torry a stern look. Torry just nodded her head. She didn't have to answer for Keys to know she was listening, and that she understood him.

Keys pulled his car to the curb and told Torry to sit still while he talked to Pete. As soon as he exited the car, he was approached by his loyal comrade Sonny. Sonny was a thorough-breed gangsta, and flat footed hustler. Everyone respected Sonny and a lot of people feared him as well. Keys and Sonny did a lot of business together. Everything from robberies to laying down their murder game. Keys liked Sonny, he also respected him because even though he had status, he understood his position when in the room with Keys. Keys was Top Dog and everyone knew better than to question his rank.. "Kiila Keys, what's happenin Jack" Sonny asked while extending his hand for some dap. "Not a whole lot Main Man, I just came through to holler at this sucka Pete" Keys answered as he slapped Sonny five. "You need ol'Sonny's assistance" Sonny asked while flashing his pistol. "Nah I can handle this sucka, just keep an eye on my lady for me" Keys said before taking off across the street. Pete was in front of his drug house entertaining an audience, while nodding off and leaning to his right side like his body was equipped with a kick stand. "Petey wee stro tell me something good Main Man

" Keys said while wrapping an arm around Petes shoulder. "Aw man I'm just punching that clock, working overtime ya dig" Pete responded "Like a shovel" Keys said. "Since you been working overtime and all that I know you got some paper to lay on me right?" Keys continued. Instantly Pete began to stutter. "Uh, oh, oh, well, well, see, see its been kind of slow Keys, but give me a couple days and I'll be ready for you" Keys upper lip began to twitch from anger. "Petey don't play with me man, I gave you that package a week ago, that's more then enough time to turn a play or two. Now if you don't come out yo nasty ass pockets with my money, I'm ah do you real dirty man". Keys pulled a .38, Revolver from his waist causing Petey's stuttering to worsen. "Ke, Ke, Ke, Keys man, I, I, I, I swear man. . . . "."Save that swearing for the chapel, you no good sucka. Didn't I tell you if you played with my money again, I'd kill you?!" Torry watched as Keys pointed at Pete with his gun. She had only heard of the crazy things Keys did in the streets, but she was now about to see him live and in action. She almost jumped out of her skin when Keys smacked Pete on top of his head with the pistol. While simultaneously squeezing off a shot. She thought Pete was dead when his body hit the ground. Keys had only smacked Pete, but blood leaked from his skull like he'd been shot. As Keys stood over top of Pete with his pistol aimed, Pete's audience begged and pleaded with Keys, trying to stop what they knew was about to happen. "Do any of you mutha fuckas wanna take his place?" Keys yelled with fury. The crowd went silent as Keys waved his pistol. "Iight then, don't put cha'self in my mutha fuckin business!" when Keys swung the pistol back on Pete, Pete balled up and covered his head from the blow he thought was coming. Instead, Keys squeezed off two shots, hitting Pete twice in the chest. As Pete lay in a puddle of blood, Keys made his last announcement. "If I hear a peep out of any of you mutha fuckas, I'll be back for you wit magician speed and magical quickness. You got it!"

Torry was in shock. She couldn't believe her eyes, Keys had just shot a man in broad day light, and returned to the car with a calmness as if nothing had happened. The ride home was in complete silence. Not a word was spoken until Keys pulled up in front of Torry's mothers house and said "Tee, you aint seen nothing and don't know nothing". "I know Tony" she replied. "Okay, I love you baby, and I'll be here in the morning to take you to school" "I love you too Tony and be careful okay". "Alright baby, take this bag and put it up for me until the morning". He handed her a bag filled with the money he'd collected, and the drugs he had left after his drop-offs. They kissed and Torry hurried in the house. Little did Keys know, he wouldn't be picking Torry up the next morning nor any other morning for a long time.

Later that night while hanging out on the corner of Main and Berkley, Keys got ambushed by the Cops. Pete had lived and just like a lowdown rat, he squealed. After six months of fighting for his life, Keys was lucky enough to only get three years. Since he was not yet 18 years of age. He couldn't be tried as an adult, so he was shipped to a Juvenile Facility to serve his time.

Torry's life flashed before her eyes when she heard of Keys arrest. She felt like she was dying. She had no idea how she would make it without Keys, being that she had become so dependent on him. Not only financially, but mentally and emotionally as well. Her heart felt like it had been ripped out of her chest. She continuously had to remind herself of Keys words, " A woman who cant take care of herself and her family in her mans absence is nothing more than a child playing grown up games. She is more a daughter to her man than a partner. No strong man wants a weak woman". Keys schooled her to so many things that it was difficult for her to remember them all, but now that Keys was gone, all his lessons were coming back to her like she were a musician and they were old songs she had wrote. She could hear him as if he was sitting next to her. "Tee, never become so dependent on me or anyone else that you forget how to take care of ya'self. You don't need a man for anything, you have all the tools you need to be successful on your own. And know that things like this, I have never told another woman because with juice like this. The average female may walk out of her mans life and possibly take everything he's taught her and use it against him. I share all my knowledge with you because I view you as my equal, and I want us to be equally strong and I trust you. Our love and loyalty to one another is enough to know that you will never betray me or abandoned me".

Keys words empowered Torry. She knew that she had to stay strong for her and Keys both. His first few months were stressful, because he had no phone privileges and Torry was to young to visit him on her own, but they literally wrote letters to one another everyday. A couple weeks before receiving his phone privileges. He sent Torry a letter telling her that he'd be calling. He gave her the exact date and time. And stressed how important it was for her to be home. When the day came, Torry sat by the phone impatiently awaiting his call. After snatching the phone up on the first ring for what seemed to be at least the hundredth call. She dosed off angry that none of them were Keys.

Twenty minutes into her nap. She was awakened by her mother's voice. "Torry!! Torry!!" Her mother yelled from upstairs. Torry jumped up in a hurry. "Maam" She yelled back. "Pick up the phone child, it's Tony" Her mother yelled. Torry snatched the phone off the hook with the speed of a cheetah. "I love you Tony and I miss you so much" She yelled into the receiver. "I love and miss you too" Keys replied just as quickly. "Oh hush, the two of you don't even know what love is" Her mother kidded. Keys started laughing, and then thanked her for accepting his call. "Don't worry about it baby, you just be strong in there, and hurry up home so you can get this girl before she drives me crazy." "Alright Ms. Mills, and thanks again. "Keys responded before she hung the phone up, giving the two love birds some privacy. "What's happenin baby? You get my letter?" Keys asked. "Yeah I got it." Torry answered. "So you understand what you gotta do right?" "Yes Tony." Keys laughed, after all this time, being called Tony by her still amused him. "Iight then, I am having some people get wit you for a minute, just to show you the ropes." "I don't need nobody to show me the ropes, you showed me all I need to know Tony, and a lot of your people been hollering at me in the streets already." Torry replied with sassiness. "Okay baby, then its all on you, let's make it do what it do, but this is not a game to be played lightly, you remember everything I told you and showed you right?" "Yes Tony, just chill out, yo wife got this, you worry about what you gotta do in there, and let me worry about business out here, I got this." "Iight baby, but be careful." They used the rest of their phone call to talk about how much they missed one another while trading I love you's through out the conversation. When the call ended, Torry wanted to cry, but she held back her tears for Keys sake. They had become so close, that even though Keys wasn't there, she knew he could see, and she wanted him to see his woman being strong. The next day Torry's life as a drug dealer began. She hooked up with a lot of Keys people, and bought in a few of her own. She quickly became good at it. After two months of hustling, she dropped out of school and became a full fledged hustler. With Keys in jail, Buckshot was back roaming the streets. His hustle had changed as well. Usually he would make his money shooting dice, and making store runs, but now he started selling bundles of heroine for a small time pimp. Once Torry got wind of it, she quickly put a stop to his dealings with the pimp. She knew Keys wouldn't approve of it, and he purposely kept Buckshot from selling drugs. He didn't feel Buckshot was ready, and neither did Torry. She looked at Buckshot as a younger brother, and often let him sleep at her mother's house with her. Ms. Mills quickly took a liking to the little man child, and welcomed him into her home with open arms. Buckshot still kept an eye on his mother, although their relationship was non existent. Keys taught him that no matter how much wrong his mother did, she would always be his mother, and for that reason alone, she deserved his respect. He also taught him that drugs and the streets had the power to rape a person of their morals, principles, and self-respect, so he excused his mothers neglect and lack of parenting. Even at such a young age he understood that his mother had been raped by the street life, and the ever-so powerful drug, known as heroine. By the time Keys came home, Torry had mastered her craft. She was all business. Being that she was easier to deal with then Keys, she widened their clientele. She had bust the game wide open for the two of them. She also had young Buckshot ready for the finishing touches that only Keys could give him. Keys came home in the summer of 78'. Torry threw him a home coming party in which he was greeted by all the Hustlers, Pimps, Prostitutes and Junkies. Keys was the man of the night, and his time in jail only made him more confident. The females lusted after his toned frame, pretty eyes, and bright white smile. As he walked throughout the party with his chest out, like a true king of the jungle. Torry and young Buckshot stuck by his side as he mingled with all the play turners and money earners. Keys enjoyed the sight of Torry moving throughout the party with such confidence. He could feel the respect his baby had earned in his absence. She was a qualified woman, and the missing piece to his puzzle. She complemented his lifestyle perfectly, and after he took care of Pete, they'd locked the game down.

That night Torry gave Keys her virginity, causing them to fall deeper in love. The next day Keys hit the streets bright and early. He had learned some new tricks while in jail, and he was ready to put them into play. In no time, he and Torry were closing in on the game, locking down the East Side, and parts of the South and North. Keys felt untouchable. His word was law. And all those who opposed were shot, pistol whipped and/or thoroughly beat down. Six months after the day Keys was released from juvy, Pete's body was found in an alley with a hole in his head. No one actually seen Keys pull the trigger, but everyone knew who was responsible…

Torry often tried to slow Keys down. Warning him of the heat from the cops, and Keys would just as often assure Torry that he was the Judge and Jury and what he was doing "was serving justice".

Keys started this morning the same as every other morning. He checked on his drug houses and monitored his street workers. Keys called it "Checking traps and taken no naps". Whatever it was called, it was done robotically every morning. Buckshot rode shotgun as he almost always did. And like any other time, school was in session. "What's the number one Rule Buck?" Keys asked sternly. "Never get high off ya own supply" Buckshot answered. "That's right, aint nothing more backwards than a hustler using his own product, where's the money in that?" Keys said. He paused for a few seconds, allowing his young protégé to take a moment to rotate with the knowledge before throwing another question at him. "Who can you trust?" Keys asked. "No one, its hard enough trusting ya'self to always do the right thang, but its iight to have a little faith in people, because no one can accomplish great things alone". Bucks answers rolled off the tip of his tongue. He didn't have to search his memory bank for the answers, because Keys force fed him the game on a daily basis. Keys shook his head in approval. He was pleased with his young soldier. "What's Rule number two?" Keys asked when he noticed Buck relaxing. "You either peep game or get gamed. Never let any one play you like a sucka, or like you aint hip to game. Never ask for respect. Demand it. And take it if necessary". Buck said confidently. Keys was now satisfied with Buck's knowledge. His young Gee was ready to show and prove. So it was now time for Keys to take the training wheels off.

Keys pulled up to one of his stash houses, and told Buck to follow him inside. He fed Buck a few more grapes, then threw a package on his lap and turned his back on him. Usually turning your back on someone would be a form of disrespect, but in this case it was a form of honoring. Keys turned his back on Buck to let him know that there was nothing more to be said. Buck was no longer a pup, he was now a big dogg.

In 1980, Keys and Torry had their first child. Of course Keys wanted him to be a junior, but like Keys own mother, Torry wanted to be as much apart of her sons name as her childs father was. They came to a compromise and named their son Tony Mills. Giving him his father's first name and his mother's last name. Young Tony was a spitting image of his mother with a few of his fathers' features. Such as his brown eyes and curly hair. With a new born baby, Torry fell back from her hustling. She only dealt with a few of their best customers. Keys on the other hand, dug deeper into the game. While his hunger for more money and power grew, his violent streak and sloppy unfaithfulness grew as well.

Torry had grown tired of his cheating, but she love and respected him to much to ever betray him. She knew he loved her unconditionally, but for some reason, one woman just wouldn't suffice for Tony Keys. Arguments over his unfaithfulness became the norm.

As the drug cocaine became more reputable, Keys joined the trend and started sniffing blow. He broke Rule number one. Not only did he get high off his own supply. He became addicted to it. The drug only enhanced his temper, yet and still he never laid a hand on Torry during any of their heated arguments. Not even when she attacked him.

As the 80's moved on, Keys body count grew. He had the streets so terrified that no one would tell on him. Snitching went against the code of the streets. Snitches got ditches and fakes got found in lakes.

In 83' Torry became pregnant again with Keys second child. One would think that a 3 year old son and a pregnant wife would slow a man down, but not Killa Keys. He only knew one speed and that was maximum.

Keys now hung out in the parking lot of a local spot called Joe's Hoes. He leant up against his Cocaine White 1980 Cadillac Coop. with a female under each arm and another one standing between his legs. Young Buckshot sat on the hood while serving a few addicts, as Keys styled and profiled, Keys was higher than Rick James and twice as fly. The female standing between his legs whispered something in his ear as Torry pulled into the lot. It was as if she appeared out of thin air as she jumped out her car and sprung into action. Stomach protruding and all, she grabbed a handful of hair, snatched the girl to the ground, and went to work on her face. Keys was stoned out of his mind. He just stood there watching as Torry beat the blood out of the hookers' mouth. The two ladies under Keys arms went to grab Torry off of their friend, and both received back handed slaps. Keys stared down on them as they hugged the pavement. "If I don't put my hands on her, what makes you think you got the right to put your nasty ass hands on her" He said with tightened jaws and a curled upper lip. At that moment an up and coming pimp Slash Gangster strolled over to Keys. "Slow ya roll cat daddy, don't nobody put they paws on my broads but me, Now check ya'self nigga". Candyman said with authority. He was well aware of who Keys was, but his up and coming status had gone to his head. Candyman was a large man, standing at 6'2, two hundred plus pounds. He looked down on Keys 5'8 ½ inch frame. Keys didn't waste any time chopping the man down to his size. He pulled his .357 Magnum from his waist and hit Candyman with all six shots. Candyman's body slumped to the pavement. Torry stopped her punch in mid-air, jumped to her feet and tried to pull Keys in the car. Keys stood with his gun in his hand while talking to a dead man. "I'm Tony Keys sucka, and I touch whoever I please. This is my strip and don't none of you mutha fucka's forget that!". Keys screamed at Candyman's corpse. And everyone else that was in hearing range. Young Buckshot stood by his side with his .38' special drawn. Torry yanked on Keys coat as the sounds of sirens got closer. "C'mon Tony, don't you hear the Fuckin Cops?" she yelled. Torry snatched the gun from his hand, gave it to Buckshot and told him to disappear. Buckshot got ghost immediately.

Keys on the other hand, was running out of time. Just as Torry had him in his Cadillac and was ready to peel away from the scene. The cops closed in on them.

Torry gave birth to their second son while Keys stood trial, eventually being sentenced to life in prison with no chance of parole. With Keys in prison, Torry was in control of their drug empire.

She knew she could never love again. To love another man would be a betrayal, and she meant it when she made the promise to never betray Keys. Even in his absence she'd keep her promise. No man would ever be able to have her heart, because it forever belonged to Tony Keys.

Torry formed a small army with her brothers and a few of Keys' soldiers. Although the majority of her circle was family or friends of the family. She knew that money had the tendency to turn a straight person crooked, which is why Buckshot was the only person she trusted.

After two years of being alone, Torry finally allowed a man's charm to entice her. Most men who stepped to her seemed simple. They were no match for her, but when comparing another man to Tony Keys, they all seemed simple. Not to mention small time. D-Man, which was short for Dopeman, was another story altogether. He was smooth, tall, dark, and handsome. He was also earning top dawg rank on the strip. D-Man was from Alabama. He had come to Columbus a year before Tony Keys run-in with Candyman. He laid low on the strip, doing a little small time pimping and hustling. With Tony Keys being the top dog, and Candyman on the rise he knew his time to shine was far off, but he remained patient while positioning himself. Lucky for him, Tony Keys and

Candyman were taken out at the same time. He studied Torry for a year before he mustered up enough courage to approach her. He knew his money had to be right, his game had to be tight, and his name had to hold weight. So he stayed patient, while watching her turn down one sucker after another. When he became comfortable with his all around status, he stepped to the infamous Torry Mills. After a few months of work, Torry gave in to his southern hospitality. D-Man was no Tony Keys by far, but he put it down with his own style. After being with D-Man for six months, Torry moved out of her mother's house and bought a home with D-Man. Like her mother, she refused to move out of the hood that raised her. So they moved a couple streets over from her mother. D-Man was nice to her children and besides putting his hands on Torry he treated her like a queen. D-Man's status was going to his head and he started to catch the Tony Keys syndrome. He was applying pressure to all in opposition. He became more violent by the day, and his once low key position became overly prominent. The Feds caught on to D-Man's status, and infiltrated their way into his organization. Although he and Torry's business was kept separate, he brought the heat to Torry and her team as well. One day while Torry was out of town on business, the Feds raided her and D-Man's home. Fortunate for Torry she had left her boys with her mother. The Feds found guns and drug related utensils. The next day Torry's hotel room was raided by the Feds as well. She was caught dirty, along with her brothers who accompanied her. Warrants were issued for many of her workers as well. The Feds came to Torry first with a snitch deal. She refused to talk just as Keys had taught her. D-Man on the other hand, cooperated with the government. He told on Torry and her workers. In turn, some of Torry's workers leaked information on her as well. When the Feds came to Torry with another snitch plea, she still refused to talk. She was taught the code of silence. And that is what she lived by. Unlike a lot of weak-minded individuals, Torry was prepared for both sides of her lifestyle. Tony warned her of the dark side of the game, and prepared her for it. Both mentally and emotionally. While a lot of people refuse to believe that the game has a flip side. Torry was a true player of the game and she accepted the cards she was dealt. Even when threaten with losing her kids, she stood firm. D-Man was a rat, a coward, and a man with a pink heart. The part that hurt Torry the most was that she didn't see through his hard exterior and recognize him for the charming yet weak brotha that he was. Torry was sentenced to 20 years in the Feds, while D-Man received 10 years on a snitches plea. Just about Torry's whole team went down. Her brothers and sister were even dragged into the raid. While her brothers were locked-up, they were also hit with some old murder raps. Buckshot was the only one from Torry's crew to escape the raid unscathed. While Torry and Tony served their time, their sons were in Ms. Mills's custody. The Boys would be raised right on the same streets as their father and mother, where they could possibly one day be sucked in by the same strip. Bang Bang East Main, The strip where everything is fair game. Where the weak are ate alive, and only the strong survive!!

-CHAPTER ONE-

As Mills ran into the house, he was met by his younger brother. "Where my candy at Mills?" Jimmy asked looking at the brown bag that protruded from his waist. "Not right now Jim." Mills answered as he dashed up the stairs to his bedroom, quickly closing the door. As jimmy pouted downstairs, Mills explored inside the bag. He removed sandwich baggies filled with rocks the size of his fist. He knew what dime and twenty rocks looked like, but these rocks were huge. Thoughts of how much money they were worth ran through his mind, as his grandmother screamed his name from the kitchen. "TONY! TONY! Boy don't make me come up there." "Ma'am" Mills yelled back while trying to find a hiding place for the bag. He hid the bag in one of his winter coats hanging in his closet, and then ran down the steps at full speed. "Grandma I said Ma'am" Mills said as he entered the kitchen. "Boy did you tell your little brother you was gone bring him some candy back?" She asked while stirring her mashed potatoes. "Yes ma'am, but I didn't…" she cut Mills off " No you don't, don't stand here with no excuses, we don't lie to each other in this house, you told Jimmy you was gone buy him some candy. Now you take him to the store and do just that." She ordered. Mills looked up at his brother and said, "C'mon cry baby. What I tell you about telling on people?" "I aint no cry baby, and I aint no tattle teller." Jimmy said looking mad that his idol had called him that. Jimmy lived to impress his brother. He wanted to be just like Mills. As they walked out the front door, their grandmother yelled after them, "Tony, don't let that boy eat all that candy at once. Dinner will be done after a while." "Iight Momma" Mills replied. He looked over his baby brother's wardrobe before they stepped off the porch. "Tie ya shoes up Jim." He said after fixing his shirt. When Jimmy was finished tying his shoes Mills said, "Look Jim, we brothers and brothers don't lie to each other, besides grandma and Buck, we all we got. I love you more than life, so don't ever think I'm lying to you. I aint never told you a lie, have I?" "No." Jim replied "and I aint gone start now. Now let's go get you some candy big head, and stop tattle telling. "Mills said teasing his little brother. "I aint no tattle tale man, I'm a Gee." Jimmy replied. "Iight then start acting like it." Mills said while laughing at his little brothers reply.

On the way back from the store, Mills ran into Fella, Peko, and Shawn Shawn again. "What up Mills, how much shit was in that bag bro?" Fella asked. Mills gave Fella a funny look before replying. "Man, don't you see my little brother right here?" "Aw shit, my bad" Fella said. Then put his hand over his mouth. Realizing he said the wrong thing again. Mills, Fella, Peko and Shawn Shawn all grew up together, but Mills and Fella were always the tightest. "What up J-Pimp" Fella said, Acknowledging Jimmy by the name they had given him because he attracted all the girleys for them when ever Mills allowed him to tag along. "Aye Mills you know the police took Buck to jail anyway?" Peko blurted out. "Word" Mills replied. "Word" Peko shot back. "Oh yeah, Mek said for you to come see her immediately." Fella added "Alright man, I'm ah catch up wit ya'll later" Mills said as he hurried home to drop his little brother off. Once in front of the house, Jimmy started whining about why he couldn't roll with his big brother. Their debate was quickly put to an end when grandma Mills appeared in the doorway. "Jimmy come in the house boy. You bout to eat dinner. Go wash yo hands, and Mills, you hurry back cause dinners almost ready." "Yes ma'am" Mills said as he ran off. He quickly made it to Bucks apartment on Liley, and was greeted by Ta'meka's little sister.

Tanesha was four years older than Mills, but he still had the biggest crush on her. "Whats up lil Mills" Tanesha said. "Whats up Neesh, ya sister here?" Mills replied. "Nah she went to pick Buck up, but she said for you to stay here until she gets back." "I thought the cops took Buck to jail?" Mills inquired. "They did, but only for some old traffic tickets, so Mek followed them downtown to pay the tickets off. They should be pulling up any minute." Mills Took a seat on the steps next to Neesh. And sat there quietly. He inhaled the scent of her fruity fragrance and secretly promised himself that she'd one day be his. As he drifted off into the future. His thoughts of Neesh were quickly smothered by thoughts of him becoming a hustler. He looked down the street at all the young hustlers standing on the corner, and pictured himself amongst them surrounded by all the big money spenders. "Mills, I don't know why you sitting here acting shy wit yo bad self. And I saw what you did today too." Neesh said, interrupting his dope boy day-dream. "Mills why you be running around with Buckshot anyway? I mean he's like my big brother and I love him to death, and appreciate everything he does for me, and my sister, but he's into things that you're to young to be around, and he's hot too." Neesh continued matter of factually. "C'mon Neesh. I be around Buck cause that's my big bro. and just like he takes care of you and your family, he takes care of me and mine, I'll do anything for my big bro. he takes care of this whole neighborhood, he makes sure everybody has money in their pocket, roof over their head, and food in their fridge, and although he does things around me that aren't good, he teaches me a lot of things. He hold the whole hood down Neesh." Mills said defending his idol. "Whatever Mills, that's what wrong with D-Rocs stupid butt, running around trying to be like Buck, calling himself holding the hood down." Neesh said referring to her boyfriend. Neesh was game tight for a 14 year old, but she's been around the game since she was born. Her mother was a dope fiend that died from an overdose. Her sister has been dealing drugs since she was Neesh's age, and on top of all this, she's been living with Buck for the last 5 years. Buck made it his duty to school everyone he allowed in his life to the game. Not that he wanted everybody to become a drug dealer, but just that he related everything that had to do with life to the game. When he spoke of the educational system, he related it to the game in a since that he felt the educational system taught children how to become an employee, instead of an employer, where as the game taught one how to conduct business, how to operate their own establishment and employ workers instead of becoming employed. He said that all the educational system was good for was math and history. Math, so one could count their own paper, and History so one could know the real from the fake where the black nation and our ancestry is concerned. He always got real passionate when talking about African history. He said schools portrayed black people as frivolous slaves, with frivolous civilization and culture. When in fact, the black nation had one of the most advanced civilizations, culture, and upbringing. The Egyptians, known as the ancient kemitians (which means people of the black land) were some of the most intelligent people in the world. They mastered mathematics, science, medicines, philosophy, and created the first system of salvation. He said that black people were in a wealth race, with other diversity groups. He said that the black nation only owned one half of one percent of the world's economical assets, while Caucasians own 80 percent and the Jews, Hispanics, Asians, and Arabs control the remaining 20 percent. He would go on for hours when speaking about the history of blacks.

Mek and Buck pulled up as Mills and Neesh's conversation went silent. Buck stepped out his Blazer followed by a cloud of smoke, and Eazy-E's voice screaming "Fuck The Police" He bobbed his bald head, while taking one last puff of the blunt before flicking it to the ground. Bucks bald head complemented his 6 foot toned frame, which he now exposed as he stood shirtless. Buck didn't workout, his body was just one of his blessing from the creator. He did a year in juvy, in which he played a lot of basketball, and did push-ups but that was 4 years ago. Buck was only 21, but like his mentor " Tony Keys" he was way beyond his years. He gravitated towards the porch while smiling at Mills. "T-Money, C'mere lil bro, you know you saved ya big bro's ass today, right?" Buck said, calling Mills by the nickname he had given him. We gone shop till we drop tomorrow, Iight." "What's up lil sis?" Buck said speaking to Neesh. "What's up, Bro" She replied. "C'mon lil bro let's go inside, you tryna to smoke a blunt?" "Nah bro, Momma got dinner ready, I just came to see what Mek wanted, and to holler at you about something important." Mills replied. "Aw I told Mek I wanted you here when I got here, I wanted to let you know how much I appreciated you being there for ya big bro today. So what's up, what you wanna talk about?" "Wont you drive me home bro, so I can make it there on time for dinner, and we can talk on the ride there." Mills suggested. "Aight lil bro, let me grab my car keys." Buck ran in the apartment, grabbed the keys to his Cadillac Coop, and hurried back outside. Him and Mills entered the Coop and quickly pulled from in front of the row of apartments. Buck didn't waste any time finding out what Mills had on the surface. "What's happenin T-Money, lay it on me" Mills didn't procrastinate either, he got straight to the point. "Bro, I'm tryna hustle, I'm ready to get my own money." Buck looked at Mills as if he were crazy. "Man you trippin T-Money, yo moms and pops ah kill me, not to mention Grandma Mills." "C'mon bro, my mom and pops ah kill you if they knew you had me smoking weed, and you know Grandma would lose it, who's gonna tell'em anyways? Not me, not you, And if you dont put me down Im gone do it on my own anyway. C'mon bro, I'm tryna get money." Mills spoke smoothly, and it bought a smile to Bucks face, because he knew Mills had learnt it from him. "Damn T-Money, you gone use reverse psychology on ya bro like that. I gotta stop teachin you shit. You got a point though Mills, and if you are that determined you leave me no choice, cause I'd never forgive myself if I sat back and let you get fucked around in the game, but understand something Mills, this shit aint all flowers and teddy bears, this is a game where ya life is at stake. Not everybody obtains wealth, and sometimes those who do, They still lose. Shid jus look at ya moms and pops, and ya uncles and all the youngsters out here dying on the strip. I'm ah work wit you, but you gatta promise me that your not gonna make a move with out me, until I say your ready, aight." Mills quickly answered "Iight bro. I promise not to make a move without you." As Buck pulled in front of Mills Grandmother's house he thought of the mistake he may be making. He thought back to how old he was when Mills father put him in the game. Then he thought about the small time pimp he used to work for before Mills mother rescued him, and he said to himself, "Better me than some other nigga." He looked at Mills for a few seconds before asking him, "What you do with that bag T-Money?" I hid it in my closet." Mills responded. "Aight, don't let Grandma Mills see that bag. I'll get it from you when I come through to take you and lil Keys to the mall in the morning." Buck said while holding his fist out for Mills to hit the rock. They dapped it up, and Mills entered the house.

The following day Mills was up bright and early. The sound of Bucks phone awakened him. "Ring. Ring. Ring." "Hello." Buck said with a cracking voice. "Let's go bro, its time to make it do what it do." Mills replied from the other end. Buck looked at the clock on the nightstand, "Slow down T-Money. Its seven O'clock in the morning. The mall doesn't open till nine." "Man forget the mall, I'm tryna to hit the block. Like you always say "the early bird get the first worm" and "don't nothing come to a sleeper but a dream." Mills shot back with determination. Buck started laughing, Mill's determination, and slick talk amused him. "T-Money chill baby bro, rushing things leaves room for too many mistakes, and you know I'm a man of my word and I promised you we would tare da mall up so that's what we gone do. The game aint going nowhere. So go head and get you and Jimmy dressed and I'll be there in about two hours aight?" "Aight man." Mills said sounding disappointed. Mills went through his closet, and pulled out one of his favorite outfits. He matched the outfit up with a pair of his slickest Nikes. Then he went into Jimmy's room and did the same for him. He woke his little brother up and escorted him to the bathroom. They brushed their teeth, showered, got dressed, and stood if front of the mirror putting the finishing touches on their tight fades. Mills put a little grease in his and Jim's hair, then gave their heads an equal amount of strokes. A few minutes later, Grandma Mills was yelling their names out telling them that Daylon, which was Bucks real name, was down stairs. When Jimmy took off, Mills ran to the closet, grabbed the paperbag, and stuffed it under his shirt. As he descended the stairs, he saw Buck lifting Jimmy off his feet, "What's up lil Keys, you looking real fresh boy, you gone drive the girly's crazy." Lil Keys is what Buck calls Jimmy, because he's a spitting image of his father. When Mills hoped off the last step, Jimmy was all smiles. "What's up T-Money, you ready to roll?" "Yep." Mills replied. "You got everything you need?" Buck asked insinuating about the bag. "Yea, I'm ready to roll." Mills said while winking his eye to let Buck know they were on the same page. All three of them hugged Grandma Mills before walking out the door. Buck gave her a kiss on the cheek and slipped a bankroll in her pocket, while winking his eye at her. As they walked out the house Grandma Mills said, "Tony, you and Jimmy behave yourselves, and Daylon, take care of my babies." "Yes ma'am.' Mills and Jimmy yelled back, "They're in good hands momma" Buck said. After spending a few hours at the mall, Buck took them to McDonalds, before heading home. When he pulled in front of the house, he parked the car and grabbed Jimmy from the backseat. He knew Jimmy wanted to roll with the big boys, so he sat him on his lap and said "Did you have fun?" "Yep." Jimmy replied "You better have had fun, wit all that money you had me spending on arcade games." Buck said jokingly. "Look lil Keys, me and Mills have to go take care of something, but since you been a big boy all day, we gone go to the arcade this weekend, and I'm a kick yo butt in that football game." As Jimmy smiled at the thought of going back to the arcade, Buck pulled ten dollars out his pocket, handed it to Jimmy and told him to help Mills carry their bags into the house. "Hurry up T-Money." Buck said as Mills filled his hands with shopping bags. Mills quickly returned and Buck headed for his apartment. Although Buck and Tameka slept at the apartment on occasions, they didn't live there. They had a huge three bedroom home on 161, where Neesh stayed with them. Buck pulled his Fleetwood to the curb, killed the engine, and he and Mills entered the apartment. Buck was a Cadillac lover. He had just about every Cadillac that existed, and two of the ones he liked the most. Major pain and B-N-E met Buck and Mills in the living room as soon as they stepped in the apartment. Major Pain which was a male red nose, and B-N-E, which stands for Bitch Nigga Eater, she was a black Koby with a snow white head. Buck had his dogs trained, they hid in the apartment until they seen who entered. If it wasn't a familiar face, they would jump out of nowhere and go for the kill. "Pain! B-N-E! Doors!" Bucked yelled and the beautiful but vicious dogs stood on guard. Major Pain ran to the front door, while B-N-E ran to the back door in the kitchen. Buck and Mills went in the kitchen as well. Buck grabbed a plate, a razor, and a seat at the table next to Mills. He grabbed the brown paperbag from under his shirt, sat it on the table, and extracted a large block of dope from the bag. He popped a smaller block off of it, and put it on the plate. Buck had a half a kilo of cooked crack in the bag. To some people, that would be a large amount, but to Buck, it was crumbs that he looked out for his little homies with. Buck hit the small block, known in the streets as an eight ball, right in the center with the razor, splitting it in half. "Watch me close Mills, cause I'm ah cut this half up, then you gone cut the other half up." Buck said as he went to work on the small half. He cut it into a bunch of smaller rocks. Then held one of the stones in his hand. "How much is this worth?" He asked Mills "That's a nick." Mills quickly responded. "That's right, this is a five dollar bop." Buck said. "Why you cut all five dollar pieces, what about the dimes, and twenties?" Mills asked. "I was hoping you asked that question. Dig it though lil bro, this is a trick I learnt when I use to be on the block bustin all nighters. You cut all your work into nickels, that way you able to look out for the geeks with little money, cause its going to be a lot of custies coming to you with 3 dollars, 5 dollars, and sometimes nothing, and you don't wanna be out there all day tryna bust down a twenty wit cha hands in order to get that small paper, or in order to look out for one of ya loyal customers who down on they luck, and need a piece to get them started ya dig." "I dig." Mills said with a smile as he soaked up the game. Buck continued, "If somebody comes for a dime, you give them two nickels, sometimes 3, it depends on how much money they spend with you. If they come for twenty, give them four nickels, sometimes 5. Another trick is this, when you put a lot of pieces in a dope fiend hands, they feel like their getting more for their money, than if you just put one stone in they hand. " Buck winked at Mills and said, "Let me see what you know how to do." Mills grabbed the razor, and quickly went to digging into his half. "Whoa.

Whoa, Whoa, slow down T-Money what you rushing for? It's an art to cutting dope, you gotta look at it, spin it around, find that special spot, and hit that shit just right. If you're really good at cutting dope, you'll cut more out of your shit than you suppose to." Mills listened to Buck's words carefully. He started examining the small block. He spun it around, flipped it a few times and when he thought he found the spot he was looking for, he dug the razor into it, while looking up at Buck. "Go head T-Money, make it do what it do." Buck said reassuring him that he was on the right track. Mills cut his work up like a pro and looked at Buck for further instructions. Buck said, "Aight. Now T-Money, what we just cut up was a eight ball, which weighs 3.5 grams, you should cut anywhere from 300 to 350 out of an eight ball. So I want you to add all of this up and tell me how we did." Mills went to counting the nickels a piece at a time. While he did that, B-N-E took off for the living room at the sound of the front door being tampered with. Major Pain was already hidden by the steps; B-N-E took her hiding place on the side of the couch. When Tameka opened the door, her, Neesh and D-Roc walked in. Major Pain and B-N-E both rushed to D-Roc. "Major Pain, B-N-E, Doors!" Mek yelled as D-Roc body went stiff. The dogs went back to their positions. Mek yelled for Buck while D-Roc and Neesh went back to arguing. "I'm in the kitchen baby, who you got wit you?" Mek stopped in her tracks at the sight of Mills baggin dope. "Un, un, Buck? What is you doin?" Mek said. "Chill out baby, T-Money is a natural. Come over here and give me a kiss." Buck ordered. Mek walked over and slipped her tongue into his mouth. "Who is that in the living room?" Buck asked "Oh that's D-Roc and Neesh. They goin at it again, cause that boy been foolin around with some lil trick." Mek answered. "A Dee." Buck yelled from the kitchen. "What's up homie." D-Roc yelled back. "C'mere man." D-Roc walked into the kitchen shaking his head saying, "Man, yo lil sis is a trip. Why every time a nigga don't call a bit…, I mean a female pages back, they automatically assume a nigga is with another bitch." Buck gave him a look that said "slow down, that's my lil sister you are talking about." "my bad big homie, but you fell me doe right?" D-Roc said apologetically. "No he don't feel you, cause he calls all of his girls pages back." Tameka said answering for Buck. Buck started laughing as D-Roc gave Mek a look similar to the one he just received from Buck. D-Roc was one of the youngest hustlers on the block. He was young, wild and down for whatever. All the young hustlers ran up under him. He reminded Buck of himself, besides the fact that D-Roc was hard headed. They both started hustling at the young age of eleven. "Man this shit aint funny bro, Neesh gonna drive a nigga crazy" D-Roc said seriously" "Stop trippen lil homie, that's the way puppy love goes. Especially when you can't keep ya lil dick in ya pants." Buck replied. D-Roc started laughing. "Aw that's how you gone front on yo lil bro? It's cool. I got some money for you though." D-Roc pulled out a stack of cash from his pockets. He put the money on the table and said, "That's what I owe you, and enough for another four and a half ounces." Buck tossed the money to Mek and said, "Grab Dee one of those 4 ways out of the bag." Buck had Mills bag his 330 dollars in stones into 3-hundred dollar packs. He told Mills there was no need for him to keep more than a hundred on him at a time for the time being. As D-Roc looked at his work, Buck pushed the plate and the razor in front of him and said, "Go head and handle ya business Dee. Me and Mills bout to step out front." "What sup lil Mills, I see you bout to get ya feet wet boy, be careful out there." D-Roc said recognizing the process Buck was taking Mills through, because Buck had took him through the same steps 3 years ago. Buck tossed Mills two odd hundred dollar packs to Mek and said, "I'll be out front wit Mills baby." Buck showed Mills how to hide his dope in his draw pocket, and then they took off. They walked across the street to one of Bucks loyal dope fiend's house. As they stood in his front yard, Buck saw Lucky walking through the alley on the side of his apartment building. Lucky was a dope fiend who had been on the block since Buck was a youngster. He was the best runner the neighborhood had to offer. "Ay yo" Buck yelled getting Lucky's attention. As Lucky saw Buck, he ran across the street knowing he had a blast coming. "What's going on Buck, you pitching stones?" Lucky said hoping that he was. "Nah, I'm out here with my lil bro, I want you to run for em, and watch out for him while he out here on the strip. You take care of him and he gone take care of you. Ain't that right Mills?" Buck said "Thats right." Mills answered. "Ain't that Torry and Tony Keys lil boy?" Lucky asked "Yea, you know he ah natural." Buck answered. Lucky said, "Aw man. He gone have all the business in no time, his momma and daddy is legends, and you know I'm ah get him rich, the same way I got you where you are now. Shit to think of it, you never thanked me for making you rich." Buck started laughing at Lucky's humor, though Lucky words did have some truth to them. Buck told Mills to give Lucky a couple of pieces to get him started. Mills started reaching for his package right in the open. "Naw, Naw T-Money, don't ever do business out in the open. Yo business is yo business, not show business, feel me?" Buck said. He didn't give Mills a chance to respond before he continued. "Look around you Mills, the police can be anywhere, they can be behind the houses over there or parked up the street in an unmarked car, shid the police can be any and everywhere. Never handle yo business in the open. Go over there on the other side of the house, and get Lucky together." Mills did as he was told, and Buck stood there joking with Lucky until Mills returned. Mills dropped two nickel pieces in Lucky's hand. "Aight youngster, you just chill and I'm a show you how to make a million, ask Buck, he know about me." Lucky said as he got excited by the dope in his hand. Lucky took off as quick as he came. D-Roc's right hand man, walked up as Lucky walked off. "What up big homie. What up lil Mills." Slim said greeting them both. "What's happenin Slim gangsta." Buck replied. "What's up Slim." Mills added. D-Roc came walking out of Bucks apartment as Buck talked to Slim. "Man Neesh a trip, all she wanna do is kiss and play footsies. Man I know thats ya lil sis but I aint on that shit big homie. I aint fuckin wit no more virgins, cause they aint coming off no skins." D-Roc said causing Slim, Buck and Mills to bust into laughter. "I told you, you was too advanced for Neesh man, but you kept horn doggin." Slim said while laughing. "Man ya'll niggas laughing and shit, I'm dead serious bro, Neesh the poster girl for blue balls." D-Roc said seriously, not knowing it was more his serious manner, than what he was saying that was so funny. Buck controlled his laughter long enough to throw some game under his lil homies hat. "I feel you Dee, but if you really knew what you had, you'd put cha sex life on hold for a while, because Neesh is most definitely gone by a qualified woman. She has strong morals and principals, and she understands a hustler's lifestyle, which is uncommon in a lot of females, especially the young ladies in your age group. Neesh is gonna be real successful, and you gone miss her when she gone, but I feel you, I was a young nigga before too, so I know how fascinated you've become wit sex, and ya love muscle, but I tell you what, you better strap ya Jimmy up, cause these girls out here is fast as fuck." Slim cut in before D-Roc could reply. Aye big homie, I got a couple dollars for you. I need two and a quarter." "Aight baby that's what I'm talking about, for a minute I thought you was gone stay on an ounce forever. Buck said kidding with his lil homie. "Aw yeah big homie. I'm tryna get my money right." Slim shot back. "Shit, you, Dee, and lil Walt should have been had ya'll paper right, what happen to the spot I had setup for ya'll?" Buck inquired. "I'm on top of that as we speak" D-Roc said. Maybe if you keep your dick in your pants long enough, or stop shooting up night clubs, you could really get on top of it." Buck said as he headed across the street to his apartment to get Slim's package. "Keep an eye on Mills till I get back Dee." Buck said before he got too far away. Lucky returned with a lady who wanted a twenty. Mills went on the side of the house and got 4 stones out of his bag. When he dropped it in the ladies hand, she whispered to Lucky, "Aint that Torry and Keys boy?" Mills looked at D-Roc as he stood in the middle of the street with a hand full of rocks in one hand, a blunt in his mouth, a gun on his hip, and a line of customers. Mills said to himself, "D-Roc is doing everything Buck said not to do, but he's getting all the money." Buck came walking out the apartment shaking has head at the sight of D-Roc. He handed Slim a baggie, and said, "That's 4 and a half ounces, just pay me for the extra two when you get done." "Good looking Buck." Slim replied. "Don't worry about it baby, we in this shit together, just get your money, and go hard, ya dig." "I dig, and good looking out again big homie." Slim said before walking off to join D-Roc. "Let's go sit on the porch and smoke a blunt T-Money." As they headed for the porch Buck said, "I don't ever wanna see you handling business like D-Roc, that shit don't last long lil bro, dig me." Mills shook his head yes. As they sat on the porch smoking that good green, Neesh stepped outside. She looked at D-Roc in the middle of the street and said, "Look at that stupid boy, he can't even sell dope right, he so stupid." As Buck laughed at his little sister he saw a cop car bend the corner, and yelled out, "A Dee!" As D-Roc looked at Buck, Buck pointed to the cop car,

D-Roc took off running. The police car tried to pursue him, but the pursuit was to no avail. D-Roc ran through one yard, hopped a fence, cut through another yard, and disappeared right before the cops eyes.

-CHAPTER TWO-

Meks deep Breaths started to settle as the after math from her first orgasm caused her body to jerk. She had been on top all morning so Buck took control of their power hour of afternoon sex. He plunged deeper into her from the missionary position, watching her close her eyes and open her mouth as if she wanted to scream, but couldn't muffle out a sound. He looked down on her beautiful body as she enticed him further with her sex faces. Mek's 5'7 frame was stacked. 36 Double D's, with nipples half the size of Tootsie Rolls, and just as chocolate. Her stomach was ironing board flat, and it descended right onto her hips, that rolled off of her body connecting perfectly with her apple bottom. Her jet black hair stopped just below her ears, and though Buck was mad that she cut it, he had to admit, "His lady was rocking the shit out of her short hair do. Her caramel skin was now covered in sweat as she wrapped her legs around Buck's back while he shoved his full 8 ½ inches into her. "Oh Buck, Oh shit, I'm cumming" Mek yelled "Damn baby, I'm cumming too" Buck said as he felt his manhood blow up inside of her.

⁂ ⁂ ⑧ ⑧ ⑧ ⑧ ⑧ ⁂ ⁂

Meanwhile Mills is posted up on Main and Wilson with D-Roc and Slim. After two months of being under Bucks watchful eye, Mills was finally making moves on his own. As D-Roc and Slim bullied the block, rushing every customer in sight, Mills spotted one of his loyal customers. Lucky hung out of a car window flagging Mills down with an urgency. Mills left his bike leant up against the brick wall, and hopped in the car with Lucky. After a spin around the corner, Mills was hopping out of the car with Lucky, and rushing to the car of one of his other loyal customers. The block was booming, and Mills was super charged. The first day of school was creeping up, and the more money Mills made, the more money he had to shop with. He knew he would be the flyest dressed sixth grader in the whole school. He'd maybe even win best dressed all around the board.

As he served his customer, he heard D-Roc yell out "Hit The Dirt!" When he looked up, he noticed a white Bronco flying up the street with its passenger hanging out the window blasting off shots, "Bloom! Bloom! Bloom!" Mills dove to the ground as D-Roc and Slim, ran to the middle of the street returning fire. "Pop! Pop! Pop!. . ."Pop! Pop!" "Get up Mills and come the fuck on" D-Roc yelled as he and Slim ran to his 70's Cutlass. Mills rose from the ground and ran for his bike. "Mills leave the bike, and get in the car" D-Roc yelled as he brought the engine to life. Mills looked at the bike one last time before running to the car. "Them Hoe Ass Nigga's T-Bone and Fresh thought we was slippin Slim. We ridden on them North Side niggas tonight" D-Roc was charged up. His demeanor confused Mills, because after being shot at, D-Roc was laughing and turning his music up in celebration. D-Roc parked his Cutlass in the alley directly behind Bucks apartment, and the trio quickly exited the vehicle. "Boom! Boom! Boom!" D-Roc banged on Bucks back door with an urgency. "Who the fuck is it" Buck yelled while grabbing his Four Five Torros. "It's Roc man, Hurry up and open the door!" Buck snatched the door open with B-N-E and Major Pain by his side.   D-Roc and Slim stopped in their tracks, while Mills blew right passed the dogs patting them on their heads. "C'mon man ya'll cool" Buck said while snapping his fingers and pointing to the living room, sending the dogs on their way. Buck stuck his head out the door. He looked left, then right before shutting the door and locking it. "Why da fuck you knocking on the door like the police Dee?" "Man them hoe ass niggas just came through Main and Wilson blasting." D-Roc answered, still hyped up from the shoot out. "Ya'll aint strapped? Buck inquired. "HELL YEA! Bro you know we don't leave home with out it. We dumped on them fools. And we riding on them bitch ass niggas tonight." D-Roc said while showing Buck his empty nine millimeter. "Slow down Dee, what I tell you about using your head? Them niggas is expecting ya'll to come through tonight. They'll be waiting for ya'll, and no smart warrior walks into a trap like that you dig." Buck said schooling his little homie. "I dig, but fuck them Buck. Them niggas in violation coming through our hood like shit sweet, me, Slim, and Lil Walt, got in to it with them niggas at the skating ring last night. They started yelling that North Side, fuck East shit, so we started screaming fuck the North Side, this is East Main. Then that big nigga Deuce walk up and throw some money at us talking bout tell Buck's hoe ass to buy him some. I spit in the niggas face and all hell broke loose. Make a long story brief, we shot that bitch up last night." D-Roc said with a smile on his face. Buck instantly became furious. He hated Deuce just as much as Deuce hated him. Deuce was a North Side O.G. he held the same rank out north as Buck held on the East Side. T-Bone and Fresh was his lil Homies, and right hand men. Buck kept his emotions under control, not wanting to set a bad example for his lil homies, especially Mills. "Fuck Deuce and the rest of them niggas Dee. We bout dis money, and we aint gone let them or any other niggas interfere with our paper. Now you right, them niggas in violation, but there's a time and place for everything, be patient Dee. When the time comes, we gone get them niggas missing, feel me?" Buck said trying to rationalize with D-Roc. D-Roc agreed just to end the discussion, but his mind was already made up, him, Slim, and Walt were riding on Deuce and his crew tonight. "Oh yea Big Homie, me and Slim need some shells, and lil Mills need a strap. Cause you know how crazy shit can be in the hood. Shit if it aint some niggas coming through blastin, you always gotta have that metal for them thirsty ass fiends that be out to rob a nigga." D-Roc said. Buck looked at Mills. "T-Money you aight?" "Yea I'm cool bro." Mills answered. Buck reached in the cabinet. He grabbed a .32 special and a box of nine shells. He tossed the box of shells to D-Roc, and held the small pistol in front of Mills. "Now listen Mills, this is not a toy, and its not for show. If you pull this out, you use it. When your on the block, you put it in a bag and hide it somewhere close to you. Can you handle this?" Mills assured Buck that he could handle this part of the game, and that he'd be extra careful. D-Roc and Slim loaded their weapons and headed back to the strip. Buck kept mills behind. He wanted to talk to him a little longer. He told Mills he didn't want him hanging out with D-Roc and his crew anymore. He explained to Mills that no one man could accomplish great things alone, but that he would one day have to form his own team. Mills knew Buck would feel that his friends weren't ready for the game, but if he was going to formulate a team, he couldn't think of any better draft picks than his friends who had been down with him from day one.

As Mills, Fella, Peko, and Shawn Shawn sat on Fella's porch, Mills imitated Coach K in the middle of a time out. His squad rallied around him as he layed out their game plan. "I got ya'll bro, but we gone slow roll it cause I have to run this move by Buck, but this is how we gone run it…Pee, I'm let you hold the pack while I sell it, you stay close to the house away from the heat, Fella, you gone be like the muscle, you gone hold down the pistol and watch my back. Its yo job to protect us while were out her getting money, you gotta watch everybody and everything. Shawn Shawn, you gone be the look out. You let us know when ever the police is getting close". Mills knew that Peko and Shawn Shawn were a package deal. Although Shawn Shawn was 2 yrs younger. He and Peko did everything together. Their mom was struggling as a single parent trying to raise 2 boys. Her pay check barely paid the bills, and put food on the table. Their father died in a bank robbery that ended in a shootout with the police. Fella on the other hand was an only child. He was the biggest and most aggressive of all the youngins. He wanted to be a gangster like his cousin Slim, but Slim always ran him off the strip. Fella's mother was the coolest mother in the hood. She took care of Fella with her Government Assistance, and part time hustles on the side. Mills and his friends were all products of the struggle, but Mills had a safety net, and that safety net was Buckshot. "We gone get this money ya'll, but we gotta promise to stay loyal to one another, and never allow anything to come between us. None of that arguing over money and girls like D-Roc and them, Iight?" Mills said to all his friends. "Iight" they all said in unison. "Now lets say it together" "say what?" Fella asked. "Just repeat after me" Mills answered. "I promise to stay loyal to this family, and never allow anything to come between us". They eagerly followed Mills lead, repeating every word he said. From that day on they where inseparable. They hustled hard for a month leading up to the first day of school. And when they walked through the hallways they made jaws drop with their attire. Things were going so smoothly that Mills had forgot to run things by Buck. Mills had slowed down with going on the strip, and with the help of Lucky and a couple more of his loyal customers, he started bringing money from the strip over to Berkley where he and his crew hung out at. Mills and his friends were turning Berkley into a strip of its own. Putting their stamp on that street as Buck had done with Liley.

One day after school Mills received a page from Buck. He noticed Buck's code with 911 behind it, so he rushed to a phone. "Whats up Big Bro, this T-Money" Mills said as Buck answered the phone. "Where you at" Buck inquired. "On Berk" Mills answered. "Come around here and see me, I need to speak with you ASAP" Buck ordered. "I'm on my way" Mills said before they disconnected. Mills thought this would be as good a time as any to fill Buck in on his latest moves, so he told his crew to roll with him.

When they arrived. Buck was standing in front of his apartment with D-Roc, Slim, and Lil Walt. D-Roc stood off to one side with Neesh. They were in a heated argument as usual. "What up big bro?" Mills said to Buck. "Whats up T-Money." Buck replied. He looked at Mills crew "What up Fella, Pee, lil Shawn" "Sup Big homie" They replied in unison. "Walk with me Mills" Buck ordered as he strolled up the street. Mills followed behind him, and Buck slowed his stroll until they were side by side. "Where the Fuck you been at T-Money?" Buck asked, seriously concerned. "What you mean bro?" Mills asked in return. "Why haven't I seen you on the strip, or right here on Liley? Mills carefully began explaining his relocation to Berkley, along with his new recruits. Buck was impressed with Mills leadership. He knew Mills was a natural, but he didn't think he would build his own block from the ground up. Buck didn't like the idea of Mills bringing his friends into the fold. He viewed them as three bad little niggas who stole shit and stayed in trouble. He knew they had heart, and would be loyal to Mills, but he didn't feel they were ready for the game just yet. Mills convinced him that they were, and Buck said. "Aight T-Money, I'm ah let you make this decision on ya own, cause I believe a mans ability to make good decisions is a major part of what prepares him for the obstacles that life will throw at him. But don't ever make a move like that again without at least talking to me about it, and know that I won't sell them anything until I feel they're ready. All their business will go through you." Mills accepted the terms and promised to inform him beforehand on any future moves. They walked back up the street, and joined the rest of the crew. Fella was talking to his cousin Slim, while Peko and Shawn Shawn quietly awaited Mills return. D-Roc had done enough arguing with Neesh and left her sitting on the porch alone. "What up lil Mills?" D-Roc said. "What up Roc" Mills shot back. D-Roc looked at the rest of his lil homies, "What up Pee, lil Shawn, fat ass Fella." "Lets roll out" He said to Walt and Slim before the youngins could respond. Lil Walt was really from Gilbert and Mound, but he's been hanging tough with D-Roc and Slim ever since his Big Homie Black got locked up. Lil Walt was a real live Goon; He was only thirteen, and had at least three bodies under his belt. He and his Big Homie Black would hook up with D-Roc and Slim on occasions. And the foursome would wreck havoc where ever they went. Lil Walt barred none, and loved drama more than anyone, which is why he and D-Roc were a perfect fit.

Buck rounded up Mills crew for a much needed sit down with them, and Mills took that as his clue to slide under Neesh. "Whats up Mills?" Neesh said as he joined her on the porch. "You." Mills replied. "What?" Neesh responded clearly caught off guard by Mills response. "You what's up Neesh. You always been what's up an when I get a little older, I'm a make you mine watch and see." Mills said with confidence. Neesh was blushing; she couldn't believe Mills was coming onto her. She had Mills by 4 years, and no matter how handsome he was or how grown he portrayed to be, he was a child. Neesh laughed, "Stop playin boy, you know you is too young, who told you to say that, Buck?" "Nah. Buck aint tell me to say nothing. I've always had a crush on you, I just never said anything because of our age difference, but I'm telling you Neesh, you better wait on me, cause I know how to treat you." Mills said with the same confidence. Neesh couldn't believe the words coming out of Mills mouth. She thought his little crush was cute, so she played along. "Oh you know how to treat me, huh? Tell me how I want to be treated then Mills." "Like a queen is how you need to be treated, because that's what you are to me, but I can tell you one thing, I will never treat you like D-Roc does." Buck walked up as Mills stunned Neesh with his response. " I'm done speaking with your team, like I told them, ya'll stay tight, and grounded on loyalty. I'm bout to go in, ya'll wanna come in and smoke something?" Buck asked. "Nah bro, we gotta get back to the block, it's money to be made you dig?" Mills said hitting Buck with his own words. Buck started laughing, because he recognized himself in Mills. "I dig, get yo money lil bro, and call me later, Aight?" Buck said proudly. "Aight." Mills replied. Before leaving, He looked at Neesh and said, "For real Neesh, wait on me." She laughed as Mills walked off with his boys. The next day Mills school was shattered by the sound of Walt's twelve gauge. As students dove to the ground, Walt hung out the window dumping on some guys him, D-Roc, and Slim had beef with from Livingston Ave. The guys were caught off guard, but their swift reflexes allowed them to return fire. One of Walt's slugs hit one of its targets. The boy lay on the ground shaking as blood leaked from his mid-section. Mills, Fella, Peko, and Brandy, received cold stares as they walked home. Everyone knew they were from Main Street, and Walt was screaming East Main as he unloaded the shotgun. That made Mills and his crew just as much their enemy as D-Roc, Walt and Slim were. Mills knew he may have adopted Some enemies by being on the block with D-Roc and his crew for these couple of months, so he already brought his gun to school with him, having Brandy hold it in her locker. He hoped he wouldn't have to use it, but if it came down to one of them, or one of his, he wouldn't hesitate. Mills and his crew had also made enemies unknowingly just by the way they dressed. They wore the flyest gear in the school. Everything from Guess, Used & Damaged to Cross Color, Karl Kani, and Exhaust. They also flossed Triple Fat Goose, and MCM leathers. They were saucy for sure. Fella and Peko did all the mingling, mostly with the females, taking advantage of their fame, but Mills didn't socialize at all. He paid the females no attention, and the guys were non-existent to him. The only person Mills talked to other than Fella, and Peko was Brandy. Brandy stayed next door to Fella on Berkley. She was beautiful, but to Mills she was just one of the guys. She was a true tomboy. She wanted to get down on her hustle with the boys, but Mills turned her down. he let her roll with them in the hood sometimes though. She would hold his pack for him, while he was on the block, and often times keep some of his money, and extra dope at her house, because Mills was afraid his grandmother would find it. A lot of people thought they were a couple but, they were just real cool. Mills wasn't thinking about girls, except for Neesh that is, and Brandy wasn't thinking of guys either. Mills didn't want to beef or party. He just wanted to get money. The school was closed for a couple of days after the shooting. The boy who felt Walt's 12 gauge slug, had lived, but he would be paralyzed from the waist down. When the school did reopen, D-Roc, Walt, and Slim frequently came to the school to start trouble, only making things worse for Mills and his crew. The guys envy for Mills and his crew deepened, while the girly's lust grew.

By Mills 12th birthday, and the middle of the school year, Mills and his crew were public enemy number one. Out side of school Mills had problems as well. His grandmother was becoming suspicious of his behavior. Mills ran in and out of the house, and started staying out way past his curfew. She was also suspicious of all the new things he had accumulated. He and his little brother's wardrobe had become very extensive. Mills spoiled his little brother. He brought Jimmy every video game, and more clothes than he could wear. He hated that he spent little to no time with his little brother, but Jimmy really couldn't roll with him now that he hustled. He vowed to never let his little brother fall victim to the streets. He would make sure Jimmy never wanted for anything, that way he would have no need to hustle. Mills was stopped by his grandmother on his way out the door. "Tony. You hold up just a minute, I need to speak to you." Mills stopped in his tracks. "Boy you been doing a lot of running in and out this house lately, coming in past ya curfew, and popping up with all kinds of clothes, shoes, videogames, and carrying on. I know you aint in them streets selling that stuff." She said seriously. "No ma'am. Momma you know Buck takes care of us, he buys us everything. Why would I have to sell that stuff?" Mills said lying to his grandmother. It hurt to lie to her, but he couldn't tell her the truth, and he refused to stop hustling. "You better not boy, cause God don't like ugly, and this is a house of the Lord, and I wont have the devil or the devils belongings in my house. Do you hear me Tony!" "Yes Ma'am" Mills said respectfully. "Alright now, go on where you was headed, but be back in here on time tonight. You done missed your mothers call 3 days in a row. Don't you miss it tonight, you hear?" "Yes Ma'am." Mills said. "Oh my Lord sweet Jesus." Miss. Mills said under her breath. Mills headed back to the block with the thought of him lying to his grandma on his mind. He not only lied to her about not selling drugs, but he also had money and drugs hid in her house. Ever since the day Buck gave him half of his money and drugs, telling him that it was time for him to start learning how to manage his own money he had a stash of money and drugs hid in a shoe box inside his closet. The fact that he had over twenty shoe boxes in his closet made the hiding place perfect. Mills figured he could at least take the drugs out of his grandmother's house. He'd keep his drugs at Brandy's house, where he already kept part of them.

The next day at school, Mills stood at Brandy's locker talking to her about moving his drugs over to her house. Of course she was game. Brandy was down for anything, and Mills had become the brother she never had. While Mills and Brandy conversed between classes, Mills was approached by Shawn'tae. Shawn'tae is in the eighth grade, which is a couple grades higher than Mills. She's one of the fastest females in the school, meaning she had a lot of sexual experience. She was also from the neighborhood of the guys D-Roc, Slim, and Walt had beef with. Mills knew Shawn'tae liked him, because she always made little remarks when ever he was in hearing distance. Mills always paid her no attention like he did all the other girls who dug his style. "What up Mills. Can I get you to come to my party?" Shawn'tae said while handing him a flyer. Mills looked at the flyer. "I don't know Shawn'tae, parties aint really my cup of tea." "C'mon Mills, you know I like you, why you be acting like you scared of me? You aint scared of pussy are you?" Shawn'tae said bluntly. Mills hated having his courage put on Front Street. Although he was a virgin, he wasn't scared of pussy or anything else. "T-Mills aint scared of shit. Definitely not no pussy, you just be around niggas I know don't like me, so how I know you aint tryna set me up" Mills shot back with authority. "Mills…I'm not tryna set you up. I'm more like tryna sex you up, but if you think I'm too much for you, I understand." Shawn'tae shot back. "I'll tell you what Shawn'tae, my pager number is 456-3600. You hit me up and we will see where it goes." Mills said bringing the conversation to an end. Brandy rolled her eyes at Shawn'tae, as she walked off, hoping she could get her to say something smart, so she could kick her ass. Peko and Fella walked up at the end of the conversation. They dapped it up with Mills on the way to class, while joking with him about Shawn'tae being too much for him. Later that day Mills, Peko, Fella, Brandy, and Shawn Shawn were posted up on Main and Berkley in front of the corner store. Mills pager went off. He didn't recognize the number. The number was followed by the code 69 which was also foreign to Mills. As Peko and Fella jumped in and out of cars, Mills went to use the payphone to call the number back. "Ring! Ring! Ring!" "Hello"

Shawn'tae said. "Yeah, who dis?" Mills said. "You called my house, so who dis?" Shawn'tae said sarcastically "This T-Mills, somebody over there call a pager?" "Damn Mills, you don't recognize a bitch's voice? This Shawn'tae." "Aw. What's up Baby girl?" He replied smoothly. "You what's up, I was hoping you could come over and keep me company while my moms at work, unless you scared to be in a house alone with me." Shawn'tae said knowing how to press Mills buttons. "I told you before Baby girl, Young Mills aint scared of shit. Where you live at?" Shawn'tae smiled at the thought of Mills coming to see her. "1206 Oakwood. Don't be playing with me Mills." She answered. "Damn. You right in the middle of them niggas huh? Mills said referring to the adversaries he'd adopted from his involvement with D-Roc. "Mills aint nobody thinking about them niggas, and them niggas don't be at my house, they be all the way down the street." Shawn'tae said getting angry at the thought of Mills not coming. "Dig, I'll be over there in about a half hour. I hope you aint on no bullshit, for the both of our sake." Mills said giving her a fair warning. "Mills, chill out, I aint on that type of shit." Shawn'tae replied seriously. "Aight Baby girl, I'll be der in a minute." They disconnected. "Who was you talking to bro?" Fella asked while offering Mills a blunt. Mills grabbed the weed and took a few puffs before answering. "Man that was that lil freak Shawn'tae. I'm bout to go by her crib." "Man you know that bitch stay on the same street a lot of them niggas hustle on, right?" Peko said joining the conversation. "Yeah I know that, how'd you know that?" Mills said playfully. "Her address was on the flyer she passed out for her party next week." Peko answered. "Man fuck that bro, you want us to roll with you?" Fella asked as he gripped the baby nine on his waist. "Nah I'm Cool bro. I got the other burner, but I'm a need ya'll to come scoop me up when it is time to leave."

"Aight bro just hit me up and we will be there with magician speed, and magical quickness." Fella said, mocking one of Bucks favorite one liners. Mills flagged one of his customers down as he drove by. He grabbed his 32 special from Brandy and hopped in the car. As the car neared Oakwood, Mills pulled on his hoody, and gripped his gun. He saw a pack of boys all in front of the store hustling. When the car turned on Oakwood, Mills saw the faces of a few of the boys from his school as they stared into the car. None of them noticed Mills, if they did they didn't show it. Shawn'tae stayed four blocks away from the store. Mills told the driver not to pull off until he gave him the signal. Mills hopped up the stairs that lead to Shawn'tae's door. He knocked three hard times. Without asking who it was, Shawn'tae yanked the door open. Mills peered into the house as she stood there with the door wide open. She had on a pair of daisy duke shorts that exposed the bottoms of her cheeks and a halter top that pressed tightly up against her breast, and exposed her flat stomach. She stood in a pair of footy socks, with a pink ball hanging from the back, which matched her halter top and the bandana she had tied around her ponytail. Shawn'tae's body was banging, and she had a beautiful face to compliment it. "Are you coming in? Or do you see something you don't like?" Shawn'tae said as she saw his eyes shoot right pass her, into the house. "Aint nobody in here boy, gosh." Mills threw his hand up to the driver as he walked in the house. "Can we smoke in here?" Mills asked as he finally allowed himself to relax. "Roll it up nigga." Shawn'tae shot back. They sat on the couch smoking some good weed, and holding small talk for almost a half hour. Shawn'tae being the more experienced, took control of the situation. She caressed his thigh until she felt his half hard penis. She was satisfied with what she felt, so she unzipped his pants and pulled his manhood out. She flicked her tongue at his penis a few times, making him fully erect. She stared at his six inches of steal and thought, "This lil nigga packing." Shawn'tae was only fourteen, but she had slept with a number of eighteen year olds, so she knew a good size penis when she saw one. She helped Mills out of his coat and clothes. Mills layed his pistol beside him on the couch, and his gangsterism only turned her on more. When she removed her clothes, Mills became so hard, his pole started to throb. Shawn'tae was more intrigued with his girth than she was his length. She slid a condom on to his manhood, and pushed him back on the couch. She slid down on his pole, and rode him like a wild bull. She moaned. "Oh Mills, you got a fat dick" Mills not knowing what to do, just sat there, and let her ride herself into an orgasm. She stood up and bent over, and guided Mills pole into her cave from the back. Mills slowly went in and out of her, watching her womanhood swallow the full length of his manhood. "Faster Mills faster." She said in between heavy breaths. Mills started pushing in her and pulling out of her at a fast pace. She screamed his name while yelling "Yes, right there Mills don't stop." Mills dug as deep as he could go before his knees buckled from his first nut. He could barely hold his self up as Shawn'tae continued to back her thang up. After fifteen minutes of sex, Mills was weak. He and Shawn'tae got dressed and Mills paged Fella. Fella called back immediately. Mills and Shawn'tae smoked a blunt while he waited for his ride. When Mills heard a knock at the door, he gripped his pistol, while peeking through the curtains. He gave Shawn'tae the go head to open the door, as he saw Fella standing on the porch. From that day on having sex with Shawn'tae was an everyday thing with Mills.

-CHAPTER THREE-

Young Mills and his crew were making their mark in the game. A whole year had passed, and Brandy and Shawn Shawn were now in full swing. Along with Mills, Fella, and Peko they've turned Berkley into a major money strip. Young Mill's hustle was ahead of its time. He made moves that would have him and his crew on top in no time. Mills quickly realized that by sitting at Lisa's house, he made himself easily available for all the smokers who went there to get high. He'd pay Lisa a couple stones to sit in her house for a few hours, and all the smokers that came there to get high spent all their money with him, smoking up his product until their money was gone, and they were a few hundred dollars in debt on their pay checks.

Mills eventually worked out a deal with Lisa for him and his crew to sell drugs out of her house. Lisa had practically watched Mills and his crew grow up. She lived on Berkley for as far back as they could remember. She was the kind of smoker that never had much money of her own, but for some reason all the other smokers went to her house to smoke dope with her. Yet-N-Still, to much crack is never enough crack for a true smoker, so when Mills offered her a hundred dollars worth of stones daily, for him and his squad to post up, she quickly agreed.

Mills rounded up the best dope runners in the hood, and had Lisa's house moving thousands of dollars in stones on the daily. Not only did selling their drugs out of Lisa's house stopp Mills and is squad from having to compete with other corner hustlers. It also kept them out of the cops eye sight, and therefore off of Pacman's radar. Pacman is the most scandalous police officer the game had ever seen. He robbed drug dealers, planted drugs on others, and didn't mind breaking every law in the book just to get a bust. He harassed the strip from 3 P.M. to 11 P.M. everyday. No days off! The 12th Precincts most feared officer and every hustler on Main Street's worst nightmare.

As Mills sat in Lisa's house watching Fella and Peko play Sega Genesis's NBA Live. His grandmother was in his bedroom acting on her suspicion. She rummaged through his dresser drawers until his clothes were in disarray. Nothing came up, but she wasn't satisfied so she tiptoed through her grandson's room, moving things around, lifting tops and lids from anything that was covered. Searching under the bed's mattress and every other hiding spot that she could think of. When she reached the closest, she searched all the pockets of his coats, pants, and shirts. She was amazed by all the shoe boxes her grandson had neatly stacked from floor to ceiling. "ooh Lord Jesus, my arthritis is killing me, and this boy got enough clothes to open a clothing store" she said, While wiping the sweat from her forehead. As she wiped the perspiration from her face, her elbow hit one of the shoe boxes causing the mountain of boxes to come tumbling down. Most of the boxes were empty, but a few of them hit the floor and money rolls poured out of them. She was astonished by thee amount of dead presidents staring back at her. "Jesus!" Oh my Lord Jesus!" I knew it, I knew it, I knew it, that boy done brought the devil in your house." She said, while pacing the floor , uncertain of her next move.

Meanwhile, Mills kicked his feet up, while puffing on a fat blunt and listening to Fella and Peko crack jokes on one another. He, Brandy, and Shawn Shawn laughed so hard tears were forming in the corner of their eyes. The sound of his pager caught him off guard, as his laughter caused him to choke on the marijuana smoke. Sitting upright in the recliner, he braced his pager until the screen steadied in front of him. He quickly gained his composure after noticing his grandmother's number followed by 911. He grabbed the phone and walked into the kitchen to avoid the noise. Mills was thrown back by his grandmother's tone. Not only was her tone disturbing, but she also demanded that he come home immediately, and that was unlike her. Instantly he became worried and concerned for her health and safety. "A yo, I'm bout to run to the crib, momma trippin bout something, I'll be right back, ya'll hold it down" Mills said before rushing out the door.

When he entered the house, his heart dropped into his stomach. His grandmother stood in the middle of the floor with a shoe box in her hand. . . Instantly, Mills knew his stash had been discovered. What is this Tony? I guess Daylon gave you this too huh?" She said as she held the box in front of him. "Momma I can. . . " "I don't wanna hear it. You brought the devil in my house, and lied to my face. God don't like ugly and this is as ugly as it gets. I want it out and I want it out now! You wanna be grown, and run the streets? Well I'm tellen you like I told your mother, I can't watch what you do in them streets, and I wont lock you in the house like some prisoner, but I wont have the devil in or around my home, now get this box and get it out of here!!" She spoke with authority. "Momma I'm sorry for lying, but I. . ." "I don't want to hear it Tony, you gone learn the hard way like yo momma and daddy, money aint the root of evil, it's the love for money that's demonic." She slowly strolled out of the living room, talking under her breath about her arthritis and diabetes. Mills got straight on the phone and called Buck. Buck arrived within minutes, and Mills hurried out to the car. "Damn T-Money, how you let Momma find ya stash? What she say? Do she know I had anything to do with it?" Buck asked one question after another leaving no time for Mills to answer any of them. "Damn bro slow down, you aint giving me a chance to answer the first question." Mills said, "Aight I feel you lil bro, but if Momma Mills finds out I'm the one giving you drugs to sell, she'll never forgive me, and I aint even got to tell you how ya moms and pops gonna react." "Just chill big bro, she don't know where I got the shit from, she didn't even ask, she just flipped out, and said she wants it out of her house." Mills explained. "Okay, so what all did she say?" Mills did his best impersonation of Momma Mills for Buck. "God don't like ugly, Lord sweet Lord, Blazah, skip, and carrying on/" They both busted into laughter, as they headed for Bucks home on 161. When they pulled into the driveway, Buck told Mills to put his blunt out until they got inside, because he didn't want his neighbors in his business. Once they entered, Mek was yelling Buck's name from the kitchen. Mills took a seat on the couch next to Neesh, who was on the phone with Tasha, her one and only homegirl. "What's going on Mills." Neesh said as she ended her call. "Nothing much. What's up with you?" Mills replied after putting fire back to the blunt he put out in the car. Buck came walking out of the kitchen just in time to help Mills finish the blunt. "Damn T-Money, let me smoke with you like I joke wit you." Mills quickly passed the blunt, while laughing at Bucks slick one liner. In between puffs, Buck said, "You want me to grab the rest of ya paper, so you can see what. . ." He took two more puffs from the blunt before finishing. "You workin wit?" "Yeah." Mills replied knowing his paper was shorter than it should be because of is shopping habits. Buck ran upstairs and quickly returned with a shoe box, to match the one Mills held on his lap. "What ever you got in this box you should have in that box if you been following your plan. Half at Momma Mills and half here wit me" Buck said giving Mills a look of curiosity. Mills smiled at Bucks look knowing that Buck knew him like the back of his hand. Mills emptied Buck's box out first, and counted his money. He had forty-five hundred dollars, which meant he should have an identical amount in his shoe box. When Mills finished counting the money in his box, he had seventy-five hundred dollars total. "Damn T-Money, what you done spent fifteen hundred dollars on?" Buck asked as he calculated the differences. Mills looked at his Cross Color outfit, his Deion Sanders edition Nikes, and smiled. "Listen T-Money, hard work deserves a reward, so I aint gone beat yo ears up about yo spending habits, but know that after you reward ya'self its time to grind harder. So let's tighten up. Aight!" "We on the same page bro." Mills replied. "And let me ask you something, while you spending money on new treads for ya'self, what you done bought lil Keys?" Buck asked in reference to Mills little brother. "C'mon big bro, you know I'm not gone buy me something and not buy lil Jim anything. I was raised better than that." Mills replied seriously. Buck smiled, knowing that he played a big part in raising Mills. Neesh sat on the couch fascinated by how fast Mills was growing up. She had to admit, if Mills was a couple years older, she would surely take a chance with him. He was smooth, way beyond his twelve years, and she liked the way he carried himself. Neesh wasn't the only person who noticed that Mills was up and coming. His name, and the name of his strip was starting to make a lot of noise throughout the hood, and unbeknownst toMills, the G.I. Boys wanted a piece of the pie.

The G.I. Boys were a crew of dope boys from Gary, Indiana. They had adopted that name since arriving in Columbus a few months ago. They instantly started making a name for themselves with their fancy cars, and cheap dope prices. D-Roc, Slim, and lil Walt brought the beef their way as soon as they migrated from across the bridge. Although Buck was the hood's boss, D-Roc felt that he owned the turf, because Buck no longer put in work. So whenever the hood was violated or D-Roc felt it was, he did whatever it took to defend the turfs honor.

Only three weeks into the summer, and the G.I. Boys made their move on Mills small real estate. From Lisa's porch, Mills watched Spider, Man-Man, and lil Timmy stand on the corner of Mound and Berkley short stopping his customers. "These niggas got me fucked up" Mills said to himself, before yelling in the house, telling his crew to strap up. They all grabbed their pistols and ran out the front door. Mills filled them in on what was happening, then started giving orders. "Fella, you cross the street, cut through Brandy's yard and start walking up Mound. Pee, you cut through Lisa's back yard, and come walking up Mound in the opposite direction. Shawn Shawn, you take the bike and ride pass them niggas, when you get up the street, act like you gotta tie your shoe or something, you our safety net. Brandy, you call Buck and tell him to hurry over here. I'm a pull down on these Niggas" "Cmon Mills let me roll, I aint afraid to bust my gun, stop treating me like I'm some scared little girl" Brandy pleaded. "Aight Bee, Call Buck then tail me, but you come up the opposite side of the street, and if it go down, you better not hesitate" Mills said adamantly before taking off.

Mills approached the G.I. Boys and wasted no time with small talk. "Look Homie, I don't know what ya'll think ya'll doing. But ya'll got the wrong strip for that shit. It's best that ya'l bounce" Mills said while flashing his Iron. "you must wanna die shorty" Spider said, and before Mills could react lil Timmy had his own Iron drawn and ready for action. "We taking this strip over shorty" Spider said, "Yeah lil nigga, Now step off" lil Timmy added with authority.

Brandy crept up the opposite side of the street. From a distance she spotted Timmy's gun, and with no hesitation she opened fire. "Pocka! Pocka! Pocka!" The G.I. Boys were caught off guard. Lil Timmy turned for a split second trying to locate the shooter, and Mills made his move. He drew his weapon with the speed of a gun slinger "Blowl! Blowl! Blowl!" Two of Mills slugs hit Timmy in the gut from close range. The impact from the slugs knocked him to the pavement. Spider and Man-Man returned fire, while fading away in opposite directions. Fella and Peko tried gunning Spider and Man-Man down, but Spider made it difficult as he aired the strip out, unloading on everyone in his sight. Man-Man fell for Mills trick, running straight into Shawn Shawn. Shawn Shawn watched Man-Man's body jerk as the slugs from his .380 entered its target. Man-Man ducked his head, covered the hole in his stomach and ran for cover while squeezing off aimless shots.

Spider took off through Peko's yard as his gun clicked, and he watched his last shell hit the concrete. He thought he was home free, but he ran into Buck, D-Roc, Slim, and lil Walt on the next street over. Lil Walt chopped him down, and left him stretched out in someone's front yard. Man-Man finally hit the ground, as Peko and Shawn Shawn boxed him in. They sent bullets ripping through his flesh. Lil Timmy's body made a trail of blood as he crawled for his weapon, but no matter how close his hand got to that iron, he would never reach it, Mills, Fella, and Brandy closed in on him, and Fella wasted no time waiting for orders. "Boom! A single shot from Fella's steel ripped through the back of lil

Timmy's skull gluing his head to the concrete with blood and brain matter.

The cops had been alerted and the sirens could be heard from a distance, but before panic could settle in on the youngsters, their saviour arrived. Slim slid the side door open on Bucks conversion van, "Hurry the fuck up and get in" D-Roc yelled. The youngsters wasted no time piling into the van, and Buck wasted no time smashing the peddle to the metal.

Law enforcement filled the street in no time. Yellow tape outlined the area as D.T. Brown and his partner White went door to door searching for any cooperative witnesses. It wasn't until after deep scrutiny that they discovered Spider's corpse on the next street over. The D.T.'s were furious. Over fifty shell casings were found scattered throughout the block. And not one by-stander nor resident had seen a single shooter. It was cases like these that made law enforcement look bad.

Pacman, the neighborhood asshole / super-cop didn't need any resident, nor by-standers cooperation. He knew who was behind the slayings just as he knew how hard it'd be to get any one in a twenty block radius to roll over on him. Buckshots name was written all over this crime scene and Pacman wasted no time relaying his thoughts and knowledge of the area to the detectives. The D.T.'s were already familiar with Daylon Braggs a.k.a. Buckshot. The state and federal police have been trying to build a case against him for years. While the detectives and local law enforcement worked together in an attempt to piece together the horrendous crime scene. Buckshot was on another side of town, pulling his van into Radissons Hotel parking lot. He purchased a room using his fake I.D., then destroyed the fraudulent identification.

Once inside the room, Buck called his homie Stone, and told him that he needed some garbage taken out. Stone knew exactly what Buck was referring to and told him he'd be there in about 15 to 20 minutes. Stone was a technician with guns of all sorts. He cleaned, dismantled, and got rid of all of Bucks dirty weapons.

Stone arrived and got straight down to business. He grabbed the trash bag out the can, wrapped the guns inside the hotel towels, and stuffed them inside the bag. "Listen, I don't want nobody to leave this room until ya'll receive word from me. Don't use the phone, Don't leave the room. Just chill, I'm bout to get rid of the burners and make some calls to the hood to assure that no one spoke to the police. Ya'll keep ya'lls eyes on the news, and wait on my page" Buck said before leaving out the room with Stone.

Two days had passed, and everyone in the hotel room was becoming aggravated. Peko and Shawn Shawn lay across one bed while Mills and Brandy occupied the other. Fella sat at the table with his cousin Slim, D-Roc, and lil Walt. While everyone else's mind was occupied with their situation, D-Roc's mind had drifted elsewhere. Brandy's youthful yet stacked anatomy was becoming more appealing to him by the minute. "Whats up lil Brandy, when you gone let me bust that lil thang open for you?" D-Roc said with a devious smile on his face. Brandy furrowed her brow, then rolled her eyes. If looks could kill, D-Roc would've dropped dead right on the spot. "I.m saying baby, Its bout time you let Roc pop that cherry" D-Roc continued. "D-Roc I don't know who you think your talking to like that, I aint one of them lil bitches you be fucking wit. You better check ya'self nigga!" Brandy shot back with more attitude. "My bad baby, I do need to treat the ladies with more respect. So can I open that little thang up please?" D-Roc replied sarcastically. Slim and Walt busted out laughing. "Roc man you silly as fuck. Leave lil Brandy alone." Slim said in between laughs. Brandy snapped "D-Roc I don't know who the fuck you think you are, you got yo home boys fooled, but I know you can't fight a lick, so you betta save that shit before I open yo ass up." "You lil bitch you better recognize who you talking to before I beat yo lil red ass in here." D-Roc said seriously. "Bitch? Nigga, you the bitch." Brandy said firmly. D-Roc jumped up, but Slim grabbed him. "C'mon Roc, chill out bro, she still a baby." D-Roc looked at Slim like he was crazy, but because Slim was his closet home boy he maintained his composure. Brandy jumped to her feet as well. Mills finally heard enough. "Bee chill the fuck out, you trippin Roc, we in here looking at a triple homicide, and ya'll bugging out on each other, I told you we aint about all that talking shit anyway Bee." Mills said with authority. His words only infuriated D-Roc more. "Lil Mills you better watch who the fuck you talking to lil homie, I aint one of ya soldiers, so you can save that Buck routine, cause you aint running shit, and I aint about no talking either lil nigga. You know how Roc get down!" D-Roc said loud enough for the neighbors to hear. Mills didn't respond, but that didn't stop D-Roc. "Ya'll lil niggas start getting a little money, and start getting besides ya'll self. I run that mutha fucking strip. I let ya'll lil niggas get money, but I'll shut that shit down, and there aint nothing that Buck or anybody else can do about it. You know why, cause D-Roc says so nigga. Matta fact I'm bout to rise up out this room, before I strangle one of ya'll lil niggas. . . .or Bitches" D-Roc said as he cut his eyes at Brandy. Mills pager went off. He saw the code 007 and knew it was Buck. "C'mon Bee lets go use the phone, this Buck right here." Mills said loud enough for D-Roc to hear. "I don't need Bucks say so to do shit, I'm leaving cause I wanna leave, when I wanna leave, you know why? Cause Roc says so lil nigga." D-Roc yelled as Mills and Brandy walked out the door. "You aight Bee?" Mills asked as they walked to the pay phone. "Yeah I'm straight, fuck D-Roc bro." Brandy replied. Mills called Buck and got confirmation that everything was cool, and that they could go home now. Buck also told Mills that the police were asking questions about him but he wasn't sweating it, cause his money was too long to go on a cops haunch. He also told them to stay off the strip for a few days and that if the police tried to question them, say nothing. Mills and Brandy returned to the room, to an even more fired up D-Roc. He now stood in the middle of the room smoking a fat blunt. He didn't want anybody to think he had talked behind Mills back so he started talking loudly again. This time he spoke directly to Mills. "Lil Mills you better start watching yo mouth lil homie, you starting to get a little big for your britches. I'm a let that shit you and ya lil girl friend was talking bout slide cause ya'll don't know no better, but you better tell yo lil girl friend to check herself before I treat her like a man and make her touch everything in this room." "Buck said we cool, we can go home, but be careful cause Pacman lerkin." Mills said disregarding D-Roc's speech. As D-Roc was about to respond to Mills demeanor, his ride arrived. He was hushed by the sound of one of his girlfriend's horn. He, Slim, and lil Walt left Mills and his crew in the room alone. When Mills arrived home, he heard the blues from his Grandmother. He had been gone for two days with out calling, and she was both relieved and fired up by the sight of him. Mills stayed in the house for a few days. He used the time for quality time with his little brother. They played video games and ate pizza just about everyday. When Mills finally left the house, he spent every second at Lisa's house. He and his crew punched that clock over time. The incident with the G.I. Boys drew Mills and his crew closer together. Mills knew the day would come when he would have to use his gun, but he didn't think he would handle taking a life so stoically. Mills was all in, and as far as he was concerned, there was no turning back. He was all in. In a life that he consciously knew would bring him wealth, prison, or death. Maybe even a combination of all three, but whatever the outcome, he was prepared to except the cards he was dealt.

It was nice outside so Mills, Fella, and Peko decided to take a walk to the corner store. While Brandy and Shawn Shawn held down the trap. They waved at Fella's mother on one side of the street, Peko and Shawn Shawn's mother on the other side of the street, and neared Brandy's mother, as she entered her own home. This wasn't just their neighborhood, East Main was their home. They were born and raised on the same street that they were presently running, and everyone who watched the trio. Knew it wouldn't be long before they owned these same streets.

Mills and Fella entered the store as Peko rushed over to a customer that flagged him down. Mills purchased a bottle of Ever Fresh Fruit Juice, and a pack of Now And Laters, while Fella grabbed a bag of Grippo's, a Sprite, and playfully talked a little trash to the store owner who playfully reciprocated the trash talk. Fella and Mills exited the store just in time to see Peko being strong armed by Big Bruce. Big Bruce was a neighborhood dope fiend that was known for robbing young dope boys. He stood at 6'4, 250 pounds. He was huge and his face was just as frightening.

Big Bruce had Peko by the neck with one hand, while his other hand was buried deep in

Peko's pocket. Peko's feet kicked in the air as he tried to tussle with the huge man. Mills quickly ran to Peko's aid, jumping in the air and smacking Bruce in the face with his Iron. The blow barely fazed Bruce. He slightly stumbled, instantly dropping Peko and grabbing a hold of Mills. He wrapped his large hands around Mills neck and said, "What you gone do wit that pistol lil Nigga, I'm Big Bruce, I eat bullets for breakfast" He gritted his teeth while tightening his grip. Fella jumped in the air and busted a bottle over the back of Bruce's head. The bottle exploded and blood leaked down the back of Bruce's neck. Unfazed, he grabbed a handful of Fella's shirt, while still holding on to Mills neck with his other hand. Mills shoved his Iron in Bruce's ribcage, and blasted off a shot, "Blowl!" Big Bruce stumbled backwards, looked at the hole in his side, then charged at Mills. "Blowl! Blowl!" Mills squeezed off two more shots hitting Bruce in the chest with both rounds. The Giant finally hit the pavement. As the onlookers watched in awe. The trio took off running. They entered Lisa's house through the back door bringing Brandy and Shawn Shawn quickly to their feet. Peko and Fella explained what had taken place, while Mills called Buckshot. Within minutes Bucks BMW was out front. Mills rushed out to the car and instantly noticed the police and ambulance down the street in front of the store. Buck wasted no time pulling away from the crime scene. "What the fuck happen T-Money?" Buck asked while making a dangerous right turn off of Berkley. "Some big ass fiend name Big Bruce was trying to rob Pee. Me and Fella tried to help and dude grabbed me by the neck. He was choking the life out of me, so I popped'em, but he kept coming at me so I hit'em two more times" Mills explained as his heart raced. "What you do with the burner?" Buck asked as his mind went into overdrive and he began analyzing the situation like a seasoned vet. Mills pulled the gun from his waist.

Buck didn't say a word, he just shook his head and headed for Stone's house.

After dropping off the gun, Buck headed for his home on 161, where he would keep Mills hid until he knew things were safe. Mills didn't mind laying low at Bucks house, he used the time to get closer to Neesh. Buck spent most of his time at the house along with Mills. When he wasn't making runs of his own, he was checking on the hood, making sure everyone stayed quiet about Mills involvement with Big Bruce's shooting. The whole time Mills was at Bucks house, he avoided school, but class stayed in session because Buck never stopped schooling him on the game, and life as he perceived it. "T-Money, I want you to understand something…" Buck hit the blunt a couple times before he continued. "Any man can take a life. That don't make him a Gangsta. Depending on the reason behind the man taking the life, it can make him a fool. Don't confuse being foolish with being a Gangsta. I'm telling you this because I don't want you to become controlled by your burner, and the feeling of power it gives you. Ya gun is for protection, not flexin, be smart." Mills sat there attentively. He knew the difference between a lesson he was expected to elaborate on and one that he was not.

Buck always gave it to Mills in the rawest form, just as Mills father had always given it to him. "Mills I don't want you to gain gratification from taking a life, especially a black life. And I don't say that to say that its aiight to cause harm to a white life, because I'm not prejudice in any way, shape, form or fashion. But I need you to understand that black on black crime doesn't just happen. The way blacks treat one another, speak to each other, and feel about each other, has been planted into our minds by design. Every since the black race has been plagued by slavery, we've been programmed to turn against one another, to hate or brothers and sisters of the same struggle. Jim Crow, and Willie Lynch are the founders and masterminds of this corrupt black mind set, starting with the separation of Negroes by the color of our skin, and the texture of our hair. Rewarding some of our brothers and sisters with the "Imaginary" privilege of living and working in the house close to the white family slave masters, deceiving them into believing that they were worth more, better off, and treated better than their Negro brothers and sisters who lived and worked out side in the fields. "House Negro's" is what those living and working in the house were called. It was their job to snitch, and rebel against their brothers and sisters who maybe trying to escape, learn how to read, or steal a little food. Thus turning black against black, slave against slave. . . this is the core to the problem of why blacks are so quick to feud with one another. We are doing the white man's job for him by taking each other out, and rebelling against our own kind." Buck spoke strongly, but he always did when speaking about the black race and their struggle.

He and Mills spent the majority of the night at the kitchen table, conversing about life, both inside and outside the game. Buck made sure he did everything in his power to groom Mills into a well rounded young man, and not just a game savvy street Hustler. He wanted Mills to be everything he, Mills father and mother was, plus more.

The next day Mills got to spend a little alone time with Neesh. Buck was out making his runs, while Mek was out running a few errands of her own.

Mills sat on the couch smoking on some lime green as Neesh entered the house. She dropped her books at the front door, and plopped down on the couch next to him. "Dang boy is that all you do?" She said while fanning smoke clouds from in front of her and coughing into her hand. Mills sat the blunt in the ashtray out of respect. "Nah, this aint all I do, but I do a lot of it" He said, then blew out the last cloud of smoke from his lungs.

Neesh shook her head in amusement, while Mills smiled at her in adoration. "Mills you need to be careful because everybody at my school has been talking about what you did at that store" Neesh said. "Yeah" Mills replied. "Yeah" Neesh said. "They talk about it like its something cool, but its really not" Neesh rolled her eyes to emphasize her disapproval. Mills had no rebuttal. So he just listened while she expressed her concerns. "You better watch out for those chicken heads too. They all say they're gonna get you while your young, everybody thinks your up and coming" Neesh continued. "You know I aint thinking bout them chicken heads. My eyes is on one girl and one girl only. And you know who she is" Mills insinuated. "Boy you is crazy" Neesh playfully replied, while blushing from ear to ear. Their conversation was interrupted by the sound of keys at the front door. Mek came walking through the door with both hands filled with shopping bags. "Whats up Mills, Whats happening lil sis?" Mek said while giving Neesh a funny look that caused them both to laugh.

Mills helped Mek carry her bags up stairs, then rushed back down the steps as his pager screamed for attention. He grabbed it off the living room table, and noticed Lisa's phone number, with Fella's code behind it. He wasted no time calling his ace. "Yo" Fella said answering the phone. "Whats up bro?" Mills replied. "You, Why you aint come out the crib yet homie, I told Buck I hollard at Abdullah, the arab who owned the store, and he said shit cool, dude aint tell the cops nothing. He already out the hospital. He found out who ya moms and pops is, and he choked up. He know that if he went back to the joint he gone run into yo pops, and yo pops really gone kill his ass!" They both burst into laughter. "Yeah, Buck told me everything was cool a couple days ago. I be out today, my G.Ma been tripping about me missing school anyway. Soons Buck get back, I'm ah have him drop me off" Mills said. "Aiight Homie, hurry up though cause the trap slapping

bro" Fella responded before they disconnected. "I smell it, let me inhale it lil nigga" Mek

said as she entered the living room. Mills handed her the half blunt he put out in the

ashtray and Neesh took off up stairs, headed for her bedroom to avoid the smoke.

A few minutes later, Buck walked through the door with his home boy Butter. Butter has

been Bucks homeboy since middle school. While Buck was heavy in the dope game,

Butter was selling Weed. He started out selling already rolled joints. Now he was the man

in the weed game, much like Buck is in the game of Cain.

Mek and Butter didn't get along. She hated when he and Buck hung out together, because

Butter was single, and a well known man whore.

Butter's a bona fide player. The pretty boy type, light skin, wavy hair, six foot two inches

in height. He got his name from the hoop court. His jumpshot was smooth like Butter. A

lot of Mek's homegirls had fell for Butter's smooth talk, and they all told Mek of the ten

inches of blessings he had in his pants, which made her dislike him even more.

As soon as Mek saw Butter walk through the door behind Buck, she smacked her lips,

rolled her eyes then stomped out of the living room. "Bae, get off that bullshit and come

give daddy a kiss" Buck said, after noticing her instant attitude.

Mills saved the couple an argument when he told Buck that he needed a ride to the hood.

Buck followed Mek into the kitchen, gave her a bag of money, joked with her about her

attitude, brushed off her response, then he, Mills and Butter were out the door. Escaping

the wrath of an angry black woman.

-CHAPTER FOUR-

"93" was closing in fast, and things were going good for Mills and his crew. Mills

kicked his feet up. While smoking on a fat blunt, and daydreaming about the new whip he

had plans to cop for his up coming birthday. Things couldn't be going better for him, yet

he had an unsettling felling in his gut that he couldn't explain. As comfortable as he was

in his favorite chair, it was something inside him pulling him towards the front window.

When he peered through the curtains, he noticed a U-haul pull to a stop in front of Lisa's

house. Before he knew it, men in black were jumping out the back of the U-haul. "OH

SHIT, SWAT!" Mills yelled. He threw his dope in one direction, and ran in another. Fella

wasted no time following his lead. He slid his nine millimeter under the couch, threw his

sack across the room, and shot up the stairs behind Mills. Brandy, Peko and Shawn

Shawn were quickly on Fella's heels. The front and back door could be heard hitting the

floor along with the officers voices "Columbus's SWAT Team, everybody get on the

floor". The youngsters stomped around up stairs looking for places to hide, as the SWAT

Team made their way up the steps.

The youngsters decided on a back room, where they all dove on one bed. Lisa and a few

other smokers finished their crack off with no other worries then having their drugs taken

from them. So they smashed stones into their stems, and pulled on the glass pipe like it

would be their last hit.

Everyone in the house was brought out in handcuffs. Fella's mother, along with Peko and

Shawn Shawn's mother, followed by Brandy's mom. Rushed the cruiser's their children were in.

The lady's rescue attempt was to no avail. As officers exited the house carrying ziplock bags with drugs, cash and handguns. The youngsters watched their mothers figures disappear as the cop cars pulled away from the scene. Instead of being taken to the Detention Center for Youths, they were all placed in separate interrogation rooms. Detective Brown and White took turns questioning the kids. After being left in the small room alone for hours, the Detectives strolled through the door. "SO Mr. Mills, do you have anything to tell us?" Detective Brown asked, playing the good cop. Mills was taught never to speak to the cops without a lawyer present, so he sat there quietly with out responding. "He wants to act tough Browny, take the little shit to jail and book him for all three murders." White said in a very nasty tone. Mills heart started to race, but he remained silent. "No Whitey, Mr. Mills here isn't a bad guy, he's smart, aren't you Tony, can I call you Tony?" Brown inquired. Mills still remained silent. Brown continued "Mr. Mills I know you don't wanna go to prison for some murders you didn't commit. All you have to do is give up your friend Daylon, or should I call him Buckshot, we know he killed those guys from Gary, Indiana. Even though the word is out that you did it, we know better than that, so whatah ya say, you wanna cooperate or you wanna take the rap for your buddy." Mills was scared, and it took everything in him to remain silent after hearing the Detectives talk about the G.I. Boys. The questioning lasted for an hour, but Mills stuck to the code of silence. The Detective went from room to room questioning Mills and his crew one person at a time. After five hours of questioning, the Detectives had nothing. No one cooperated. Mills and his crew didn't say a word. Detective Brown and White were furious. Mills and his crew had just made some new enemies. They were all taken to the Detention Center. Peko, Shawn Shawn, Fella, and Brandy were processed first. Mills went in last since his grandmother was not yet notified. When he called her, he got straight to the point. "Momma I'm in jail, I need you to come to court for me in the morning." "Oh Lord Jesus Tony, I knew it, I knew it, I told you God don't like ugly, sweet Jesus not my baby." Grandma Mills said hysterically. "Mr. Mills you need to end your call." The lady processing him said. "Momma I gotta go, I love you, and make sure you come to court in the morning." Mills said before hanging up. Mills lucked up and was placed in the same tank with Fella and Peko. Shawn Shawn was placed in a unit for the younger kids, while Brandy was stationed with the young ladies.

Back in the hood, D-Roc, Slim, and lil Walt were on their way to a night club on the cities north side. When D-Roc pulled his Bronco into the clubs parking lot, heads turned as his system rattled the ground. 2-Pac's-"How Long Will They Morn Me", screamed from the speakers and everyone stared as the truck glided into its parking space.

D-Roc, Slim, and lil Walt stepped out the truck Fly as always. D-Roc's walk exuded confidence. He was the epitome of the term "Prettyboy Gangster". He wore a simple dark green jogging suit, white and green Delta Force Nikes, and a green and white Boston Celtics hat sat nicely on top of his French Braids. A thick Herring Bone necklace with an iced out name plate hung from his neck. D-Roc and his crew were always over the top with everything they did, so one necklace, no matter how big was never enough. He coupled his Herring Bone with a Figgero necklace that had a solid gold Ozzi Medallion hanging from it. His wrist sported a thick Herring Bone bracelet, and six of his fingers were flooded with Diamond Rings.

Slim Gangster, better known as Slim, was named after his tall, slim frame. He stood at 6'2, 175 pounds, and sported his hair style in a small afro, with a razor sharp line up. Slim wore dark blue jeans, a white Tee, and baby blue Patton Leather Georgia Bertini sneakers. A Leather North Carolina Varsity Jacket blended perfectly with his sneakers and he sported layers of blinding jewelry as well.

Lil Walt was 5'6 with a head full of plaits that hung down to his shoulders. His dark skin and grayish colored eyes assisted his plaits with making his mean mug look meaner. Although D-Roc was the crew's leader, Lil Walt was the bigger threat, and most feared. He sported a black Guess Jean outfit, a black Tee, and black low cut Nikes. He had four gold teeth in his mouth that covered up his chipped teeth, and accommodated his many other gold accessories.

As the trio scanned the parking lot for any of their adversaries. D-Roc spotted Neesh's best friend Tasha, and a few of her going out buddies. He called out her name, and waved her and her entourage over to his truck. "Whats up D-Roc, Slim, and lil Walt" Tasha said. Her and her girls had price scanners embedded into their eyes, so it didn't take them long to appraise the young Ghetto superstars riches. "Whats up Baby", D-Roc replied "Dig baby doll wont you and yo girls carry me and my homeboy's pistols in the club for us? We got a hunnit a pop, and drinks on us" D-Roc said hoping they were guided by greed.

"I don't know D-Roc, what if they search us?" Tasha responded. "C'mon good looking, you know I aint gone let nothing happen to you." D-Roc persuaded. "Shit girl for two hundred I'll carry one of them bitches in." Tasha's homegirl said. "Shit me too." "And me three." Said Tasha's other two homegirls. "Well there you go D-Roc, and you better be good in there." Tasha said letting him know that if she seen him talking to any girls she'd be the first to tell her best friend. D-Roc started laughing. "Ha Ha Ha, yeah aight." He replied. They gave the girls their guns and headed for the club.

Once inside, the girls walked up to D-Roc, Slim, and lil Walt giving them hugs while stuffing their guns in there waste band. Lil Walt rubbed on Tasha's homegirl's bodonka donk as she hugged him. "I'm tryna hit that tonight" He whispered in her ear." "And I'm tryna let you." She whispered back. Slim on the other hand was a chick magnet, so it was only natural that he was being hit on by Tasha's friend Lauren. As they exchanged flirtatious words, D-Roc slid a few insinuations under Tasha's hat, causing her to blush, and glance at the bulge in his sweat pants. "Damn is that his gun or is that all him." She thought. They all went their separate ways. Tasha and her girls headed for the dance floor, while D-Roc and his boys headed for the bar. After ordering their drinks, they found an isolated corner of the club, and stood there bobbing there heads to Mc Breeds "Just Shake Ya Rump". As the music changed to Celly Cells "Its Going Down". D-Roc noticed the dance floor parting like the Red Sea. T-Bone, Fresh, and several of their homeboys came walking through the crowd. They met up with Big Duece and some more of their homeboys in the middle of the dance floor.

A fine redbone came walking over to D-Roc as he stared down his adversaries. "Big Duece and T-Bone said you can walkout, or get carried out" Redbone said, while standing in front of D-Roc with her hands on her hips. D-Roc threw his drink in her face, and mugged her to the ground. "Tell T-Bone and Duece I said Suck My Dick" He said grabbing his crotch and flicking T-Bone and Duece the middle finger.

Two guys appeared out of nowhere. The first guy swung on D-Roc, but missed his vicious blow. Slim busted him in the head with his beer bottle, sending glass flying across the room. D-Roc and his boys were swarmed from all angles. Lil Walt pulled his nine mm and smacked everyone within reach up side their head. He sent one guy after another to the pavement. T-Bone opened fire in the club, and Walt wasted no time firing back. D-Roc followed suit, sending shots in the direction of his adversaries and the club erupted with gunfire.

Slims long body dove through the air while blasting off shots. He landed behind a table which he used for cover. All the gunmen lost their targets as the party goers ran through the club like a herd of elephants trying to escape a mouse. D-Roc and his comrades tried to make it out the club before their adversaries, but Fresh took aim on the front entrance. Bullets whizzed by Walt's head as he pushed by a flock of females, and slid out the door. D-Roc and Slim ran for cover as innocent people felt the wrath of Fresh's Smith and Wesson. Bullets ripped through the flesh of the innocent, sending the crowd at the door falling to the floor, and diving for cover.

D-Roc spotted T-Bone running for another exit, and opened fire. T-Bone hit the deck and crawled for cover. Pandemonium broke out in the club again as D-Roc and Slim traded shots with T-Bone and his posse. Slim spotted a few girls running out the back exit. "C'mon Roc, We gotta get the fuck outta here" He yelled while grabbing D-Roc shirt. D-Roc recklessly emptied his clip as they ran for the back door.

They made it out, but bullets followed behind them. "Aw shit, I think I'm hit" D-Roc

yelled as they ran through the parking lot. Lil Walt had the engine running as D-Roc and

Slim quickly loaded into the Bronco. Lil Walt sped out the lot with the music blasting. He

emptied his clip on T-Bone and Fresh as they came running out the club, once again

sending them diving for cover. Lil Walt pulled up to Grant Hospital and let D-Roc out at

the emergency entrance. Then sped out of that parking lot as well. D-Roc took a bullet to

the shoulder blade. Lucky for him the bullet went in and out.

After the doctors patched him up, he was visited by Detectives Brown and White.

Sticking to the G-Code, D-Roc refused to Cooperate with the law, but ladyluck was on

the D.T.'s side this time, D-Roc had a Warrant. So the remainder of his night would be

spent in an Interrogation Room.

Instead of questioning D-Roc about the shooting at the Night Club, the Detectives

focused on the Triple Homicide of the G.I. Boys. "So. . .Mr. Turner lets skip the bullshit

and talk about your involvement in the killing of those guys from Gary, Indiana." Brown

said breaking the ice. "Pha ha ha ha ha ha ha ha!" D-Roc busted out in laughter. "C'mon

man, you got to do better than that." D-Roc said. "Listen here muther fucker. You think

this is a god damn game? Well your little buddies have already told on you and your

friend Buckshot. So we'll see how much of a game it is when your little pretty yellow ass

is being fucked by some big dick mother fucker in the penitentiary." White said angrily.

D-Roc laughed in his face again. White hated being ridiculed, so D-Roc's laughter sent

him over board. He grabbed D-Roc by his shirt. "Ahh Shit!!" D-Roc yelled as White

smashed his hand into D-Roc's wound. Brown grabbed his partner, but he too was afraid

of White. White was Brown's superior. He had been a cop for 10 years, and a Detective for 5. Brown knew his partner had a prejudice against people of color, but he valued his job too much to speak on it. White was never to zealous about colored people's justice. He would let black murders go uninvestigated. The same as he did with the black break-ins or any other case where blacks were the victims. Brown became a victim to his position, as most people of color did when they were awarded a good paying job. They often over looked the injustice done to other people of color when they worked for the one's doing the injustice. Oftentimes they viewed themselves as being superior, much like the "House Negro" was deceived into believing about his / or herself during slavery. D-Roc ridiculed the Detectives throughout their interrogation. And they did everything in their power to make him uncomfortable before taking him to the Detention Center.

D-Roc was famous throughout the juvenile facility. To be honest, DYC was like his second home. He spent months at a time there. Feuding with his many adversaries and befriending J.C.O's, so whenever he came through DYC's gates. It was like a reunion for him, the staff, and all the youngsters who idolized him and his legend.

As D-Roc was escorted to D-Unit, he spotted Mills, Fella, and Peko in B-Unit. He quickly ordered the J.C.O to place him in the unit with his little homies, and the J.C.O obliged after making him promise not to cause any trouble. As D-Roc dapped it up with is little homies. They all examined his arm as it rested like a chicken wing in a sling." Don't worry bout it, its just a love tap" D-Roc said. "Did ya'll talk to the D.T.'s" He asked, referring to the Detectives. "HELL NAW!" They answered in unison. "I mean they questioned us, but we all kept it Gee" Mills added. "Aiight ya'll nigga's make sure ya'll keep it that way, cause they gone come at us every chance they get. But don't pay those pigs no mind. If they had anything on us we'd be in jail by now" D-Roc said. The next day D-Roc went to court, and was released to himself. He was now eighteen, and his Warrant was for Violation of Probation that he was on a year ago as a juvenile.

The next time Mills and his crew went to court they were all released with two years probation. After a few days in the house, they were right back on the strip. Now that Lisa's house was boarded up, they were once again block monsters. Mills birthday was in a few weeks and he still wanted to purchase his first car. So he hugged the block everyday after school. He was having a party at the Residence Inn and wanted it to be live, so he made flyers which he passed out in the hood and at school.

When his birthday hit, Buck took him and Fella to a special car connect. Mills purchased a Red 70's Cutlass with T-Tops red and white pen striped bucket seats, chrome McClain rims, and two twelve-inch speakers with a Punch 1000 Watt Amp. Fella copped a Money Green Box Shaped Regal with T-Tops green bucket seats, chrome rims, and a sound system identical to Mills. They now trailed through the hood showing off their cars before Mills party tonight. Brandy rode shotgun with Mills while Peko and Shawn Shawn rode with Fella. They stopped in front of D-Roc, Slim, and lil Walt's spot on Liley as they stood on the porch. "What up Roc? Ya'll coming to my party tonight?" Mills yelled after turning down his music. "You gone have some hoes up in there? D-Roc yelled back. "Fa'Sho." Mills replied. "Count us in then homie." " Aight then. . .peace." Mills said and threw up the deuces.

Later that night Mills party was everything he expected it to be. The females out numbered the males two to one. The party was small, but sufficient. The only guys there were from Main Street. There were no outsiders, which meant the chances of gunplay were very slim. Mills stood by the stereo playing DJ, while Fella, Peko, Shawn Shawn, and Brandy stood by the homemade bar smoking weed. Buck was in the middle of a big dice game with D-Roc and the rest of the hustlers. Slim stood in the corner entertaining a crowd of females, while Walt stood over top of D-Roc assisting him in his trash talk. Neesh and her sister Mek shared a loveseat by the door, while Tasha sat on the couch adjacent to them, with a few admirers and couch potatoes. As Mills changed the tape from 2-Pac to Biggie Smalls, he mumbled curse words under his breath at the sight of Shawn'tae sashaying over his way. "What up Mills, you still mad at me." Shawn'tae asked while showing Mills her tongue seductively. "C'mon Shawn'tae, I told you I aint mad at you, I just don't fuck with you like that, cause you run yo mouth to much." Mills said. "Damn Mills, why you want everything to be such a big secret? I said I was sorry, let me make it up to you." She proposed. "Nah I'm cool baby girl." Mills said as he brushed her hand off his thigh. Mills felt he was being watched, so he glanced over his shoulder and spotted Neesh checking him out. She rolled her eyes and smiled at him. "Dig Shawn'tae, you just a lil bit too much for me, but I got somebody you should meet." Mills said persuasively. Before Shawn'tae could reply, Mills yelled out D-Roc's name. D-Roc looked up from the dice game and Mills waved him over, D-Roc held up a finger telling Mills to hold on a minute. D-Roc held the dice to his ear as he shook them. "Nine my favorite point, cause I keeps mine on me, get'em Nena." He said as he threw the dice in the middle of the floor. He hit his point and picked up his money from several spots on the floor. "I need a fader not a friend; I take the shit that fold and the shit that jingle." D-Roc said as he shook the dice by his ear again. As he got a fader he let the dice roll out of his hand. The dice landed on a three and one. "Bet fifty you don't ten or four.." His fader yelled out. "Bet it nigga." D-Roc said as he slid a fifty-dollar bill by his faders feet."

Back doe lil Joe." D-Roc yelled as he threw the dice out his hand backwards. D-Roc hit a few nines before crapping out. He stood up with a stack of bills in his hand. He counted the money as he made his way over to Mills. "What's happenin lil homie?" He said while giving Shawn'tae a glance over. "Aint shit happenin bro, I got somebody I want you to meet. . .Shawn'tae this is D-Roc, D-Roc this is Shawn'tae." Mills said as he gave Shawn'tae a little nudge towards D-Roc. Shawn'tae appraised D-Roc as he stood before her looking like a million bucks. "That's how you wanna play it Mills?" Shawn'tae asked . she grabbed D-Roc by the hand and said, "Aight then." As they walked off, D-Roc looked at Shawn'tae ass and said, "I owe you one lil homie." Neesh watched from the other side of the room as D-Roc walked into the bathroom with Shawn'tae. "I hope his thang fall off." She said to her sister with a hint of jealousy. Mills walked over to join his crew as Peko opened the door for two more females. Brandy passed Mills the blunt she was smoking on and said, "Happy Birthday Bro." Peko watched both of the girls backside jiggle as they walked through the door. He shook his head and bit down on his bottom lip as he fantasized about drilling the both of them from behind. The girls were a couple of years older than Mills. They went to Neesh's high school where Mills name was a little heavy in the hallways, because of all the girls from his neighborhood that went there. "Whats up Mills, Happy Birthday from me and my girl Chrissie." La'Shay said doing the talking for her and her friend. La'Shay and Chrissie were both fine. La'Shay was abrown skin beauty, while Chrissie was a cold light skin wavy, which meant a fine light skin sister with wavy hair. "Thanks." Mills said smoothly. "Mills my girl is kind of shy, but she likes you." La'Shay said referring to Chrissie. Mills spotted Neesh looking again. This time they locked eyes and Neesh stuck her tongue out while rolling her eyes at him. Mills knew Neesh was digging him, and he smiled back at her. "Chrissie you fine and so are you La'Shay, but I'm kind of seeing somebody. Wont ya'll holla at my bros. La'Shay this is Fella, Chrissie this Peko." Mills said pointing at both of his homeboys. Mek caught her sister exchanging looks with Mills and said, "Girl you better get him before one of these scavenger ass bitches get him." "Mek you know Mills is too young for me." Neesh replied. "Says who? And who says you cant get him now and put him up for later. Psssssh, girl you better quit playin and it aint like you coming off of none of that lil coo coo noway." Mek said causing her and her sister to start laughing. "Mek you is a trip." Neesh said in between laughs. Mills walked up as their laughter ended. "What's up Mek. What's up Neesh." "Shit smoke something nigga." Mek replied "You the Birthday Boy, this is yo day. Did you get everything you wished for?" Neesh added. "I don't know, it all depends." Mills answered. "What do you mean you don't know?" Neesh asked. "I mean you could answer that question better than I could." Mills insinuated. "How can I answer it? I don't know what you wished for?" Neesh said. "All I want for my birthday is you, so tell me. . . do I got everything I wished for?" Neesh couldn't stop smiling. She was clearly drawn to the youngster. Stevie Wonder and Ray Charles both could see that. "Boy you is something else" Neesh said. Mills took it as a compliment and squeezed into the seat next to Neesh and her sister. He stayed there smoking weed with Mek, and kicking flavor with Neesh for the remainder of his party. From the other side of the room, D-Roc watched Mills and Neesh with envy. Even though he was no longer with Neesh, he couldn't stand seeing her with anyone else. He doubted if Neesh would give Mills any play considering their age difference and Neesh's "Holier Than Thou" attitude, but two thangs were for sure. Age is nothing but a number and Mills was definitely becoming a problem.

       ⁑   ⁑   ⑧   ⑧   ⑧   ⑧   ⑧   ⁑   ⁑

The very next day, the young hustlers were right back on the block. Getting high and kicking it was cool, and very much needed. Since being placed on probation and warned about drug testing, they hadn't done much of anything. But for a True Hustler, there was no better feeling than being on your grind. For a True Hustler, making money was a high within itself. The more money you made, the higher you felt. This corresponds with that saying "High On Life!"

Everyone beside Peko took heed to their probation officers warnings. But for Peko, smoking weed was apart of who he is. So not smoking wasn't even an option he had to weigh. He and that green leaf were married until death did them part.

As Mother Nature would have it. The season quickly changed which allowed Mills and Fella to showcase their rides. They parked their cars on the strip, letting their systems flood the street with Hip Hop while they hopped in and out of cars or hid on the side of houses serving different customers.

Hustling on the block was cool for Mills and his crew, but they wanted badly to be back hustling out of a house. It was a safer hustle and it awarded more cash. Hustling out of a house made the grind more business oriented, than standing on the corner competing with numerous other Hustlers for crack sales.

Hustling on the corner made slanging Dee seem "Savage Like" when in all actuality the "Dope Game" was a business. An ongoing enterprise that extended way beyond the corner and house hustlers that are more widely portrayed with the dope game than the Bolivian, Argentinian, Cuban, Columbian, and other out of the country producers and distributors that are the fathers and mothers of this never-ending world wide enterprise. As Mill sat on the hood of his car, Lucky pulled up in a truck with a white man, and two prostitutes. "C'mere Mills" Lucky yelled. Mills had never before seen the white man that Lucky was rolling with which made him leery about approaching the truck. "Hey Fella, you ever seen that cracker befoe" "Not at all" Fella answered. "Get out the car Luck" Mills yelled back as him and his friends stared at the white man. That was the irony of the game. A brother or sister that no one in the hood has ever seen in their life, could pull up on any strip and get served. But a white person was automatically perceived as the law, as if smoking crack was a black thang and the white race was above addiction. Lucky could since Mills concern from a distance. "He straight Mills, This is one of my big spenders" Lucky yelled back. "Iight, just get out the car, I need to holler at you bout something." Mills said encouragingly. Lucky got out the car and met Mills on the sidewalk where he now stood. "Dude straight Mills, Now sell me a fat hundred and make it look like something" Lucky said while twitching his lips and doing the dope fiend rock. " I got you baby, but what's up with Lolly, did you holler at her about me and my crew posting up in her crib?" Mills asked. "Mills you know Lolly will let you come over and make a few dollars." Lucky answered. "Yeah Yeah, I know, but I'm talking about me and my crew, and I aint talking bout for no few hours, we tryna get this money, you know we gone pay swell." Mills persuaded. "I don't know Mills, you know how Lolly is about her house, she don't allow anybody to sell out of there, but you and that lil dude from Studer, and she only let ya'll stay for a few hours." As Lucky and Mills talked, Pacman turned onto the street. Fella quickly turned his system off, and jumped out of the car. Pacman pulled to a stop in front of Mills and Lucky. He hopped out his cruiser with his weapon drawn. "Both of you put your hands up and don't move." He said with authority. His partner hopped out with his weapon on the white man and two prostitutes in the truck. "Don't fuckin move." He said as the prostitutes moved around in the backseat. Pacman did a thorough shake down on Lucky and Mills, than he started stepping on trash that layed on the ground around them. He knew hustlers kept their dope hid in potato chip bags, cigar packs, candy bags, and boxes so it could blend with the trash on the ground. Lucky for Mills, he kept his dope in a cigar box across the street in Fella's front yard. "Where's your dope Mills? You got it in your ass like your boy D-Roc." Pacman said as he pushed Mills and Lucky up against the cruiser to frisk them once again. "I aint got no dope." Mills said loud enough for everyone to hear, because Pacman was known for planting drugs on people if he wanted them bad enough. "C'mon Mills you don't expect me to believe that. You're talking to one of the biggest smokers in the hood, and you don't have any dope. C'mon Mills you're moving big dope for your boy Buck." Pacman said trying to get a certain response from Mills. "I aint got no drugs man." Mills continued to say loudly. Pacman's harassment was cut short when Fella's mother came out her house raising hell. "Pacman, you take your bullshit somewhere else. These boys aint bothering nobody, you gone quit fucking with my son and my nephews or I'm a have that file ass badge of yours." "Ms. Stargell I'm going to ask you to back away from my car, before you join your nephew here." Pacman said as he aggressively stuffed Mills in the back seat. "Put me in the mutha fucking back seat, it aint gone get you nowhere. What you gone do, plant some drugs on me like you did the boy up the street the other day? Fella's mother yelled. "Ms. Stargell I'm going to ask you one more time to back away from my car, and lower your fucking tone of voice, if your so called nephew doesn't have any drugs on him, than I'll let him go." Pacman said in a nasty tone. "DRUGS. . . you done searched the boy a thousand times, now I'm calling the damn precinct on your ass." Fella's mother yelled as she dialed numbers on her cordless phone. Pacman paid her no attention and walked over to the truck to assist his partner. After frisking the trucks passengers and thoroughly searching the truck. He then tried to get the white man and prostitutes to say that Mills had sold them drugs. Pacman and his partner headed to the cruiser empty handed. They let Mills and Lucky out the back seat of the cruiser and sped off. "Mills C'mon and take care of me so I can get the fuck from around here." Lucky said. " Dig Luck, you know Pacman probably somewhere watching us right now, so wont you go over Lolly's and wait on me, I'll be there in about five minutes. I'm a put something real special together for you and I'm a brang Lolly something." Mills said as he looked around paranoidingly . "Aight Mills, but hurry up, and you better make me famous." Lucky said referring to the amount of dope he was expecting to receive. When Lucky pulled off, Mills grabbed his work off the ground and told Brandy to follow him in her house. Mills grabbed the several pieces he needed to take care of Lucky and Lolly. Then gave the rest of his pack to Brandy. While Brandy ran upstairs to stash Mills pack, Mills wrapped the work he kept in some paper. He had intentions to go over Lolly's on his own, but he thought better of it. When Brandy came downstairs, he tossed her the small pack and told her to stuff it and ride with him over to Lolly's house. They grabbed two bikes from Fella's front yard and rode inconspicuously through the allys and cuts.

When Mills and Brandy arrived, Lucky snatched the door open before they had a chance to knock. After a half hour of Mills slick talk, and a few bolders of his hard white critty Lolly was persuaded. Mills left Brandy there with a few stones, while he headed back to the strip to inform the rest of his crew of the good news, and grab more work. When Mills arrived. Peko and Shawn Shawn were on the side of their house with a few customers, and Fella was hopping out of one car into another. Fella made it back before Peko and Shawn Shawn finished with their customers. "Dig Fells, we back in action, I got Lolly to let us open up shop at her house." Mills said. "Word?" Fella replied. "Word." Mills shot back. "SO what's the plan?" Fella asked. Peko and Shawn Shawn walked up right on time. "The plan for what?" Peko asked. "I got Lolly to let us open shop at her crib." Mills Answered. "This is how we gone do it, Bee around there right now holding it down wit a few stones. I'm bout to grab some more work and shoot back to Lolly's with her. Since ya'll already crankin here, ya'll stay here and let all the custy's know we at Lolly's. then tomorrow me and Bee gone play the strip and shoot the custy's to Lolly's while ya'll post up. We'll do it like this for a couple days until everybody knows where we at. With Lucky's help, we should have that spot boomin in 2 weeks tops." "Mills said. "What about the fiends that don't know where Lolly stay?" Shawn Shawn asked. "Every fiend know where Lolly stay lil bro. If you smoke dope, you've been over Lolly's before." Mills assured Shawn Shawn. "Lets make it do what it do then bro." Fella said. "AIght, I'm bout to grab some work and head back over Lolly's, let's get this paper baby!" Mills said, playfully throwing punches at Fella's stomach.

-CHAPTER FIVE-

Lolly's house became a million dollar spot in no time. For the last three months, Mills and his crew did nothing but hustle and go to school. Now that school was out, Brandy felt the crew could use a little time off. "Bro lets go out tonight, we been goin hard for months with no time off. I'm tryna get my party on." She said while snapping her fingers to the music that filled Lolly's living room. "Aint nothing going on sis, we getting this money, stack-N-grind, you know the name of the game." Mills replied. "Shid bro, the skating ring popping tonight and you know hard work shouldn't go unrewarded." Brandy said using Buck's logic. "Yea T-Money, lightin up, aint nothing wrong with a party now and then." Fella added. Mills looked at Shawn Shawn. Shawn Shawn shrugged his shoulders as if to say he was down with whatever. Peko came strolling in the living room counting the money he just received from one of his customers. As always he was smoking on a fat blunt of killer weed. He sensed the tension in the air. "What the fuck going on in here?" He asked. "We trying to go to the rink tonight Pee and Mills is being stubborn as always." Brandy said while playfully shoving Mills. "I know Pee agrees wit me, he's a block monster for real, huh Pee." Mills said. "I'm always down with banging a few bitches." Peko said while dapping it up with Fella who always agreed when it came to the females. "Well T-Money, it looks like you and Shawn Shawn are out voted." Aight man, look like we going to the rink. I mean I understand why you and Pee wanna go, ya'll some horndogs, but Bee aint gone give no nigga no holler noway. She gone be actin all mean and shit. Then as soon as some nigga try to holler at her, she gone flip." Mills started doing his impression of Brandy, and they all busted out laughing. Brandy couldn't help but laugh, but she punched Mills in the arm letting him know that she didn't like the joke being on her.

Later that evening they all went home to get dressed for the night out. When they arrived at the skating rink, the first people they ran into were D-Roc, Slim, and lil Walt. Mills was dressed completely in Tommy Hillfiger. He wore 14k gold Gucci link necklace with a solid gold lion head hanging from it. His right wrist was accommodated with a matching Gucci link bracelet, while his left wrist sported a Tommy Hillfiger sports watch. Unlike D-Roc who wore a ring on every finger, Mills only wore one ring on his pinky finger. It was an iced out lion head, like his medallion. Mills sported a tight fade with waves drilling on the top. His light brown skin accommodated his baby face. Mills was mature beyond his years and the majority of his quietly smooth style was inherited from Buck.

Peko was as smooth. At 5'8 he was the tallest out of the crew. His build was similar to slim, being that he was lean, weighing only 130 pounds. Peko had hazel brown eyes to go with his golden brown complexion. All the weed he smoked coupled with his naturally droopy eyes made it hard for his pretty eyes to be admired. Peko walked with a slow stroll, somewhat dragging his feet. He had natural curly hair like his deceased father, which added to his pimp demeanor. Peko stood tall in a pair of blue Guess jeans shorts, a white v-neck T-Shirt, white ankle socks, and some white low cut Canvass Nikes. He wore a white fitted cap with East Main airbrushed on the front of it. His short trimmed curly afro stuck out the sides of his hat like a Jerry Curl. He sported a terquish link around his neck, with a Jesus piece medallion outlined in crushed ice. A matching bracelet rested on his left wrist. Shawn Shawn resembled his older brother in looks and style. They shared the same hazel eyes with the same sleepy eye stigma. His hair was curly, which he wore in a tiny afro like his older brother. He was 3 inches shorter than Peko and he now stood next to him in black Guess jean shorts, a white Crew-neck shirt, black ankle socks, and black Canvass Nikes. He wore a black White-Sox baseball cap with a 1 inch wide Hairing Bone necklace, and matching bracelet.

D-Roc, Slim, and lil Walt stood with a click of guys from East Main. They stood strong by the food stand, while the dance floor was packed with guys from across the bridge. As Mills and his crew approached D-Roc and his homeboys, Mills could feel the tension in the air. "What up Roc." "What up lil homie, ya'll be careful in here tonight, them niggas from across the bridge in here deep. It's about to go down." D-Roc said while laughing at the drama that awaited him. Peko tapped Mills and pointed across the room to Neesh and her friend Tasha. "We bout to hit the dance floor." D-Roc said as he bobbed his head to the music while charging himself up. "Shit, we bout to hit the dance floor too. I'm tryna get some bitches." Fella said before Mills had a chance to reply. Fella, unlike the rest of his crew was a live wire. Before getting into the game, Fella thrived on stealing bikes, beating people up, and occasional B-n-E's. his cousin Slim would have been put him in the game, but he knew Fella was too undisciplined and he didn't want to hear his Aunt's mouth if Fella went to jail. Fella wasn't as fat as everyone made him seem. He was just chubby with a block head. He was big for his age. Standing at 5'6, 180 pounds give or take a few. He had brownish green eyes that attracted the ladies. He had a dark brown skin complexion, with a lighter brown birthmark on the left side of his face that stretched from his forehead to the top of his neck. He wore his hair evenly cut with a two blade and razor sharp line up. Fella wore a brown crew neck t-shirt, some black Eddie Bower jean shorts, and a pair of brown Suede ACG mid-cut Nikes, with a black sow. He also wore a Cleveland Browns fitted cap, cocked to the back. Fella was just as flashy as D-Roc, Slim, and lil Walt, so he not only had on his jewelry; he had on a few of Mills and Peko's extra pieces as well. "Ya'll go head man, I'm a catch up wit ya'll in a minute." Mills said as he made his way over to Neesh. "You sprung and you aint even got none." Brandy said playfully as she noticed where Mills was headed. "You be careful bro." Fella said as he led the pack to the dance floor. Brandy, Shawn Shawn, and Peko played the background. "You stay close to me lil bro." Peko whispered to Shawn Shawn as they hit the dance floor. As the two different clickes had a stare off, the people on the skates started making their way off the floor. "Whats up lil Mills." Neesh said as he approached her and Tasha. "You. What you doing out? I didn't think partying was your cup of tea." Mills said. "It's not. Tasha made me come since I'm bout to go to Atlanta for college, after this coming school year." "Damn you just gone leave before you give me a chance huh?" Mills asked. "Chance for what?" Neesh asked playing dumb. "My chance to be your man, to show you that I know how to treat you." Mills answered smoothly while licking his lips. "Boy you crazy, and I don't remember me saying I would give you a chance. But you talking like I'm a be gone forever. I'll still be coming home on the holidays and school breaks. I'm just tryna to get away from all this craziness in the hood." Neesh said adamantly. Before Mills could respond, Tasha was yanking Neesh's arm saying, "Oh girl he all in my shit." Talking about some guy she was exchanging dirty looks with across the room. "Well go on over there girl, you aint gone get nowhere playing who can look the longest." Neesh said. "You right girl, I'm bout to go put my mack hand down." Tasha said while fluffing her curly hair. "What's up Tasha, you aint speaking tonight?" Mills said sarcastically knowing her attention was elsewhere. "What's up lil Mills, you know you my homie." Tasha said before walking off and throwing up a peace sign. "Peace Out" She said in a funny voice. Neesh and Tasha were both fine. They were by far the finest females on the set tonight and there were some fine sisters out. Neesh stood at 5'2, with a compact petite frame. Her legs were smooth, with a slight muscular build from being on the drill team. Her hips rolled perfectly off her body, complementing her small but sufficient apple bottom. She had a caramel brown skin complexion that stayed radiant. Her hair was jet black, and it hung just below her shoulders. She was beautifully dressed in some red thigh high shorts by Limited that squeezed her ass tight enough for it to be admired, but not enough to be slutty. Her red and white pen stripped halter top by Limited complemented her breast perfectly, and exposed her flat stomach, from the belly button down. Her small feet stood in a pair of all white K-Swiss with no socks. Her hair was pulled behind her ears showcasing her diamond earrings, which complemented her other accessories. She was shinning from her ears to her ankle bracelet. Tanesha Walker was fine, and she knew it. Tasha was what one would call bootylicious. She was a thick red bone, with a body made especially for a strip club. She was an inch taller than Neesh, at 5'3. she weighed close to 140 pounds with a flat stomach and lumps and bumps in all the right places. Her hair was a redish blonde color. She wore it in a curly like afro, which she now had parted down the middle letting her curly hair hang down to her shoulders. Her attire was identical to Neesh's, except for the color. She wore yellow shorts that hugged her jelly tight enough for anyone to see that she was pantiless tonight. Her halter top was yellow and white, and it clung to her jugs like magnets to metal. As

Neesh and Mills conversed, R. Kelly' crooned "you're thee only one I wanna slow dance with". "OH my goodness, this is my jam" Neesh said while throwing her arms in the air and snapping her fingers. "C'mon Mills dance with me" Neesh said while grabbing his hand and leading him to the dance floor. She pulled Mills close to her and put his hands at the small of her back, as they rocked side to side. Mills inhaled Neesh's vanilla Fields perfume. To Mills, she was an angel and she both felt and smelled like heaven.

Neesh enjoyed the smell of Mills cool water cologne, as she rubbed the back of his head, and smiled at the thought of them as an item. Mills had went from a ten year old boy to a thirteen year old man-child almost over night. It was impossible for her not to acknowledge his growth. Not only physically, but mentally as well. The youngin had an old soul, and she'd be lying if she said she wasn't attracted to him. Even now, she felt safe within his embrace. "Damn Mills, Why couldn't you be a couple years older" She thought.

The song ended, but Mills kept dancing. R. Kelly was singing, but he was moving and grooving to a whole nother tune. "The song is over Mills" Neesh said, with a big smile on her face. "Yo song maybe over, but the song I hear whenever I'm close to you will never end" Mills said while staring into her eyes. Neesh shook her head in an attempt to clear her mind of her sisters voice, "Girl you better get'em while he's young." Her sister words echoed in her head.

D-Roc stared the pair down. while contemplating menacing thoughts. But before his emotions could take over, the music switched from R. Kelly to Spice One's hit, featuring none other than 2-Pac, "Jealous Got Me Strapped", and the party went crazy with various sections yelling out their neighborhood. D-Roc joined his posse in yelling out "Main

Street" while throwing his hands in the air, and bouncing recklessly to the beat. The dance floor became rowdy as the boys began pushing and shoving one another and Mills took that as his cue to lead Neesh off the dance floor. "Uh uh Mills hold up" Neesh said as she spotted Tasha in a cat fight with two females.

She ran to her best friends' aid, grabbing one of the girls by the hair, and going to work on her face with her free hand. Neesh was definitely the "Girly Girl" type, but she was no stranger to a throw down. She had fought many girls throughout the neighborhood. Some over D-Roc, others for her respect, so she had no problem holding her own.

Mills followed behind her, arriving just as a third girl jumped into the fight. She tagged Neesh a few times in the back of her head before being grabbed by Mills and shoved into a wall. Mills had seen enough of the cat fight. He separated Neesh from her opponent and backed into a vicious blow from his blindside. He stumbled to his left, but quickly shook the blow off as he caught sight of his attacker charging after him.

Mills and his attacker squared off, while three girls joined in the rally against Neesh and Tasha. Mills fainted the guy, causing him to flinch. Then rushed him with a flurry of punches. The Skating rink turned into an old western brawl, as the two sides collided. Mills was stole on again from behind as he used the guys head for a punching bag. The blow knocked Mills into the wall, but Fella appeared out of nowhere sending one of the guys to the ground with a vicious hook, Shawn Shawn, and Brandy were close behind. Brandy assisted the girls, while Shawn Shawn did the A-Town Stomp on the face of the guy Fella had knocked to the ground. Peko took Mills position squaring off with the guy Tasha was talking to. Peko's long arms were too much, he picked the guy apart. Mills bounced off the wall and assisted Peko, hitting the guy with a combination of quick blows. The cops quickly took charge of the melee, spraying mase everywhere. Everyone who was on their feet took off running, jumping rails, walls, and hitting side exits. Some people lay on the ground sleep, while others leaked blood from to many blows to the head or an old fashioned razor job.

Neesh and Brandy had one of the females trapped in a corner punishing her with a combination of punches, knees, and kicks. Women were violent like that when fighting. There was nothing pretty about their arsenal, but their method was always effective. "C'mon we gotta get outta here" Mills yelled while tugging on their shirts. Peko scooped up Tasha, and they all made their escape.

Once outside, they all ducked and dodged their way through the parking lot as D-Roc and his Goons traded shots with their adversaries. Neesh and Tasha were pulling out the parking lot as Brandy and Mills hopped in his whip. Fella, Peko, and Shawn Shawn quickly packed into Fella's ride and D-Roc and his Goons were already peeling out the lot with lil Walt hanging out the window letting off rounds "Doom, Doom, Doom!!" was the sound of Walts canon. "Fells" Mills yelled out as he and Brandy changed seats. Fella nodded his head as Mills pointed to the guys from across the bridge loading into their cars. Mills cocked one into the head of his nine.mm as Brandy turned left out the lot with two cars hot on her tail. Fella went in the opposite direction with a couple of tailers as well. Fella hit the freeway, while Brandy sped up Refugee.

Brandy had put a little distance between her vehicle and the vehicles of her tailers, but she had to slow down in order to make the quick left Mills told her to make "SKEEERRRTT!" were the sounds of the screeching tires. ",Pocka, Pocka, Pocka!!" shots rang out from behind as she yanked on the stirring wheel. "make a quick right, right here" Mills said while preparing to return fire. Brandy made the turn just as bullets ripped through the back windshield. "Boom, Boom, Boom!" . . . "Boom, Boom!" Mills adversaries slowed down as he sent bullets flying through their front windshield. One of the gunners had been hit. Mills watched the gun fall from his hand and breathed a sigh of relief, but the chase was still on.

As the car stopped and the gunner hopped out to retrieve his weapon, the driver in the second car swerved around his partners and smashed the gas, quickly closing the gap between his ride and that of his assailants.

Mills whip had 350 Turbo horse power under the hood, so he knew his ride would leave his attackers in the dust on a straight away. Lucky for Mills he knew the neighborhood. "Make a quick left on the next street Bee" Mills yelled as they ducked their heads from the bullets flying through the car.

Brandy made the left without slowing down, causing the car to drift. "Boom! Boom, Boom, Boom, Boom!!" Mills emptied his clip as the car drifted the corner behind them. "Floor this Bitch Bee" Mills yelled. Brandy pushed the petal to the metal, and the car became more powerful by the second.

She clutched the wheel with two hands as the car flew through the red light. She never noticed the police cars parked in the stores parking lot. Before the cops could pull out behind the flying vehicle, two more cars soared past them. "Voom, Voom!!" Now all three cars were chased down by the red and blue lights. Each car swerved through the neighborhoods curvy streets with the precision of Indy 500 drivers.

Mills directed Brandy to the freeway hoping to lose the cops there, but as the car fishtailed on to the highway he noticed the roadblocks the cops had waiting up ahead. At the last second he slung his gun out the window into a nearby field.

Meanwhile Fella swerved in and out of traffic on another highway. His pursuers swerved through traffic behind him while taking turns trying to pick off his car. Peko told Shawn Shawn to stay on the floor as he stayed low in his seat waiting for a chance to exchange fire. Fella smiled and laughed as he dodged bullets and cars both. Once he had seen the Miller and Kelton exit, he knew he had made it home free. "Pee, soon as I make this turn on Miller, light they shit up." Fella yelled. The two cars flew up the ramp behind Fella. Fella made a quick turn avoiding the stop sign and stopped the car completely. Peko sat up on the window seal and picked both cars apart. "Pucka, Pucka, Pucka!". . . "Pucka, Pucka, Pucka!" Peko held the browning nine.mm with both hands, aiming with precision. He watched each bullet fly into the vehicle, busting out windows, and ripping through the cars armor.

He hit the passenger of the first car in the chest and leg, while sending another bullet ripping through the drivers shoulder.

Bullets whizzed into the second car, hitting the front passenger in the leg. one of the guys in the back seat slid out the car unnoticed.

As Fella pulled away, the guy came running off the side of the car firing shots. "TAT, TAT, TAT!" . . . "TAT!" . . ."TAT, TAT!" "Ahh shit Fells, I'm Hit!" Peko yelled while grabbing his shoulder.

"Hold on Pee, we gotta get the fuck out of this car" Fella yelled as the gunner continued blasting off rounds. Police sirens could be heard from a distance as Fella pulled in front of Peko's mothers house. "Have yo mom take you to the hospital Pee, I gotta hide my whip and get rid of that strap" Fella said. As soon as Peko and Shawn Shawn had both feet on the pavement, Fella was speeding away in his bullet riddled Monte Carlo.

❧❧ ❧❧ ⑧ ⑧ ⑧ ⑧ ⑧ ❧❧ ❧❧

Mills and Brandy sat in separate interrogation rooms hand cuffed to the table, while waiting for Detectives White and Brown to arrive with their latest good cop, bad cop routine. The Detectives entered Interrogation Room Number One with smirks on their faces. "So Mr. Mills, here we are again." Brown said. Mills remained silent. "So you're not going to talk to us again huh, Mr. Mills! That's fine because you and your little girlfriend can't get out of this one. There are bullet casings in the car that prove you guys were doing some shooting. So where's the gun." Brown asked. "You're a dumb little fuck." White added while puffing on a cigarette. "That pretty little girlfriend of yours will be a bull dagger bout time she comes home, and you'll have slept with more men then her, smart guy." White said devilishly. Mills was worried about Brandy. He cared about her too much to let her go to jail with him. He knew he would takeout before he allowed her to go down. "Don't worry, we're goin to go talk to your little girlfriend, surely she will tell on your little black ass." He and Brown prepared to leave. Before walking out the door, White said, "Oh, by the way tuff guy, a couple of your buddies got shot on the freeway, their in critical condition, so some of your little enemies will be goin to jail with you and 9 times out of 10, they will kick your ass while your in there." They left Mills in the room alone with his thoughts. He wondered had one of his road dawgs been shot, or was the Detectives words, just more of their tactics. The Detectives went to Brandy's room and received the same silent treatment. Brandy was a soldier and going to jail didn't scare her one bit. She was down with her crew until they got layed down, especially Mills. After giving the Detectives the silent treatment for over three hours, Mills and Brandy were escorted to the Juvenile Detention Center. Brandy's mother handled the situation a lot better than Mills grandmother, who cried and called upon her Jesus for help. Mills had to be pulled off the phone by the authorities once again. As him and Brandy sat down waiting for their escort, Mills told Brandy that he was taking the rap for all the charges. "No bro, fuck that. If we go down, we go down together." Brandy pleaded. "C'mon sis, you know I can't let you go down for no shit like this. People got shot Bee, this shit is serious and it aint no use in both of us going down." "Fuck that bro, we in this together man." Brandy shot back. Their dispute was broken up as the J.C.O's came in to escort them to their pods. A female came for Brandy, while a cool cat named Steve came for Mills.

The next day, Peko was out of the hospital with his arm in a sling. He, Fella, and Shawn Shawn were back in the spot getting money, while Mills and Brandy faced a long list of charges, including Feloniest Assault. Though Peko was free right now, his situation wasn't pretty. His probation officer tightened the rules on him. He was given a urine test today and he was dirty forsure. "Man this fake ass bitch done piss me today. I'm dirty as fuck bro." Pekosaid to Fella and his younger brother. "I told you bro, you a marijuana junky, a baby weed fiend, now that bitch gone lock you up." Fella said while laughing at his homeboys habit. "Damn bro, they gone try and lock you up for that shit." Shawn Shawn asked, as he thought about being without his brother. "Look at em, he still smoking. He hard headed." Fella said as Peko paced the floor while smoking on a blunt of fire weed. "Shid bro, it's too late to quit now, I'm like the gingerbread man, them hoes gone have to catch Pee." Peko said while pausing in a run motion with his blunt hanging from his mouth. They all started laughing, but the joke definitely was on Peko, who looked silly with his arm in a sling, and smoke coming out his mouth.

-CHAPTER SIX -

After spending a month in the Detention Center, Brandy was released with six months of house arrest. The third time Mills and Brandy went in front of the Judge. They were threatened with three years. That was enough to make Mills step up, and clear Brandy of all charges. Brandy was furious. Her and Mills were like brother and sister. If he had to do three years she wanted to do it with him. As Brandy sat in her PO's office waiting for her mother to pick her up, Mills stepped out his cell for Rec and noticed three new faces in his pod. Some guys from Livingston Avenue were moved to his unit after putting in work on some guys from the North side in their unit. Them and Mills had been exchanging words and cold stares as they passed each other in the hallways. Mills noticed that the guy he had shot in the hand had his cast removed from his arm, and he now only wore a bandage on his hand to support his wrist. All three of the guys gave Mills their mean mugs. Mills returned their mean mugs with one of his own. He knew he had a fight on his hands, but he didn't care because at his next court hearing he would be receiving three years, so he needed to release some anger.

The guys let a few days pass before they attacked. Mills was on the phone talking to his crew who took turns talking to him on the telephone in Brandy's bedroom. As he laughed at one of Fella's jokes, he lost sight of his three adversaries. When he looked over his shoulder trying to locate them, he was hit hard. He dropped the phone and squared off with the guy who hit him. The guy's friends stood off to the side letting Mills get a fair fight. Mills rushed the guy with a wild combination. He landed two of his punches, and the guy went under him in an attempt to wrap Mills legs up. Mills got out the way and the guy only managed to grab one of his legs. Mills unloaded on his face, causing him to ball up. Mills felt what he knew was coming. He received a blow from his blind side. When he turned to face the second man, the third guy hit him from behind. "Ya'll bitch ass niggas gotta jay Young Mills huh?" Mills said loud enough for his friends on the phone to hear. They listened as the phone hung by the cord, and Mills battled it out with all three guys. Mills faked one guy with a right, and scooped the other off his feet. He slammed him to the ground, and beat the blood out of him. While Mills worked on him, the guy's buddies worked on Mills. The staff member had to call for back up. When help arrived, Mills was lumped up, and spitting blood from his mouth, while blood leaked from his nose. The guy Mills had on the ground was just as bloody. He had a black eye, and a few lumps and bumps of his own. "Ya'll some busters, all three of ya'll cant whoop me! That's how East Main Niggas get down" Mills said in between spats of blood.

"Livingston Ave. "Fuck Main Street!," "You see how we get down!" The guys fired back. They were all restrained, and locked in their cells, where they awaited the institutions nurse.

Mills was eventually moved to another unit to stop the constant fighting between the youths. He spent another month at the Detention Center before being transferred to Circleville's Juvenile Holding Facility. He'd spend a month or two in Circleville before being shipped to the facility that he would serve the remainder of his time at.

Back in the hood, Brandy sat on her front porch, flagging down customers as she waited for Fella, Peko, and Shawn Shawn to come and kick it with her. Brandy's ankle monitor wouldn't allow her to go further than her front yard. Lucky for her, she stayed right on the strip. So she had no problems getting rid of her work and the four and a half ounces Mills had left her. Peko and Shawn Shawn hopped out of a car in front of Brandy's house and quickly ran up on her porch. "Damn, it's about time ya'll came to kick it with me. I aint seen ya'll in days." Brandy said. "We just been chillin at Lolly's getting that money Bee, you know we love you." Shawn Shawn said with a smile on his face. "Yea Bee, you know we love you, but I'm on the run and you know if Pacman see me, I'm through, so let's go in the crib." Peko said as he looked up and down the street. "Aight, C'mon wit yo spooky ass." Where Fells at?" Brandy asked as they were entering the house. "Nicole, I'm right here in the living room, you better watch your filthy mouth." Her mom said calling her by her middle name. "My bad, Ma." Brandy said while tucking her head into her chest, and smiling a devilish grin. "What up auntie." Peko and Shawn Shawn said in unison. "What's up nephews." She replied as they climbed the stairs headed for Brandy's room. "Why ya'll aint answer my question? Where Fells at?" Brandy said as she plopped down on her bed. "Aw shit, he been hanging out with D-Roc and his cousin Slim lately. Fells off the hook they shot some night club up last night." Peko said as he pulled out a fat bag of weed. "Fells been hanging with D-Roc. WHAT!" Brandy said loudly. "That's some bullshit, he know D-Roc and them be into a lot of BS. They beefin with half the city. I heard they robbed some guy in front of the store the other day, took his rims off his car and everything." Brandy continued. "Mills gone flip out when he hear that shit, huh?" Peko said as he licked his blunt shut. "You already know." Shawn Shawn said answering the question for Brandy. "Pee you is one hard headed brother, you still smoking weed." Brandy said, while giving Peko a funny look. "Shid I'm on the run now Bee, they gone take me to jail when they catch me anyway, so aint no use in me trying to stop now. Shid truthfully I wouldn't stop smoking anyway, I need this shit to cope." Peko said as he fired up the blunt. "Cope with what, and go by the window wit that. Me and Shawn Shawn aint tryna be on the run wit you" Brandy said while waving smoke out the air.

While Brandy, Peko, and Shawn Shawn chilled out, Fella was in a gambling house with D-Roc, Slim, and lil Walt. Fella's forehead and hands were moist from perspiration. He was nervous because the Houseman was standing over top of the dice game with a 40 caliber in his hand. This would be Fella's first robbery, and the fact of pulling a gun on a man who already had his drawn was giving him bad vibes. D-Roc had a stack of bills piled up by his side, along with a stack of bills in front of him which he needed to roll a nine to win. He held the dice to his ear while shaking them, "C'mon baby talk to daddy. This the lick that' killed Poe Dick" D-Roc said talking in third person. Lil Walt stood next to the house man, Slim stood by the liquor table with his eyes locked on the house mans Goons. While Fella stood to the side talking to a couple of dime pieces. D-Roc hit his point, then arrogantly snatched the piles of money from the floor. "Hold up, Hold the Fuck Up. I was fading you for three hunnit, I had two side bets over here for three hunnit on a straight five, two side bets over here for two hunnit on a five or nine, this shit aint right. Don't nobody move, House straighten yo game out" D-Roc said aggressively. The Houseman had been running illegal gambling houses for over 20 years. He was known as "Willie the Rambler, All Night Scrambler, The Compulsive Cotton Pickin Dog On Gambler". He missed nothing, no hands were quicker than his eyes. He scanned the room looking for any sudden movement. "Calm down, just relax youngin', you say ya money aint right, whats missin?" Old Man Willie said. "Hell yeah my money right" D-Roc shot back. "Well what's all this about" Old Man Willie said, confused by D-Roc's out burst. "THIS IS A MUTHA FUCKIN ROBBERY" Lil Walt said while shoving his Four Five in Old Man Willie's face.

Before his Goons could react, Fella had his nine.mm Rougar to the back of the taller one's head. "If you move you lose Big Dawg" Fella warned him. The man froze up instantly. Slim had a Tech Nine concealed inside his jacket. He waved it in front of the bulkier Goon as he reached for his weapon. "Slow your roll homie for I heat that ass up" Slim ordered.

D-Roc slung his Tech Nine from his jacket and yelled. "Everybody reach for the sky, and drop to ya knees!" One guy was hesitant with following D-Roc's instructions. "C'mon D-Roc we pose to be boys" The guy pleaded. D-Roc swung his Tech Nine, smacking the guy across his face with it." You wanna Die Pussy!" D-Roc yelled, then shoved the guy to the floor. "Everybody get on the floor, Gangsta grab some bags" D-Roc yelled to Slim. Slim found a few trash bags and passed one to each of his homies. They removed everyone's jewelry and pocket cash, then hit the House's safe, and quickly dashed out the front door.

After spending a month in Circleville, Mills was finally transferred to Cuyahoga Hills Boys School in Cleveland Ohio.

He stepped off the bus in an orange jumpsuit along with nineteen other juveniles. They all wore handcuffs on their wrist and shackles around their ankles. A hard nose J.C.O by the name of Taylor walked back and forth as he instructed the boys to make a single file line.

Taylor looked just as mean as the words he spoke. He stared all the juveniles in the face as he walked by them. Two guys behind Mills whispered to one another, causing Taylor to quickly turn in their direction. "Who the fuck is talking in my line? I see I got a group of hard-headed Mutha Fuka's!" Taylor said. He slowly walked by Mills and looked him up and down before moving on to the next juvenile.

"Man what's this jerks problem" Mills whispered to the guy in front of him. "Chill out Homie, this dude is a dick head." Nasty whispered back. Nasty was a few years older than Mills, and this was his third time doing a juvy bid, he knew most of the staff at the facility. He and Mills were cellies at Circleville, and being that they were both from Columbus, they became pretty tight in the few short weeks they celled together. As Mills and the other nineteen juveniles walked up the long hallway, juveniles the size of grown men came running out of their classrooms. Some juveniles were already in the hallway awaiting the intakes arrival. They stared at Mills and the rest of the intake with the meanest faces. Some of them threw up gang signs, while some spoke with gang lingo. "What up folks?" one of the guys said to the boys behind Mills. "Seven foe gangsta." They replied. "Man these niggas trippin on this gang shit, get money." Mills thought. By the time they made it to the end of the hallway, and turned down another hallway, Mills had heard the name of just about every gang yelled out. They walked down a second hallway and J.C.O. Taylor started yelling out orders. "In this hallway there will be a door to your right, stand next to that door. There will be a lady sitting at the desk. She'll give you your bed number, and ya bed roll. Ya'll make ya beds, and stand next to them quietly, until given further instructions." J.C.O. Taylor put special emphasis on the word quietly. When Mills finally got his cuffs removed, he stepped in the dorm and scanned the room looking for familiar faces. He received another set of mean mugs, but he also noticed some faces that he'd seen before. Out of the familiar faces Mills recognized, he could only put a name to one. While all the other boys sat two, three, and even four to a couch, Black was stretched out on a couch by himself. Mills nodded his head at Black.

Black returned his nod with a smile and said. "What's up lil homie, get your shit together, I'll be back there in a minute." Mills got his bed roll and headed to his bunk. While Mills made his bed, Black walked up behind him with a care package. "What's up Black?" Mills said. "Aint shit my nig, here go a few things you gone need, it's some hygiene, and a few goodies in there. What yo lil ass doin in here man?" "It's a long story bro." Mills answered. "How much time you got?" Asked Black. "Three years." Mills said while shaking his head in disgust. "Aw I'm a let you get yo shit together then we can kick it. You only gone be in this pod for like a week though. Since it is your first time being locked up, they gone send you to the first time offender's dorm, them lil niggas down there wild'n out too, so guard ya grill" Black said while playfully throwing a jab at Mills. J.C.O. Taylor came walking in as Black and Mills was finishing off their conversation. "Aye! I thought I told you I wanted it quiet until I gave further instructions. What the fuck don't you understand about being quiet." Taylor yelled at Mills. "What the fuck is dudes problem?" Mills whispered to Black. "Now you hard of hearing huh lil nigga, you gone start yo time off in isolation." Taylor continued. "Chill out Mills. I gotchu, this dude soft for real. He just hard on the intake." Black whispered. "My bad Taylor man, it's my fault, I mislead him. It wont happen again." Black said smooth talking the J.C.O. "You saying it's your fault like that makes things alright. You aint running shit, you gone make me take you in that box and bend yo lil ass up again." Taylor said as he gravitated towards Mills and Black. Once he got close he and Black squared off on each other, and playfully threw a few jabs at one another. "Aight Taylor, I'm a put you on yo ass again." Black said playfully as he slipped Taylor's punches and tapped him with a combination to the body. They both started laughing as Taylor grabbed Black in a Bear Hug. When they separated, Taylor looked at Mills and said, "And don't think just because you cool with Black you can do what the fuck you wanna do, cause Black aint the one runnin shit, this my unit." He looked at Black and said, "Go to the T.V. room pully, while I go over the rules with these new jacks." Taylor went over the rules and released the new jacks into the T.V. room with the rest of the juveniles. Black petted the couch like a dog, and told Mills "Have a seat lil nigga." "Why everybody else squeezing two, three, and four people on a couch and you got one to yourself?" Mills asked as he sat down. "Cause these niggas know, if they sit on my couch, I'm a beat they ass. I aint bout to be sittin shoulder to shoulder with some niggas unless I'm cool with them like that, you dig." Black answered. "I Dug." Mills said with a smile. "And fuck what Taylor's soft ass talking about, this my unit. He don't run shit but his mouth." Black added. Black was D-Roc and Slim's age. He hung out on Main and Gilbert, which was a few blocks down from Liley, where D-Roc and Slim hung out at. Lil Walt was from Black's crew. They'd hook up with D-Roc and Slim and cause havoc everywhere they went. When Black got juvenile life at the age of fourteen for aggravated robbery and murder, lil Walt teamed up with D-Roc and Slim. The three eventually became inseperable. Black knew Mills as Buckshot's younger brother. He, like everyone else on Main Street, bought dope from Buck. Mills was just entering the game when Black got knocked, so he never got to witness Mills transition. As Mills caught Black up on everything that he's missed in the hood, including the events that lead up to him being in jail, Nasty walked up. "What's up homie?" Black said, cutting Mills off. "What's happenin?" Nasty responded. "You tell me nigga, you over here standing over top of my couch." Black said while jumping to his feet ready to rumble. "Nah Nah. Hold up Black. This is my homie, he cool." Mills said as he jumped in between them. "Black this ma dude Nasty. He from Mount Vernon. Nasty, this ma big homie Black from the hood." Mills said introducing the two. Black let some of the air out of his already blew up chest. "What's happenin' bro." Black said as he extended his hand for some dap. Nasty dapped it up with Black and returned his greeting. "You gotta' excuse ma' hostility homie, but I put in so much work on them streets, I don't even remember some of the niggas I had beef with, but if you a friend of Mills you cool with me, you can have a seat bro." Black said as he pointed to an empty spot on the couch. As they sat on the couch conversing, Black and Nasty hit it off. They knew a lot of the same females, and Black finally remembered Nasty from the first time he visited Cuyahoga Hills Boys School two years ago. After spending a week in the unit with Black, Mills was transferred to the first time offender's dorm. Once he walked in the unit, all the juveniles were beside their beds, on their knees, with their hands on their heads. J.C.O. Whitaker was just as mean as Taylor. He yelled at Mills, Drop your shit on your bunk and join the rest of the dorm on ya knees. I'll let the boys tell you why they're on their knees, and the rules in this unit, that way when you break the rules, and everyone pays for it, you can answer to them, so I hope you can fight." He paced the floor, up and down each isle. "A dorm. Tell Mr. Mills here, why you are all on your knees right now." J.C.O Whitaker ordered. "Because a dorm that stays together pays together Sir." The boys answered in unison. "That's right, so if one person fucks up, everyone pays for that fuckup, so I say again, Mr. Mills I hope you can fight." Whitaker said as he looked down on Mills while passing his bunk.

It took Mills a few days to find some guys he could relate to. Out of the sixty inmates the dorm housed, only ten of them were from Columbus. Twenty-five were from Cleveland, ten were from Cincinnati and the remaining fifteen were from a mixture of Akron, Dayton, and Toledo. Out of the ten guys from Columbus only four of them were thorough, five including Mills. The other five guys were punked on a daily basis, and Mills quickly saw who not to hang around. Black told Mills that although there were gang bangers in Cuyahoga Hills, the color of a person's flag aint mean nothing when they were from the same city. He told Mills it didn't matter what hood a person was from, Columbus boys stuck together, and the same rules applied to boys from every other city. B-Nut, Law, Rash, and H.T. stuck together like glue, and Mills could tell they were respected, although it was clear that Rex and the Cleveland boys owned the dorm. Mills was confused, he couldn't understand why B-Nut, Rash, Law, and H.T. sat back and let the Cleveland boys pick on the other guys from Columbus. It didn't take Mills long to see why the guys didn't mix. After standing up for one of the guys, and watching him run off when the drama popped, Mills understood at that moment that they were cut from a different cloth, and no longer tried to mix their fabric.

Lucky for Mills, B-Nut, Law, Rash and H.T. ran to his aid that day. Afterwards, they explained why they didn't mix and mingle with the other boys from Columbus.

After getting into a brawl with the Cleveland boys over them extorting some of the weak guys from Columbus, and having those same guys turn their backs and run when the fight broke out, they vowed to never deal with those guys again. "Real Gees never allow squares into their circle." That was an unwritten rule for true gangsters. Mills began working out with H.T, Rash, and B-Nut, while Law did what he did best… "Showcase his skills on the hoop court"

Law was the oldest of the five, at seventeen. He was from the south side of

Columbus, he could've played high school and possibly college ball, if he didn't get sucked into the dope game. He was serving 5 years for shooting two guys that robbed him. He already had two of the five years in. Besides talking about females and street gossip, shooting hoops was all he did.

H.T was next in age, at fifteen, but only because his birthday was a few months before Rash's. H.T. was short for Hill Top, which was a neighborhood on Columbus' west side. He was truly a black guy trapped in a white boy's body. He was the gangsterest, and smoothest white boy Mills had ever seen. He was also serving 5 years for an aggravated robbery and car jacking. "Now tell me that white boy aint a brother!" H.T had been stealing and jacking cars since he was eleven. He had a crew of car jackers, and if he wasn't thorough he could've brought his team down with him, but he took his time and kept his mouth shut. Unlike Law, H.T. was halfway through his bid.

Rash was from Livingston Avenue, and although he was aware of the beef with him and Mills' hood, he had been locked up before the beef got thick. Rash was sentenced to juvenile life, which was until he was eighteen or twenty one. He had three years in on his murder charge. Like B-Nut, Rash liked cracking on people, telling jokes and laughing. A lot of times his humor had him misconstrued for a local joker, but the boy's hands were cold. B-Nut was only a year older than Mills, at fourteen. He was a blood, from Columbus Lincoln Park project housing. B-Nut was off the hook. He had no respect for authority, and barred none. Everything was funny to him. He was the kind of guy that made being in jail less strenuous, and stressful, because all he knew how to do was have fun. B-Nut was serving four and a half years for killing his mother's boyfriend in self-defense.

As Mills got his set in on the weight bench, B-Nut and Rash attacked one another with jokes.

"B-Nut, Yo lil ass always capping, with them lil ass locks. You ol fake ass Jamaican, with that nasty ass chipped tooth." Rash said causing Mills to put the weights down and burst into laughter. B-Nut and H.T. laughed as well, but Rash rarely won a cracking battle against B-Nut. "Aw blood, you tryna send me." B-nut said in between his laughter. "Rash, you got me fucked up, I knew I seen you somewhere before too, you was that dude at club Teen Scene wit a halter top on and some biker shorts with Sagittarius going across the ass in glittery letters." B-Nut said while acting out the scene at the club. They all fell out laughing again. "Mills you sure is getting a good laugh today. I aint heard this much out of you since you been here." Rash said. "Yeah he always sittin around all quiet, like some monk meditating and shit." B-Nut said while dropping to the floor Indian style, clasping his hands together, and bowing his head like a monk. The laughter continued as B-Nut put on a show. "Nah man, I just be thinking. I been here almost a month and Whitaker soft ass aint let me make a phone call yet." Mills said "What you tryna chase down some little hood rat." B-Nut asked "Hell nah bro, I'm trying to check on my peoples, let um know where I'm at and that I'm aight, my grandma a trip. She probably talking to Jesus right now." Mills said, while shaking his head at the thought of his grandmother's strong belief in God. He and B-Nut's conversation was cut short when H.T. jumped to his feet. "Aw shit, Rex and nem bout to jump Law" He, B-Nut, Rash and Mills rushed off the stage just as Law hit Rex with a wicked combination.

Rex stumbled, but quickly gained his composure. B-White came from Law's blind side, and sent him to the pavement with a thunderous right hand. As quickly as Law fell, he was just as quickly back to his feet. "Ya'll gotta jump ole Law dawg huh?" Law said as he pivoted out of the circle that was being formed around him. "Boom!" B-Nut yelled as he slid B-White across the gym floor with a treacherous hook. "Yeah Blood!" he screamed as guys from Cleveland started appearing from every angle. They quickly filled the gym floor and wasted no time putting in work. Rash hit Rex with a pretty one-two before being swarmed. H.T. rumbled with Flannigan, while Mills went toe to toe with Scooter, but it didn't take long before the numbers became to vast for the Columbus boys. Though the guys from Cleveland had the boys from Columbus out nubered 3 to 1, the Columbus boys held their own, refusing to hit the floor and be stomped out.

The J.C.Os called for backup as the brawl become too much for J.C.O Whitaker and the Rec staff to handle alone.

Although Mills and his boys were leaking blood, their blood wasn't the only blood shed. Several of the Cleveland boys had war wounds of their own.

While Mills and the rest of the boys who were caught was being escorted out the gymnasium, Black was walking up the hallway with J.C.O Taylor and the rest of his unit. He mean mugged Rex and the rest of the Cleveland boys, "You know ya'll done fucked up right?" Black said to Rex while cracking his knuckles. Rex looked at Black in confusion, having no knowledge of how close he and Mills were. All the boys were placed in Isolation, known throughout the institution as the box. Mills and his new homeboys were questioned first by authorities, because they were clearly outnumbered, and Rex was known to be a trouble maker throughout the camp. There were so many Cleveland guys involved, that they couldn't catch them all. Mills and his homeboys didn't give the staff any help identifying the stragglers. They simply said it was a misunderstanding over basketball, and they didn't know who all was involved. The boys spent a few days in Isolation. When they were released, five of the guys from Cleveland were placed in another unit, Rex included. Unfortunately for them they were placed in the same unit as Black. Black, Nasty and the rest of the guys from Columbus didn't waste any time avenging Mills and the rest of their homies. Unlike his crew, Rex managed to escape a hospital visit. After being moved to another unit, Rex and some other guys from Cleveland returned Black's favor, by breaking some jaws and stomping out some guys from Columbus in their unit. For the next few months Cleveland and Columbus went back and forth exchanging beatings on one another. By the beginning of 94' the whole camp was placed on lockdown. They had no privileges, and were escorted everywhere they had to go. Mills did his push ups, while finishing his time in isolation. He thought of how worried his grandmother must be. With all the beef going on, he had no time to write letters to anyone, because he was either in the box, marching up and down hallways for hours with the rest of the dorm, or standing on his knees with his hands behind his head. After being in the camp for thirty days, Mills was supposed to receive his phone privileges, but after the constant fighting the camps phone privileges were taken. After spending close to a hundred days on lockdown, the camp had calmed down and were gradually being given the privileges back. As Mills and his homies occupied two couches for movie day, the unit manager announced that the camp had finally been given back their phone privileges. Mills dashed to the phone, racing past thirty other juveniles. There was only four phones, so the juveniles were allowed only one call then they had to get back in line. Mills was happy he made it to one of the four phones first. He dialed his grandmother's number and watched a lengthy line form behind him. Mills' grandmother accepted the call before the recording could go all the way through. "Oh lord Tony, why aint you called home?"

"Hi to you too mama." Mills responded.

"Oh I'm sorry baby but you had me worried sick."

"Don't worry momma I'm aight, but why I haven't called is a long story. One I'd rather not tell." Mills said, hoping his grandmother would leave it at that. "Where's my lil brother at?"

"He's upstairs playing that video game. Daylon brought him some new games for scoring three touchdowns in every last one of his football games this past season." Mills grandmother spoke with so much pride in her voice that he could feel her energy through the phone.

"My lil bro playing football and I'm in here missing it. I'm hurt momma, I can't believe I'm not there for Him right now. Three touchdowns a game. He's that good huh?" Mills said proudly.

"My baby's the bomb! But Ima let him tell you his self" his grandmother said with enthusiasm. "Jimmy get the phone, its your brother" she yelled upstairs.

Jimmy snatched the phone off the receiver and yelled into it overzealously. "What's up big bro, I love you man, when you coming home?" The question touched Mills, but he maintained his composure.

"I love you too big head, and I'll be home shortly" Mills replied. He conversed with his little brother for a while, then told him to put their grandmother back on the phone before the call ended.

He gave his grandmother the address to the facility and the recording said "Sixty seconds". "Well momma the phones bout to hang up I love you, and I'll call again next weekend."

"I love you too, you be good and go to church while you're in there. Get right with the Lord Tony". she said adamantly.

"Yes ma'am." Mills replied. "Okay baby. Oh before I forget call Brandy and Daylon, they been calling over here driving me crazy." She said before the phone hung up. Mills looked behind him and shook his head at the sight of the line he had to get back in. He quickly dialed Brandy's number. "Hold up Pimp, I gotta use that phone too." A guy named T-Bone from Cincinnati said. "I feel you homie, I don't mean no disrespect but this call is real important." Mills responded. "Aight Pimp, Ima let you get this one off, but my shit is important too dawg." T-Bone said strongly. Mills didn't like T-Bone's tone of voice, nor his demeanor but the sound of Brandy's voice caused him to disregard it.

"What's up bro, why you just now calling a bitch?" Brandy said. Mills laughed before responding. "You crazy Bee, but shit been wild down here, we been on lockdown for fighting these Cleveland niggas, I keep a lump or bump on my shit sis." They both started laughing. "Man I miss you bro, them bitches extended my house arrest for six more months, I been in this house sick, but I'm off this shit next week, I'm pumped. I got rid of your shit too, so you got a few stacks over here when you get out too nigga." Brandy said. "What's up with the fam" Mills asked.

"They chillen, getting money and shit. You know Pee on the run for smoking weed. That's messed up too because me, Fells and Shawn Shawn bout to get off paper early."

"Oh yeah?" Mills said. "What Fells fat ass been up to?"

"Oh my God, what aint he been up to. He been hanging out with D-Roc and them, and they been into all types of shit. They been robbing niggas and everything."

"BRANDY!" Watch your mouth. I told you about all that cussing, you aint mutha fucking grown." Her mother yelled from her bedroom. "My bad ma." Brandy yelled back. "Where fells and them at now?" Mills asked.

"They at Lolly's, hold on I'm bout to call over there." Brandy clicked over and called Lolly's on three way. Lolly answered the phone as Brandy clicked Mills back on the line. "Who the fuck is it."

"Dang auntie, what's wrong with you?" Brandy answered. "Brandy? Excuse me baby, Fella's fat ass get on my nerve, he always playing and shit." Lolly said sounding frustrated. Mills and Brandy both started laughing knowing how playful Fella was. "Is that my nephew I hear?" Lolly asked noticing Mills voice.

"Yeah this me auntie, what's happenin?" Mills answered.

"You, you happenin, baby, when you coming home?"

"I got a couple more years left, where my bros at?" Mills said.

"Peko and Shawn right here playing the game, Fella in the back wit some lil girl he bought over, he just walked in the door about half an hour ago, and he's already pissed me off." Let me speak to my bros auntie, before my call ends."

"Aight baby, you stay strong, and hurry home. Here nigga' Mills on the phone." Lolly said as she threw the phone on Peko's lap. "What's up bro, you know we miss you out here." Peko said. "Yeah bro I miss ya'll too. Bee told me Fella been tripping."

"Aw man, that dude off the hook, he in the back room wit some freak right now."

"Get that dude for me before the phone hang up bro." Mills said. "Hold up, holler at Shawn while I get Fells."

Peko pitched the phone to Shawn Shawn. "What up big bro, we miss you out here man." Shawn Shawn said.

"I miss ya'll too lil bro. You keeping them fools together out there right?" Mills said.

"Man you know these boys off the hook, especially Fells bro, he all over the place, hold up. Here he go right here." Shawn Shawn passed the phone to Fella.

"AHHHH! What's up nigga?" Fella said.

"I don't know you tell me, I hear you rolling with Rock now. You know dude aint nothing but trouble bro." Mills said.

"Stop tripping bro, it aint even like that." Fella said as the recording informed him that Mills had sixty seconds left. "A my nig don't worry, I'm holding it down out here. I hollered at them hoe ass niggas for you too, tighten they ass all the way up boy. Fella said while laughing as he remembered the bullets he put in the guys that followed them from the skating rink a year ago. "Get money bro fuck that bullshit." Mills said with authority. He was furious that his right hand man was turning into D-Roc. "Aye don't go nowhere bro, I'm bout to call right back." Mills said when the recording told him he had ten seconds. Mills hung up the phone, and looked over his shoulder, he noticed T-Bone conversating with one of his homies and quickly dialed Brandy's number again. "Aye hold up Pimp, I told you I need to get on that phone." T-Bone said.

"This the last one homie, I'm in the middle of an important conversation." Mills said, not paying T-Bone any attention. "Nah, you got me fucked up Pimp, my shit important too, if I aint using that phone, aint nobody using it." T-Bone said. He walked up behind Mills and hung the phone up. Mills was already mad about Fella's decision to hang out with D-Roc. Now T-Bone was testing his courage by hanging his call up. "So what you wanna work about this shit?" Mills said while sizing up T-Bone. "Whatever Pimp, I know you aint bout to use that phone again." T-Bone replied while standing his ground. Mills dropped the phone and rushed T-Bone with a quick jab, followed by a left hook. He landed his jab but missed the hook, as T-Bone faded away from it. Before T-Bone could fully recuperate, Mills was under him, taking his body to the air. T-Bone tried to wiggle out of Mills lock on his legs, but it was too late. Mills slammed him to the ground hard, and climbed on top of him. As Mills went to work on his face, B-Nut, H.T., Law, and Rash came running out of the movie room.

"Beat that ass blood!" B-Nut yelled. Mills was carried off to the box while T-Bone was escorted to medical bay. Mills had already spent so much time in the box, that being locked in the cold room didn't bother him anymore. He had long ago accepted the box as his second home, so once the door was slammed and locked, he removed his shirt and started doing push-ups, which he would do until he was tired enough to stretch out on the floor and sleep.

-CHAPTER SEVEN-

"Oh my God, I'm finally free. I can't wait to spread my wings" Brandy said while stretching her arms out and basking in her reclaimed freedom. "Okay Nicole, you take yo grown ass in them streets and get in some more shit it if you want to. Ima let your ass sit in jail next time." Her mother scolded.

"Dag Ma. Go head and jinx me why don't you." Brandy playfully rolled her eyes at her mother. "I aint playing with you Brandy" her mother responded, with a sassy look of her own.

"I know Ma, it just feel so good to finally be off of house arrest, add that to the early termination of my probation, and you can understand ah sista's enthusiasm." Brandy's mother didn't respond. Instead she playfully stared her daughter down, then rolled her eyes and gave her a neck roll of her own.

"Plus I know you aint just gone let your babygirl sit in no jail. So… Trick no good" Brandy said teasingly.

"Try me" her mother shot back. Brandy and her mother had a beautiful relationship. Her mother had her young, so although she guided Brandy like a parent, they vibed like sisters. And Brandy loved that about their relationship.

Brandy played with the radio until she found 106.3. "Jodeci's hit single titled "Stay" filled the car. "C'mon Ma, this my jam" Brandy said while throwing her hands in the air and snapping her fingers. Her mother rolled her eyes again while saying "Your grown butt get on my nerves, you think I'm playing with you". They both burst into laughter as the car pulled into traffic.

When Brandy's mother turned onto Berkley, the strip was packed. Young hustlers and crack addicts were scattered up and down the street while ghetto superstars like D-Roc and his crew profiled in front of their newly purchased vehicles. D-Roc sat on the hood of his all white '94 Maximum. The gold flakes glittered throughout his paint job, while his sixteen inch gold moe moes reflected the sun's light. Fella sat in the driver's seat of his

'87 Monte Carlo while playing with the deck to his system. His Monte was equipped with a green and gold marble paint job, green and gold leather bucket seats, a matching race car steering wheel, chrome McClain rims with gold spinners, and a 350 turbo horse powered engine.

What's up auntie? What's up Bee?" Fella yelled over the top of him and D-Roc's systems.

"What's up Nephew." Brandy's mother replied as she climbed up the steps leading to her front door. What's up Fells, let me hit something." Brandy said referring to the fat blunt Fella held between his fingers. Fella took a couple puffs before passing it. "Feels good to be off that probation shit, huh?" Fella said while blowing smoke in the air. Brandy looked at D-Roc, Slim and Walt as she hit the weed. She could feel D-Roc's eyes on her. "What's up Slim and Walt." She said. "What's happening." Slim said smoothly. Walt returned her greeting with a simple head nod. "What you getting into today Bee? You tryna roll up to the coming home?" Fella asked. The coming home is a large block party held every year on one of Columbus' drug infested strips, known as Money Earning Mount Vernon. "I don't know… who you rolling up there with Pee and Shawn Shawn?" Brandy inquired.

"Nah, I'm rolling with D-Roc, Slim and Walt. You know Pee and Shawn Shawn don't know nothing but Lolly's They act like that money going somewhere." Fella said. "They might roll up there though, cause Pee just bought a sick ass Regal." Brandy was turned off by the thought of rolling with D-Roc and his crew. She didn't dislike them; she just knew that wherever they went, trouble seemed to follow. After all, half the city was at war with them, while the other half feared them. "I don't know Fells, I might roll if Pee and Shawn go but I gotta' call Buck so I can get right feel me."

Brandy said her see you laters and headed in her house. She paged Buck, Putting in her code, followed by 911. Buck quickly returned her page. After a couple minutes of encoded conversation, Buck told her he'd be there shortly and they disconnected. Brandy pulled two shoe boxes out of her closet, and dumped stacks of money from both of them onto her bed. She counted out fourteen thousand, not including the six thousand she had of Mills. She put eight thousand aside, then put the remains back in one shoe box, and hid it in the closet. She wondered if D-roc and his crew knew she had twenty thousand dollars in her house, would they rob her and her mother. She was unsure about Slim, because he was the most polished, and cool of the three, but she knew for sure D-Roc and Walt would have to have it. She was sure the both of them had twenty thousand of their own, if not more, but that never stopped them, they robbed people with less than them everyday. More or less didn't matter to them, if the person had it and they wanted it they were coming to get it! Brandy separated the seventy five hundred she was about to pay Buck for nine ounces and put half in each of her front pocket. She put the remaining five hundred from the eight thousand in her back pocket for spending cash, and headed to the front porch to wait on Buck. After standing on her porch for five minutes, a candy painted, cherry red 5.0 Mustang with a peanut butter brown leather drop top, gold flakes, triple gold hundred spoke daytons, and a thunderous system bent the corner. Computer love filled the street from the car speakers. Heads turned, mouths dropped, and D-Roc, Slim, Walt and Fella gripped their pistols. Although the car was a big deal to everyone else, it was only one of Bucks newest toys. One he'd more than likely get rid of in a few weeks. Lucky for Buck he rode with the top down because had Walt not of seen his bald head, he would've filled the vehicle up with holes just for riding down the street and stealing him and his boys shine. Buck stopped in front of Brandy's house and motioned for her to come to the car. After Brandy hopped in, Buck backed up to acknowledge his little homies. "What's up Roc, Slim, Walt and Fella."

"What up big homie." They replied in unison. "Damn Roc, that Max clean as a bitch." Buck said complementing D-Roc on his ride. Yea its aight." D-Roc said modestly.

"Who's SS is that with the wet as marble paint." Buck asked. "Fuck this SS, I'm tryna get that right there." Fella replied while pointing to Buck's 5.0.

"Shit that Monte clean lil Fells, that's a bad ma fucka, but if you wanna upgrade, you know the name of the game Stack N Grind baby." Buck smiled. "What ya'll getting into tonight Roc?"

"Shid, we gone slide up to that coming home a little later, why what's up?" D-Roc answered.

"Aint nothing up, I'm probably gone roll up through with ya'll, flick it up for T-Money." Buck said.

"I can dig it." D-Roc shot back. "Call me before ya'll take off."

"You got it." D-Roc replied. Buck turned his system back up, and threw up the peace sign, as he bobbed his head and pulled off. When he dropped Brandy off she didn't waste any time getting back to business. She threw Buck the peace sign then nodded at a few young hustlers who stood on the corner before running in her house. She took one ounce from the nine she purchased then put the rest in her stash spot, and took off down the steps, passing her mother in the living room and back out the door headed for Lolly's. She knocked on the door a few times, before hearing Lolly on her way to answer the door. She knew it was Lolly, because Lolly was cursing someone out as she approached. "Who the fuck is it" Lolly yelled while snatching the door open.

"Damn Auntie, who done pist you off now" Brandy said while standing with her hands on her hips. "Awe shit, C'mon in Brandy" Brandy entered the house laughing because Lolly was the type of person who was always mad about something so more than likely she was screaming and cursing for no reason. "My niece here now, ya'll boys better tighten up. " Lolly yelled as Brandy walked through the living room. Shawn Shawn sat on the couch by himself smoking on a fat blunt, while counting a stack of bills. "What up lil Bro, where Pee at?" Brandy asked.

"What up sis. Pee ah be here in a minute, you know he don't come out till Pac-Man gets off work, he at the crib wit his girl." "That boy whipped too." Shawn Shawn said, causing him and Brandy to laugh.

Brandy passed the blunt back to Shawn, then threw him a bag of weed that she copped from Buck. "Roll up." She said before heading for the kitchen. After busting her blocks down, she gave Lolly a plate full of crumbs, then dropped a couple extra twenties on the plate. "That's why you're my favorite." Lolly said. Brandy winked at her, washed her hands and rejoined Shawn Shawn in the living room. Shawn Shawn had the spot to hisself all day, so he laid back letting Brandy serve all the customers as the back door got knocked on non-stop.

Now that Mills was locked up, Peko and Shawn Shawn had the most money out of the crew. They hustled together, so one of them was at the spot getting money at all times. After smoking and joking away a few hours it was 4 o'clock which meant Pac-Man's shift was finally over. Peko let his system rattle the house in Pac-Man's absence as he quickly pulled in Lolly's backyard and parked his car. Within a few minutes he came strolling in the living room through the kitchen. "What up lil Bro, what up light skin." Peko said. The Fire Weed Brandy purchased from Buck had her and Shawn Shawn stuck, so all they could manage to get out was a simple "Sup Bro".

Peko plopped down on the couch next to Brandy, pulled a blunt from behind his ear, and sat fire to it. "Plug the game up bro so I can bust yo ass in that Madden." Peko said as he took a few quick puffs of the weed. As Shawn Shawn hooked up the Super Nintendo, Brandy asked Peko about the coming home block party.

"Shit, I don't give a fuck sis, if you wanna roll up there we can."

"Yea we might as well, I been cooped up in the house for a year bro, I'm tryna go somewhere, anywhere." Brandy replied.

"Aight, let me bust Shawn Shawn ass in Madden a few times, then we can roll out." Peko said.

"C'mon bro, you know you can't fuck wit me." Shawn Shawn replied. "Yeah we bout to see." Peko said while laughing, because he knew his little brother was telling the truth. After losing a few games of John Madden's football, and smoking a few blunts, the session was interrupted by Fella's call. He informed the crew that him, D-Roc, Slim, Walt, and Buck were on their way to the block party. Peko and Shawn ended their fourth game with Peko up a touchdown. Although it was only half time, Peko swore his seven point lead as a victory. They headed out the back door to Peko's sky blue 84 Regal. It was accommodated with a white rag top, sky blue interior, chrome trimming and hundred spoke daytons. Peko kept his Regal clean inside and out. The rims and the paint were both sparkling clean. "Pee this a nice ass ride." Brandy said.

"Shit for five large it better be tight." He responded. Peko's pager started screaming as he popped the face on his system. Once he looked at the number he began shaking his head. "Damn....this girl is crazy." He said.

"Who dat...Shy?" Brandy said in a funny voice. "Hell yea... how you know about my Shy?" Peko answered.

"Damn. Yo Shy huh?" Brandy said inquisitively. "Yeah. That's my baby, but she always paging me for no reason. Where you at? Who you wit? I think she addicted to what the dick did." Peko said playfully. Brandy punched him in his arm. "Nah she cool though Bee. I love her and shit, she down for Pee dawg." Peko said speaking in third person. "I hope so." Brandy replied. "Shit light skin you need to get you a nigga so you can loosen up" Peko said playfully. "Psssh. I don't need no nigga. I aint thinking about no nigga, my mind is on my bread. Anyway with the way you and Fella treating bitches, I'm cool, I don't need no nigga lying and cheating on me." Brandy said in sassy tone. Peko's pager started screaming again as he started the car up. He looked at the pager, once again shaking his head. "Hold up ya'll, let me run in here and call this girl back for she breaks my pager. Huh roll up." Peko threw a bag of weed on Brandy's lap before hopping out the car.

"So where ya girly at lil bro?" Brandy asked Shawn Shawn while breaking open a Backwood Cigar. "My girl's name is Reese, she cool, you probably know her sister Sa'sha ya'll go to the same school." "Sa'sha the head doctor." Brandy said while turning completely around to face Shawn Shawn in the backseat. Shawn Shawn started laughing. "Yea that's her." "Lil bro you better be careful, cause you know what they say, like mother, like daughter, like sister." Shawn Shawn continued to laugh. "I aint playing

Shawn, you better be wearing condoms, and thinking twice before you put yo thang in these lil girls, cause they nasty, and they will give you some shit you can't get rid of." Brandy preached. "Yeah I know big sis, and I'm being careful, but me and Reese aint even went that far yet, she still a virgin."

Peko came running back to the car interrupting their conversation as he hopped in saying, "I told ya'll that girl aint want shit, she lucky I love her." He backed out the yard, as eight balls "Mr. Bigs" shook the ground. When Peko turned onto the crowded street heads turned as his fifteens roared. He quickly spotted Fella and D-Roc's cars parked at Tooney's drive thru. He pulled in the parking lot, and parked next to Bucks 5.0 Mustang. Buck sat on the hood of his car snapping off pictures as Fella entertained two females by the pay phones, while D-Roc, Slim, and Walt held the attention of another flock of half dressed females. The scene was packed with ballers, and females of all shapes, sizes and colors. As soon as Peko, Brandy and Shawn exited the car, Buck turned the camera on them and snapped off a few pictures. He passed Peko the blunt of expensive weed he was smoking on, and tossed Brandy one of his cameras. They both flicked it up for Mills until the cameras were empty. Buck finished his film off by taking pictures of the two girls Fella had flashing the camera. Fella waved Peko over to where he and the two hood rats stood. "What's up bro. This is Kita and Rita, they twins." Fella said with a big smile on his face. "Rita this my bro Peko. Pee this is Rita she feeling you." Fella said as he pushed Rita closer to him. D-Roc, Slim and Walt had enough fun with the gold diggers they were with, so they joined Buck, Brandy and Shawn over by the cars. "Roc, Gangsta, look at this bitch ass nigga." Walt said as he saw a white box Chevy on gold daytons starting to pull in the lot, then back up after spotting D-Roc and his crew, who were well known

Jack Boys. The three burst out in laughter as Walt grabbed his pager and aimed at the car like a gun, causing the driver to duck. "HA! HA! HA! Coward ass nigga. He a hoe and a coward." Walt said loudly. Brandy watched as Peko and Fella fondled the twins, and it made her think about the conversation her and Peko had about her finding a partner of her own. She remembered him saying how much he loved his girlfriend Shy, but she watched him cheat on her with no regrets, or empathy for his girlfriend at home. Being around the boys so much gave her an understanding of men that she didn't like, and that made her distrustful of all men when it came to dating and relationships. Fella and Peko joined the crew after setting up booty calls with the girls for later that night. As buck gave Brandy a few bills to grab a couple of disposable cameras from the drive thru, a black Camero, with jet black tint, gold flakes, and some triple gold hundred spoke daytons pulled into the parking lot. The driver of the Camero stared at Brandy as she walked in the drive thru. He obviously didn't know who D-Roc and his crew were because he parked right in front of them and hopped out of the car blinging. D-Roc, Slim, Walt, and Fella stared at him with greed in their eyes. Buck felt their vibe, "Be easy Roc, right now aint the time for that." "What you talking about big homie." D-Roc said with a sinister grin on his face. Buck gave him a look that said "C'mon Roc, I know you." As Brandy stood in front of the cash register awaiting her cameras, the driver of the Camero stared a hole in her back side. Brandy was a tomboy, but she was drop dead gorgeous, and her young body screamed 100% woman!

Brandy wore an airbrushed T-shirt, with Main Streets Boss Lady on the back of it, and her name going across her breast on the front. She wore white wind breakers, with a pair of red biker shorts beneath them. Brandy's body was well proportioned, and her ass demanded attention through her wind breakers. On her feet, she wore a pair of crispy red and white Jordans. Her skin complexion was high yellow, and her jet black hair rested on her shoulders. She wore a diamond ring on every finger, a thick herring bone bracelet, and matching necklace with her name hanging from it, in crushed ice. Brandy could feel the guy's eyes undressing her from behind, and after she purchased the cameras, she turned around with attitude. "Damn! Did you lose something?"

"As a matter of fact I did... I lost control of myself when I seen you. But I apologize if I offended you, but I think you're a very beautiful young lady Brandy." The guy said smoothly. Brandy was caught off guard by his response. Most guys were ignorant, and screamed out things like "Let me kill it" or "When you gone let me hit that?" but this guy was smooth, and he spoke respectfully. Although Brandy felt violated by his wandering eyes she thought the guy was attractive, as he stood before her with his shirt off, exposing his genetically acquired six pack. He was dark skinned, with some blue jean Nautica shorts on, some white ankle socks, and a pair of high top Air Force Ones. He rocked a skin tight fade with a few waves on the top. Around his neck was a very thick Gucci link chain, with an iced out Jesus piece. On his wrist was a matching bracelet complementing his 3 karat diamond pinky ring. Brandy still refused to fall for his slick talk, but before she could gun em down, his words froze her. "brandy is yo name right boss lady..." Brandy looked down at her shirt, and thought of the words on her back, "Look man, I aint impressed by your jewelry, your car, or your money, so you wasting your time." "Damn Brandy, why you being so mean, you too beautiful to be acting so ugly. Give a brother a chance, all men aint full of shit. How about we start over? How you doing Brandy, my name is Chris." Chris said as he extended his hand for a handshake. Brandy couldn't help, but to laugh. "C'mon Brandy. I promise if you give me a chance I can keep you smiling." Chris poured his game on heavy. Brandy accepted his hand, "SO where do we go from here?" She said. "Well I'm hoping you'll give me your number and allow me to call you and hopefully take you out sometime." Chris said. "Let me guess, you carry a pen and paper in yo pocket for a moment like this huh?" Brandy replied sarcastically. "Ha! Ha! Ha!" Chris laughed. "Nah, not exactly, but I do have a pen and paper in my car, but I'm ah business man, so I give my number out a few times a day feel me." "Yeah, you felt." Brandy said with a smile on her face. Chris bought a pack of back woods, and escorted Brandy back to his car. He gave her his pen and paper, and emptied out one of his back wood cigars while she wrote down her number. She gave his pen and paper back to him and said "Be careful with that." He looked at her and smiled. "Aight Brandy, I'm bout to get out of here because I see yo killers over there aint feeling me." He motioned over to the guys. "You stay beautiful Brandy, and stop being so mean." He said before pulling off. Brandy and the guys spent a couple more hours at the block party, but as the day turned into night they loaded into the cars and left.

The next day Brandy was the last one to make it to Lolly's. As she knocked on the door she noticed Fella's car parked on the street. She was happy to finally see him at the spot, because she was starting to feel as if he'd just abandoned the crew. When she entered the house, Peko and Shawn were going at it in John Madden football as usual. "What's up Pee. What's up lil bro?"

"What up light skin." Peko shot back. "Sup sis." Shawn Shawn added. Neither of them took their eyes off the game.

"Where Fells at?" Brandy asked.

"Shid... who knows. He ran in and right back out Fells don't really hustle no more Bee, he on that stick up shit with Roc and them now." Peko said still not taking his eyes off the game.

"Yeah sis, big bro off the hook for sure." Shawn Shawn added.

"Well aint that his car out there on the street?" Brandy asked. "Probably so, I think he left with his cousin Slim." Peko answered.

While Fella was the topic at Lolly's, he and Slim had two females they met at the club a few nights ago, at the hotel room giving them the business. Fella held Lisa's legs in the air as he pushed his manhood into her with force. "Oooh, get this pussy Fella. Yea! Right there!" Lisa yelled as Fella dug deeper. Slim plunged into India from the back. She yelled, "Oooh Slim you got a big dick." Her moans and screams got louder with every stroke. Fella was more turned on by India's screaming and moaning than he was his own encounter. The deeper Fella dug in Lisa, the more she yelled for him to dig deeper. As Slim flipped India over, Fella became competitive. He dragged Lisa to the end of the bed, and put her legs around his shoulders as he stood on the floor. He dove into her with force, and watched her large breasts bounce all over the place with every stroke he made. He was through trying to please her; he wanted her to scream like her home girl in the other bed. Lisa was a freak. She grabbed Fella by the waist, and tried to pull him deeper into her with every stroke.

"Whose pussy is this" Fella asked.

"Yours." She yelled back "Tell me you love this Main Street Dick." Fella ordered as he plunged into her at jack rabbit speed. "I love this Main Street Dick. I'm cumin again Fella don't stop. Harder! Harder!" she yelled. Fella looked down at his piece as it slid in and out of her hairy vagina. "God damn I'm giving her everything but my balls." Fella thought as his manhood swelled up with excitement. Slim was now on the bottom, guiding India by the waist as she took as much of his large piece into her cave as she could. Slim released one hand from her waist, and smacked it on her ass as she closed her eyes to enhance the pain and pleasure of the ride. Slim's pager started vibrating as India's body started to shake. He let her take control of the ride as he checked his pager. He saw D-Roc's girl's phone number followed by 911, and D-Roc's code. Slim had D-Roc's Maximum, but by D-Roc putting 911 in his pager he knew he was calling for more than his car. He stopped India right at the end of her orgasm and grabbed the phone. "Ring! Ring!" D-Roc answered after the first ring. "Slim" He yelled into the phone "Yeah." "What up nigga, you ready to roll." Slim said. "Man hurry the fuck up and come get me before I kill this bitch! This stupid ass hoe done stabbed me dawg." D-Roc shot back. "I'm on ma way bro" "Aiight man hurry up." D-Roc ordered. "Fells lets ride, it's a 911 call." Slim said as he got dressed. Slim looked at India as she pulled her panties on, and thought about climbing back into her tight cave. He snapped out of the daze her body had him in, and finished dressing. Slim dropped the girls off at the bus stop before heading to D-Roc's girl's house. When Slim pulled in front of Tee Tee's her lil cousin Stanley stood in front of the corner store, across the street from her house. Fella stayed in the car while Slim went to retrieve D-Roc. Slim noticed the door was cracked, but the house was silent. He pulled out his nine millimeter Taurus and peeked into the house. He walked in as he saw D-Roc sitting on top of Tee Tee with her arms pinned to the floor. D-Roc had scratches on his face and his shirt soaked with blood from the hole Tee Tee put in his stomach with a steak knife. Tee Tee's face was covered in blood, her body was bruised, and the house was a mess. D-Roc's nine mm lay on the couch in front of him. While Tee Tee's steak knife lay on the floor a few inches away from her pinned down hands. "Roc what up bro? What the fuck… you and Tee Tee done tried to kill each other in this bitch." Slim said as he put his gun away.

"Nah bro, this stupid crazy ass bitch done stabbed me, burned my clothes, and threatened me with the police." D-Roc said. Man lets go bro, you bleeding badly my nig. Let's get the fuck outta here." Slim said as he scanned the messy living room. D-Roc grabbed his nine with one hand, but before he got off Tee Tee he pulled his hand back and slapped blood out of her mouth. He stood over top of her with his nine pointed down at her. "I should kill this bitch bro, look at me, I'm bleeding to death." D-Roc said angrily. Slim was a bonafide gangster, and he was down for whatever, but he didn't believe in putting his hands on a woman. His father used to beat on his mother, and he had no respect for the man for that reason. He felt sorry for Tee Tee, but he was loyal to D-Roc, so he couldn't show any sympathy for the injured woman on the floor. "C'mon Roc, fuck that bullshit, let's go my nig." Slim urged. D-Roc snatched the phone cord out the wall before walking out the door, but Tee Tee made her way upstairs to the phone in her bedroom. She called the cops, and pressed domestic violence charges against D-Roc. She gave the cops his full name, and the description of the car. D-Roc had a feeling Tee Tee would call the cops so he refused to go to the hospital. He and Tee Tee always got into fights, but today things had gotten out of hand, and the two really hurt each other badly. Slim dropped Fella off at Lolly's, and took D-Roc to his mother's house.

Fella strolled in Lolly's being loud a usual. Peko laughed as Fella told the story of him and Lisa's encounter. "I love this Main Street Dick." Fella said in a funny voice, imitating Lisa, causing Shawn Shawn to join Peko in laughter. Brandy didn't find anything funny. It had been a long time since the four of them were together, so Brandy took advantage of the opportunity. "Fells what's up wit you bro?" Brandy asked with concern. "What you mean what's up wit me? Don't start trippin Bee." Fella said "I'm sayin, you changed bro, you don't even hustle no more, you out here robbing, and shooting it out wit niggas, you know that aint even what we about, you don't even fuck wit the family no more, we sure don't get money together no more, I'm sayin bro you changed." "C'mon Bee, you tripping, I'm still the same ole fells, huh Pee?" Fells looked at Peko for some backup. "Man bro, you know you my nig, and I love you dawg, but Bee right, you aint been about your paper or the fam lately." Peko said. "What, man ya'll trippin, tell em lil bro." Fella said moving on to Shawn Shawn for some backup. "I don't know bro. If you getting money, you sure aint getting it with us, and you know you been off the hook lately big bro, it wasn't like this when Mills was home." Shawn Shawn said putting an end to Fella's search for support. Fella was both angry, and hurt. His pockets weren't hurting by a long shot, but it had been a while since he'd kicked it with his crew. "Aight man, maybe ya'll right, but we all together now, so let's do it like we use to." Fella said. He pulled out a fat bag of weed, "Lets blow till we can't blow no more. Roll something fat for my nigga T-Money." As they kicked it, money came through non stop, and they took turns serving customers like they did in the old days. Brandy's pager went off as she served one of her personal customers in the kitchen. After Lolly let the smoker out, Brandy called the unfamiliar number back. A male voice answered the phone after a few rings. "Who dis?" The male voice said. "This Bee, somebody call my pager?" Brandy said inquisitively. "Yeah this Chris and I hope that Bee is short for Brandy." He said sounding smooth as ever. Brandy smiled "Yeah, that Bee's for Brandy, what's up Chris?" "You, I was hoping we could go to the movies tonight." "Oh you were, were you?" Brandy said playfully. "Yeah C'mon Bee, don't tell me your turning me down already." Brandy laughed at the sound of him calling her Bee already.

"Nah I aint say that, but what time you talking about going?" "The movie start at nine, I was hoping I could pick you up around eight?" "I guess that can work." Brandy said trying not to sound too anxious about her first date. "Well it's about seven now. Can I call you back at this number in about an hour, and get your address?" "Yea that can work." Brandy said. "Aight Bee see you in an hour, you stay beautiful."

An hour later, Chris called on scheduled. He was hoping to hear Brandy's voice, but Fella answered the phone. After hearing the male voice ask for Brandy, he reacted like a protective older brother, but before he could go too far with his questioning, Brandy snatched the phone from him, gave Chris the address and quickly ended the call. Fifteen minutes later, Chris's system announced his arrival before his knock on the door. As Fella rushed to the door, Brandy flew by him. Just as she opened the door, Fella appeared beside her with his Gloc nine in hand. "What's up homie, where you taking my sister to?" Fella asked Chris, who was confused by Fella's demeanor, and large pistol. Brandy rolled her eyes and smacked her lips before saying, "Fella put that gun up and quit acting stupid. Chris this Is my brother Fella, that's my brother Peko, and my brother Shawn. Everybody this is my friend Chris, say what's up." She said while playfully elbowing Fella in the stomach. "What up dawg." Peko said. "Sup bro." Shawn Shawn added. "Fella." Brandy said "Whats happenin homie? You da dude from the drive thru huh?" Fella asked. "Yeah." Chris said before Brandy pulled him away by his arm. "Bye Fella." Brandy said as her and Chris headed to the car. Once inside the car Brandy apologized for Fella's behavior. "It's cool, if I had a sister as cute as you I would be protective too." Chris responded. "So that's where you live huh?" Chris said sparking conversation. "No…that's a spot." Brandy replied while giving Chris a look that said "Nigga I live better than that." "A spot? Like a drug spot…?" Chris asked. "Yea. What other kind of spot is there?" Brandy answered. "Ya brothers let you chill up in a drug house and shit?" Chris inquired. "Let me? Psssshh! Nigga I get money too." Brandy said with a funny look on her face. "Excuse me. It aint everyday that A brother meet a female as beautiful as you, and hood too." Chris said while winking his eye at Brandy. "My name Brandy nigga, you better recognize." She said playfully mimicking a skit from Snoop Dogg's album. On that note Brandy and Chris shared their first laugh together. As Chris pulled off, he grabbed the half backwood filled with weed from his ashtray "You don't mind me smoking do you?" "As long as it's Chronic and you sharing, I don't." Brandy answered. Chris smiled, and put fire to the weed. He took a few puffs before passing it to Brandy, "Be careful how you hit that baby, that aint that reggie, that's the best weed on the east side." Chris chided. Brandy playfully rolled her eyes before taking a pull on the backwood. The hydro Chronic instantly caused her to choke on its smoke. Chris let out a little laugh while pulling her hair behind her ear.

"You aight?" he asked.

"Yeah I'm cool." Brandy said, feeling a little embarrassed. "Don't be acting all bashful boss lady, I told you it was some killer." Chris said causing the two to share a second laugh. Brandy quickly passed the weed back to Chris. "Where you get that from, that's some chronic. My brother Peko gone want some of that for sure." "I got a little for sale." Chris said modestly. He was really the weed man, and had pounds on top of pounds. Chris's pager had been screaming since they got in the car. He had put it on vibrate not wanting it to interfere with him and Brandy's date, but the pager continued to go off. "You better call whoever that is back cause they aint playing" Brandy said. Chris smiled "It aint nothing like that, this about some money, you don't mind if we make a quick stop do you?" "Nah, its cool, gotta get that money right." Brandy replied. Chris drove straight to his weed house. They expected to be in and out quickly, but every time they prepared to leave, there was someone else knocking on the door. They ended up having to catch a later movie, but Brandy didn't mind. Her and Chris clicked immediately. They enjoyed each others company a lot, and from that day on made it a point to hang out together on the regular.

-CHAPTER EIGHT -

Now two months free from isolation, Mills sat on his bunk impatiently awaiting mail call. "MILLS!" J.C.O Whitaker yelled from his desk. Mills rushed to the mail line and scooped up a stack of envelopes from Whitaker's desk top. He fingered through the names on each envelope as he rushed back to his bunk.

The first envelope contained a card, signed by his grandmother and little brother. His grandmother enclosed a couple pictures of herself and Jimmy after one of Jimmy's football games. Mills smiled at the sight of his family. Jimmy's football uniform fitted him perfectly. He looked like a star.

The next envelope contained pictures from Buck, along with a card and his new phone number. Buck had laced him with photos of the block party, and a couple pictures of Fella, D-Roc, lil Walt, and Slim at some club. Mills shook his head at that sight. Fella was blinded, and Mills just hoped that his friend didn't have to fall too hard for his eyes to open.

He breezed through the pictures, and moved on to an envelope with the name Chrissie on it. He had no idea who the letter was from, until he saw the picture enclosed. He smiled at the sight of Chrissie, as he remembered how fine she looked the night of his party. Chrissie's picture became less intriguing as mills spotted an envelope with the name Ta'Nesha Walker on it. The envelope smelled just like Neesh causing him to get lost in the scent of her perfume, before ripping through the envelope like a wild animal.

A picture fell from the envelope as he snatched the letter from inside. Neesh looked gorgeous standing in front of her dormitory at Moreheads college. He stared at the picture for a moment, before reading her letter:

Dear Mills,

I bet you never thought you'd be hearing from me, huh? I hope you're healthy, and behaving yourself in there. Me, I'm healthy, and I always behave myself.

Mills, I want to apologize for what happened that night at the skating ring. I find myself feeling like your being in jail is all my fault, and I feel really crappy because of that. However, this is not a sympathy letter. I'm writing because I care, because I think about you, and because I wanted you to know that I'm sorry, and you're missed. Well Mills, Its time for me to go to my next class, so I have to cut this one short. I hope you liked the picture, write me sometime, I promise I'll make time to write back.

With Love,

Neesh

Mills was in a daze and BNut caught him zoning. "Damn Blood, we like pictures too" B-Nut yelled. His voice brought Mills back to reality. "C'mon homie what's mine is ya'lls" Mills said as he passed the pictures around to his homeboys.

As they looked at the pictures, Mills tore through the remaining envelopes, which were all from Brandy. The first three were nothing but pictures. Mills reminisced as he stared at the picture of him sitting on the hood of his car in front of Brandy's house. Then he looked at the picture of him and Brandy sitting in his car smoking a blunt. The pictures brought back memories that he cherished. He missed his crew and he couldn't wait to get back to the money.

The last envelope contained a letter from Brandy and he couldn't wait to read it:

What up bro?

Man, we miss you out here.

I'm still mad at you for putting all them charges on yourself, but I know you did it because you love me. Me and mommy been babysitting Jimmy a lot lately, just to give grandma Mills a break and some time to herself. He starting to look just like you too. He's been hanging with some friend from school named Leon. I haven't met him yet, but I guess he cool. Mommy be kidnapping the boy, sometimes I think she loves him more than me, I'm smiling but I aint joking. Oh yeah, I got pictures posted up in my locker at school, and you know all the lil hoochies be on ya heels. They be wanting to write you and shit, but I will never hook you up with none of them nasty ass bitches bro. Other than that, ain't shit changed, oh Pee got a sick ass Regal, and Fella gota nice ass Monte. I'm bout to buy me something too, you know a bitch gotta go hard. I know you salty about your ride, but don't trip bro, you know you gone come harder when you get out. We'll I'm gone bro but I love you and you better call me.

Your sister,

Bee, The Boss Lady <3

P.S. I did give this one girl named Tiffany your information, she cool though bro, and she aint no hood rat, she cute too! Peace Out.

Mills folded the letter up, grabbed the rest of his pictures and joined his homies on B-Nut's bed. "Who this lil bitch right here blood, she cold." B-Nut said speaking about Chrissie. "That's this one female I met at my party, she's a little older, I never got a chance to fuck with her though." Mills said. "Yea she nice, but who is this?" Law asked while holding Nesh's picture in his hand. "Now that's my wife right there nigga, let me get that." Mills said playfully snatching the picture out of Law's hand. "Now that right there is a dime." Law said speaking of Nesh. "I would eat her pussy on the first night" "What!" Mills said with a funny look on his face "Yea nigga, ya'll lil niggas better start eating ya'lls girls pussy. Before a young skinny fly nigga like myself come along and take ya bitch with a swift flick of the tongue." Law responded. "You nasty booty mouth having ass nigga, that's why yo breath always stink and shit." Rash said causing the boys to break out in laughter. "Yeah you yuck mouth, garbage truck mouth havin ass nigga." B-Nut added, but Law wasn't laughing, because it was never funny to the person who was getting cracked on, especially when they were getting teamed up on by Rash and B-Nut. While Mills and his homies laughed themselves to tears, Rex and some of his Cleveland homies were in another unit stomping Nasty out. Nasty had been moved to Rex's dorm a month ago in an attempt to split him and Black up to stop them from jumping the boys from Cleveland. Rex and his homies laid on Nasty allowing him to get comfortable before they bomb rushed him, but Nasty didn't go out without a fight. The J.C.O in charge of their dorm was from Rex's neighborhood, so the beating wasn't reported. When Nasty came to church on Sunday to meet Black and the rest of the Columbus boys, his face told the story for him. The boys were already warned that the next riot would result in immediate transfers to different camps of higher security for all parties involved. Black told the crew that it would be best to use the element of surprise. "We gone lay on these niggas for a few months, then when we attack we going all out, we gone hit every dorm them niggas in, cause after this one we getting transferred anyway. But in the meantime lets get this money and rock these niggas to sleep." Black pulled out a few cartons of cigarettes from under his shirt, then he tapped his partner

Roscoe, and motioned for him to pull out the bricks of Black and Mild cigars. "The cigarettes go for a dollar a square, that's twenty dollars a pack, and the milds go for five a stick, twenty five dollars a box. Ya'll giveme ten off each pack and fifteen off each box. Black passed the tobacco out to all the Columbus boys, making sure to give them all at least one pack and one box.

Back in the hood, Brandy, Peko, Shawn and Fella sat in Lolly's getting money as usual. Brandy and Chris had become serious over the months. While Peko and Chris had hit it off because Chris kept the best weed in the city. Fella still had a dislike for Chris, more so because him, D-Roc, Walt and Slim wanted to rob him, than Fella actually disliking him. As Peko set fire to his Swisher filled with Chris's expensive weed he said, "Man that nigga chris got the best weed on the east side for sure. This shit killer!" "I'm glad somebody like him." Brandy said while rolling her eyes at Fella. "Shid, that nigga Pee like whoever got weed. Let that nigga Chris run out of that weed, and Pee a forget his name." Fella said butting in. "Ha! Ha! Ha! That's cold Fells, you got me fucked up too." Peko responded while laughing because Fella was probably right. "Shut up Fella, Chris dig Pee, he always asking about em. Him and Pee is cool." Brandy said. "Shid I would dig em too, and ask about em every chance I get if he spent two, three hunit a day wit me. He lucky a nigga don't take the shit from him, jewels and all." Fella said seeing how

Brandy would react. "Aint nobody taking shit from him, Fella stop hatin." Brandy said in Chris's defense. "Hatin? Shit you better check me out, I'm blinding shit." Fella said as he fixed his jewelry.

Although Brandy and Chris haven't yet had sex, their relationship was most definitely serious. Chris showered Brandy with gifts, such as clothes, shoes, and pieces of moderate jewelry. When Brandy spoke of buying herself a car, Chris told her to save her money, that he'd get her a car for her birthday, which was a few months away in December. Meanwhile, Buck was on the other side of town in a big dice game, at the crap house known only by the ballers. No one shot dice for less than $500 a shot. Buck was up thirty five thousand, and still held the dice. This shot was worth close to ten thousand dollars. Him and another guy talked trash to one another as Buck clicked the dice in his hand. "Bet another stack nigga." Polo said to Buck while taunting him with a stack of cash in his hands. "That shits chump change dawg, with a shot like mine, I can break the bank, pay attention I might teach you something." Buck said as he shook the dice. "Teach me something? Shid if I wanted to learn something I would have kept my ass in school." Polo responded. "Well you know what they say…lose yo books, you lose yo lessons, pay me in bud, straight seven." Buck said as he released the dice. The dice rolled out of Bucks' hand perfectly, and stopped with a five and a three facing upward. "Yous a lucky brother" Polo said as Buck picked the money up from all his bets. "You know what I learnt Polo man? Sometimes its better to be lucky than to be good." Buck said issuing out more slick talk than Polo could reciprocate. As Buck rounded the money up, T-Bone and Fresh walked through the door. Once they made eye contact T-Bone scanned the room and smiled at the fact of Buck being by his self. T-Bone and Fresh were younger than

Buck but they were well aware of who he was. Buckshot and their Big Homie Duece had been in a rift with one another since their early teens.

Once Buck and Duece became rich, they became too focused on making money to even think about their childhood beef, but mostly because they rarely crossed one another's path. Duece kept his movement up north, and Buck kept his out east.

T-Bone and Fresh took over Dueces beef, like D-Roc and his crew took over Buck's. It was an east side north side thing, you'd have to be involved to fully understand it. T-Bone stepped in Buck's path, and bumped shoulders with him. Buck stumbled into Fresh, but with lightning speed he threw a two piece, landing both punches on Fresh's chin, sending him to the ground ass first. Then he quickly pulled his Colt four five and aimed it at T-Bone. "C'mon lil homie don't make me give it to you" Buck said. He backed out the door with a smirk on his face and his pistol aimed at T-Bone's head.

Once the door closed, Buck ran to his car and made a quick get away. He cursed Butter under his breath as he smashed on the gas pedal. Butter was supposed to meet him at the gambling house, but he stood buck up. This was the second time Butter didn't meet him when they had made plans to meet. "I gotta' have a serious sit down with this nigga, I could've lost my life tonight" Buck thought.

"Oh my gosh Butter…. Shit you in my stomach!" The girl screamed as he shoved his 10 ½ inches of steel into her bushy entrance. Butter and the Girl went at it with all the backed up anger and hatred, they thought they had for one another.

Butter felt hisself coming to his climax, so he pulled out of her tight hole, flipped her over on her stomach and re-entered her from behind.

He couldn't believe how wet her cave had become. Although her hole fitted around his pole like a glove, she was so wet that he re-entered her with ease. She moaned his name as they both reached their climax, and when it was finally over, they were both hit with a guilt that weighed down on them like a ton of bricks.

Butter hopped off the bed, while Mek rolled off the other side. As they both put their clothes on in silence, Mek stole one last peek at Butter's God like penis. "What have I gotten myself into?" She thought. "Butter we can't do this anymore" Mek said.

She couldn't believe she was cheating on Buck. He treated her like a queen. He took care of her, and her little sister. She loved Buck to death, and he more than satisfied her in the bedroom. "So why am I in a hotel room having sex with his one and only friend" She thought. You right Mek, this shit is wrong, Buck is my homie, He's like a brother to me, this can never happen again." Butter said, but he and Mek both knew that the dirt had been done, and not doing it again could not make things right.

Neither of them were sure if they could control this newfound lust for one another, but the one thing they were for sure about was, Buck could never find out about them, and that if he ever did, they would both see a side of him that they never wanted to see. They both knew that to Buckshot "Disloyalty was unforgivable"

-CHAPTER NINE -

Mills laid in bed with his eyes closed, but it was difficult for him to sleep with tomorrow's agenda on his mental. After four months it was finally time for the last ride on the Cleveland boys. Black's plan had worked perfectly. Through selling tobacco to the guys from Cleveland, they had become under the impression that the two cities had established a rapport, after all, their attack on Nasty was revenge for Black and Nasty's attack on Rex. Mills dozed off playing out his actions for tomorrow's battle. When he awoke the next morning, the clock seemed to stand still. He had been moved from the first time offender's dorm, to G dorm, which was right across the hall from H dorm, where Rex and the majority of the Cleveland boys bunked. Black pulled some strings and got moved to H dorm because he didn't like Nasty being in the dorm all by himself, nor did he like the idea of Mills being across the hall alone. The rest of the guys from Cleveland bunked in E dorm which was right below G and H so the attack would be easy once the guys from Columbus met and split into groups. When the clock hit ten o'clock, Mills slipped out the door while the J.C.O wasn't looking. As he crept down the steps he was met by Black and the rest of his homies.

Everyone already knew the plan, so the groups split up. Black, Nasty, Mills, Rash, B-Nut, Law, H.T., Roscoe, Big Dawg, and Doughboy headed upstairs to H-dorm while Big Trav, Tim-Tim, Lee Ray B-Knight, Tone Capone, Strong Arm, D-MAC, White Side, Tee Streets, and Lil Bobby stayed at the bottom of the stairs awaiting the signal to raid E-Dorm.

Black and Nasty entered the dorm like any other day. Several of Rex's homies sat in the television room, while several of them laid in bed.

Rex, B-White, Flannigan, and several others were deep in a dice game. The laundry room was packed and loud as all out doors, but that was the norm.

As Black and Nasty walked towards the dice game, Rex spotted them coming. "What's up Black, you and Nasty tryna lose some of that money on these stones" Rex teased.

"Yeah who got last shot" Black answered.

"Young Flannigan got the stones last" Rex said, as he rolled the dice and hit his point.

"Point seen, money gone". Rex trash talked while snatching his winnings from the ground.

A vicious uppercut from Black lifted Rex's whole body up. The overhand right that followed, sent Rex's body melting to the floor. B-White reacted quickly, landing a swift right to Black's jaw.

Nasty knocked Flannigan to the ground with a left hook, then squared off with another one of Rex's homies. Black shook off B-Whites blow, then pivoted, placing his back against the wall as B-White and another guy rushed him.

B-White was too frail to stand up under the two piece Black delivered to his chin. His body crumbled to the floor. Black faked the other guy with a right hand, and went under him. The guy never had a chance, his feet almost touched the ceiling when Black lifted him into the air. The sound of his back crashing into the floor woke the guys in bed from their sleep.

On his way to the melee, the J.C.O was startled by Black and Nasty's troops, as they came running through the door. Part of the troops bombed on the guys in the T.V room, while the others raided the back of the dormitory to assist Black and Nasty.

Although the Columbus boys were outnumbered, the element of surprise evened out the odds. Just as Nasty was being cornered by three guys, Mills ran to his rescue with a leaping hook. The hook sent one guy sliding across the floor, but his homeboy delivered a mean blow to Mills' jaw. Mills staggered into the wall, but B-Nut rushed to his aid. H.T got Black out of a jam, as he ran freely, splitting everyone he hit with the lock he held tightly in his hand.

Rash danced around with one guy, patiently waiting for an opening. When he found it, he slipped under the guy's lazy jab and laid him out with a crispy three piece.

It didn't take long for blood to fill the floor, nor for the J.C.O to hit his man down button calling for backup.

Big Trav, and his group of soldiers hid behind the doorway that led to the steps. They watched countless J.C.Os rush by them headed for the royal rumble in H-Dorm.

As soon as they were sure that all of the cavalry had passed them Tim Tim, and Lee Ray walked into E-Dorm and set it off. Tim Tim punched B.G in the face with a vicious blow, knocking him out his seat. Lee Ray slid the person closest to him, then rushed another guy. They were quickly swarmed, and the blows they endured were worth it, as Big Trav and the rest of their backup came charging through the door. Big Trav was huge for his age. He put every guy he hit down with one blow. He grabbed one guy by the throat, and slung him into a wall as the rest of his homies went to work. The J.C.O didn't know what to do. He watched his dorm being torn to pieces and decided to called for backup, but all the troops were upstairs in H dorm. Tee Streets ran around with the J.C.O's steel chair clobbering everyone in his path. By the time the J.C.O's backup came, bodies were laid out all over the place, while some of the boys were still slugging it out. A lot of the boys were hospitalized, but those who weren't were immediately transferred to different juvenile prison camps. Mills, B-Nut, H.T., and Black, lucked up. They got transferred to Tyko, which was closer to home. Rash, Law and a lot of others were transferred to Indian River. While Big Trav, Tim Tim, and Lee Ray were sent to RiverView with the majority of the Cleveland guys who survived the storm.

Meanwhile, Peko was at home with his girlfriend Shy. Had it not been for Peko, Shy would be in school this morning. But instead she was in the shower rinsing the smell of morning sex from her young body.

A few days ago Peko had learnt that he was about to be a father, and since that day, he hasn't been able to keep his hands off Shy. Knowing that she was carrying his child increased his attraction to her by one thousand.

She was already beautiful, standing at 5'2" 125 pounds. Her frame had already outgrown her fifteen years of age, and she was well on her way to becoming a brick house. Her reddish brown hair complemented her golden brown skin complexion, while the mushroom hairstyle that she wore it in shaped her face perfectly.

Shy entered the room with a towel wrapped around her young goddess like body and Peko instantly became aroused. Her flat stomach accentuated her hips, that seem to roll off her body forming a perfect Coca Cola bottle shape.

"Oh my goodness Peko, why you always smoking?" Shy said as she fanned the room with her hand "Cause I can't think sober" Peko answered. "Every time somebody see you, you got a cigar in ya mouth, that is not attractive" Shy said while checking herself out in the mirror. "Give me something else to put in my mouth then" Peko said while putting the blunt out in the ashtray. "That's why I'm pregnant now, you and that dirty mind of yours."

Peko walked up behind her as she went through her panty drawer.

The sight of her apple bottom protruding form beneath the towel had Peko excited. He wrapped his hands around her and rubbed on her belly, while poking her with his excitement from behind. "Peko don't start that, I'm tryna get dressed." Shy whimpered. Peko put his hand under her towel, and began caressing her inner thigh. "C'mon baby, you know I can't get enough of that gushy stuff" Peko whispered into her ear, while kissing her neck.

Shy did a one eighty, and stared Peko directly in his eyes. "Pee don't look at me like that, you know that turns me on" Shy said while rubbing on his earlobe. "You know that's my spot" Peko said, while removing her towel.

He slid his tongue in her mouth, then quickly moved on to her breast. He teased each one with his tongue, then nibbled on her nipples "C'mon Peko lets do it." She whispered in a sexy voice. Peko picked her up and carried her to the bed. Once he laid her down, he went back to work on her breast. Peko and Shy had never done oral sex, but they watched enough porno's to know what to do. Peko replayed the porn in his mind and kissed on Shy's inner thigh. As he opened her lips to get a better view of her clit, she became afraid of the pleasure she was about to feel. "Peko Noo!" she whimpered as he flicked his tongue at her clit. He stuck two fingers in her opening and made a "Come here" motion. As he licked on her pearl tongue. "OH MY GOD!" Peko I'm bout to cum!!" She yelled while trying to get away from his tongue.

Her body shook uncontrollably, and Peko wasted no time removing his clothes and climbing on top of her…

Brandy laid still with her eyes closed, as Chris worked his tongue from her mouth to her ear. He craved her virginity and could taste her innocence through the perspiration from her skin.

Her high yellow tone looked radiant as he looked down on her. He removed her bra, and stared lustfully at her pink nipples. He took her left breast into his mouth, while using his hand to massage the right breast. He pinched her nipple, but maintained his gentle approach with Brandy. He wanted her first time to be memorable.

"Hold on Chris, I don't think I'm ready" Brandy said as he began to remove her panties. Chris had never been with a virgin before, but he talked many females out of the twat, so he didn't panic. "Listen Brandy, if you don't want to do this, then we don't have to. I love you and I'm willing to wait, but understand I am only a man and being in a non sexual relationship is very new and hard for me. I know you're probably scared, and doubtful about how things will be after we have sex, but you have to trust me. You love me don't you?" Chris said. "Yes" Brandy replied. "Do you trust me?" Chris asked, knowing that if her answer was yes, her virginity was his. "Yes Chris but..." Chris cut her off, "There is no buts baby, either you trust me or you don't." Brandy thought for a moment. Everything Chris had told her he'd do, he done. He told her he would get her a car for her birthday, and he did. He told her that if they were together she wouldn't have to hustle, because he'd take care of her, and he did, although it didn't stop her from getting her grind on. Most importantly he both loved and respected her. "You bet not hurt me Chris." Brandy said as she allowed her panties to slide off. Chris removed all his clothing and slipped out of his boxers. His love muscle was at full attention, and Brandy looked at the large piece before her and throught "What did I just get myself into." He hovered over top of her while taking in the beautiful sight beneath him. Brandy's body didn't have a scratch on it, and the hair on her vagina matched the hair on her head. It was soft and silky.

Chris gently kissed her on her thigh as he opened her legs. He sucked, licked and gently bit on her inner thighs, blowing on her vagina as he switched from one thigh to the other. "Chris no, I aint ready for all that" She said, as he opened the entrance to her love box. "It's gone feel good, trust me." Chris said as he looked at the muffin with hunger in his eyes. Brandy's love box was pinker than bubble yums chewing gum, and Chris licked his lips before tasting her. He licked around her cave before going to her clit. He wanted to relax her body before he took her to ecstasy. He stuck his tongue in her hole, and twirled it around for a minute then he pulled out and went to work on the clit. Chris licked her at rapid speed causing her to run from the feeling. "Chris, please nooo!" Brandy yelled as she became wetter, hotter, and hornier than ever before. Christ locked her in, as he nibbled on her clit. When Brandy started cumming, she grabbed Chris's head, while locking her legs around his neck. Her juices squirted out of her fountain and Chris drank them up. He entered her slowly, causing her to close her eyes, and bite down on her bottom lip to endure the pain.

HE put half of his manhood in her, and stroked her slowly. She was so wet and tight that the feeling was driving him insane.

As he pushed more of himself into her cave, she clawed his back with her finger nails. The deeper he dug in her hole, the deeper she dug her nails into his back. "Awwweee shiiittt Bee, you killin me" Chris said as he felt both pleasure and pain. Brandy's only response was heavy moans, and high pitched screams. Chris picked up on the pace with his motion as he felt his rod about to explode and Brandy's screams grew louder with each stroke.

After he released himself into her, he collapsed on top of her. They were both tired and out of breath, not to mention sore. Brandy stared at the ceiling in shock, while Chris basked in the glory of his first virgin conquest.

After being in isolation for two weeks, Mills and the others who were transferred to Tyko's juvenile facility were released into population. All the boys were placed in different units, so they rarely saw one another, except for when passing in the hallways. For the first few days Mills watched his surroundings very closely. He noticed one guy in particular keeping a watchful eye on him. The guy didn't look familiar at all, so Mills watched the guy's movements like a hawk. "You don't watch people, you watch the way they move" Buck once told him, so he didn't focus on the guy, as much as he did the things the guy did, who he associated with, etc etc.

The guy came and went as he pleased. He also gave a lot of handshakes and hugs before and after his brief conversations.

Game recognized game, so it was clear to Mills that this guy had something going on. What exactly that something is, Mills had yet to figure that out, but as the saying goes, "The proof is in the pudding and the pudding is in the eating".

"What's up lil homie. What city you from?" Mills heard the words, and felt the presence, but there was no familiarity in the voice, so he slowly made his way up from the weight bench. He spotted the guy he'd been watching and cursed hisself for slipping. "No need to get on the defensive, I come in peace, I'm from Columbus, and I thought you looked familiar. My name is Rio." The guy extended his hand for some dap. "T-Money. I'm from Columbus too, but I don't think you know me homie" Mills said. "T-Money huh? I been noticing you watching me T-Money am I in any kind of trouble that I'm not aware of" Rio said. "I been meaning to ask you the same thing" Was Mills response.

Rio laughed, because he knew Mills had noticed him peeping him out. "How old are you man? You look hella young." Mills was confused by Rio's easiness. He wasn't comfortable with the guys questioning, and felt it was time to end the conversation. "Listen bro, I don't mean no disrespect, but you sure are asking a lot of questions to a nigga you don't know." Mills said. "Asking questions is the only way to get answers homie. Think about it. How else does a person get to know another person?" Rio had a point, but Mills wasn't sure he wanted to get to know the guy. "Listen man it was nice meeting you, but I think that's enough conversating for one day." Rio smiled. "Communication breeds understanding but too much of anything can be bad for you, so I guess I'll catch you some other time Mills." Rio said as he walked off. Mills watched as Rio strolled over to the J.C.O that ran their unit. The two kicked it like they were buddies while taking a quick glance at Mills. Mills didn't know what it was, but there was something real familiar about the J.C.O.

Later that night, Mills replayed him and Ri0's conversation in his head. He remembered Rio calling him Mills before walking off, but he was sure he had introduced himself as T-Money. There was something unsettling about he and Rio's encounter and tomorrow, he planned on getting to the bottom of it. The next morning, Mills watched Rio as he made his rounds, issuing out daps and hugs. The moment Mills caught Rio by himself he pulled down on him. "What up homie?" Mills said as Rio walked out of his cell "Not a whole lot, what's up wit you?" Rio shot back. "I don't know you tell me seeing as how you know more about me than you led me to believe." Rio smiled. He called Mills by that name purposely last night hoping that he would catch onto it. "I don't get what you mean man, what do I know." Rio said continuing his mind games. It was Mills turn to smile and he did sinisterly, because game recognized game. "Well seeing how you called me Mills before leaving yesterday when I told you my name was T-Money you obviously know something, So tell me… what is this all about?" Mills said as he played the wall. "I don't get what you mean my nig, yo last name is Mills, and that's what I called you." Rio said trying to sound innocent. "Dig bro, two can play the game you playing, I got a phone call to make so I'm bout to pull out, but from one hustler to another, you should handle your business a little more discreet than you do, Stevie Wonder can see through yo dap, and hug front. Peace." Mills said as he walked off, leaving Rio with something to think about this time.

Later that day, second shift came on; Mills watched Rio and the J.C.O with the familiar face closely. Mills wasn't stupid, or slow to the game, so he knew that there was more to Rio and the J.C.O's relationship than they let on, While at rec later that day, Mills was approached by Rio, as he watched the J.C.O spray shots from all over the basketball court, running circles around some of the best ballplayers In the unit. "So you back for more already?" Mills said as Rio took a seat next to him on the weight bench. Rio laughed, "Nah homie, the game is over, the J.C.O Butter is real cool with your brother Buckshot. Buckshot told him to holler at you, but he wasn't sure who you are, so he had me holler at you, he wanted me to talk to you yesterday, but I was having too much fun playing mind games with you." Rio said. "Is that right?" Mills said, clearly bothered by Rio's mind tricks. "C'mon lil homie aint nothing wrong wit a little mental sparring match, it keeps you on your toes, you dig." Mills and Rio kicked it until rec was over. Once they got back to their unit, Rio escorted Mills to J.C.O Butter's desk. "What's happening shorty?" Butter said to Mills. "Not much, Rio tells me you know my big bro" Mills replied. "Yeah, that's my ace; don't tell me you don't remember me, all that fire ass weed I sold your brother. I think you was at the house the day I came by, Buck said you was laying low because you popped some dope fiend who tried to rob you of yo shit." Butter said. "Aw shit, that is you. I knew I remembered you from somewhere, I think

Buck took me to yo crib wit em one day too, off of Brice road?" Mills said. "Ssshhh!"

Butter said looking around to see if anyone was listening. "Yeah that's me, and damn boy

you getting big as fuck, how long you been down?"

"Almost two years. I got one more to go man." Mills said while shaking his head in

disgust. "Don't look so down shorty, that year gone fly by, you down here wit family

now. I'm ah make sure you aight." Butter said. Rio walked off to handle some business

while Mills and Butter kicked it. By the time he returned, Mills had his photo albums at

the desk. He and Butter laughed at some of the photos as they flipped through the pages.

Butter looking at an inmates pictures wasn't unusual. He was only twenty five and still

youthful at heart. So he vibed with the juveniles on a special level. A lot of the juveniles

viewed him no differently than they did their peers, which had its pros and cons, but this

connection gave him a level of understanding with the youngsters, that no other J.C.O

had.

Buck pulled his casket gray '94 Lexus coop onto a side street. He could barely

control the steering wheel as Mek took his 8 ½ inches into her hot wet mouth. "Damn bae

that shit feel so good, hold up, let me pull over real quick" He said while pulling in

behind a dark blue celebrity.

Mek didn't stop. She played with the head of his pole, slowly licking around it, then picking up the speed. Buck jerked as she made her way down his shaft, and onto his ball sack, before licking her way back up then slowly deep throating his manhood.

Buck laid his seat back so he could enjoy the moment. His girl was a beast with her mouth, and she knew just how he liked it. As buck played with her clit, she moaned with pleasure, and drenched his fingers with her juices. Buck pulled his hand from under her dress and licked her juices from hisr fingers. He loved the way his woman tasted. And she could see the pleasure in his eyes as he devoured his fingers. "Mmmmm! Baby you taste so good" he whispered.

Mek couldn't take it anymore, she needed to feel him inside of her. she climbed on top of him, and easily slid down his pole. She looked buck directly in his eyes as she arched her back, and bounced up and down on his rod with rhythmic motion.

"Daddy I wanna' have your baby" She whispered while picking up the pace in her rhythm. Buck gripped her cheeks, spreading them apart so he could dig deeper. "Lets have a beautiful lil girl" Buck whispered through deep breaths and gritted teeth. "Buck I'm cumming! I'm cumming! I'm cumming! I love you boy!" she grunted out as she reached her climax.

-CHAPTER TEN-

As spring slowly manifested itself, the jack boys rode up Cleveland Avenue thinking about Slim and Fella's customized MPV mini vans. They had just left the bodyshop and their vans were coming along nicely.

After going on a robbing spree throughout the winter, the crew was ready to come hard with their new vehicles for the summer.

D-Roc had been laying low for the last few months due to his domestic violence warrants. Although he and Tee Tee had made up, and were back sleeping together, the state wouldn't let her drop the charges.

With the sun beaming down on this late March afternoon, D-Roc couldn't resist the urge to break his Maxima back out for the ladies. "Aye Roc, Check out these lil freaks beside us bro" Lil Walt said from the backseat. D-Roc looked to his right and smiled a gold grilled smile at the three ladies in the vehicle next to him. He motioned for the brown skin beauty in the passenger seat to roll down her window, and got her and her friend in the backseat to do so. "Follow us!" the females yelled, then hopped over two lanes. D-roc swerved around a couple cars and squeezed in front of another one, to keep up with the car full of chicks.

He never noticed the police cruiser a few cars behind. Until he bent the corner behind the females, and caught a glimpse of the cruisers lights. The cruiser hit the corner just as the females pulled into an open lot to meet up with the boys. The females watched D-Roc pull right past them with the police cruiser hot on his tail.

The chase was on. D-Roc had several pistols, along with the cocaine and marijuana in his ride. Add that to his warrant and it was clear to see why pulling over wasn't an option.

D-Roc bent a few corners, and once out of the officer's sight the guns, and drugs went out the windows. The cruiser quickly came back into view and D-Roc pulled over like he'd done nothing wrong and was completely legit.

The officers hopped out the cruiser with their weapons drawn. "Turn the car off and step out with your hands where I can see them" The officers ordered. The boys did as they were told, and the officers held them there until backup arrived. All four of the boys were handcuffed and placed in the back of a cruiser, while the officers ran ID checks on them.

D-Roc's alias came back clean, but he was taken downtown for fleeing and traffic violations. Once he was fingerprinted he knew he had to face the music, but he was cool about it, and past ready to have the warrants resolved.

The next morning, Slim, Fella, and Lil Walt sat next to a bondsman along with D-Roc's mother. They were prepared to pay his bond, and have him released ASAP, but to their surprise, D-Roc was held without a bond. D-Roc cursed the judge on the way out of the courtroom, and continued to do so all the way back to his cell.

Later that night, Peko sat in Lolly's counting the cash he made for the day. Shawn

Shawn was at his girlfriends house, while Brandy was out with Chris, but Peko didn't mind. He took advantage of the alone time, and ran through several ounces in seven hours.

Now at 11:30pm, he sat on the couch smoking a fat stogie. He had close to eight grand stacked on the table in front of him and was ready to call it a night, but first he had to call Shy and wake her up, because Shy's mother hated when he woke the whole house up knocking on her door late at night.

"Ring! Ring! Ring!" "Hello" Shy said with sleep in her voice. "What's up Baby why you aint wait for me" Peko said. "Peko you know I gotta got to school in the morning" Shy answered. "I know, but I left my key, and I'm on my way home. I need you to come let me in so get up." Peko ordered. "Pee, why you wait so late to tell me you left your key? Now you want me to get up out my sleep, and sit up till you bring yo butt home?"

"Yeah, you know how yo mom be tripping about me waking her up, by knocking on her door late at night" Peko answered. "I know, that's why she gave you a key boy" Shy exclaimed. "Ha! Ha! Ha! Ha!" Peko laughed in her ear. He was always tickled by her attitude. "Stop tripping Shyrah, you know I'm gonna wake you up so I can get me some of that gushy before I go to sleep anyway."

You aint getting nothing if you don't hurry up." Peko laughed in her ear once again. "You can't stop me from getting what's mine. I got my name all over that" Peko said. "You get on my nerves, you think everything's funny" she exclaimed. "NO I don't, I just think you funny when you mad" Peko said in between giggles. "Whatever, you better hurry up" Shy replied. "I'm on my way" Peko said. "Alright, I hate you" Shy said "I hate you more" Peko said before hanging up.

"I hate you was their way of telling each other that they loved one another. They came up with that after a heated argument in which Shy whispered the words I hate you in Peko's ear during make up sex.

Peko stuffed his money in his pockets, slid his gun under the couch, and relit his blunt, he usually took his gun with him, but for some reason his instincts told him to leave the gun behind tonight. As Peko walked out the back door he had a funny feeling in his gut. He scanned the dark backyard as he unlocked his car door, and out of nowhere a black truck pulled up blocking him in, and men in black ran out the truck's sliding door. Peko took off towards the house. When he heard the men yell, "Columbus SWAT team get the fuck on the ground" HE ran back off the porch and headed for the front of the house, but was stopped in his tracks as the men in black filled the front yard as well. He shot back towards the backyard, so he could leap the neighbor's fence, but never made it as the men in black boxed him in.

After months of rolling with Mario, Mills had the camp's movement down pat. He had also become cool with some more of the J.C.O's on behalf of his relationship with Butter, and Mario both. Mario was known all through the camp. He was sentenced to juvenile life at the age of fourteen and for the last five years of his life he's been living in TYKO juvenile prison camp. Like Mills, Rio was a young hustler. Even now at the age of nineteen all he thought about was different ways to get money. In Rio's mind, he had the dope game down to a science. Rio and Law's case was very similar, Rio was robbed at a dope house but the robbers never searched him for a gun. As the robbers ran out the door headed for their get away car, Rio emptied his clip on the jackboys, paralyzing one with a shot to the back and killing the other one instantly as bullets ripped through his neck.

Mills walked up the hall with his drawers full of weed. He had to do most of his hustling through Black, B-Nut, and H.T. since Rio had their side of the camp on lock, and Mills didn't want to step on his new homies toes. Mills stopped by H.T.'S unit, then B-Nut's. He gave them both an ounce of good green, for a grand a piece. Only asking for a grand was showing love, because when broken down, one could make anywhere from two to three grand off of one ounce. Mills made a few other stops, so he could take care of a few customers Rio hooked him up with, and then he headed for the rec department where Black was at. He didn't spot him, which meant he was in the weight room. J.C.O Hudson was one of Butter's homies and Mills nodded his head at him while pointing to the weight room. Hudson knew Mills was looking for Black. He held up five fingers, which let Mills know he had five minutes. Mills rushed to the weight room, and caught Black off guard throwing up two hundred pounds on the chest machine. When he spotted Mills he hopped off the machine and motioned for his workout partner to take over. "What up T-Money?" Black said as he and Mills embraced each other. "Not a whole lot, lets step outside the door for a minute, Hudson only gave me five minutes." Mills said. Mills and black shared a few words, and when they felt no one was looking Mills passed him the last ounce of weed. Black quickly stuffed it. He and Mills embraced one another again and said their see you laters. Mills held his fist in the air to Hudson showing appreciation and saying see you later at the same time, then walked out of the gym. When Mills made it back to the unit Rio was on the phone, in what seemed to be a deep conversation. ON the way to his cell, Mill was stopped by a guy from Akron named D-Boy.

"Hold up Mills" D-Boy said, "let me get a fifty" he whispered in Mills ear while passing him fifty dollars in a handshake. "I don't know what you're talking about homie." Mills said as he wondered how D-Boy knew about his business. "Rio told me to holler at you." D-Boy said as he felt Mills putting a spin move on him. Mills looked over at Rio, who gave him a thumbs up. "Aight homie, just give me a minute. I'll be right back." Mills walked to his cell and returned a few minutes later with a fifty pack cuffed in his palm. He dropped the paper the weed was wrapped in on the floor next to D-Boy's feet, and kept walking. He headed to the phone next to Rio, dialed Brandy's number, and quickly got through.

"What's up nigga, you aint call to wish a bitch happy birthday or nothing?" Brandy said. "My bad Bee, but yo bro can't stay out of isolation, I'm in a whole nother camp and everything now." Mills replied. "Yeah I know, Buck told me they transferred you to the place on the west side. At least you closer to home" Brandy said matter-of-factly.

"Yeah, I like it better her anyway, what's up with the fam though?" Mills inquired. "Damn you aint heard about Pee yet?" Brandy said. "Heard what about Pee?" Mills questioned. "He got caught in a SWAT raid at Lolly's a few weeks ago. He aint have no drugs or nothing on him, but you know he had that warrant. His P.O. talking about making him do six months for probation violation, so he'll probably be down there with you in a few months. That's fucked up cause he got a baby on the way too." Brandy explained with empathy. "What! Bro got a baby on the way, you bullshitin." Mills said enthusiastically. "His girl like three months pregnant." Brandy said. "Damn a lot has changed." Mills replied. Mills and Brandy talked for a few more minutes. Then he had

her call his grandmother. He conversed with his grandmother for a while, since his little

brother wasn't home. When Mills call was over Rio was ending his second call. "I see ole

girl got you pissed off again huh bro?" Mills asked Rio as he watched him slam the

phone down. "Lightweight man, fuck that bucket head though, lets go smoke something.

I got some new numbers for you anyway." Rio said. Rio liked to break drugs down to

grams, and come up with the best prices to sell them for. He wanted a price that would

make the supplier a lot of money and sow up the whole strip, so every other day he came

up with some new prices, sales schemes, and projections. He called this doing numbers.

Mario was a few years older than Mills, and a lot of things he said made sense, so Mills

loved listening, and trading ideas with him. Mario wasn't necessarily the smartest guy,

but he was sharp because he asked alot of questions, and paid attention when someone

was speaking. When they entered Mills cell, his celly was laying back on his bed reading

a book. "What up Junebug?" Rio said to Mills celly. His name was Julius Braxton, but

people called him J.B for short. Rio and Mills joked with him saying that J.B. stood for

Junebug and the name just stuck with him.

"What up Rio? Sup Mills?" Junebug said as he put the book away. He knew it was time

to get high whenever Rio walked in the cell with Mills, so he played his position by

stuffing the bottom of the door with towels, and opening the window. Rio pulled a fat top

joint out of his pocket and set fire to it. He hit it a couple times, and passed it to Mills.

After making it around the room three times, the joint was gone; Mills threw a small bag

of weed in Junebug's lap and told him to roll another one up. While Junebug rolled

another joint Mills asked Rio about his new numbers. "Oh yeah, peep this, say you cop a brick for twenty six gees, a brick is a thousand grams, you turn that thousand to twelve sixty, that's straight mack, some of the best dope in the city for sure, you sell twenty eight grams for seven hundred, that's thirty one fifty a brick, that's a profit of fifty one fifty, five thousand, one hundred and fifty dollars, now here's where the flip comes in at, ounces are being sold for seven fifty to nine hundred dollars a pop, and a lot of that shit niggas be selling aint mack. They turning one into one and a half, greedy niggas you feel me?"

"I feel you." Mills said to show Mario he was being attentive. "You selling ounces for seven hundred, which is at least fifty dollars cheaper than the cheapest Dee around, and you got the best in quality, you sowing up the whole strip lil homie no lie, you gone run through those forty five ounces in five days tops, that's thirty thousand a month all profit!!! Three hundred and sixty thousand a year all profit!! Let's say you run through a brick in three days instead of five, this is just for a little extra motivation, something more to reach for, nah mean, if you run through a brick every three days that's fifty thousand a month all profit!! That's six hundred gees in a year all profit!! You could be a millionaire in two years, can you buy that?" Rio asked seriously. Mills shook his head in agreement. Rio was helping Mills take his hustle to a whole nother level, and Mills loved every minute of it, because it sort of reminded him of the talks he and Buck used to have. Mills had a little over a year left in Juvy and he planned on soaking up all the game he could, because once he touched the turf again, he was taking his game to a whole nother level…

-CHAPTER ELEVEN-

Young L's and Pimp stood in the apartment complex's doorway as cars rode up and down Miller Avenue. As Liley walked up, L's ran out to catch one of his big spenders. "Where you going little L's? I need some shit." Liley said as L's ran by her. "Holler at my homie." L's shot back while pointing at Pimp. "What's happening baby, you got the same shit L's got?" Liley asked as she approached Pimp. "Yeah I got that, what you need?" Pimp asked while scanning the scene. "I got seventeen dollars and I'm tryna get twenty." "I got you step inside." Pimp said as he pulled his pack from his draw pocket. He gave Liley a fat twenty and pocketed the seventeen dollars. "Boy you is fine, if you was a little older mmmhm." Liley said causing Pimp to smile. "I might have to introduce you to my daughter." She continued as L's walked up. "Damn what about me Liley?" L's said butting in. "Mm mm you is too bad and too fast for Leslie." Liley said as she walked off. "That's cold." L's said while laughing. "You better get her daughter bro, I'm telling you Leslie is cold, and she got a fat ass." L's whispered to Pimp. Liley smoked dope but she kept herself up. Everyone could tell she was the one back in her day. Leslie was only thirteen, but it was clear to see, she would one day become a hustler's wife. She was gorgeous, and the only chance she had at escaping "some hustler's game" was to be moved out the hood… That wouldn't be happening any time soon. Her and L's were cool, mostly because they grew up together. If L's wouldn't have treated all the girls in the neighborhood so disrespectfully, Leslie might have given him a chance, but L's was wild, and every girl that he had sex with, he dissed afterward, and moved on to their friend. "C'mon man we got to get out here in the open where we can be seen, or else all the geeks gone go up the street." L's said,

"C'mon bro you know I can't be in the open like that, if one of my big bro's homies catch me out here pumping I'm ass out, not to mention my big bro Buck, or my grandmother, maaan shid." Pimp said with a funny look on his face. I feel you bro, I gotta look out for my mom, its like she know I'm out here doin something, but she hasn't caught me yet, and I aint tryna find out what will happen if she does. Feel me." "You know I feel you bro" Pimp replied. L's started splitting a swisher so he could fill it up with weed. He didn't smoke as much as he would like because Pimp didn't smoke, and he didn't like smoking alone. "What up Pimp you gone blow this one with me?" L's said as he filled the Swisher. "Hell nah man, football season is coming up this summer and that shit aint good for my gas. I don't know about you but this hustling is temporary for me, I'm going to the pro's baby." Pimp said while doing his Heisman pose.

L's real name is Leon Pittman. He's a couple years older than Pimp, but because of Pimp's skill in football they played on the same football team. They also went to the same high school in which L's was known throughout as a live wire. He didn't do much fighting but he was known for letting his gun go.

It took Liley a few weeks to bring her daughter around, but the more she dealt with Pimp the more she liked him for her daughter. Pimp and L's stood in front of Big Looney's house with Big Looney, lil Looney, and the rest of L's big homies. Liley pulled up hanging out the passenger window of a black Escort. C'mere Pimp she yelled. Pimp walked up to the car. "What's happening Liley how you doing today?" Pimp said as he leaned in the car. "Aint nothing happening baby I just wanted to introduce you to my daughter" Liley looked in the back seat where Leslie sat. Leslie this is… boy what is your real name?" She said directing her attention back to Pimp. "Jimmy" he replied. "Leslie this is Jimmy, Jimmy this is Leslie." "Hi" Leslie said. "What up." Pimp replied. "Isn't he the bomb?" Liley asked her daughter. "Mom!" Leslie said in her please don't embarrass me voice. "Alright but ya'll can at least exchange numbers or something" Liley urged one last time. "Mom!!" Leslie said again. "Okay" Liley replied.

Pimp was laughing as the two went back and forth. "Excuse my mom, she can't help herself" Leslie said "Don't worry about it. I would like to call you sometime tho, if that's cool with you?" Pimp smoothly replied. On that note, he and Leslie swapped pager numbers. Then Leslie and her mother drove off.

So what's up, you knock her off or what?" L's asked. "C'mon man, my name aint Pimp for nothing." Pimp arrogantly answered, causing everyone to burst into laughter. "Awe, that's cold, you gone send me like that bro" L's said in between his own laughter.

Big Looney and the rest of L's homies were taking to Pimp pretty quickly. Big Looney loved being surrounded by his little homies. They were his young killers, his team of wolves, but as with every alpha male who led the pack, he had to do most of the thinking, because the youngsters were easily distracted.

Like now, they were all sharing shits and giggles totally oblivious to an adversary cruising by the block in an unknown vehicle. Big Looney shared the moment of laughter with his youngins, but he always stayed on point.

He was in the middle of a turf war with the Detroit boys. They were moving in on his territory and multiplying in numbers at a rapid speed.

Not being the one to wait for potential enemies to strike first, Big Looney had sent some of his soldiers to do a number on the Detroit boys dope spot. A few of the Detroit boys had felt the steel. One of which was still recovering in his hospital bed.

Big Looney knew that it wouldn't take long for the Detroit boys to retaliate, so he was on high alert.

As he rounded up his best gunners, to inform them of the vehicle circling the block, shots rang out, and bullets ripped through the crowd of youngsters.

Big Looney spotted the unknown vehicle pulling out of an alley with shooters hanging out the windows. He, lil Looney, and Hawk ran for cover while returning fire.

L's snatched Pimp to the ground, then popped back up with his baby gloc in hand.

"Pocka! Pocka! Pocka!" L's chased after the vehicle letting off rounds until his clip was empty.

When the smoke cleared, L's noticed Lil Looney on the ground. His body was shaking as blood leaked from his abdomen. His gun lay a few feet away from him, as any soldier's weapon should. "Big Loon, they got Lil Loon! He's hit!" L's yelled.

Big Looney and Hawk came running to Lil Looney's aid. Get the car started, we gotta' get 'em to a hospital." Big Looney said. Hawk ran across the street, hopped in Looney's old school and quickly brought the car to life. "Hold on lil bro, I got you , fight for me" Big Looney said as he picked his little brother up and carried him to the car.

"Lil L's grab those straps and get out of here, I'll get with you later" Big Looney ordered. L's grabbed the guns from off the ground and he and Pimp ran up the alley headed for his mother's house.

～ ～ ⑧ ⑧ ⑧ ⑧ ⑧ ～ ～

D-Roc, Slim, Lil Walt, and Fella sat in an unknown vehicle, parked down the street from Chris's weed house. They came to rob the place, but was interrupted by Brandy's sudden appearance.

She pulled up in her new '93 Probe, and all hell broke loose. She had caught Chris with another girl, and instantly snapped.

Brandy beat the girl from the porch to the sidewalk. Chris tried to intervene and received a few combos upside his head as well.

"Get yo nasty ass hands off of me!" Brandy said as she yanked away from Chris' grasp. As Brandy stormed to her car, the girl jumped up off the ground and took off ruuning in the opposite direction.

"Hold up Bee let me holler at you baby, it aint what you think." Chris said as he ran after her. Chris snatched Brandy's keys out her hand as she went to put them in the ignition.

"Give me my muthafucking keys Chris." Brandy screamed. "Hold up baby I don't want you leaving like this, fuck that bitch I love you, she aint nothing." Chris pleaded. "No fuck you Chris, now give me my keys before I start acting a fool out here." Brandy said as she reached for her keys.

"Aw shit aint that that bitch India lil cuzz?" Slim said as India took off up the street.

"Hell yea that's the freak." Fella said. Then he and Slim burst into laughter. Brandy started throwing blows at Chris' face, as he tried to restrain her. Her punches were a little too much for Chris to continue enduring, so he smacked her full force, then grabbed her by the throat. The keys now lay on the ground as Chris tried shaking the life out of her. "What the fuck is wrong wit you girl, putting yo motha fucking hands on me like that?" Chris yelled. Brandy wasn't an easy woman to restrain, and she continued to fight Chris. Fella didn't like what he was seeing, and rather Brandy liked it or not, Fella was bout to bring it to Chris the gee way. Fella hopped out the fan and ran down on Chris. When Brandy saw Fella she knew it meant trouble for Chris. She didn't know where Fella had come from, or what he was doing there, but she loved Chris and she didn't want to see him hurt in the way Fella was going to hurt him. Brandy spotted the big boy gloc in Fella's hand. "Fella no its cool!" she yelled. Chris never spotted Fella running up the street from his blind side, and when he turned to see who Brandy was yelling at, he felt the butt of Fella's gloc nine. Chris dropped to one knee and Fella continued to beat blood out of him. As brandy tried to stop Fella, D-Roc, Slim, and Walt ran up. D-Roc snatched Chris up by the neck, and put his forty five Smith and Wesson to his temple while saying, "Get the fuck up. You make one more move and I'll blow ya brains out." Slim and Walt ran straight in the house with their weapons drawn. Brandy was confused. She didn't know rather to help Chris or grab her keys and get out of there. Fella was like a brother to her, even though they seemed to be growing apart, she still loved him. "Bee get yo keys and get the fuck out of here." Fella said. Brandy was crying, and her heart raced, but she did as she was told. She wasn't frightened by the situation because she was no stranger to gangster shit, but she loved Chris and the fact that his life was in the hands of some killers scared her. By the time D-Roc and Fella made it into the house, Walt and Slim had assured them the house was empty. "Where the fuck is the shit at?" D-Roc asked Chris, as Fella slammed the door closed. "Its upstairs man, just please don't kill me." Chris whined. "Gangsta, Walt lets go, the shit upstairs." D-Roc said. "Fells watch the door bro." D-Roc ordered as he, Slim and Walt escorted Chris up the steps. "Is anybody else in this house?" D-Roc asked as he peeked in the two bedrooms with open doors. "Nah man, aint nobody here but me." Chris answered through his bloody mouth. D-Roc knew there was weed in one of the rooms, because it reeked so bad he could smell it once he got to the top of the steps. Chris told them it was in the room directly in front of them. The door to the room had different locks on it, but Chris willingly handed over the keys. Slim quickly unlocked all the locks. When he pushed open the door two pitbulls came charging at him. He let off a couple rounds but one of the guard dogs was too fast. He grabbed a hold of Slim's arm and shook it until his gun hit the floor. Boom! Boom! Boom! Walt knocked the other dog out the air with his top of the line nine. The dog let out a whimper as it hit the floor. Walt grabbed the other dog by its tail, as it hung by Slim's arm. He shoved the nine in the Dog's throat and let off nine rounds into the dog's skull. The dog died before it hit the ground. Slim grabbed his pistol off the ground and backhanded Chris with it. "Bitch ass nigga, I should kill yo stupid ass." Slim yelled. D-Roc followed Slim's smack across the face with one of his own. He let Chris' body fall then stood over top of him with his Smith and Wesson aimed at his head. "Just give me the word gangsta, and I'll finish this bitch nigga off." D-Roc said. "I'm sorry man, please don't kill me I got kids." Chris begged. As Fella heard the shots, he started to climb the steps but the knock at the door stopped him. He peeked out the window and saw a gold Cadillac with triple gold hundred spoke Daytons parked in front of the house. A guy stood on the porch draped in gold and diamonds. Fella knew he should have let the guy leave but his greed took over him. Fella opened the door with his gun behind his back.

"What up bro?" Fella said to the guy on the porch. "What's happening man, is Chris here?" "Yeah he upstairs, C'mon in" Fella said as he stepped to the side to let the guy in. The guy fell for his trick and walked in the house checking his pager. Fella shut the door and aimed the gun at the guys head. "Don't move unless I say so, or I'm a send you to meet Jesus." Fella said while moving closer to the guy who stood frozen like a statue. "Get on yo knees and put yo hands on your head bitch." Fella ordered. The guy did as he was told. Fella stripped him of his jewelry, cash, and car keys. Upstairs, Slim and Walt had hit the jackpot. They opened the closet door and found a small safe, and four duffle bags filled with blocks of compressed weed. "Jackpot baby." Walt yelled with a devilish grin on his face. D-Roc ordered Chris to get up and walk over to the closet. Once they moved the safe and duffle bags of weed out the closet, D-Roc pushed Chris in the closet and told him "If you open this fucking door while I'm still in this house, It'll be the last door you open bro, you hear me?" Chris shook his head yes. D-roc slammed the door shut in Chris' face. Slim and Walt grabbed the duffle bags, D-Roc picked up the safe, and they took off. When they got downstairs Fella had the guy face down on the ground. "Where you find that nigga at?" D-Roc asked as Slim yanked the door open. "He was coming to buy some herb." Fella said with a smile on his face. "We'll do something with'em and let's cut." D-Roc said. "Ya'll go head, I'm a follow ya'll in this his ride. I gotta have his rims." Fella said as he rushed the guy into the bathroom. D-Roc, Slim, and Walt ran out the house and Fella was right behind them after telling the guy to get in the tub and count to a hundred. Fella laughed as he ran to the guy's Cadillac. He fumbled with the keys for a moment until he found the right one. Once he got the car started Slim pulled up beside him to make sure he was cool, then pulled off. Fella pulled out right

behind him, making a smooth getaway.

-CHAPTER TWELVE-

After two months of being involved with Leslie, Liley decided to let Pimp pump

out of her house. Of course he and L's were a package deal, but Liley didn't mind

because L's always looked out for her, even when her money was funny. As Pimp sat on

the sofa across from L's, Leslie came strolling into the living room. "Pimp I need a few

dollars so I can grab a few things for dinner tonight." She said while taking a seat on

Pimp's lap. Pimp gave her a twenty dollar bill. She walked out the front door as the back

was being knocked on. L's rushed to it, because he knew the knock on the back door

meant money. He peeked through the window before opening the door. Once he saw

magic Mike who got the name from making a hustler's dope sack disappear so quickly,

he put his baby nine in his back pocket and opened the door. "What's up fool?" L's said

as Magic Mike walked in. "Not you, I'm looking for Pimp." Magic Mike said while

twitching his mouth from left to right, and rocking his body back and forth. "Don't start

that shit Mike; you know it's all the same dope in here." L's said "C'mon L's you know I fucks wit Pimp, why you gotta give me a hard time?" Magic Mike replied. L's pulled his piece from his back pocket while saying, "You lucky you watched me grow up nigga or else I would pistol whip yo ass Mike." "Pimp! Come get this nigga Mike before I shoot em in his knee cap." L's yelled. Pimp came walking into the kitchen laughing because he knew L's was giving Mike a hard time. "What's up money Mike?" Pimp said while dapping it up with him like he was one of the fellas instead of a smoker. "Sometimes you sometimes me, all the time us." "Let me get like sixty in bricks." Magic replied with his usual slick talk. Pimp dropped three fat stones in his hand. "C'mon pimpin you got more love for Money Mike than this." Magic mike said even though he was already satisfied with the boulders he held in his hand. Pimp always gave Mike extra, so he knew he was spoiled. Pimp dropped another stone in his hand that was half the size of the other three. Magic Mike shuffled his feet, while singing a song. "Late night candle light fiend with a crack pipe, its only right." "Get yo ass out of here Mike, this aint no soul train ma'fucka." L's said while snatching the door open and laughing at Mike's performance. As he walked out he looked at L's and said, "That's why I deals with Pimp because you is a evil mutha fucka." L's tried to kick him in his ass before slamming the door on him. Pimp and L's laughed as they headed back into the living room. Magic brought entertainment along with a few dollars. Leslie came rushing in the front door with tears in her eyes, immediately putting a stop to their laughter. "What's up Les, what's wrong?" Pimp asked as she ran into his arms. "What the fuck happened?" L's added. "That punk Monster just slapped me cause I wouldn't let him feel my ass, I tried to fight him but he threw me on the ground and kicked me in my butt in front of his homeboys." Leslie explained as shameful tears streamed down her face. Leslie wasn't a soft girl, she wasn't one to do a lot of fighting, because she didn't want to mess her pretty face up, but the few fights she got into with neighborhood girls she had been victorious. Monster on the other hand was supposedly the toughest youngster on Oak Street. He was a few years older than L's and Pimp, bigger in size as well, and his fighting record was flawless. He didn't bar L's but he didn't try him either, because it was known that although L's was not quick to fight, he was quick to pop that tooley. That was the reason big Looney, and a lot of older hustlers liked him. L's grabbed Pimp's 380 Lugar off the couch, handed it to him, and said , "Let's roll bro, Monster got us twisted. Leslie knew L's was off the hook, and she wanted Monster touched, but not like what L's had in mind. "No L's it aint that serious." She pleaded. "Just chill Les, Monster know you Pimps girl so he basically saying fuck all of us, and he got it twisted." L's said as he and Pimp headed out the front door. Leslie ran up the steps calling her mother, because she knew things were bout to get out of control. As Pimp and L's marched up the street to the corner store, Monster stood in the middle of Stanley and the rest of his homeboys, while rubbing his hands together in anticipation. "What up homie?" Put yo hands on me like you did my girl." Pimp said strongly. "Lil L's you betta tell this lil nigga who he fucking with fore he get his ass beat." Monster said calmly, still rubbing his hands together. "I aint telling him shit." L's said as Pimp pulled out his chrome 380. All of Monster's boys stepped back at the sight of the gun. Monster stood his ground even though his heart was racing. "Damn L's you gone brang this nigga to the hood and just let him shoot ah nigga you grew up with?" Monster said. L's drew his baby nine, letting his actions speak for him. Pimp stopped L's and passed him his 380. "Hold this L's I'm bout to beat this niggas ass." L's placed Pimp's gun on his waist, while keeping his in his hand exposed to the world as if it were legal. Monster laughed at the sight of Pimp as he stepped in the middle of the street. "I'm bout to beat the fuck out of you bro." Monster said as he met Pimp in the middle of the street. Monster was bigger and stronger than Pimp, but like his father, Pimp was naturally good with his hands. The two squared off, toe to toe. Monster stalked Pimp looking for the quick knock out blow, but Pimp never stayed still. He was bouncing around, shuffling his feet, while switching his style up with every movement. Pimp feinted Monster, and got the response he was looking for. Monster threw a wild blow, and Pimp was under it sliding into his chest as he delivered a three piece combination that Monster shook off. "You hit like a lil bitch." Monster said as he spit blood from his lip. He rushed Pimp with two sloppy hooks, and once again Pimp was under them. This time he delivered a right upper cut, right hook and left hand straight down the pipe. Monster staggered back, now leaking from his mouth and nose. Once again he shook Pimp's blows off. "Lil nigga you know something huh?" Monster said. Pimp answered him with a leaping hook that swelled his eye up instantly. Leslie and Liley watched as Pimp went to work on the neighborhood bully. L's stood on the side with his homeboys. They were all astonished by Pimp's performance. L's knew pimp had some go in him, but the way he threw his hands today made L's think Pimp should be in a boxing ring instead of football. L's had a sinister grin on his face "Hell yea my boy a tiger, I knew he had that killer instinct in him, it's really on now." He thought as he started coaching Pimp on. Monster had finally gotten his hands on Pimp, but it wasn't for long. Monster grabbed a hold of Pimp's shirt, but Pimp slithered out of his shirt and went back to work on his face. "That's enough man, c'mon L's break that shit up." Stanley said while trying to pull Monster out the way of Pimp's flurries. "Don't nobody touch my boy." L's said as he flashed his gun. "C'mon man you know it aint like that L's." Stanley said while throwing his hands in the air. "You cool Pimp?" L's asked, as Pimp stood in the middle of the street with his shirt off. "Yeah I'm cool." Pimp answered. "You touch my girl again, I'm a stomp a mud hole in yo ass. That goes for all you chumps." Pimp continued as Monster stood there looking like the elephant man, from all kinds of speed knots from Pimp's quick hands. Leslie was already feeling Pimp, but to see the pretty boy go from smooth to hardcore in honor of her, sent her head over heels. Liley was proud of both Pimp and herself. Pimp for defending her daughter against a young hustler that was feared by many, and proud of herself for picking such a winner for her daughter.

Slim and D-Roc bobbed their heads to crime boss as he screamed from Slim's four twelves. Fella and Walt trailed behind them bobbing their heads to C-Bo's straight killer as it harmonized through Fella's four twelves. Slim and Fella had their vans out the shop for two days now, and they've yet to park them for longer than an hour. Slim's MPV was candy green, with gold flakes in the paint, a peanut butter brown rag top accommodate his triple gold hundred spoke Daytons, Gold grill, bumper and door handles. The inside was plushed out with peanut butter soft brown leather seats, matching floors, ceilings and doors. The dashboard, steering wheel, and radio deck were all decked out in wood grain marble brown. Slim flashed his gold and diamonds as he mean mugged all the onlookers. The top of his mouth had Slim spelled out in diamonds, while the bottom spelled gangsta in even more diamonds. Slim wore a gold Rolex on his left wrist, with a couple of gold and diamond bracelets on his right wrist, matching the chains around his neck. He wore two nice sized diamond rings on each hand, and the sun complemented them as he controlled the wheel with both hands, swerving from one side of the street to the next. D-Roc rode shotgun with even more jewelry on. His teeth were cluttered with gold and diamonds, while he wore a huge Rolex chain around his neck with crushed ice all through it. On his left wrist he had a gold Movado time piece, with a diamond ring on every finger. On his right wrist he wore a thick gold Rolex bracelet flooded with diamond chips. His long cornrows hung on his back as he bounced to the sound of crime boss, while smoking a fat blunt of expensive hydro. His eleven shot Taurus sat on his lap ready for action if it occurred. Slim's gloc nine rested under his leg. Behind them, Fella and Walt blinged as well. Fella's truck was identical to Slim's except that his color was raspberry blue with gold flakes. Fella had a fitted hat cocked to the back as he showcased his gold and diamond grill. He had the whole top row flooded while the bottom only had four teeth in the front of his mouth blinging. Walt had his whole mouth filled with 14 karat gold while only two fangs at the top and bottom of his mouth were iced out. He and Fella were draped with plenty of other accessories as well. Both cars were bedazzling both inside and out. Walt shook his plaits as they hung in his face, and rested on his shoulders. He had twin glocs on his lap, while Fella carried a P.94 Ruger. As Walt looked through his rearview mirror he noticed the cars being chased by three gunmen. One directly behind the van, while two chased the vehicle on the opposite side of the street. "Oh shit we getting dumped on." Walt said while tapping on Fella's leg and pointing to the rearview mirror. The music was up so loud that neither Slim, D-Roc, Walt, nor Fella could hear the gun shots. Walt hung out the window, and returned fire. D-Roc thought he heard gunshots, and noticed Walt hanging out the window. He tapped Slim and pointed to the gunman on the side of the vehicle, while catching a glimpse of two gunmen running off the side of a house. He leaned towards Slim while recklessly blasting several shots. Both vans picked up their speed leaving the gunmen further behind. Fella followed Slim as he swerved right and they both made a quick left turn, leaving Mt. Vernon and the gunmen in the wind.

Mills paced the hallways awaiting the intake. He was out of place because he didn't have a pass to be out of the unit, but he was cool, since Butter was the J.C.O in charge of bringing in the intake. As Butter lead the long line of juveniles up the hallway, Mills spotted who he was looking for, and a big smile covered his face. "What's up bro?" Mills yelled to get his attention. Peko's poker face instantly changed to a smile. "T-Money what's up bro?" he replied. Butter was cool unlike the J.C.O in charge of the Cuyahoga Hills intake. He didn't mind the juveniles talking as long as they weren't too loud; Butter saw one of the ranking authorities coming, so he gave Mills a look while nodding in the authorities' direction. Mills peeped game. Butter pulled him over to the side to avoid him being stopped by the administration. "Mr. Mills do you have a pass to be out here in the hallway?" Butter asked. Mills flashed him a piece of paper as the administration walked by. "I'm back from med bay." Mills answered. Butter winked at him and quietly asked which one of them was his homies. Mills showed him Peko and Butter told him he'd make sure they got a chance to kick it with each other later, but now he needed him to go back in his unit. Later that evening Butter gave Mills a pass to Peko's unit. Peko was placed in the same unit as B-Nut, and Mills couldn't wait to introduce them to each other. Mills entered the unit with no problem, since Butter called the J.C.O in charge of the unit in advance. "What up blood." B-Nut said to Mills as he scanned the room looking for Peko. Mills laughed before replying, because even though he wasn't in a gang, B-Nut always acknowledged him like he was. Mills didn't mind though, because B-Nut used his blood lingo on everyone, even opposing gang members, which was naturally the cause of his fights. "What up bro." Mills said as they embraced each other. "Shit blood jus bicken it." B-Nut replied. Mills spotted Peko walking out of the bathroom as he and B-Nut conversed. "C'mon bro I want you to meet somebody." Mills said. He locked eyes with Peko, and flagged him down. They met in the middle of the floor with a strong embrace. "Got damn bro you getting big as fuck." Peko said a he stepped back to take a look at Mills. Mills smiled. "Shid bro look at you, you as tall as a fucking tree." Mills said as he looked at Peko's now 5' 10" frame. They both laughed. "Oh shit…bro dis B-Nut, he family…B-Nut this my bro Peko, he was in a lot of my pictures." Mills said as he stepped to the side so the two could dap it up. "What's up bro." Peko said as he and B-Nut shook hands. "Shid I bant ball it, I heard a lot about you dawg, blood talk about you, Fella, Shawn, and uh what's her name… Brandy." Peko said. "Yeah Brandy all the time, it's all love blood." B-Nut said. Peko was lost by his lingo and Mills could tell by the expression on his face. "You'll get used to it B-Nut crazy bro, or should I say brazy." Mills said as he smiled and elbowed B-Nut in his rib cage. They kicked it for a while, in which Peko told Mills he only had a couple months left to serve, Mills wasn't too affected by his short amount of time he had with one of his closest friends, because he only had eleven months left himself, and B-nut was right behind him with eighteen. H.T. was down to four months, and Black was at twenty. Before leaving Mills told B-Nut to lace Peko up with hygiene and goodies then slid a half ounce of weed to Peko while hugging him. Peko looked in his hand and quickly closed it. "What am I supposed to do with this bro?" he asked as he nervously scanned the room. "Do what you do best, B-Nut got you." Mills said with a big smile on his face. "Yeah I got you blood. We bick it like that everyday, my head in the blouds right now." B-nut said. Mills laughed as he took off, headed back to his unit.

Back in the hood, Brandy and Shawn continued to grind and stack. Although they didn't have a drug house their pager rewarded them just as much money as the drug house could. On top of that, just sitting on either one of their porches was enough to make the strip do Nino Brown numbers. Their only need for a spot was to hide themselves from Pacman and his cop buddies that continuously harassed the neighborhood.

As usual, the strip was packed. With Mills and Peko being locked down and Fella now a full time Jackboy, Berkley as a real estate belonged to Shawn Shawn and Brandy. And they now sat on their thrones on Shawn Shawn's mother's porch watching Baby Tone, lil Scoob , and a few other young hustlers compete for crack sales.

As they battled over one customer, another car hit the corner and pulled to a stop in front of Shawn Shawn's mother's house. "I got that fire! I got that Crit! I got two for one's!" the young block monsters yelled out as they bomb rushed the vehicle.

"Brandy! Lil Shawn!" The passenger of the vehicle yelled out. "Is that Lisa" Brandy asked. "I think so" Shawn Shawn answered. Lisa climbed through the car's window. "Ya'll better not be acting like ya'll don't remember ya'll auntie Lisa." She began while squeezing through the window's opening. "After all the shit ya'll done put me through" Lisa continued while straightening out her disheveled clothes.

They hadn't seen Lisa since having her house raided by the Columbus Police Department's SWAT team. She kept her mouth closed when questioned about the drugs and guns found in her house and as a result she was convicted of all charges, including aiding and abetting and corruption of a minor. She was sentenced to three years, in which she had put on hella weight, but that voice was unmistakable. Brandy and Shawn Shawn rushed off the porch to greet her. "What's up auntie?" Brandy said, "How long you been home?" Shawn Shawn added.

"Bout four months, I just got me an apartment down the street on Oakwood and Fulton" Lisa said happily. "Auntie you right on time, we lookin for somewhere to post up at." Shawn Shawn said. "You know ya'll welcome 325 Oakwood but right now , I'm tryna get something fat for this twenty dollars." Lisa responded. "Keep yo money auntie, you know yo money aint no good here girl." Brandy said while placing her hands on her hips and playfully rolling her eyes. Lisa smiled, but she figured she'd be leaving with something free anyway. After all she had just done years in prison for them. Brandy and Shawn dropped a couple of stones in her hand and told her they'd be by her apartment later. Just like that Brandy and Shawn were back in a spot. As soon as Lisa pulled off, Pacman bent the corner with his door cracked ready to jump out his cruiser and snatch up anybody who looked nervous. Brandy and Shawn hurried back up to the porch, where they could run in the house if need be. As Baby Tone and lil Scoob tried to walk off, Pacman threw his car in park in the middle of the street, and rushed the two younguns. Lil Scoob took off in one direction, while Baby Tone shot off in another. Too bad for Pacman because he was without a partner today, and the youngsters were through one yard and over a fence before he could decide which one to chase. The other younguns on the strip disappeared as well, leaving Pacman to stare off with Brandy and Shawn.

Later that evening Brandy and Shawn stopped by Lisa's. Although Lisa only had an apartment for a month, she already had a little traffic coming in and out. With the help of their pagers, Brandy and Shawn had Lisa's apartment doing numbers in no time.

As fall closed winter prepared to open, Peko was finishing off the last couple weeks of his six month sentence. Mills made his way over to Peko's unit every chance he got. They also spent every Sunday together in church, along with Black, B-Nut and H.T.

Mills enjoyed his time with Peko, but he was happy to see him leaving. Not only did Peko have a new born child to go home to, but the quicker Peko left, the closer Mills was to following behind him with his own freedom walk.

Mills and Peko had already discussed all the business they needed to discuss, so they spent their last Sunday together reminiscing, and laughing at B-Nut's wild stories. Later that night while Peko lay in his bed unable to sleep, D-roc, Slim, Walt and Fella were dodging bullets. They ran through the club's parking lot ducking behind cars, as they rushed to their own vehicles. When they finally made it to their artillery, more of T-Bone's and Fresh's crew had opened fire from across the street. D-Roc grabbed his mini Mac ten off the passenger seat and returned fire. Slim focused on getting the van started, while Fella did the same thing with his van. Walt stuffed one fifty round clip in his pocket, before spinning around with his chopper in hand. HE ran off the side of the van letting loose rapid fire from the A.K He sent everyone diving for cover as he swung his body back and forth letting the chopper chop everything in sight to pieces. As the last bullet hopped out the A.K., Walt ran back to the van. Slim and Fella were already whipping out their parking spaces. D-Roc dove in the van while Slim covered him with his twenty one shot top of the line nine. Fella did the same with his Desert Eagle as Walt hopped in the van with him. As the vehicles sped out the lot, bullets riddled the van, knocking windows out, and grazing Fella on the shoulder. Walt quickly popped the second clip in the A.K. And swung back into action. Slim dumped shots into the club, sending bouncers and party goers diving to the floor, as he and Fella whizzed by the club. Police sirens filled the air as bodies lay stretched out from the club entrance to the parking lot. By the time the police and medical squad arrived, D-Roc and his crew were gone.

-CHAPTER THIRTEEN-

After spending his first few weeks at home with his newborn daughter and girlfriend, Peko was right back to the streets. Shawn Shawn had hustled hard for the both of them while Peko was locked up. Now Peko was returning the favor, as Shawn spent time with his now pregnant girlfriend. After hustling hard Peko told his little brother that he had to reward himself, and he did. His Mustang had a peanut butter brown rag top, matching interior, and dark tinted windows, sixteen inch hundred spoke Daytons, and two fifteens in the trunk, along with some killer horse power under the hood. Peko had been home for four months now, and he too was ready to cop him a mean vehicle. He wanted to have a nice ride, to match his little brother's Mustang and Brandy's Benz.

With three months left Mills stopped selling weed and focused on rounding up the money owed to him. Two weeks prior to him being released, he had all his money except two hundred dollars which was owed to him by a guy named Tyson from Cincinnati. Tyson boxed growing up as a child. He had three golden gloves titles, and would have boxed for the Olympic gold medal if he wouldn't have killed a guy from a rival neighborhood.

Tyson had been in TYKO for four years, and he quickly earned the title of a champ in juvenile prison as well. Very few people stood up to him, and even fewer attempted to fight him. For that reason, he liked to throw both his weight and rank around. It had been three months since he got four fifties from Mills, with an agreement to send the money within a month. Every time Mills asked him about his money, he blew Mills off with some drag game. Mills was starting to understand Tyson's motives. He promised himself this would be his last time asking for his money. He walked over to the table where Tyson sat playing spades with a few of his homies. "Aye Tyson, let me holla at you for a second big homie." Mills said to Tyson as he dealt the cards. "Hold up dawg, let me finish this hand." Tyson said while fixing his cards. Mills didn't say anything, he sat back until the hand was over. When Tyson's homie started dealing another hand, Mills spoke. "Tyson let me holla at you for a minute bro." Tyson knew Mills wanted to talk about his money, so he tried blowing him off with the waiting game. "Hold up lil Mills let me finish this game dawg." "And how long is that gone be." Mills said as he became more frustrated by the second. "We just started, gimme a minute man." Tyson said now becoming aggravated. "C'mon man you know what I need to holla at you about bro, it aint gone take but a few seconds." Mills responded. "Damn man, I said gimme a minute. You starting to act like my bitch, nagging me and shit." Tyson said with authority causing his homies to burst out laughing. "Yeah aight." Mills said as he walked off. Five minutes later Mills returned with a metal mop ringer. Before Tyson's homies noticed him, Mills was behind Tyson swinging the mop ringer with all his might. "Ty watch out dawg" his homie yelled as he jumped up from the table. It was too late, Mills sent blood flying across the room as he connected Tyson in the back of his head. Mills didn't stop with one swing, he continued to beat Tyson in the head until he fell out of his seat and balled up on the ground. Mills continued to beat the blood out of him while saying, "Do I still remind you of yo bitch?" Butter let Mills get his funky off for a few minutes before calling for backup. Rio dropped the phone in the middle of his conversation, and pulled Mills off of Tyson's bloody body. Mills spent his last two weeks in Disciplinary isolation. He would leave the institution the same way he came… on lockdown.

Buck leaned up against his 500 Benz, on all chrome Lorenzo's while checking the time on his iced out presidential Rolex. He shook his head in frustration because Jimmy was twenty minutes late for the time they had set to pick Mills up. Peko, Shawn Shawn, and Brandy stood on the porch, while grandma Mills worked her magic in the kitchen. Jimmy speed walked home after being dropped off around the corner from his grandmothers house. As his pager screamed for attention, he looked at the screen and saw one of his fiends codes with the number one hundred behind it. He cursed under his breath knowing that one of his big spenders were on their way over to Lily's. The pager continued to sound off as he got closer to home. He turned it off as he heard Peko saying "There go Jimmy right there." Buck turned around as Jimmy jogged across the street. "What's up big bro" Jimmy said. "I don't know you tell me? Where you been at you know we had to pick Mills up this morning." Buck said as he opened the passenger door for Jimmy and walked around the car to the driver's side. "I stayed over my friend L…I mean Leon's house last night, I'm sorry bro." Jimmy said as they ducked off inside the spaceship like vehicle. "Don't ever say you sorry lil Keys, that's an ambiguous word, and it's usually used negatively for a person who is worthless. Never use that word in reference to an apology. Just say you apologize. Furthermore your apology is accepted, but don't make being late a habit." Time is a man's most precious commodity, and the only way to stay on time is to arrive early, feel me lil daddy?" buck said as he held his fist out for Jimmy to hit the rock. Jimmy smiled, because just like Mills and everyone else, he loved hearing Buck drop his knowledge. He hit the rock as Buck pulled away from the curb.

Fifteen minutes later, they were pulling into TYKO's parking lot. When Buck and Jimmy entered the lobby they approached the only desk in sight. An attractive young lady sat behind the desk pretending to enjoy the conversation she was involved in over the phone. She was happy to see Buck awaiting her service because it was her excuse to end the phone call, which she quickly did while rolling her eyes, clearly showcasing her exasperation. "I apologize how may I help you?" the young lady asked with a hint of both boredom and frustration. "Well first let me apologize for any stress I may be adding to your day and I hope helping me doesn't cause you to work too hard but I'm here to pick up Tony Mills. He is being released today." Buck answered while pouring his charm on heavy. Buck's mannerism brought a smile to her face. As she picked up the phone to call Mill's unit, she gave Buck a once over. The VVS diamonds in Buck's presidential Rolex almost blinded her as she tried to sneak a better peek at it. Once again the young lady was rolling her eyes as the person on the other end of the phone annoyed her. "Oh my God, some people just don't let up. I apologize for the way I have been acting but I'm having a real bad day. Tony Mills will be out shortly, thank you for being so understanding." The young lady said as she smashed down the phone on the receiver. "Don't worry about it Miss…" Buck said while pausing so she could state her name. "Tonya" She said. Quickly recognizing game. "Tonya that's a pretty name, and with all due respect, you too beautiful to let a bad day at work cause you to feel so ugly. Sometimes we gotta put up with things we don't want to, in order to reap the benefits we need to live the type of life we like living." Buck said while glancing at his Rolex. Jimmy smiled as Buck charmed the attractive young lady. As they exchanged words, Buck took a sneak peek at Tonya's frame as she stood up to press a button on the a wall. Buck had to admit if he was not so committed to Tameka and their baby they had on the way, he would show Tonya what it felt like to be with a real nigga. Bucks thoughts were interrupted as Mills snuck up behind him and playfully delivered a hook to his ribs. Buck quickly spun around. He grabbed Mills up for an embrace while saying, "Damn boy, you done got big as fuck!" Mills grabbed Jimmy up next, hugging him so tight he almost cut off his circulation. "You talking bout I'm gettin big, look at lil bro." Mills said as he rubbed his hand over Jimmy's waves, and threw a few punches at him. Tonya watched as the three attractive young men reunited. She blushed as dirty thoughts traveled through her mind. "Tonya you take it easy, don't letcha job get the best of you baby girl. After the dark comes the light." Buck said while giving Tonya a wink. Tonya waved bye as the three young men walked out the door. Mills was intrigued by Buck's 500 Benz. The jet Black vehicle was roomy and the plush leather was inviting. Mills promised to get himself one of these spaceship like vehicles, once he brought his plan to life. Buck pulled out the lot with the sound of Jay-Z's reasonable doubt blasting from his speakers. As Buck turned onto Mills grandmother's street Mills looked at the fancy cars parked in front of the house, and wondered who they belonged to. As Buck parked the car Peko, Shawn Shawn, and Brandy came rushing out of his grandmother's front door. He instantly knew who the cars belonged to. "Damn, my homies getting it like this" Mills thought as he took a second to look at Peko's burgundy and gold 96 Impala with the peanut butter brown rag top, dark tinted windows and sixteen inch hundred spoke Daytons. The gold flakes in Peko's candy paint sparkled as the sun hit them from an angle. The sun complemented Shawn Shawn's Mustang and Brandy's 350 Benz as well, as they both sat pretty on clean rims. Mills wasn't fully out of the car before Brandy rushed him with a big hug. "Punk don't be actin like you aint happy to see me." Brandy said while playfully punching Mills in his rock hard chest. Peko and Shawn Shawn stood in the front yard with their arms crossed as Mills, Brandy Buck and Jimmy crossed the street. "Ya'll niggas perped out acting like ya'll aint miss my bro." Brandy said. Peko and Shawn Shawn stood firm. "Ahhh!!" Peko and Shawn Shawn yelled out as they rushed Mills with tight embraces. They all laughed as grandma Mills swung the front door open. "You better come up here and give me some love while you down there giving all my hugs away." Mills ran up the steps and squeezed his grandmother tightly, while planting a big one on her cheek. "You know I love you momma" Mills said while embracing her. "I love you too baby, don't leave me no more, now you go on down there with your friends and show them how much you appreciate them watching over your grandmother and baby brother in your absence. I got some fried chicken and thangs goin on in here and the food will be ready in a few." Grandma Mills said as she walked back in the house. Peko flashed Mills with a fat blunt of hydro as he rejoined them. "C'mon Pee, you know we can't do that with Jim right here." Mills whispered. "Aw, my bad bro, later for that." Peko said as he cuffed the blunt out of Jimmy's sight. Jimmy shook his head at Mills' attempt to keep him sheltered from drugs. "If he only knew" Jimmy thought as Mills wrapped his arm around his shoulder. "What's up little bro, what you been up to?" Mills said. "Not much, just goin to school and playing football." Jimmy replied. "What's up with the lil girlies? Mills asked while playfully squeezing his biceps tighter around Jimmy's neck. Jimmy just smiled. "Uh huh, I knew you had the girlies big head." Mills said while playfully delivering a blow to his little brother's gut. Buck interrupted their moment after ending a call on his cell phone. "Dig lil bro I gotta go take Mek to the hospital for her monthly checkup. I gotta make sure your lil niece growing inside her is healthy. If I don't make it back today, call me in the morning so we can discuss that business. Aight" "Aight big bro I love you man, Tell Mek I said what up." Mills said. "I love you too boy, get you some pu…" Buck looked at Jimmy and stopped in mid sentence. "You know what to get tonight. Get loose boy, cause tomorrow its back to the money." They embraced, and Buck said his see you laters to the rest of his little homies, then pulled out. As Buck turned off the street, a four door white Bonneville with a golden brown rag top, gold grill, gold bumper, gold door handles, gold Daytons, dark tinted windows, and a thunderous system hit the corner on three wheels. Behind it was a 70's Cutlass, with gold candy paint, a gold grill, bumper, door handles and dual exhaust pipes along with dark tinted windows, a booming system, and some triple gold hundred spokes. It was on three wheels. The show wasn't over as two more mouth dropping vehicles bent the corner on three wheels. A drop top six four Impala coated with wet green candy paint and chrome hundred spoke Daytons to accommodate its chrome grill, bumper and trimmings. It also had a system that could wake the dead. Although the top was down on the Impala, Mills could not see inside because the driver had all the dark tinted windows rolled up. Behind the Impala was a Regal, with a white and gold marble paint job, triple gold hundred spoke Daytons, dark tinted windows and a glass breaking system. All the car doors dropped to the ground in front of Mills. Two of the vehicles pancaked side to side and front to back, while the other two bounced off the ground like basketballs. As the cars pulled to the curb, Mills looked at Peko, Brandy and Shawn Shawn for an answer. "That's Fells and d-Roc and them." Peko said motioning for Mills to turn his attention back to the vehicles. Slim got out the Bonneville, D-Roc stepped out of the Cutlass, Fella rose from the Regal, and lil Walt from the Impala. The foursome looked like rap stars as they gravitated toward Mills with their jewelry blinging. "Welcome home bro." Fella said while puffing on a fat backwood filled with green. "Put that shit out Fells, you see Jim right here, and my grandmother in the house, you trippin bro" Mills said. Then he told Jimmy to go in the house. Jimmy felt the tension in the air and wanted to stay by his brother's side, but he did as he was told. Fella used the ground to knock the fire off the end of his blunt, then pulled Mills in for a hug. "Damn baby you on swole." Fella said. Out of D-Roc, Slim and lil Walt, Slim was the first to speak to Mills. "What up lil Mills you looking good boy, welcome home." Slim said while pulling a wad of cash from his pocket, peeling back five hundred dollar bills, and offering them to Mills. "I'm straight Slim, I appreciate it though big Homie. What up Roc, Sup Walt" Mills said. "What's happenin lil Mills you lookin good baby, I guess I can't offer you nothing seeing how you turned slim gangsta down" D-Roc said as him and Mills exchanged daps. "Yeah you must got a hell of a stash hid somewhere homie" Walt added with a devilish grin. Although Mills knew what Walt was insinuating, he gave a fake chuckle to accommodate the one D-Roc and Walt shared. "Dig I don't mean to be rude, but I need to holla at Fells on the one on one tip… take a walk with me Fells" Mills said while leading the way up the street. Fella exchanged daps with Peko, Brandy, and Shawn Shawn as he passed them. They conversed with D-roc, Walt, and Slim while mills and Fella stood on the corner talking. "Listen Fells fuck all that shit that's been goin on while I was locked up, I know Slim yo cousin and I aint askin you to turn ya back on ya family, but I'm home now, is you gone get back to getting money with cha ace or what?" Mills said. "I'm sayin bro, we can all get money together, we all grew up together, we from the same hood, I don't see what the problem is." Fella responded. "C'mon bro. Them and us is like water and oil. We just don't mix, them niggas aint to be trusted and I'm sayin bro, I don't knock how no nigga get his money, but I don't want them problems that type shit put too much bullshit in the game. SO I'm sayin though, is you gone get money wit the crew you came into the game wit, or is you gone keep living life on the edge?" "What is this Mills, an ultimatum or some shit?" "Pee and Bee came at me wit that same bullshit, like ya'll tryna make me choose a side. If ya'll fuck wit me, ya'll gone fuck wit me no matter who I roll wit" Fella said loud enough to turn heads. "C'mon bro, why you being so loud, this me, T-Money, yo ace, from birth to the turf, we like brother's and I'm always gone have ya back, but I aint fuckin wit Rock and them, so now what?" Mills said adamantly. Fella was frustrated. He loved Mills, but he refused to be put in a position were he had to choose between his blood kin, and his family by covenant.

He dug in his pocket extracted a thousand dollars from his roll of bills, and held them out to Mills. "Here you go I aint trying to argue wit you right now, but we aint kids no more, and I aint taking no ultimatums from nobody." Fells said. "I'm cool bro keep yo paper, but never lose sight of what's real." Mills said. Fella laid the money on the ground in front of Mills and said, "You got my number bro, as he walked off." Mills was frustrated, he never expected the conversation with his ace to end the way it did. As Fella, D-Roc, Slim and Walt lifted their vehicles off the ground, Grandma Mills called Mills and his friends in for dinner. Mills enjoyed his meal with his family along with laughter and small talk. As dawn set in, Peko, Shawn, and Brandy took off, while Mills spent some quality time with his little brother and grandmother. Mills eventually dozed off and woke up in an empty room. Jimmy had left and his grandmother had gone to her room for some much needed rest. Mills grabbed the phone, paged his little brother, then made a booty call.

Ring! Ring! Ring! "Hello." Chrissie said. "What's up girl?" Mills responded smoothly. "Mills?" Chrissie said with inquiry. "The one and only." Mills shot back. "I thought you forgot about me." Chrissie said. "After all the letters and calls we shared how could I do that?" Mills asked. "You know how niggas in jail be making false promises and shit." Chrissie said. "Hahaha" Mills laughed because Chrissie had a valid point. "Dig Chrissie, I'm a man of my word. Now is you gone come get me or what?" "I don't know you don't sound too enthused about spending the night wit me... do you want me to come and get you?" Chrissie asked in a seductive voice. Mills laughed again because he peeped her game. "Girl you better quit playing wit me." "I'm sayin Mills, do you want some of this cat as much as I want you?" Chrissie teased. "If I didn't baby, I do now, you gone let me beat it up?" Mills said joining her in the game she obviously wanted him to play. They enticed one another a little longer, then Mills gave her his grandmother's address. She said she'd be there in a half an hour which was just enough time for Mills to jump in the shower and get fresh. Chrissie arrived at 12 o'clock PM. She hit the horn on her drop top Lebaron, and Mills quickly ran out before her horn woke his grandmother. His eyes went from her face to in between her legs.

Chrissie was a thick mixed breed with long sandy brown hair. Her hazel eyes almost matched her hair color. Her breast almost hung out the bottom of her cutoff wife beater, while her nipples were protruding through it. Her flat stomach fell right into her wide hips that went with her ass in perfect harmony. She wore a pair of cut off daisy dukes that her pussy jumped out of. As Mills looked at the muff between her legs, and admired her thighs, she leaned over and kissed him on his cheek. "That's all you got for me?" Mills asked. Chrissie gave Mills a devilish smile, then opened her legs to give him a better view of the goods. Mills looked between her legs, returned her devilish smile with one of his own then leaned back in the seat and cranked up the music. Twenty minutes later, Chrissie was pulling into her apartment complex. Once inside the apartment Mills set fire to a blunt he had put out in the car. Chrissie clicked on the lights and said, "This is it, this is my little home." Chrissie's parents had money so Mills expected nothing less than the expensive furniture she had, but it was a women's own will to keep a clean house. Buck had told Mills a long time ago, that a man could tell a lot about a person by the way they took care of their house, especially a woman. Although Chrissie was fine, and had a bright future, Mills new she could never be more than a playmate, because she had too many miles on her, and too many men knew where she lived. At nineteen Chrissie had been with enough men to last her a lifetime. She took Mills on a tour of her house, and ended the tour in her bedroom. "So what do you think?" Mills looked around her bedroom. "I think your apartment is nice, and ya room has one hell of a view." He stared at her body, and licked his lips. Chrissie smiled as she walked to Mills, she kissed him gently on his lips and Mills didn't resist. He accepted her tongue as she slid it in his mouth, and twirled it around. That was all it took for Mills to rise to the occasion. His pole rubbed up against her leg as it attempted to poke a hole through his sweat pants. Chrissie felt his manhood against her leg, and she grabbed a handful of it. She wanted to taste it, so she wasted no time stripping him of his clothing, and sliding out of her own. She laid Mills back on the bed and crawled up on his body until she met the tip of his manhood with her lips. She kissed the head softly, and then flicked her tongue at it. She licked it down, then up using her tongue to explore his whole penis. She made eye contact with Mills as she went to work on his piece. Mills body tensed up as he exploded in her mouth. It didn't take Chrissie long to bring his piece back to life, and once she did, she used her mouth to put the condom on. She turned around and straddled Mills pole from the back. He spread her cheeks open as she bounced up and down on him. Her juices rained down on him as she stuffed all of his manhood inside her. Mills switched positions to stop himself from busting too quickly. He bent her over and spread her cheeks apart, and her neatly shaved peach came into view. Mills watched her lips grip his penis as he entered her slowly. He started off slowly moving with rhythm, allowing her to rock with him. She sucked her teeth, while moaning, "Ooooohhh! Mills that's my spot!!" Mills dug deeper, while pounding harder and faster causing her to grab a handful of sheets, while biting down on her bottom lip. "Oh! Oh! Oh! Oh! Oh! She screamed as Mills slammed into her with rapid speed. Before the night was over they had tried multiple positions, and brought one another to several climaxes. After half an hour of hard morning sex, and some breakfast, Chrissie took Mills home. Mills didn't waste any time showering and getting dressed. He threw another wife beater on with some black sweat pants, and some grey black and white Jordans that Peko had bought him. He slapped a coat of grease on his waves and brushed them a few times, dapped his self with some Michael Jordan cologne, and made a quick call to let Brandy know he was on his way over her house. While walking up Mound Street, he noticed all the young hustlers standing around, flagging down cars and chasing money. He smiled as he realized that all the new faces were his clientele. As he reached Berkley he finally saw some familiar faces. "What's happening Chris. Sup Var." Mills said while exchanging daps and hugs with them. "What ya'll hustlers been up to?" Mills asked. "Shyd man tryna get this money, but shit aint been right since Buck left the hood. Its like niggas don't wanna see a young hustler blow, they taxing for they work, two fifty for quarter, a grand for an ounce, and that shit only be half decent. Pee look out for a nigga wit that crit when he can but you know he rock for rock wit his shit, Pee a block monster for real." Chris said. "How much paper ya'll got right now?" "Shid, me and Var got about twelve hundred right now, but we still got a few hundred in stones left." Chris said. "Hold that shit bro, I'm bout to be right in a couple hours, Ima throw ya'll some love, we bout to eat bro, just fuck wit me." "I'm bout to go get me a pager, then go holla at a couple of my people, gimmie three hours tops." Mills said. "Man we gone be right here bro", Chris and Var said in unison. "Headup, Feet down" Mills said before exchanging more daps and hugs then taking off. As Mills approached Brandy's house he noticed Brandy standing on her porch with a dark skinned beauty.

"What's up bro?" Brandy said. "I can't call it what's up with you?" Mills replied. "Not a damn thing just chilling with my girl and you better go in there and holler at mommy because she was talking shit all night about you not coming by here to see her yesterday." Brandy explained. "Aw shit." Mills said as he walked in the house. "Damn girl he is even finer in person." Brandy's friend said. "Why you aint say nothing to him, wit yo scary ass?" Brandy said. "Cause he act like he aint even know who I was." "Pssshh! Bitch how he supposed to know who you are, when you aint send him a picture." Brandy said. "I know Bee but... she stopped as Mills came walking out the door. Mills was laughing at something Brandy's mother said when Brandy blurted out, "Nigga don't be acting like you don't know who my girl is." "What!" Mills said. "You heard me. This is Tiffany, the girl from my school that was writing you." Brandy said. "Damn my bad Tif, but you never sent me a picture so you can't hold nothing against me." "I won't." Tiffany replied. "For the record though I think you fine as hell." Mills said while seducing her with his eyes. "Feelings mutual." She replied with a hint of seduction in her voice. As Mills and Tiffany caught up, Buck arrived. He looked up and down the street as he climbed the steps to Brandy's porch. "What up Buck, why you looking so paranoid?" Brandy said. "What's happenin lil sis, aint no yellow cab drove by here has it?" Buck replied while scanning the street. "Nope." Brandy answered with a puzzled look on her face. Mills and Tiffany finished up their small talk and exchanged numbers, and then Tiffany was gone. "What's up T-Money, who's ya lil thang thang?" Buck asked with a smile on his face. "That's Brandy's home girl Tiffany, she nice huh?" Mills said with a smile on his face. "She a cute dark skin ,but I like mine with a lot more meat on they bones." Buck said "Yellow cab at nine o'clock." Brandy interrupted. The cab stopped in front of Brandy's house, and Buck signaled for the young lady in the back seat to get out. She rose from the car with a figure that was to die for. All eyes were on her as she opened Brandy's gate and joined Buck on the porch. Brandy and Mills were confused, because Buck always talked about men who abused or mistreated their women. He watched his mother be abused and mistreated and vowed to never treat a woman like that. Buck was committed to Mek and everyone knew that. So who was this flawless dime standing on Brandy's porch Mills and Brandy thought? "T-Money, Bee, this is Porcha, Porcha this my lil brother Mills and my lil sis Brandy." Buck said. "How ya'll doin?" Porcha said in her southern accent. "What up." Mills and Brandy said in unison. "Bee take Porcha in the house and grab that thang for Mills. "Buck ordered. While the ladies went in the house Buck assured Mills that him and Porcha were just cool. "C'mon lil bro you know I aint cut like that. Mek know about Porcha she do a lot of picking up and dropping off for me, loyal female and friend, and a man can never have too many of them in this game you dig?" Buck said. "Like a shovel" Mills shot back. Porcha and Brandy walked out the house as Mills and buck shared a laugh, while exchanging daps. "Guy talk huh? Shawty." Porcha said while slapping him on the back of his arm. "You know it." Buck shot back. Porcha kissed him on the cheek and sashayed back to the cab. Mills watched her ass bounce like a ball as she walked away. He shook his head while talking under his breath. Buck laughed as Brandy let her thoughts fly. "Walk nasty then bitch." Brandy said loud enough for Mills and Buck to hear her. "Ya'll crazy and I gotta go I got a few more people waiting on me." Buck said as he and Mills laughed at Brandy. Buck took off and so did Mills. He gave Mills the keys to his old weight house on Liley, so Mills went there to cook up his product. When he finished he hit the strip to let Chris, Var and a few other homies know that he was back in business, and just like that his vision was coming to life.

-CHAPTER FOURTEEN-

By the beginning of fall Mills had things on lock. His prices were cheaper, and his product was better than anyone else's on the strip. He now rode shotgun in Brandy's Benz as she headed for Buck's house. His pager had been sounding off the whole four hours he had Brandy chauffeuring him around, and she was starting to get irritated by it. "mills you need to put that damn pager on vibrate… matter of fact you need to get a fucking cell phone." "You got your nerves Bee, your shit be screaming too." Mills replied. "Yeah my shit be all about money, you got them lil hoochies blowing up yo shit." Mills burst into laughter. "You tryna send me now sis, my shit be about money too, I can't help it if hoes be addicted to what the dick did." Brandy couldn't help but to join him in laughter, while playfully punching him in his arm. "You got nerves Mills, you got me driving all the way out here, after you done had me on a tour all day, just so you can catch Neesh's call, that girl got you whipped and she aint even gave you no coochie." Now Brandy was laughing by herself. "That's cold Bee, you tryna send yo bro for real, I got you though." Brandy pulled in Buck's driveway teasing Mills all the way in the house. Once inside, Brandy sat on the couch with Tameka, while Mills followed Buck into the kitchen. They sat at the table discussing business until Neesh called. Buck told Mills he wouldn't be staying in the game much longer and that he wanted Mills to take his position. Mills gladly accepted the challenge, and dollar signs ran through his mind as Buck told him he would be taking him to meet the connect. Buck's daughter was due in a few months, and by the summer of 97, he planned to clean his hands. He told Mills the dope game wasn't a game to be played for a long period of time. A person had to set goals and get out because only a fool thought they could sell forever. He told Mills the sooner he knew what he wanted from the game the sooner he would be able to achieve it. Buck had survived in the game, while a lot of others thrived in it. At the age of twenty seven, with the exception of a two year juvenile bid, he's made it through the game without being caught. Before being interrupted by Neesh's call, Buck touched the topic of D-Roc and those of his kind, because what they have is never enough. As long as there is someone with more, they would never be satisfied. He told Mills that even though he raised D-Roc, he could feel bad vibes around him. He finished up by telling Mills that he had seen Walt's car parked down the street from his house a few nights ago, and because of that he wouldn't be staying there much longer. Mills knew D-Roc wasn't to be trusted, but he never thought he would turn on Buck... Neesh's voice made Mills realize how much he needed a cell phone. Although she was still playing the age card with him, he wanted to hear her voice more often, and he could tell that the feelings were mutual. After finding out Neesh was coming home in April for spring break, time seemed to fly by. It was now a week before Mills seventeenth birthday. He sat in his weight house waiting for H.T. to come pick him up, so they could go pick up B-Nut together. H.T. also told Mills he had something he wanted to show him. He wouldn't tell Mills what it was, but he told him he was sure he'd like it. H.T. pulled in front of Mills spot with his system on blast. Mills looked out the window as H.T.'s sound system shook the ground in his apartment. H.T.'s Acura legend was mean. The platinum gray vehicle had a white rag top, dark tinted windows, and some chrome hundred spoke Daytons. The inside was decked out as well. Mills leaned back on the plush white leather, with gray pin stripes, while he and H.T. reminisced and caught each other up on their life to date. When H.T. pulled in Lincoln Park project housing, he and Mills didn't know weather to get out the car or pull back off. Gangsters of all sizes stood in front of B-Nut's girlfriend's apartment, some of them flashed pistols, while others threw up gang signs. A few bangers inched closer to the car trying to get a better look at the passengers. H.T. rolled down his windows, and guns came out from everywhere. As he asked for B-Nut, B-Nut came running out of one of the apartments telling his homies to be bool. "What up blood." B-Nut said as he slid in the back seat. "What's up Bro, you tryna get us killed out here nigga." Mills said. "Yea fool, you tripping." H.T. added as he quickly pulled off. B-Nut burst into laughter. "Ya'll niggas aint got nothing to be scared of blood, ya'll family. Spooky niggas." They all started laughing just like old times. "So what's happening baby, what the money in the jets looking like?" Mills asked. "Shid blood its money out here but niggas be fucking shit up, with bullshit ass work, a nigga sold me some flim flam the other day. My fiends said that shit made them throw up dawg. Ima send that nigga when I be em doe." B-Nut explained. "Man what yo money looking like bro?" Mills asked seriously. "It aint too good homie, I got bout nine faces to my name and a few stones of some more bullshit work .I got a banging ass spot blood, but I can't get no good work, blood me." Mills and H.T. couldn't help but to laugh at B-Nut's lingo. B-Nut was a blood for real, where a lot of youngins were faking and breaking with their set. "Look bro, I got something real sweet for you, quality shit, and love on the price. I told you we was gone get this money when we got out nigga, shit bout to be lovely for me, which means its about to be lovely for you." Mills said while reaching in the backseat to give him some dap. "Shid I feel you bro, but blood need some help like yesterday." B-Nut said. "Well I'm a day late, because I'm bout to get you together today, as soon as we come from wherever white chocolate taking us." Mills was referring to H.T. who they said was a black man in a white man's body. H.T. cranked his system up as one of his favorite songs came on, and Mills threw a bag of expensive weed on B-Nut's lap, with a pack of Backwoods. "Roll up bro". Mills said.

Halfway through the fat blunt, H.T. was pulling up to a two door garage. Once the garage door opened and went back down to the ground, the garage was completely black. H.T. exited the car, and in a few seconds the garage was illuminated. H.T stood next to an all white 98 Eddie Bauer Expedition truck. Mills and B-Nut rose from the Acura in awe. "That bitch pretty as fuck top." Mills said to H.T. "I knew you'd like it homie, I got a special price just for you. I can get any rims you want, for this bitch, candy paint, system, the works. You name it, I can make it happen." H.T. said while opening the driver's door. Motioning for him to get in. Mills sat behind the wheel and instantly became one with the truck. "I want this bitch top." Mills said. "I knew you would that's why I let you see it before anyone else." H.T. explained. "I want the triple gold hundred on this baby, with gold flakes in the same white paint, with a fifth triple gold hundred spoke wheel on the back of this bitch, I want everything trimmed in gold from the door handles to the windshield wipers, I want the windows tinted, and King Kong in the trunk. Mills said leaning back on the plush white leather. H.T. was all smiles as Mills zoned out, picturing himself on the road in the truck. "Man that shit sound slick blood, but you gotta get the red rag top with blood paint on this bitch and come through damu riding." B-Nut said loudly. They all burst out laughing as B-Nut leant back in the passenger seat, using the dashboard for a steering wheel, showing Mills how to gangster mob. "Aight, Aight, c'mon I got something else to show ya'll niggas." H.T. said while waving them over to a large metal box sitting in the corner of the garage. It took Mills a minute to part himself from the car, but he eventually joined B-Nut and H.T. at the box. "Before I open this box, that truck with all the shit you want done to it would normally be about 40k, but because you family it'll only be about twenty stacks and Ima lay that bitch out for you… Now is ya'll sure ya'll ready for this shit?" H.T. said with a sneaky smile on his face. "Man open the box white boy, you looking really silly right now blood, like the Riddler man on Batman, wit yo cracker box built ass." B-Nut said. H.T. threw a quick two piece at B-Nut.

"Aight aight blood, I aint gone start capping on you dawg." B-Nut said while laughing and blocking H.T's two piece combination. "Mills you over there laughing like shit sweet wit yo lil Tevin Campbell looking ass." Now the joke was on Mills, H.T. and B-Nut shared the laugh. H.T. finally gained his composure and opened the box. He reached inside and pulled out two AKs. He handed one to Mills and the other to B-Nut. They both fell in love with the choppers. H.T. pushed the lid wide open so Mills and B-Nut could look at the rest of the merchandise. The box was filled with artillery. Mills reached in the box and grabbed two P.89 Rugers. B-Nut grabbed a mac-ten with a thirty shot clip, and H.T. lifted up a few choppers, and grabbed two bullet proof vests. He held one out for Mills and the other for B-Nut, and said "Try these on." They spent a few minutes at the gun shack, and was ready to leave after Mills put in his order for some artillery and vests for him and his crew. H.T. and B-Nut had already met Peko in TYKO, but Mills wanted them to meet Brandy and Shawn. After calling Peko and finding out that they were all at Lisa's, he gave H.T. directions to their next destination. A half an hour later they pulled in behind Peko's Impala. Lisa opened the door after a few knocks. If one didn't know Lisa, they would never believe her to be an all out dope fiend. Because Brandy, Peko and Shawn kept her geared up with her hair and nails done. They treated her like family, showing their appreciation and loyalty. Peko and Shawn sat on the couch smoking a fat blunt, while Brandy served one of her personal customers in the kitchen. "What the fuck is up blood!" B-Nut said while smacking Peko on his leg. Peko was so deep into the video game that he didn't notice B-Nut when he walked through the door. Peko jumped off the couch and pulled B-Nut in for an embrace. The two had become tight during their ninety days in TYKO. "What's up dawg." Peko said. "Shit just bickin it blood tryna get this money blood." B-Nut replied. "What up H.T." Peko said acknowledging him with a warm greeting as well. "I can't call it homie I see you rolling good out there, when you ready to upgrade holler at me." H.T. said advertising his services. Brandy came out of the kitchen with her nine in her hand. Her beauty froze H.T. and B-Nut both. They both stared at her with admiration and lust. Brandy sized both of them up, quickly giving them a once over. She thought they were both attractive, but not dark enough for her liking. "Well ya'll already know Pee, soo… this is his lil bro Shawn Shawn but you can call him Shawn, and this is Brandy, but ya'll can call her Bee. Bee and Shawn this is B-Nut and H.T. they family." Mills said pointing at B-Nut and then pointing at H.T. identifying them with their names. They all spoke to one another, and then had seats. They spent a few hours smoking some killer weed and sharing small talk. Mills told stories about many brawls he, H.T. and B-Nut had gotten into with guys from other cities. Peko gave H.T. and B-Nut his number before they and Mills took off. The three drove a few streets over to Mills spot, where they went inside and smoked more blunts, and took some pictures to send to all their homies who were still doing time. Before they left, Mills gave H.T. a ten thousand dollar down payment on his truck and artillery. Then gave B-Nut four and a half ounces for $3150 and told him to give him a call when he was ready for more.

Mills birthday closed fast. His intentions were to have a birthday and welcome home party for himself, instead he put it off for his next birthday. He now rode shotgun in Peko's Impala bobbing his head to Master P's crack house. While puffing on some expensive hydro weed. He, Peko and Shawn Shawn had been fitted for some gold teeth, a few weeks ago, and Mills received the call that they were ready. Instead of getting them done professionally, they kept the money in the hood, and ordered their teeth from Leroy, who had learned his craft from the best in Atlanta at the grill maker. Leroy worked in his mother's basement, so Peko turned the music off as he pulled into the driveway. Leroy was letting a few people out as Mills and Peko were walking in. They quickly entered the house, and received some of Leroy's southern hospitality. Leroy led them to the basement, where he had three bad red bones awaiting his return. The young ladies gave them looks of approval as they stood in the middle of the floor trying on their grills. "Yo shit sweet bro." Mills said while snapping his own grill in. Unlike Peko, Mills only had two iced out gold teeth in the center of his mouth. With his bottom four teeth covered in gold and diamonds. He flashed Peko with his five thousand dollar smile. "How you love that nigga." Before Peko could answer one of the females said "Mmhmmm I can love that." Mills and Peko turned around finally giving the girls their full attention. Peko tried to avoid an encounter with the beautiful young ladies, because he was just piecing back his relationship from his prior unfaithfulness. Mills was just being overly confident, playing mind games with the ladies. He saw the girl appraising him the whole time, so he intentionally avoided eye contact with her, just to see how long she could go without receiving attention. "I think that's a real good look for you." The girl said as Mills locked eyes with her. "Good looking out and the feelings mutual." Mills replied. Leroy butted in. "My bad buddy, let me introduce ya'll to each other. Mills and Peko this is Catlin, Cat fo shawt, Deedrah, of course Dee fa shawt and this is my shawty Lin. Cat, Dee, and Lin this is Peko and Mills. "Hi." The ladies sad in unison. "What's happenin?" Peko replied. "How ya'll ladies doing?" Mills added. "Well I'm doing fine now but I'd be doing a lot better if knew we had a date scheduled for sometime this week." Cat said to Mills. Cat was cold. Mills could tell she had a nice body by the way her hips and thighs filled out her spot on the couch. Her complexion was light enough to pass for white, but enough melanin to notice her African-American genes. She had green eyes, full lips that shined from the lip gloss she had on them, and her hair was jet black, cut in a short style like the lead singer from Total. Her nails were freshly manicured. She wore a simple white DKNY sweater, tight black DKNY jeans and some black, white and purple DKNY gym shoes. Mills was digging her flavor for sure, and as they hit it off, Deedrah had her eyes locked on Peko's tall frame. "Peko don't tell me you aint man enough to know when a woman is feeling you." Deedrah said while rising from her seat to show off her curvaceous figure. Deedrah was a stallion, being a few inches shorter than Peko's 6' 1" frame. Her complexion was near a redish color, complementing her long reddish brown hair and hazel eyes. Her long sleeve white shirt from Gap hugged her body showing off her handful of titties and iron board flat stomach. Her hips rolled off her body, falling into an ass that could cause a traffic jam. Her long thick legs were double jointed, making her stand firm like a horse. As Peko stared at the gap between her legs, it took everything in him to turn down her proposition. "First off baby, let me tell you, you cold as ice, and as much as I would like to take you out, I can't, cause I got a woman and a child at home, and I'm trying my best to behave for the both of them dig me?" Peko said while licking his lips, and staring her down with his chic magnets. "Aww, that's so sweet, a man tyrin to be faithful, if only there were more men like you." Deedrah said. "If she only knew." Peko thought. Mills and Cat exchanged numbers, Leroy gave Peko Shawn's grill, and he and Mills were off.

April came quickly, and as much as Mills anticipated Neesh's return. He anticipated his first encounter with Buck's connect even more. Buck pulled off highway 270 and turned onto a road that seemed to never end. As he pulled his 500 Benz up to a large fence, he rolled down his window and spoke into an intercom. After stating his name the double gate opened up to the huge estate's lengthy driveway. As Buck followed the series of curves that led to the mansion's doorway, Mills drooled over the extensive land, and humongous home that came into his view. Buck pulled behind a casket grey Rolls Royce and two men in black with fully automatic weapons approached the car, they helped Buck and Mills out the car, and escorted them in the huge mansion. After going up a hallway, down another, then another, they came to a stop in front of some double doors. The men in black gave the door a secret knock, and the left door swung open. Buck and Mills were searched thoroughly before going further. As the door closed, a Puerto Rican man with two beautiful Puerto Rican females in his arms came strolling in the room. The women were flawless, and they were wearing nothing but bikinis. The man said something in Spanish tapped them on their butt then sent them to a room on their left. "Capaso." The man said while taking Buck's hand in his. "Capaso." Buck replied as the two hugged. "Chico, this my lil brother Mills, the one I've been telling you about." Buck said while placing his hand on Mills shoulder. "Capaso, I've heard a lot about you, all true I hope." Chico said to Mills. "Me too." Mills shot back with an amicable smile. Chico pulled Mills in for a hug and said, "Don't worry everything is fine, what I have you have, familia of Bucks is familia of mine lets have a seat." Chico waved the bodyguards off as they attempted to follow behind. "Familia." He said to the guards, while nodding his head assuring them that he could be left alone with Buck and Mills. Chico spent a half hour discussing business with Mills and Buck, while the other three hours they spent watching basketball on the huge flat screen that covered almost the whole wall, and smoking weed. The beautiful ladies traveled in and out of the room as they bought appetizers, and refreshments. Before leaving Chico gave Buck a hug and told him to enjoy life, and bring his God daughter around sometime. Then hugged Mills and whispered in his ear "Welcome to the family." After that the bodyguards reappeared and escorted them to their car. Mills shook his head with intrigue, as he stared at all the expensive vehicles in the circular parking spaces. A Rolls Royce in front of him, Bentley on his left, Lamborghini to his right, and a Continental with you can't see me tint parked in front of the mansions front door. Mills palms became moist as he thought about Buck's retirement next month. He would receive ten bricks for 13.5 a piece upon Bucks departure from the life, and according to how fast he moved that product, his supplies could increase, which would naturally cause the price of his product to decrease. Mills was up and coming and he could feel himself becoming richer by the moment.

For the next couple of weeks Mills just coasted. He was slowly but surely working Peko into taking over his position with smaller weight, while searching for a house to serve as a weight house for his new position. Peko and Shawn had enough money to move some large weight of their own, but they loved the profits they made from moving their work rock for rock. Peko didn't mind taking over Mills position in Bucks old weight house because his little brother would still be going piece for piece out of Lisa's. It was like controlling two sides of the game at once, which meant more profit for them, and he could always love that. Neesh's arrival had been pushed back a month, which Mills didn't mind, because his truck would be ready for the road by then. Mills now rode shotgun in Brandy's Benz while Shawn rode shotgun in his brother's Impala. Leroy had rented a night club in the hood for his birthday party tonight, and stopping through his party was on everyone's agenda. The parking lot was packed as Brandy and Peko pulled into the last two parking spaces on the street. Although Mills and his crew couldn't get in with their weapons, that didn't stop them from wearing their vests. As they slid by security at the door, they instantly spotted Leroy and his girl Lin at the bar. Lin made Mills think of Cat, who he hadn't heard from since their encounter in Leroy's basement. She hadn't called him and he was too caught up in business to contact her. Leroy saw

Mills as he spotted Peko's tall frame sliding through the crowd. He quickly waved them over. They all exchanged daps and hugs with Leroy and respectfully acknowledged his girlfriend. Leroy embraced Shawn now sporting a 5' 9 ½ " frame and whispered in his ear, I see that grill was a perfect fit. Shawn showcased his grill with a big smile. As Mills and his crew mingled with Leroy and Lin, Cat and Dee came gliding towards them. They walked with a rhythm as they bounced to Biggie and Total's One More Chance. Peko grabbed his dick as he took in Dee's body. The white body suit she wore complemented her anatomy so well, that Peko could feel his piece growing in his hand.

Cat wore a pair of casual white Capri pants by Fendi, a matching white blouse and purple sleeveless v-neck sweater by Fendi, with some purple Fendi slip ons. Her earrings were blinging, while complementing the other pieces of jewelry she wore. She walked up to Mills and placed her soft manicured hands around his neck, and spoke directly into his ear. "Hi stranger." Her breath smelled sweet, like juicy fruit, while her hair smelled fruiter than a fruit basket. Mills was digging her, and he could tell the feeling was mutual. He smelled rich with his Polo cologne, and he looked hood rich standing in his coogi sweat suit, and all white patent leather ADIDAS forms. His grill was blinging while his 3 karat diamond earring blinged and his 360 waves made the club sea sick. An hour into the party the goons arrived. D-roc and his crew shoved their way through the crowd. Braids swinging, chains dangling, grills, watches, bracelets and rings blinging. The females loved the gangsters, and they didn't hesitate showing their intrigue. Mills and Fella had seen one another a number of times since their encounter on Mills first day home, but they were both too stubborn to speak and settle their differences. Word had been circulating through the hood that D-Roc and his crew had intentions on robbing

Mills. Mills didn't know how true the rumor was, but he knew D-Roc and his crew had started snorting coke, and anything was expected from them, especially after Buck, believing he had seen them watching his house. The further Fella fell into D-Roc's trap, the more Mills started to distrust him. As they approached Leroy at the bar they gave Mills sinister grins. Mills could tell they were high off blow by the way they continued to massage their nose. Mills didn't understand how things had become so complicated between him and his childhood friends, especially his main road dog.

It was as if they didn't want to see Mills doing good, or maybe it was that they didn't want to see Mills doing better than them. D-Roc and his crew had money in large amounts, but for jackboys, robbing was an addiction, and the only way to get that high was to put in work.

Mills brought Fella into the game, basically sharing everything he had with him. Now that Fella had made a name for himself, and had been accepted by a crew that he idolized growing up, he had flipped the script.

Its said that money is the root of all evil, but Mills had seen niggas with money stay true to the game, so he felt that that rationale had too many holes in to be solid. The real remained real, regardless of the situation and or circumstances.

Mills and Fella had now seen each other for the umpteenth time, and still no acknowledgement was given or received from either party. "Love changes, a thug changes, and sometimes best friends become strangers." Mills thought. He couldn't remember who he had heard that from, but it touched close to home at that moment.

As the party wound down, Dee stuffed her phone number in Peko's hand while whispering in his ear, "What your girl don't know won't hurt her." Peko watched her cheeks eat up the spandex as she walked away, and it was at that moment he told himself "Pee you tried with everything inside you to be good, but you gotta hit that one time." He unconsciously grabbed his crotch while biting down on his lip. "Yeah, you gotta blow those cheeks out" he thought, then giggled at the image in his head.

He gave her number to Shawn Shawn because he knew his night would end with a shakedown from Shy. He couldn't blame her though. He had given her plenty of reasons not to trust him, so he accepted her nightly shakedowns and penis sniffs without any lip. When Mills and his crew made it outside, they spotted D-Roc's G-Ride. A young hustler named Torry was leaning in the window, and Mills shook his head in disbelief of the youngster's innocence. Though the scene looked harmless, Mills knew Torry was being robbed. He watched D-Roc shove Torry out the window, minus his jewelry, and with his pockets inside out. Once again Mills shook his head. "Got to be more careful homie." He said to hisself.

Torry was a flashy young hustler who was known for keeping a few grand on him at a time. He was from Main and Kelton, and looked at D-Roc and his crew as his homies, which made him easy bait for the well known jack boys.

The Bonneville slowly rode by with Brotha Lynch Hung blasting from the speakers as the jackboys theme music. The windows were tinted, but they were rolled down far enough for Mills to see inside. Slim drove, while D-Roc rode shotgun. Fella and Walt aggressively bobbed their heads to the music in the backseat. Mills could see all of Torry belongings on D-Roc's lap, along with a large handgun.

Lil Walt had an ounce of powder on his lap, in which he dipped an I.D into the bag before shoveling a mountain of powder up his nose. He pointed an imaginary gun at Mills and Peko while jerking his hand back as if he was letting off shots. He laughed as Mills attempted to flag the car down, only to watch it turn into traffic, and speed up Main street. "Aint no love in this game."

-CHAPTER FIFTEEN-

Mills strolled through H.T.'s car garage in astonishment, he looked at all the vehicles being worked on. Some hung from the ceiling, others were at ground level. Some were finished, others were primed down. A few were missing doors, and interior, while others were without engines. H.T's crew went to work, while he sat in the passenger seat of Mills truck, with the door wide open. He tossed Mills the keys. "Hop in homie." He said while snapping his fingers at one of the workers, and motioning for them to bring him something. Mills examined the truck as he walked around to the driver's side. The white candy paint, had gold flakes neatly sparkling through it. While the 18 inch triple gold hundred spoke Daytons fit the truck perfectly, and had a special sparkle of their own. The fifth wheel on the back of the truck complemented the gold door handles, and windshield wipers, while its reflection reflected off the dark tint on the back window. Before Mills hopped behind the wheel, he checked out the interior, which was soft white leather, with gold pin stripes. The dashboard, and steering wheel were all white, while the rugs, roof and the doors were gold. The Kenwood deck was white and gold marble matching the remote that H.T.'s homie handed him. Instead of the seats having Eddie Bauer edition on the headrest it said T-Money edition in gold letters. Mills put the key in the ignition and bought the truck to life. H.T. hit a few buttons on the remote and Tupac's Picture Me Rolling blasted from the speakers. He threw the remote on Mills lap, and held out his hand for some dap. Mills hit his rock and H.T. hopped out the truck, telling Mills to call him later. Mills bobbed his head to the music as one of the garage doors ascended. He backed out, threw up a peace sign, and pulled out into the road, while cranking his system up another notch. Mills was pumped. Not only did he have the sickest truck the streets had seen, but Neesh would arrive at the airport in less than 24 hours and two days after that he'd be receiving his first ten kilos from Chico. The sun was shining, Mills had only been home now for ten months, and he had close to a hundred thousand in his stash. Minus the five thousand he carried in his pocket to pay off the money he owed on the Presidential Rolex he had on Layaway. After picking his Rolex up, he decided to give Cat a call. The night of Leroy's party he spent the night at her house, and for the past two weeks he'd been hitting that cat at least three times a week. He liked cat because she wasn't looking for more than what he was willing to give her. After informing her about his feelings for Neesh, she was still cool with just being friends, with benefits, of course. As Mills dialed her phone number, he pictured their last time together. Thinking about how her soft luscious lips wrapped around his pole had him aroused.

Ring! Ring! Ring! "Hello." "What's up girl, you thinking about daddy?" Mills said smoothly. "OF course, daddy been thinking about mommy?" Mills laughed. "Does a bear shit in the woods and wipe its ass with a furry white rabbit?" Mills said mocking Tupac, as What's Ya Phone Number played in the background. Cat laughed. "You hungry?" Mills asked. "I am if it means I get to spend some time with you." "I'm on my way to come get you, I'll be there in 10 minutes." "I'll be waiting." Cat said seductively. "Peace." Mills said before disconnecting.

When he pulled in front of Cat's house, he killed the music because she lived in a peaceful neighborhood and he didn't want to upset her neighbors. When she walked out the house she looked stunning as always.

Cat fell in love with Mills ride at first sight, but when she stepped inside the truck, the bling from his Rolex and earrings made her weak in the knees. Mills hid his eyes behind a pair of Cartier frames, but the smile on his face showed that he was pleased to see her. He kissed her on her cheek, before pulling off, and turning up his stereo. Mary! Mary! Mary! Mary! Mary! I'm happy just to hear ya name Mary Jane! Blasted from the speakers as he relit his Backwood Cigar filled with hydro. He took a couple puffs and passed it to cat. She took a few puffs and placed it in the ashtray. Then she leaned over, unzipped Mills pants, and slid his already half hard penis into her mouth. "Damn Cat, I thought you said you wanted some dinner." Mills asked as she used her tongue to play with his head. "I do but I can't have my dessert first." She replied while looking him in his eyes, and sliding her mouth down his pole. Mills just leaned back in his seat and enjoyed the warmth of her mouth. She felt so good it was hard for him to keep his eyes on the road, but he managed to swerve around a car making a left turn at the last minute. The next day Mills arrived at the airport at twelve o'clock on the nose. He continuously glanced at his iced out time piece, because Neesh was over fifteen minutes late. As he searched through the crowd of people coming out of the airport's doorway he spotted her.

She had only become more beautiful with time. She wore a two piece Coogi outfit. Her skirt stopped at her mid thigh, showing off her muscular, yet feminine legs. Her skin complexion was mocha brown, and radiated like Ra the mighty sun god. She wore her sleeveless Coogi vest open, showcasing her flat stomach, as her white halter top stopped at the top of her belly button. Her jet black hair hung 3 inches below her shoulders, and she had it pulled behind her ears to show off her two karat diamond earrings that Buck bought her. Her compact petite frame was flawless, like that of a goddess. Mills quickly relieved her of her bags. His 5' 6" frame towered hers at 5' 3". Her Bath and Body wash made her smell like peaches and cream, and Mills loved every second of   their embrace. Neesh was taken aback by how much Mills had grown. His white tee fitted him perfectly, exposing his toned frame, that Neesh was loving as he wrapped his muscular arms around her. As they walked towards the truck, the sun hit his waves, and bling just right. The Rolex was blinding all those who looked, while his diamond studded smile nearly melted Neesh as he helped her into the truck, carefully closing the door behind her. He threw her bags in the backseat, and quickly pulled away from the illegal place he was parked. "I hope that look you giving me is a good one?" Mills said while pulling into traffic. "It is, I'm just tripping off how much you grown." Neesh replied. "Nothing stays the same Neesh, I'm a young man now, and I remember, and meant everything I told you when I was a youngin." "Is that right." She replied. "C'mon Tanesha Tyreka La'nette Walker, you know how I feel about you, I'm just waiting for my chance." Neesh liked Mills confidence, and maturity, but the fact still remained that he was seventeen, and she'd be twenty one in two months. Their age difference had always been a problem for her, that and the fact that she didn't want a man who lived Mills lifestyle. She lost her mother and father to the dope game. Her mother smoking it and her father selling it, and she refused to let herself fall for a man who had so many possibilities of being taken away from her. Death and prison were the end result for the majority of the people in the game. She looked at Mills expensive earrings, watch and shiny grill. Then she examined his expensive vehicle. She was happy to see Mills doing well for himself, but she knew that he had only gotten deeper into the game that she feared. The same lifestyle she had tried to evade by going to Atlanta, Georgia for college. "I see some things don't change." Neesh said while tapping Mills wrist. Mills looked at his watch, and a smile was his only response. She shook her head and harmlessly rolled her eyes. Mill knew what Neesh was getting at, but the discussion was one he'd rather not have, especially at their first encounter in over three years. Mills called Peko to avoid the topic, before Neesh brought it back up because it wasn't like her to not speak her mind. He also wanted to make sure that Peko, Shawn and Brandy were all at Brandy's house, where he asked them to be. Mills told them he wanted them at Brandy's so he could bring Neesh by, which was true, but he also wanted to surprise them with his new truck. Mills cranked the music up and let Neesh enjoy the scenery for the rest of the ride. When he hit Main Street, Neesh felt as if she'd never left. Everything was the same. The strip was crowded with prostitutes, smokers, dealers, pimps and hustlers of all kinds. When Mills turned onto Berkley the street was packed from beginning to end. All the hustlers had their cars out, with their systems on blast, as they chased down the money, and hollered at the p.y.t's that walked nasty up and down the strip. Mills system sounded off as he neared Brandy's house, heads turned as Master P's ice cream man filled the street. Mills hid behind his tint, as onlookers drooled over his mean machine. D-Roc, Slim, Walt, and Fella stood in front of

Fella's mother's house. D-Roc had his raspberry blue 97 Explorer parked at the curb. The Explorer was mean, with gold flakes in the paint, tinted windows, and some gold hundred spokes. His Explorer was a smaller version of Mills Expedition, but not only was the truck smaller, but his rims were too. D-Roc leaned up against his truck, with Tasha standing between his legs. Tasha had on just as much shine as D-Roc and a brand new Honda Elantra to match his truck. She hadn't talked to Neesh in over a year. Not that they weren't still cool, just that they were living in two different worlds. As Mills pulled up the street, letting his system slap, D-Roc and the jackboys mouth's watered. The truck put D-Roc's to shame, and neither D-Roc nor his crew liked it. Had the truck not pulled in front of Brandy's house the jackboys would have shot it up. Neesh couldn't believe she was seeing Tasha and D-Roc hugged up. Although she was over D-Roc the sight didn't sit right with her. Tasha was her best friend, and the same person who called her every week for her first year away, telling her something new about D-Roc and his sex life. She talked about him like a dog, now she was with him." Snakes came in many different shapes and forms, sometimes in the form of a friend." Mills stepped out of the truck leaving his system on blast. A few females yelled out "I like Ice Cream" as they drooled over Mills truck.

Mills smiled, showing off his grill, while throwing up peace signs to the females, and young hustlers who acknowledged him. Mills was going to Make Neesh's visit quick so he kept the car running with her in it, but after seeing D-Roc and Tasha shining, he knew it was only right that Neesh shine with him. He opened her door, and helped her out of the truck, after telling her to kill the engine and grab the keys. Peko, Brandy, and Shawn sat on the porch laughing and joking about the look on D-Roc and his crew's faces, while

D-Roc and his crew grilled Mills with hate and envy. Fella didn't really show hate, but no emotion was just as hateful. As the saying goes," sometimes silence can be so loud." Mills Rolex shined from where he stood, all the way up the block, and D-Roc hated it, although his shine was on ten as well. Mills held Neesh's hand as Tasha yelled her name out, and came running over to her. D-Roc's mouth dropped as he stared at Neesh's beautiful face and frame. She looked flawless, fresh and innocent. Tasha dragged D-Roc along with her, holding tightly on to his hand. "Fake love." Neesh thought as Tasha embraced her. As Tasha went on explaining her and D-Roc, Neesh stopped her. "It's okay Tasha me and D-Roc haven't been together for years." "I just don't want you to think…" Neesh cut her off again. "Don't worry about it girl." She looked at D-Roc and said, "HI Derrick." D-Roc eyed her hand as it stayed locked inside Mills's. Neesh hadn't realized that Mills still held her hand, but she liked the fact that he did. "What's up Tanesha." D-Roc shot back with a smirk on his face. Mills was too busy talking to his crew, but he turned around in enough time to catch Tasha staring at him while licking her lips seductively. "I should have been sucking his dick." Tasha thought as she appraised Mills from his head to his feet. As Neesh waved at Slim, Fella and lil Walt, she caught a glimpse of Tasha flirting with Mills. She waited for Mills to throw a signal back at Tasha, but instead he brushed her off. "What up Roc?" Mills said as D-Roc sized him up. "Shit I see you finally got what you want." D-Roc said nodding at Neesh. Neesh knew D-Roc was directing that towards her, but Mills didn't give her a chance to say anything. "I wish man, Neesh is a queen, it will probably be a long time before she give me a chance." Mills replied. Then directed his attention elsewhere.

"What up Slim, Walt and Fella?" Mills said. They nodded their head, and went back to flirting with Tasha's friends. Fella took another look at Mills as if he wanted to say something, but he quickly turned away as Mills locked eyes with him. The meeting and greeting ended as Buck called Mills asking where he and Neesh were. Mills put Neesh on the phone. D-Roc and Tasha walked off while Mills and Neesh climbed the steps to Brandy's porch.

Two days later Mills sat in his new spot with his first ten kilos. He knew getting rid of them wouldn't be a problem, because he already had six of them gone with Peko, Brandy, and Shawn. They'd buy one, and he'd give them one on consignment. He had Chris and Var buying nine ounces each, which was enough for half a brick. He'd give them the other half on consignment. Then he had B-Nut, and his big homie Bear Bear. B-Nut was buying half a brick, while Bear was buying a whole thang. He'd show Bear Bear some super love on the price for his one, and take the money B-Nut had for his half a brick, and give him the other half on consignment. That would leave him with one kilo, which he'd break down into four nine ounces and look out for young hustlers with potential like lil Scoob and Tone. Ten days tops he'd be back at Chico with $130,000 he owed him and $130,000 of his own to cop with. After ridding himself of ten kilos, Mills headed for Buck's house to pick up Neesh for their movie and dinner date. Buck had upgraded his living conditions. He had a small estate of his own. His home was worth 1.5 million. He had 12 foot ceilings, six bedrooms, a large dining room, living room, sitting room and a special game room for his alone time. He had transformed one of the bedrooms into a library. The stairway in the living room had a series of curves which ascended up to a balcony that overlooked the living and sitting room. On the other side of the balcony were identical steps that lead to the sitting room and a hall way that led to the spacious kitchen. Buck had a surveillance system installed with cameras in every room, so he could monitor inside and outside his house at all times. When Mills arrived Neesh and Mek were seated on the couch with Buck and Mek's beautiful daughter, who lit up at the sight of her uncle Mills. Mills spoke to Mek, kissed Neesh on her cheek, and grabbed Daylonna off the couch. Daylonna slobbered on Mills face as he held her in the air swinging her around like a helicopter. "You love your uncle Mills don't you girl...I know you do." Mills said as he brought her in for one of her slobbery kisses. "Buck upstairs in his reading room, he wanted to talk to you before you leave Mills." Mek said. Mills sat Daylonna down on Neesh's lap, then jogged up the lengthy steps, and walked in on Buck as he was reading one of his books by the reputable black activist, Marcus Garvey. "What up T-Money?" Buck said as he swung his feet off of the desk they were propped up on. "What it is big bro." Mills said. "Have a seat, an ima tell you." Buck said while motioning to the chair that was adjacent from him. Mills took a seat while Buck fired up a blunt he had in his ashtray. Buck hit the green, held up a picture of Marcus Garvey and asked Mills "Do you know who this is?" "Nah." Mills said. "This is Marcus Garvey, he's one of the first black activists to fight for black's freedom. He's a bad man, in a good way of course. He was the first black man to come up with our nations migration back to Africa. He believed that blacks would be better off segregated, and that segregation was our best chance at progressing economically. He believed we should build our own economy, by establishing our own business in the black communities. So we can provide jobs for our own people, circulating the money amongst one another, instead of giving all our money to the white man. The majority of unemployed people are black. That's because blacks own very little, therefore we always look for help with employment from diversity groups other than African-Americans. We are so busy competing with one another, and taking from one another, that we have no time to compete with anyone else, or take from anyone else." Mills sat attentively while Buck shed light. He was lost, but hungry for understanding. "I'm telling you this T-Money because what I'm about to do is give back to the community that I've gained from. I wanna be able to help people climb up that economical ladder. I'm doing good, so why shouldn't I help my brothers and sisters succeed in life. Now I can't force anyone to succeed, they have to want success, its like the saying goes, you can lead a horse to water, but can't make him drink it. I'm bout to create opportunity, and want you to be a part of this. The thing is you can't be both a negative and positive influence at the same time. The dope game aint forever T-Money, and you are now in a position where you can start setting goals, such as a quota you want to meet before leaving the game. Sooner is always better. Because the longer you remain a participant of that lifestyle, the more susceptible you are to the negative consequences that come with that lifestyle. I aint gone beat yo eardrums up but I just thought I should enlighten you on a few things. When I was young and off the hook thinking I owned the world, an old wine-o pulled my coat and enlightened me about hour history. How I was helping bring my family down, he hip me to our brother Marcus Garvey, Carlos cook, Malcolm X, and George Jackson. Those brothers were some gangsters Mills. The library is always open, you should come pick up one of those books sometime, you'd be amazed at what you can learn outside the classroom. There's a saying that says if you wanna hide something from a black person; just hide it in a book. If you wanna find out what's hidden pick one up. Now get up out of here and enjoy ya night out with that young black princess down there. You know she headstrong boy, you better be ready to conversate on her level." Buck smiled as he dropped Marcus Garvey's book on Mills lap and left the room. Mills spent a few minutes scanning the book's pages, then placed the book back on Buck's desk and headed downstairs. Neesh was awaiting him with her purse in hand, and her I'm ready to go face. After kissing Daylonna and saying their see you laters to Buck and Mek, Mills and Neesh were gone.

-CHAPTER SIXTEEN-

On this hot early July afternoon, the corner of Oak and Morrison was packed. D-Roc and his crew were parked in front of Tee Tee's house talking to her little cousin Stanley. Pimp and L's had Oak street on lock .Since they've been pumping out of Liley's house, everyone's money on Oak Street was slowing down. Without knowing it, Pimp and L's were becoming ghetto superstars, and a lot of people did not like it. D-Roc and his crew had a perfect view of Liley's apartment, and as Pimp and L's came walking out the front door, D-Roc started laughing. "These the lil niggas you talking about Stan?" D-Roc asked with a big smile on his face. "Yep that's them niggas right there, don't be fooled by them lil niggas they in that bitch eating." Stanley said seriously. "Aw man this shit is goin to be easy, like taking candy from a baby." D-Roc said, once again laughing at the easy lick Stanley put him up on. "You mean, these the lil niggas everybody been talking about?" D-Roc asked. "Yep." Stanley said. "So which of these niggas got out on Monster?" D-Roc asked still laughing. "That one right there." Stanley said pointing at Pimp. As Pimp and L's crossed the street heading for the corner store Fella thought his eyes were deceiving him. He almost burned himself with the blunt as he threw half his body in the front seat to get a better look. "Man that's Mills little brother." Fella said shocked at the sight before him. "I was just about to say that shit but I thought I was tripping." D-Roc said. "Hell nah I aint tripping that's lil Jimmy." Fella said. "Ha! Ha! Ha! This might be the sweetest lick we done ever hit." D-Roc said laughing once again. "Nah Roc, we can't hit this one bro, I help raise that lil nigga." Fella said. "Aw shit, here Fells go with that super hero shit; you can't be everybody's Superman." Walt said. Shid looks like somebody already beating us to the punch." Slim said while pointing at Liley's apartment. Three men with black masks were forcing their way into the apartment, while the forth was in the getaway car. "There goes the neighborhood." D-Roc said while shoving a mountain of powder up his nose. "Check this shit out." D-Roc said as Pimp and L's came walking out the store. L's thought his mind was playing tricks on him as he watched three masked men running out of Liley's apartment.

He dropped his bag and opened fire immediately. "Pop! Pop! Pop!" His 9mm sounded off, as the masked men loaded into their vehicle.

The masked men recklessly returned fire as Pimp joined his road dawg in the fireworks. He and L's traded shots with the cars backseat passenger as it brazenly sped by. They both emptied their clips into the vehicle, knocking out its back window as it recklessly bent the corner on Morrison.

"Hell nah, them lil niggas goin out dumping." D-Roc said as he burst into laughter.

"Mills lil brother got more heart than him." Walt said while joining D-roc in laughter.

"Ya'll niggas silly as fuck." Slim said while adding a little giggle. Pimp and L's ran into the apartment. Once inside, Pimp rushed to Leslie's aid as she cried at the bottom of the stairs. "Leslie you aight?" Pimp asked. "My mom they beat her half to death cause she wouldn't tell them were the dope and money was." Leslie said while wiping the tears from her face.

"Where Liley at?" Pimp asked. Leslie was slow to answer clearly in shock from what she had just witnessed. "Where the fuck is yo mom Les?" L's asked aggressively. Leslie pointed upstairs as she choked on her own tears. L's shot up the steps with Pimp behind him; Liley lay on her bedroom floor bleeding. Her eyes were swollen shut and blood leaked from her skull. "God damn man!" L's yelled as Liley moaned from the pain of a simple touch. "C'mon Pimp we got to get her to the hospital!" L's yelled as Pimp stood in a small state of shock of his own. They carefully lifted Liley's body, and carried her down the steps. "Leslie grab yo mom's car keys and hurry the fuck up." L's ordered as he and Pimp rushed Liley out the back door. By the time Liley was carefully placed in the back seat, Leslie was running out with the keys. She hopped in the backseat with Pimp and her mom, while L's drove. L's helped carry Liley in to the hospital, then rushed back out the double doors. He didn't know if anyone had notified the cops, but he needed to get back to the apartment so he could get the drugs and guns out of there just in case. He also wanted to see what the streets knew about the robbery.

It took L's a little over an hour to return. When he walked into the room, Leslie sat at her mother's bedside while she rested. Tubes ran from Liley's body into an I.V. Tank, and a couple of other machines L's didn't know the name of. The sight angered him further, causing his jaws to tighten and his hands to ball into fists.

He nodded his head, motioning for Pimp to follow him into the hallway. "Word is the Detroit boys hit us." L's whispered. "Word." Pimp shot back as he scanned the hallway for any eaves droppers. "Word." L's answered. "You know we gotta handle that bro. If not niggas gone think shit sweet, like they can just take from us with no consequences." "Nough said." Pimp replied with anger and rage.

After a couple weeks, Liley's face was still swollen and her ribs were fractured, but she was expected to make a full recovery. Neither her nor Leslie felt safe going back to their apartment, especially after learning that Pimp and L's had retaliated on the Detroit boys. So instead of going to the apartment, Pimp and L's put them in a hotel room. They were already moving anyway, so hopefully they wouldn't have to be there too long. Once Liley's section eight voucher was transferred over to the house she had been approved for, they were ghost.

Pimp and L's wasn't happy about the move, because that meant they had to find another dope spot, but Leslie and her mother had become family, so if the boys had to lose out on a few dollars to ensure their safety, they had no problem doing so.

After three weeks of laying on the Detroit boys, Pimp and L's finally had their movement down to a science. They hid in the bushes across the street from the Detroit boys dope spot., waiting for them to come out the house in their flyest threads headed from the strip club, as they did every Friday night between 11 and 12 o'clock pm. L's checked the time on his pager as the vibration startled him. It was fifteen minutes after twelve. He cursed under his breath as his plan started to seem fruitless. At that moment, the Detroit boys came walking out the front door laughing and talking loudly about which stripper they would be sleeping with by the end of the night. It was only three of them but that was enough to make the hour spent in the bushes worthwhile. As they loaded into the two tone Lexus, L's and Pimp drew their weapons. "Chill for one minute bro, let em get all the way in the car, then we gone run up on they shit." L's said. The front passenger was the first in the car, then the back passenger. The driver stood outside the car talking for a couple minutes, then he too loaded in the vehicle. Before he could brang the car to life, Pimp and L's sprang from the bushes blasting off shots. Pimp ran halfway to the car and stood in the middle of the street with his hood on, picking the front seat apart. L's ran all the way up on the car. As the windows came out, glass flew everywhere. Pimp emptied his clip quickly. He had touched the driver and front passenger up pretty good, but they were still alive and moaning as they tried to get as low as possible. L's stuck his gloc inside the car and finished all three of the Detroit boys off with the last six shots from his sixteen round magazine.

His gun clicked a few times before him and Pimp took off running through a dark alley. The driver and front seat passenger met death instantly while the guy in the backseat fought for his life.

෨෩ ෨෩ ⑧ ⑧ ⑧ ⑧ ⑧ ෨෩ ෨෩

After being hooked up with some of Buckshot's loyal clientele, Mills was running through his first thirty kilos with ease. He finished his grind a little early today because tomorrow would be a long one.

Not only was it Neesh's birthday, but he had to pick Black up from TYKO tomorrow morning. Mills had been spending a lot of time with Neesh since she had been back home, and the more time they spent together the more in love with her he fell. She still hadn't given in to Mills, but Stevie Wonder could see Mills wasn't the only one falling. Mills had a special surprise for her tomorrow, and he couldn't wait to see her reaction to it. He had tickets to Martin Lawrence's stand up comedy at Nationwide Arena, then he had reservations for dinner at one of Columbus's finest restaurants, but no matter how much Neesh loved Martin or seafood neither one of them could top his surprise birthday gift.

The next morning Mills was up bright and early. He showered, groomed himself, and slid into a pair of dark blue Nautica jeans, a v-neck white tee, and some high top white on white A-1's. After grabbing his grill from the jar of cleaner beside his bed, he ran them under water, then snapped them in his mouth, put on his Rolex, and his two karat diamond earring, then rushed out the door talking to Brandy on his phone. Twenty minutes later he was pulling into TYKO's parking lot. He strolled through the door blinding Tonya with the shine from his diamonds. He and Tonya flirted with one another until Black arrived. Black was already fit, but he had become huge. His chest protruded from his shirt, while the shirt sleeves clung to his arms like a bear hug. He sagged his pants slightly, but it was still evident that they were too small for his running back type legs. His cornrows hung down his back as they zig zagged from the top of his head.

When they embraced one another, Mills could feel Black's strength as he squeezed the life out of him. As they walked out the door Black admired Mills success, from his jewels, to his ride. Mills had sent him pictures, but to see his little homie balling out of control in the flesh, was inspirational. As they pulled out the lot, Mills fired up a hydro-filled backwood and passed it to Black. Master P's Ghetto Dope blasted from his system all the way to the City Center Mall. After taking Black shopping, and to the cell phone shop, Mills headed for his weight house. While Black showered and got dressed, Mills got rid of a few kilos, and collected some of the money he had in the streets. Brandy stopped by to drop off some money she owed Mills and catch him up on the latest street gossip. While they chopped it up, and smoked on some sticky, Black came walking down the steps. Brandy stared at the dark piece of chocolate that gravitated towards her, and felt a real attraction for the first time since Chris. "Black this is… Brandy." Black said cutting Mills off. "How you doing Brandy, I been waiting a long time for this day." Black said while extending his hand for a formal greeting. "What day is that?" Brandy asked. "The day I got to meet you, Mills aint been delivering you my messages?" "No." Brandy said bashfully. "That's cold Mills." Black said. "My bad bro, you know I gotta short term memory, but dig… you can catch her up on all that shit, cause she gone be taking you to your moms' house." "What!" Brandy said butting in. "Yeah sis, you know it's Neesh's birthday today, I gotta go pick her up and show her that surprise I was telling you about, you and Black need to get acquainted anyway, cause he's been feeling you for a long time now, and I know you like em cause he's your type, so don't front." "Who the hell you think you is match maker nigga." Brandy said with sass. "Nope but you know I wouldn't plug you wit a nigga whose not official…" Mills replied as he dug into his pocket, and extracted a wad of cash. He handed the cash to Black and said, "Bro this is about four gees, just something for you to put in yo pocket, I got something heavy for you, but we'll get into that tomorrow. After you spend some time with yo mom, by the way tell her I said hi and sorry I couldn't stop by." Mills grabbed a bag full of money from the table and kissed Brandy on the cheek.

Good looking sis, ya'll a good look for each other too." He said then gave her the key to the house and told her to lock up. As he walked out the front door, Brandy and Black stood there speechless. It took Mills forty five minutes to reach Buck's house. Mills and Neesh didn't waste any time getting back on the road. Forty five minutes later they were turning into Canal Winchester's far east side condominiums. He pulled to the side of the road and grabbed a blindfold out of the glove box. "Mills what are you doing, and where are we going." Neesh asked. " It's a surprise; now turn around so I can blindfold you. " "You know I don't like surprises Mills, now please just tell me what my present is.. please." Neesh pleaded. She tried melting him with her puppy dog look, but it was to no avail. Mills blindfolded her and pulled into the condominium housing units. He helped Neesh out the truck, and into the dark condo. "Mills where are we?" Neesh asked as she stood in the dark room. Mills hit the switch on the wall and illuminated the room. He removed her blindfold and she stood in awe, while looking at the beautiful living room. Plush white Italian leather, fish tanks, luxurious lamps, and glass tables accommodated the space. Mills took her on a tour of the place starting with the kitchen. As they climbed the steps Mills held her hand while guiding her through darkness. The upper level had only two rooms, a master bedroom and a comfortable bathroom.

Neesh was confused. Mills said he had a surprise gift for her, but here they were in a strange apartment. Mills found the lamp next to the bed and lit the bedroom up. A dozen roses and a huge teddy bear holding a large card that read "Happy Birthday Neesh in big bold letters sat on the bed. "Aww, Mills this is so sweet, I've never been given roses before." Neesh said as she grabbed the roses from the bed and smelled them. "You aint gone read ya card?" Mills asked as he anticipated Neesh's reaction. "Of course I'm going to read my card, thank you for everything Mills." Neesh said before planting one on his cheek. Neesh grabbed the card from the teddy bear and opened it wide.

Neesh,

I've been in love with you since the very first time I've laid my eyes on you, and I promise to treat you like a queen if you ever give me a chance. This place isn't befitting for a queen, but I wanted you to have a place of your own to call home, when you visited. This place is yours, no strings attached.

Happy birthday my queen

T-Mills

Neesh was speechless. "Happy birthday beautiful." Mills said while holding the keys to the apartment in front of her. She jumped into his arms and tears of joy poured down her face. They peered into each other's eyes, and Mills took advantage of the moment. He leaned in for a kiss and she accepted.

It began with a peck on the lips, then another one. Then he used his tongue to part her lips and she closed her eyes while inviting his tongue into her mouth. As she sucked on his tongue, his hands traveled her body.Up her back, down her spine, over her ass, around her hips, then down her thighs. She was tired of holding out. The fire that burned between her legs whenever Mills was around was ready to be put out, so she submitted to her emotions and his will. " Mills " she said in between breaths. "What up" he answered in between kisses. Neesh didn't answer right away, she couldn't believe what she was about to say. She had fallen in love with Mills, and no matter how wrong for her he was, the way he made her feel was so right.

After sensing Neesh's change of body language, Mills stopped his attack on her neck and ear long enough to ask her was she alright. "I want you to make love to me" She answered. Those words were like music to Mills' ears. He had waited seven long years to make love to this woman, so he took his time enjoying every part of her anatomy. They made love all through the night into the wee hours of the morning.

Neesh stared at Mills while he slept. Never in a million years would she believe that Mills would have put it down on her the way he did last night. As she watched the rhythm of his breaths, she decided that going back to Atlanta wasn't an option. In her head she had already transferred her credits from Morehead to O.S.U. She wasn't leaving her man's side for anything.

D-Roc and his crew cruised up Mt. Vernon letting Nas "if I ruled the world" scream from the fifteens in his Explorer. Mt. Vernon and Graham was packed and as D-Roc pulled his truck to the curb, guys took off running in all directions. "Now that's what I call respect. That's the type of respect we supposed to have every fucking where we go, when we roll up, clear the mutha fucking set." Walt said intrigued by the fear they put in people's hearts. Slim stood outside the truck emptying a backwood, while D-Roc hung out the window talking to a few females. Walt and Fella hopped out the truck to catch another flock of females that admired the truck as they walked by. When Slim walked in the store he noticed a smoke gray Taurus driving by slowly. The windows were tinted so he couldn't see inside, but he flashed his gloc 40, just to let the passengers know he wasn't slipping. The car kept going and Slim walked in the store. "Clown ass niggas must be sweating my bro's ride." He thought. When he exited the store he laughed at the sight before him. Walt stuck his tongue out of his mouth while palming two girls asses at the same time. Slim crossed the street to join his partners and the hood rats they had attracted. He leaned up against D-Roc's truck while filling his backwood cigar with hydro chronic. The girleys were attractive but not more appealing than the sticky green he was rolling up.

The gray Taurus slowly bent the corner, unnoticed by the jackboys. Slim dug in his pocket searching for his lighter, while his boys were distracted by their female entertainment. Slim spotted the car out the corner of his eye but by the time he lifted his head he was staring down the barrel of a gun. "Roc it's a hit." Slim yelled while drawing his gloc nine.

Slim never got off a shot. His gun hit the ground before his body. The gunner hung out the window of the Taurus dumping slugs into his frail frame. Walt and Fella dashed for cover as the second gunner sprayed rounds from his Mac Eleven in their direction. Fella shielded himself with D-Roc's truck while letting his four four bulldog bark back at the gunners. Walt shielded himself with one of the females while blazing back with his 32 shot gloc nine. D-Roc managed to open his truck's door, and hit the dirt. He let off rounds from his eleven shot four five while laying stretched out on the sidewalk.

As the gunners ducked back into the window and the Taurus turned up an alley, Walt threw his female shield to the ground and chased after the car. His extended magazine sent bullets flying through the Taurus's back windshield, and thumping into its trunk. D-Roc ran to his aces aid, but it was too late. Fella held his cousin's lifeless body tightly in his arms. "Naw man, not my dawg! Not my dawg man!" D-Roc said repeatedly as tears fell from his eyes.

Walt returned quickly. He shook his head as he looked at Slim's bullet riddled body. Slim's blood drenched Fella's clothes as he rocked back and forth with his cousin's body. "Fells! Roc! C'mon man we gotta go!" Walt said as the police sirens became louder. Neither D-Roc nor Fella moved. Walt grabbed their guns off the ground and hopped behind the wheel of D-Roc's bullet riddled truck. The truck's engine came to life despite its condition and Walt yelled for his homeboys once again. "Slim gangsta gone man, hurry the fuck up. Before the cops get here." D-Roc and Fella loaded Slim's body into the backseat of the truck. They refused to leave him there. Dead or alive he was coming with them. Fella stayed in the backseat with his cousin, while D-Roc ran around to the front of the car and hopped in the passenger seat. Walt wasted no time smashing on the gas and fishtailing out into traffic.

⁊⁊ ⁊⁊ ⑧ ⑧ ⑧ ⑧ ⑧ ⁊⁊ ⁊⁊

Pimp and L's sat in Liley's new house on Long 22nd awaiting their cab. L's aunt Peaches had finally found them a new dope spot and they couldn't wait to open up shop. Aunt peaches was a smoker slash prostitute. Despite her addictions, she was a money maker, and any dope spot she touched turned into a gold mine.

When their cab arrived Pimp kissed Leslie and told her he'd be back later, while L's cracked jokes on Leslie and her mother has he ran out the door laughing. Pimp and L's had been laying low since putting that work in on the Detroit boys. Nobody actually knew who killed them, but Pimp and L's name was in heavy rotation, so they kept a low profile, and only came out at night.

The cab ride to Oak and Sherman only lasted five minutes. L's aunt Peaches answered the door with nothing but a shirt on. The shirt stopped at her waist exposing the bush between her legs as she motioned for the boys to come inside. "Damn auntie put some clothes on, don't nobody wanna see that hairy ass wolf pussy" L's said as he entered the house " You aint gave me enough dope yet to be giving out orders nephew, and until you do, I run this mutha fucka" Aunt peaches said. Two more half naked women occupied the living room, while another one came walking out of one of the back rooms.

L's pulled his dope sack out and passed out a few rocks to Peaches company. "Everybody get the fuck out of here smoking that shit. From here on out all dope gets smoked in the back rooms!" L's yelled. He dropped three stones in Peaches hand and said "Now I run this mutha fucka. Back rooms please." Aunt Peaches led the pack to the back rooms. L's smacked her on her bare hiney as she walked by and aunt Peaches stopped in the doorway and gave him the middle finger. "I love you too." L's said while laughing. Pimp fanned the smoke out the air while covering his nose and mouth, "You smell that?" He asked L's. "Yeah, it smell like money" L's answered as he came walking out of the kitchen with a plate and a razor. "Have a seat bro, this is home baby, we bout to get rich. You see all that pussy in there? The money follows trust me. L's explained. He loved teaching Pimp the little bit he knew about the game. Pimp's bloodline was so pure that the game and putting in work came to him naturally, but L's had more hands on experience.

Pimp's genes were dominated by the blood of his gangster father, but his soul was filled with the hustle of his hustling-ass mother. The more blood he filled the streets with, and the more money he made, the more he felt like he was born for the lifestyle he was living. L's was an only child, so Pimp was like the brother he never had. Their bond grew quickly, and their loyalty to one another had become bulletproof. They didn't know it yet, but that loyalty would be their greatest asset as they battled their way to the top. Unbeknownst to their knowledge, the challenges they faced currently would be nothing compared to the challenges they'd face in the future. As the old famous saying goes : Heavy is the head that wears the crown.

-CHAPTER SEVENTEEN-

Slim's funeral was stacked. It looked more like a block party than a death ceremony. The parking lot was filled to the capacity with fancy cars, and saucy mourners. Detective White and Brown were parked up the street in an unmarked car. They snapped off shots as all the Main Street Ballers, and gangsters came to show their respects to one of their most reputable products. D-Roc, Fella, and Walt sat in Walt's fire orange 96 Caprice on gold hundreds. Walt sat behind the wheel with his door wide open as he, D-Roc, and Fella snorted coke like it was legal. Mills pulled into the lot, and parked next to Tameka's Lexus truck. When he and Neesh exited the truck, he spotted D-Roc, Walt and Fella a few cars down. he told Neesh to go ahead and he would catch up with her. as he walked over to Walt's Caprice, he acknowledged a few hustlers from around the way, who stood by their cars smoking weed. When he reached the Caprice he noticed the large Desert Eagle forty four on Walt's lap. He also caught a glimpse of Fella in the backseat filling his nose with coke. "What up Walt, what's happenin Roc, I know this is a difficult time for ya'll right now and I feel ya'll pain, Slim was cool as fuck." Mills said before looking in the backseat and asking Fella for a minute of his time. Walt shoved his Desert Eagle in Mills face while saying, "Get the fuck away from my ride homie, you aint give a fuck about Slim and you don't give no fucks about Fella neither. Push on before I twist yo bitch ass cap." Mills stared down the barrel of Walt's Desert Eagle with fury. He knew Walt would pull the trigger, but for some reason his body felt no fear.

"Walt chill out bro, not at Slim's funeral." Fella said from the backseat. "You better tell this nigga to get the fuck away from my ride with that fake love shit, for it be his funeral next." Walt shot back while staring unblinkingly into Mills eyes. Fella watched Mills jaws tighten and his hands ball into fists before turning his back on Walt and walking away in the opposite direction. "Hold up Mills" Fella yelled after him. He sprang from the backseat, and met Mills in the middle of the parking lot where he now stood. "What's up bro?" Fella said. "I just wanted to check on you. I know Slim was more like an older brother to you than a cousin, so I wanted to make sure you was aight. No matter what this bullshit is we goin through, I'll always have yo back, if you need me for anything I'm here for you, and when I say anything, I mean ANYTHING! You know how to contact me. You be careful bro, and know that my love for you is always pure." Mills said adamantly. He pulled Fella in for a hug and the two embraced for the first time in a long time. Before walking off Mills used the sleeve to his suit jacket to wipe the white residue from Fella's nose. "Call me bro, I'm here for you." Mills said before walking off. Mills entered the funeral home just as the ceremony began. Brandy, Black, Mek, Buck, Peko, Shawn Shawn, and Neesh all occupied one row. Mills squeezed in next to Neesh just as the minister was handing the floor over to Slim's mother.

Her words were concise. The loss of her only child was too much to bear. She couldn't stop crying long enough to deliver her message, so her sister quickly escorted her from the podium. Everyone visited Slim's casket to have their last look at the Slim gangster before having him taken away from them forever.

He had so many proclaimed girlfriends in attendance that the young lady pregnant with his child didn't know whether to be mad at Slim or to mourn him.

A number of females filled Slim's casket with tears, while his pregnant girlfriend cried on her sister's shoulder and awaited her turn to say goodbye to her unborn seed's sire. All hell broke loose in front of Slim's casket as one of his proclaimed girlfriends continuously kissed him on the lips while trying to climb into the casket with him. Slim's baby mother lost it. She grabbed the girl by her hair and went to work on her face with her free hand.

As those two exchanged blows, the funeral turned into a melee. The pregnant one's sister joined the fight, then the other girls friend jumped in headfirst to assist her homegirl and Slim's funeral went from a ceremony to a royal rumble.

Slim's mother and his relatives started pulling the girls apart, but the girls somehow managed to lock back up. D-Roc, Fella, and Walt had to come down to the casket and regulate the situation. As they manhandled the women, the rest of those in attendance made their exit.

Those who weren't going to the burial peeled out of the lot as if terrorists had invaded the funeral, while the others patiently awaited Slim's hearse so they could fall in line.

On the way to Slim's burial, D-Roc received a disturbing call. "Yeah what up?" D-Roc said as tears poured down his face. "Ya boy look real good in a casket huh?" the caller said humorously. "Who the fuck is this?" D-Roc yelled into the phone while sniffing up his tears. "This the nigga you love to hate, hahaha! Aye I aint know gangsters cried. Hahaha!" the caller laughed. "You a dead man, bitch ass nigga! Enjoy all the laughs now, cause when I find out who you are, you dead mutha fucka!" D-Roc yelled. Walt and Fella asked in unison, "Who the fuck is that?" "Ha ha ha ya'll niggas aint no killers, and I hope yo homeboy slim run into my dogs in hell, so they can bite em in his ass, ha! Ha! Ha!" The caller said as he hung up laughing in D-Roc's ear. D-Roc continued to yell threats into the phone long after the caller disconnected. "Roc chill the fuck out!" Walt yelled as D-Roc screamed into the phone at the top of his lungs. "man that was some bitch ass nigga talking about he killed Slim, talking some shit about we aint nothing but some dog killers and he hope Slim sees his dogs in hell so they can bite him in his ass… man I'm telling you bro when I find out who that clown nigga is, I swear to God ima kill em." D-Roc yelled. Walt didn't need any time to think. He knew exactly who it was. He and Slim had only killed two dogs in their lifetime, and those dogs belonged to Brandy's old boyfriend, Chris! He calmed D-Roc down and explained his logic to him and Fella. Once Walt reminded them of Chris's dogs rushing out of the room during their robbery on him, the connection hit them over the head like a ton of bricks.

They had robbed several cats from the Mt. Vernon area, but Chris was the wealthiest, which in their minds made him the most dangerous. Chris was more than likely behind every attempt on their lives that occurred on Mt. Vernon. The boy had paper and top dawg rank on the money earning Mt. Vernon strip.

D-Roc clutched his big boy 9mm Taurus while gritting his teeth. "That niggas a dead man." D-Roc growled. "Like yesterday" Fella added.

After school Pimp skipped his grandmother's house and headed straight for he and L's dope house. He strolled through the kitchen and walked in on L's getting sucked up by a fine red bone prostitute named Roxi. Roxi was completely naked as she squatted like a frog and licked L's rod like it was a Lolly pop. "Aw shit man!" Pimp said as L's palmed the back of Roxi's head.

"Aye where you going bro?" L's said as Pimp ran out of the living room back into the kitchen. L's laughed as Roxi swallowed his juices. Once he dumped his last drop of sperm into her throat, he pushed her head out the way, pulled up his pants, and chased after Pimp.

"Ha! Ha! Ha! Aye, you silly as fuck bro." L's said as pimp made faces that showed how disgusting he thought L's was. "No you silly, you're in there getting yo dick sucked by a nasty ass dope fiend. You trippin bro!" Pimp replied. "Shid aint nothing wrong with getting yo helmet cleaned off by a smoker, dope fiends got the best head, and the best twat." L's said matter of factly. Pimp burst into laughter because his partner's rationale sounded stupid to him. "Pussy is pussy bro." Pimp said. "How would you know? You aint had no pussy but Leslie's lil young ass coochie, pussy whipped nigga." L's shot back with an explosion of laughter. "Aight, aight!" Pimp said. Not wanting to talk about he and Leslie's sex life.

"I know aight nigga." L's said while playfully grabbing pimp in a head lock." I need some Swishers bro, lets go to the store." L's said after releasing Pimp from his head lock. Oak and Wilson was packed. Jeezy, lil Breeze and a few of their homies stood in front of the store, hugging the block like true block monsters. L's was Oak street born and bred, so he was no stranger to the Oak and Wilson block. He had grown up with these guys, so they knew how one another got down, and respected each other's gangster.

"What up Jeezy, sup lil Breeze, Tuck, Domi, What ya'll niggas into?" L's asked. "Shit just pumping tryna get that bread blood." Jeezy shot back. "I can dig it. I'm bout to grab some Sweets, you tryna match one?" L's asked as he and Pimp walked in the store. "You know them Swishers don't get no play on Oak and Wil, put it in a backwood, and we can smoke and joke." Jeezy said. "Its on." L's yelled over his shoulder while laughing under his breath because he knew the guys from Oak and Wilson only smoked out of backwood cigars. It was part of their trademark and something that they took very seriously.

Meanwhile, Mills, Brandy, Peko and Shawn Shawn sat in Peko's dope house blowing on good green, and talking about Dee's fatal attraction to Peko. "Man I'm telling you bro, dat bitch Dee been tripping." Peko said "What's up wit her?" Mills asked. "This bitch be calling my phone and pager all hours of the night and shit, leaving lil freaky messages tryna get a brother hemmed up. Shy almost heard them shits one time, and you know she gone lose it if she catch the kid cheating again." Peko explained. "Ha! Ha! Ha! Ha! You just had to hit that. You should have followed yo big head instead of your little one." Mills said.

"You laughing and shit bro, but this is serious, man this bitch tryna compare herself to Shy, like I'm ah leave my family for that trick!" Peko continued. "That's what you get nigga for not being able to keep yo dick in yo pants, ya'll niggas kill me, ya'll can have a good bitch, yet and still ya'll out in the street cheating with a slut." Brandy added. Shawn was in tears, as Mills and Brandy teamed up on his brother. Peko couldn't help it, he had everything a man wanted in a woman with Shy, but he still cheated. Having sex with other women was like a sickness for him. "Man, I'm ending that shit this week bro, for sure." Peko said. "That's what you said last month Pee, that lil bitch gone bend over and you gone be through. You got a sensitive dick head nigga." Brandy said. "Aw that's cold." Peko said as Mills and Shawn shook off their laughter, "Enough about that bitch." Brandy said "Have ya'll heard about them lil niggas Pimp and L's?" "Yeah I heard them lil niggas killed those Detroit boys on Miller and Oak. Them lil niggas name is in the streets like a mutha fucka." Peko added. "Who is the lil niggas?" Mills asked. Shid if I know. Brandy said. "They some lil niggas, one of them mess wit one of my girls, home girls, lil sister, she talk about them lil niggas like they God." Shawn added. They stayed there smoking and kicking it until the sky turned black and sent them each on their individual mission.

D-Roc, Walt and Fella sat in Walt's basement filling India's nose with powder and her lungs with chronic smoke. Fella remembered India running out of Chris's house the day they robbed him, and figured she was still one of his booty calls. After picking her up, getting her high off cocaine, weed, and liquor, he got her talking. They tricked her out of all the information on Chris she knew. They had her right where they wanted her, and they delivered the killer blow by offering her a thousand dollars to set him up. She quickly agreed, thinking she was only setting him up to get robbed. All it took was one call and Chris quickly accepted her booty call. After finding out he was home alone, she ended the call, telling him she'd be there in twenty minutes. Fella loaded his nine shot Mossberg pump while Walt loaded his twin Desert Eagles, and D-Roc checked his twin Smith and Wessons. Once they were ready for action, Fella told India it was time to roll. "Ya'll gotta give me my money first." India said with greed. Fella pulled a roll of bills from his pocket, counted out a thousand dollars, and threw the stack on her lap. She counted it then said, "Alright let's roll." Little did India know she would never get to spend that money. The ride to Chris's would be her final ride. It only took ten minutes for Walt to reach Chris's apartment in Poindexter village. It was a quarter till twelve am and the g-ride blended in perfectly with the darkness of the night. Fella stood on the side of the door with his pump ready for action. D-Roc and Walt stood on the opposite side of the door with their automatics hidden behind their legs. India nervously knocked on the door "Who is it?" Chris yelled. "Its India" She yelled back. Chris snatched the door open with his tech nine clenched by his side. "Come in, why you standing there looking stupid?" Chris said with a big "I'm bout to get some pussy" smile on his face.

As Chris held the door open for India, Fella bounced off the wall and hit him in the chest with the pump. "BLOWL!" The sound of the Mossberg along with the sight of Chris's insides jumping out of his body scared India half to death. She tried to back out the doorway, but Walt slumped her with a shot to the back of her head.

Fella kicked the door open wider and stepped over Chris's body. Chris's young black

Koby pit-bull stood by the couch barking at the intruders. Fella sent two Mossberg slugs into the pups skull. Blood and bone matter splattered on the couch. D-Roc stood over Chris's already dead body emptying his twin Smith and Wessons into the corpse. It wasn't until the sound of his empty chambers clicking that he snapped back to reality. Before fleeing the scene, Walt dug in India's pocket and took the thousand dollars Fella had given her. Then dumped two slugs into Chris's corpse. "That's for Slim gangsta pussy." Walt growled before running out the door.

Revenge cleansed the soul, and relieved one of stress. Tupac said it best: "Revenge is the sweetest joy next to getting pussy!"   "Peaceful Journey Slim".

-CHAPTER EIGHTEEN-

Pimp had a funny feeling as he walked to the store. He didn't know why but his intuition was telling him to be alert as he walked up Oak street. The street was clear which was strange for a crack strip. Pimp fixed his fifteen shot nine millimeter as it slid around his waist. He gained a sense of security from the feel of his steel. His pager sounded off distracting him for the few seconds it took for an old school galaxy to turn onto the street. Pimp looked up just in time to dive out of the way of the first shot. He landed behind the car parked by the curb as the gunman continued letting off rounds. Bullets tore through the car as Pimp fumbled for his nine. He didn't know how he was going to get out of this ambush, but he knew whatever happened he was going out blazing. The shots stopped for a few seconds, but Pimp could hear the gunmen reloading their weapons. "It's now or never." Pimp said to himself. He rose to his feet, and backpedaled through the field directly behind him while unloading his clip at his attackers. The driver of the Galaxy had no choice but to pull off as Pimp's nine millimeter shells thumped up against his ride. Pimp dashed through the field, over a fence and through a backyard. He pressed his back up against the side of the house he hid behind, then peeked his head from behind the wall. The coast was clear. "That's why I love you baby, you never let me down." Pimp said to the barrel of his nine. Then gave the tip of it a kiss.

L's was pulling up as Pimp ran up the steps. He knew something wasn't right, because Pimp still had his nine out as he ran in the house. L's quickly killed the engine and ran in behind him. Pimp sat on the couch with his hand covering his shoulder. "What up bro, what the fuck is going on?" L's yelled as he became frantic at the sight of his main man's blood. "I came out the store, and got dumped on by some niggas in a blue Galaxy!" Pimp said as L's assisted him with removing his shirt. "It's only a graze." L's said as he spotted the small gash Pimp was bleeding from. "Stand up and check yo self for any other holes bro." L's said with anger in his voice, and tears in his eyes. "Who the fuck was it, I swear to God we gone kill the mutha fuckas!" L's said while pulling an AK from under the couch. "I don't know who it was bro, they wore ski masks and I aint never seen that car before." Pimp answered. "Fuck man!" L's yelled with anger in him. He seemed to be more touched by the situation than Pimp. Although Pimp was a year younger he was always the calmer of the two. "Just chill bro, as I've always heard my big bro say everything in the dark comes to light. We gone find them pussies, then we gone Kill'um!" Pimp said Calmly.

❧ ❧ ⑧ ⑧ ⑧ ⑧ ⑧ ❧ ❧

On the other side of town, Peko sat in front of Dee's apartment, thinking of the words to say to her. He flicked his roach to the ground as he knocked on the door. Dee opened the door wearing thin linen high rider shorts, with a matching sports bra. Peko could tell she didn't have any panties on, and he was already becoming aroused. Dee's body was to die for, and she knew it. This was Peko's third time visiting her this month, every time he had come over to break up with her, he got hypnotized by her body and turned it into a booty call. Peko was so high, he was eating stars, and the drugs made his little head easy to influence. He could feel his manhood growing in his boxers, as he stared at the deep gap between her legs, but he snapped out of his horny rage before he walked through the door. "What up Pee?" Dee said after running her tongue over her soft luscious lips. "Not a whole lot." Peko replied. Dee locked the door behind him while grabbing his hand. "Hold up Dee, Ima cut to the chase, cause I see where you tryna go with this, and I aint tryna go there." "You mean to tell me you don't want to have recess on this playground?" Dee said while putting one of Peko's hands on her ass. "Dig Dee, I told you I got a girl, and a family, and you starting to get beside yourself wit calling my phone all hours of the night, and tryna compare ya self to my family. This shit is over, this aint no ass call, this is goodbye." Peko said adamantly, while pulling his hand from her ass. "Alright Peko, I am tired of fighting for something I can't have anyway, but we can at least end this on a good note right?" Dee was back in Peko's face. She grabbed a handful of his half hard penis while whispering in his ear. "Looks like somebody don't want to leave." She pulled his manhood through his boxer hole with ease, due to his low sagging jeans. She squatted and cocked her legs open so he could get a good look at the muff between her legs. She flicked her tongue at the head of his penis a few times then wrapped her mouth around his pole. Peko couldn't control himself. His full nine inches grew in her mouth, and he stopped resisting. Dee pulled his pants down to his ankles and pushed him back on the couch, Peko was quickly mesmerized as she slid off her tight shorts. She slid down on Peko's pole, and rode him like a wild bull. Dee was so wet, her juices drenched his boxers, as she slammed down on him. Peko didn't like being dominated, nor did he want to cum yet, so he stopped her long enough to bend her over the couch. He had let Dee trick him a few times, into having sex without a condom. She said she didn't like the way it felt, and swore she was on the pill, he never trusted her, but her love muffin was so good that he always gave into her game. He pulled his boxers down to his knees, put his pole halfway in, adjusted his position, pushed her cheeks apart, then slammed his pole in her cave at rapid speed. Dee was a freak, and she loved pain. She backed into every one of Peko's strokes with force, while biting down on her bottom lip and looking at him over her shoulder. "Oh Peko, don't stop I'm bout to cum!" She yelled. Peko was in the act of exploding himself, but as he tried to pull out of her, she wrapped her hands around his waist holding him in her while she backed up on him, until he released his fluids in her. "What the fuck is you doing Dee! That's the shit I be talking about, that's why I'm through fucking with you, I know you tryna get pregnant bitch!" Peko said while fixing his clothes. "I aint gotta try, I already am nigga, and its yours now tell yo precious bitch Shy dat!" "Shiid no you aint!" Peko screamed. "Yes I am!" Dee replied. "It aint mine, bitch you be fucking outta both draw legs!" Peko said. "Yeah nigga it's yours and you gone take care of me and my baby." Dee replied. "Imagine that, you car hoppin ass hoe. Cum thirsty, once a month bleeding bitch!" Peko screamed back at Dee. "Yea I'm a car hopper, and I hopped my ass right in to yo car and yo stupid ass got me pregnant, and you gone take care of us too." Dee said. "Imagine that." Peko said as he walked out the door.

It took only a few days for Pimp to get the 411 on who was behind his assassination attempt. Jeezy's girlfriend Ty'eisha learned from one of her homegirls that the Galaxy belonged to the Detroit boys. Ty'eisha immediately informed Jeezy, and he didn't waste any time telling his homeboys. He startled Pimp and L's as he ran up the steps. Pimp grabbed his nine, while L's rushed to the window with his Mac eleven. "Be cool Pimp, its Jeezy." L's said as he snatched the door open. "What up bro?" L's said as Jeezy stepped in the house. "Them coward as Detroit boys is what's up." Jeezy replied. "What's up with em Jay?" Pimp asked. "That's who dumped on you in the Galaxy last week, my lil flame's homegirl fuck wit the niggas, and when she heard them talking about it she told my girl, and the rest is self explanatory. Them niggas on Linwood and Fulton right now bringing spring in with a barbecue, they slipping homie." Jeezy explained. "Like a mutha fucka." L's said. "Strap up Pimp and lets go get these niggas." L's said while running to the back room. Pimp grabbed the AK from under the couch, L's came running back into the living room with one of Peaches trick's car keys in his hand. He threw the keys to Jeezy and said, "We need you to grip the wheel." "Say no more my nig, lets ride." Jeezy replied. L's tucked his Mack under his shirt, while throwing an extra clip in his back pocket. Pimp wrapped his AK up in a towel, and they ran out the back door. In a matter of minutes they were creeping up on the house from the back side. Jeezy crept up real slow, letting the car cruise. Pimp scanned the back yard, noticing more females than males. He spotted most of the Detroit boys in the front yard drinking and smoking. "Pull up in front and hit the brakes Jay." Pimp ordered from the backseat. L's never gave the car a chance to make it to the front. As they passed the guys on the side of the house, he rose out the window and yelled, "Aye, Aye! What up bro." They turned to look, and L's opened fire. Pimp let the chopper go as the guys hit the deck, Pimp kept his head tucked tightly in the car, while chopping down everything in sight. L's aimed for the ground as he watched his victims dive for the dirt.

Mills was driving up Fulton in the opposite direction. He had his system blasting, so he never heard the artillery sounding off. He pulled to the corner of Fulton and Linwood, and noticed a car directly across the street, splashing with heavy artillery. He pushed Neesh's head down and quickly bent the corner. Jeezy turned right behind Mills as Pimp and L's emptied their clips. As Pimp pulled his chopper back in the window he noticed Mills truck in front of him. He hit the floor just as Mills made another quick turn and floored the engine up the street. Jeezy kept the pedal to the metal as he sped across Mound Street, and swerved through traffic crossing Main.

After hearing of the three dead bodies, and seven wounded at the house on Linwood, Pimp and L's were laying low. Pimp spent most of his time at home, while L's bounced around from place to place. Mills had been seeing very little of his brother. He spent most of his nights with Neesh at her place. His business distracted him from his grandmother as well. Had he been around more often he would have noticed the change in his brother's behavior, and his grandmother's health. Grandma Mills was stubborn, and stuck in her ways. When Mills offered to get her a new house she refused. She said she would live in her house until death did them part. She was old fashioned and worked for everything she had. Trading it in for something new was not an option. Her old home, and her old car was as good as it got for her. She hid her cancer from her grandsons, because she didn't want to worry them, or be put in the hospital, no matter how bad her health was. She felt that when it was her time to go there was nothing she could do to stop it. In a way, she was ready. After stopping by his grandmother's and seeing jimmy home again, Mills decided this would be a good night to stay home. While Mills and jimmy played NBA Live on Playstation, D-Roc and his crew were driving up his grandmother's street. As they passed Mills truck, Walt let off a few shots into the vehicle. Mills jumped to his feet at the sound of the gunshots. "Stay right here Jim. I'll be right back." Mills said as he ran out the room. Mills ran outside his grandmother's house with his gun ready for action. He caught a glimpse of the back of the car as it turned off the street. Jimmy followed Mills down the steps without him knowing it. He peeked through the window, with his nine tucked under his shirt, ready to back his brother up if needed. Mills circled his truck, checking out the damage. Most of the windows had been shot out, and a line of holes trailed up the driver's side of the vehicle, leading to a large hole in the hood of the truck. Mills knew his engine was totaled, so he didn't waste his time checking it. As he ran back in the house, Jimmy took off up the steps.

Fella didn't like what had just taken place back at Mills grandmothers' house. He would never agree to doing anything to harm Mills, especially at his grandmother's home. "Fuck that lil Fells, you wit us or him?" Nigga its us against the world" D-Roc said as Fella yelled at him and Walt. "For real Fells you starting to get on my nerves with saving that nigga, you can't be his soldier for life." D-Roc continued knowing that would press

Fella's buttons. "Fella aint nobodies soldier, I'm a fucking gee, but it's lines you just

don't cross, and even though we aint fucking with each other no more, I'm a never bring

harm to Mills, we go too far back for that." Fella explained. "Man fuck that nigga bro, he

aint eating with us, break bread, or play dead out this bitch, and that goes for Mills, Buck

and whoever else aint breaking us off!" D-Roc screamed. Walt wasn't one to use a lot of

words. HE was all action. But he too was tired of Fella saving Mills. He liked Fella but

he knew he would never cross Mills. If it wasn't for him being Slim's cousin, Walt knew

he would've been slumped Fella and left him in an alley to die. Now that Slim was gone,

he didn't see any reason to keep Fella around. If Fella wasn't all in with him and D-Roc

he had to go. … No ifs ands or buts. Walt rubbed his hands together, while cutting his

eyes at Fella. D-Roc noticed the look on Walt's face, and knew exactly what was on his

mind. "I'm sorry Slim, you my nigga, but yo cousin has ran his course." D-Roc said to

himself, as him and Walt locked eyes. What was understood didn't need to be explained.

-CHAPTER NINETEEN-

It had been a few weeks since Mills truck had been shot up. He didn't have any

proof but he knew D-Roc and Walt were behind it. Instead of feeding into their jealousy,

he decided to make them more jealous. He was now with H.T. looking at a 97 Lexus

coop. Mills pushed his rental through traffic while smiling at the thought of D-Roc's face

when he laid eyes on his new whip. Mills pulled in behind Peko's Impala, as Peko paced the sidewalk. All of the windows were busted out, his tires were flat, and key marks trailed around the vehicle, stopping at the front of his car. "Yo stupid ass Dee! Why you fuck wit my car!" He yelled into his phone. "Fuck yo car nigga, what about me and my baby." Dee replied. "Bitch fuck you, and that aint my baby. You so stupid that's why I aint given you shit, you think you did something by fucking up my ride, wait till you see the new one I replace it with. You dumb ass bitch." Peko screamed. "I'm stupid huh? Well you stupid too cause you let a bitch like me get the number to yo house, and I left yo Shy a little message too, so say goodbye to yo happy home, rookie." Dee said then immediately gave Peko the dial tone.

Mills stood to the side of him as he dialed the number back. "Fuck man!" He screamed repeatedly. "Pee chill the fuck out bro, you letting this bitch drive you crazy." Mills said while grabbing his shirt. "Man this bitch batty bro; look at my window on the driver side." Peko said. Mills walked around the car and reached in the window and pulled out a brick. Attached were pictures of an ultrasound, and a piece of paper that read congratulations. "So what bro, just because a bitch is pregnant don't mean it's yours." Mills said as he walked back around the car with the brick in hand. "Man that aint even half of it bro, that bitch said she called my house and left Shy a message on the machine. Bro Shy gone wig out if she find out I'm cheating again. She pregnant wit my second child, and we getting our relationship back on track. I don't need this shit right now bro." Peko explained. "Well, what you waiting for, call the crib and see if she got the message, if not run home and erase the message." Mills said. "Damn good thinking bro, I don't know what I would do without you." Peko said as he quickly dialed the number to he and Shy's apartment. Shy snatched the phone up on the second ring. "Hello." Shy answered in an irritated tone. "What up babe." Peko said. "Don't what up bae me Peko, I'm through playing games with you, come and get your shit and take it to yo other baby mama house." Shy said. "That aint my fucking baby Shy, and me and her only happened once, it was a mistake you know I love you bae." "Apparently not enough and I'm tired of being cheated on, so just come get your stuff, before I get pissed and start fucking shit up. I'm not playing with you." Shy screamed. "Hold the fuck up bae, you acting like you the only one hurt behind this shit, I'm hurt too." Peko said. Shy slammed the phone down as he tried to use reverse psychology. "Shy! Shy! Shy!" His yells were to no avail; the only response he got was a dial tone.

Pimp sat on Leslie's bed waiting for L's .It was early July, and the beginning of a sick drought. L's was over a half hour late and Pimp was beginning to worry. He paged L's a number of times and L's had yet to page him back. Pimp called a cab and went downstairs to await its arrival. Liley sat on the couch with her new man friend. They were both nodding off while scratching like they had been bitten by a thousand mosquitoes. Pimp didn't really like Liley's new friend, because every time he came around Liley ended up getting higher than Rick James. Pimp didn't' have enough knowledge of any other drug other than crack or cain, but he knew the drug Liley and the man where high off of was neither one of the two. He caught her injecting herself with a needle one evening but before he could question her she passed out. Pimp's cab arrived quickly and he was out the door. He wanted to keep an eye on Liley until Leslie got home from school but L's came first, and his gut was telling him that L's needed him. When the cab turned down Sherman, Pimp's intuition was verified. Peaches, Roxi and a few other hookers were being walked out the house in handcuffs. Behind them were a few smokers, and several tricks. The whole house was surrounded by men in black, while regular uniformed police assisted them with taping off the street. Onlookers crowded the sidewalk as the men in black tore through L's car. They ripped out speakers, dash boards, carpeting and the whole nine. Pimp stopped the cab a block away, and watched the scene for a moment, searching for L's in the back of numerous police vehicles. L's was the last person escorted out in cuffs. Pimp's heart raced as his only friend was being taken away from him. He directed the cab back to Liley's house. He went back up in Leslie's room, and called L's mother to inform her of the bad news. Pimp's situation had gone from bad to worse. Not only was he suffering a drought but his right hand man was gone.

L's sat in the juvenile detention center for a month and a half before receiving a year sentence for CCW and trafficking a gram of crack to an undercover. In that month and a half Pimp had been sold plenty of garbage work. Liley's man friend had been hearing Pimp, and Liley talk about the drought, and the garbage he's been getting. He had been watching Pimp closely for the past few months, and he liked his style. Pimp was quiet, watchful, attentive, and serious about his grind. He wanted to talk to Pimp but, Liley told him Pimp wasn't big on strangers. After telling Liley, he had a connect with some good product for Pimp, she agreed to introduce him.

Late one evening, Pimp came strolling through the front door as Liley and her man friend watched television. The first thing Pimp noticed was that they were sober.

"Sup son, let me talk to you for a minute." Liley said. "What's goin on?" Pimp asked. "I wanna introduce you to my friend Sonny, he says he knows where you can get some good shit at." Liley explained. Pimp didn't say a word. He was puzzled, because he always heard Mills say, "Very little people offer their help without wanting something in return." "Pimp this is Sonny, Sonny this is Pimp."

"Sup" Pimp replied.

"What's happening youngin." "Liley won't you give us two men a few minutes alone." Sonny said. Liley headed into the kitchen. "Have a seat youngin." Sonny said while patting on the couch. "I'm cool." Pimp said. "How old are you main man?" Sonny asked. "Check it out O.G. I don't mean no disrespect, but what exactly is this about? Is this about me, or is it about you hooking me up with some good product?" Pimp asked. "Actually youngin its about both, I like yo style, and no matter how things may seem, there's more to this old head than what you see at face value. It's a lot of money out here and because of my habit I can't get it no more, I aint always have this monkey on my back, but that's neither here nor there, I see a lot of the young me in you. You got a lot of potential to go far in the game, and because I care about Liley, and she care about you, I felt the least I could do was hip you to a few tricks." Sonny explained. "And what does being hipped to new tricks cost me? And where do you profit from it?" Pimp asked. Sonny smiled at Pimp's wittiness. "That's a good question, because very few people give, without the intention of receiving, and in this case, all I wanna receive is the satisfaction of seeing money made. You see I've took a liking to a few different youngsters, and I've offered them the same opportunity, but because I am a heroin addict, they feel it's nothing to be learned from me, but a wise person knows, a lesson lies within everyone. Even if the lesson is learning what not to do. You dig what I'm saying youngin?" Pimp could relate to Sonny's situation. He thought of everything he learned from Magic Mike, who was an all-out dope fiend that all the hustlers disrespected, including L's. Pimp still had his guard up, but he lowered his defenses a little. "Fourteen, I'm fourteen." Pimp said. "Come again?" Sonny replied. "I'm fourteen, you asked me my age right?" Sonny smiled. "I guess that's our icebreaker huh." Sonny said. "I guess so, what's up wit them tricks, and that connect?" Pimp said. "Tell me something young Pimp, what do you know about heroin?" Sonny asked. "Heri what?" Pimp replied. Sonny was surprised by Pimp's ignorance to the oldest drug known to man. "You got me on that O.G. I'm lost." Pimp said. "Listen young Pimp, the money you making from crack, that can't even compare to the money you can make from heroin. You right here in the middle of Mount Vernon, and Long Street. And you don't know about dog food? Listen Pimp this is the heroin capital, because heroin is capital around here. If you give me thirty days with showing you about this heroin and you don't make more money than you can estimate making off that crack, I'll plug you wit some of my guys from California that never run out of cocaine, and despite my habit, they love me, and owe me plenty of favors, so whatever you buy I can have them front you the same thing." Pimp pondered the proposition for a moment, weighing the pros and cons of accepting and denying the proposal. "So when does our thirty days start?" Pimp asked.

⤲⤲   ⤲⤲   ⑧   ⑧   ⑧   ⑧   ⑧   ⤲⤲   ⤲⤲

Three months had passed since Shy had learned of Peko's involvement with Deedrah. Peko was back living at his mother's. Shy had calmed down, and started talking to him again, but Peko didn't leave her much of a choice. He purposely left pieces of his clothing and jewelry at he and Shy's apartment so he would have reason to stop by other than his son. After a month Shy was giving in to his apologies, and after two months she was allowing him back in between her legs. She still hadn't allowed him to move back in, nor had she allowed them to become a couple. Peko wanted Shy back, but for now, he enjoyed the benefits of having two baby mothers. He finally accepted Dee, and their baby, Dee didn't mind being second place to Shy. Peko had a key to her apartment and a key to the muffin between her legs, and Deedrah didn't mind him coming and going as he pleased. Peko pulled his Deville into Grant hospital with a smile on his face, as two nurses stood by the door admiring his vehicle. H.T. had the Cadillac loaded. It has wet purple candy paint, a white rag top, chrome grill, bumper and trimmings, with a dark tint, and some chrome eighteen inch blades. The interior was leather, with purple pinstripes, and the trunk was on boom bam blast!!

Peko flicked the last of his hydro filled blunt to the ground as he entered the hospital. His heart was racing as he thought of Shy pushing his daughter out on her own. As the elevator skipped from one floor to the next Peko prayed he was on time.

&ℴ& &ℴ& ⑧ ⑧ ⑧ ⑧ ⑧ &ℴ& &ℴ&

Shawn Shawn shuffled through his music looking for no limit's latest album. He inserted the CD and listened to C-Murder's deep voice talk about that tru shit as he pulled away from Lisa's apartment. As he neared the stop sign at the corner he thought his eyes were deceiving him. He watched a black van with the letters D.E.A plastered on the side of it in big white letters turn into the alley behind Lisa's apartment. He smashed the gas wasting no time looking for intersecting traffic. "Damn!" He cursed under his breath. Lisa was like family and he felt bad knowing she was on her way back to prison. He shook his head out of empathy. Five minutes sooner and he would have been in cuffs as well. Thanks to the game God for the timing of the birth of his brother's second child. Had Peko not have called him and told him to meet him at the hospital he would've been a sitting duck, and headed up shit creek without a paddle.

Ten minutes later Shawn Shawn's phone began to ring. "Yeah what up?" He answered on the second ring. "What's up nephew it's Lisa, you got some big spenders here waiting on you." Shawn Shawn couldn't respond. He couldn't believe Lisa was trying to set him up. Lisa had always been true to the game and handled the game's adversity like a true soldier. Up until this point she had always been loyal, and it hurt to witness her fold.

"Hello, Shawn Shawn you there?" Lisa yelled into the phone. Shawn Shawn rolled down his window and tossed his phone out into traffic. "Not today Lisa baby." He said to himself.

᷾᷾᷾ ᷾᷾᷾ ⑧ ⑧ ⑧ ⑧ ⑧ ᷾᷾᷾ ᷾᷾᷾

Mills pulled out of H.T.'s car garage in his money green Lexus coop. The vehicle was fully loaded, with gold flakes, a peanut butter brown rag top, you can't see me tint, some eighteen inch gold, Lorenzo's, and King Kong in the trunk. The interior was all beige, soft leather seats, flat screen TV in the dashboard, with a VHL VCR built into the floor next to the automatic shift handle. As Mills rode up Mound Street, he thought about stopping at Brandy's but quickly changed his mind when he noticed Berkley filled with police and detectives. Fella's house was surrounded, while detective White and Brown escorted him out in cuffs. The sound of Mills phone snapped him back to reality, as he sat at the corner causing traffic to pile up behind him. "Hello?" "What's up bro it's Bee." "What up Bee, what the fuck is goin on at Fells crib?" Mills asked. "You aint seen the news this evening?" Brandy inquired. "Nah why?" Mills replied. "bro they charge him with Chris and that girl's murder. They just snatched him out of his mom's crib." Brandy answered with a cracking voice. Mills had no response. He parked in front of his grandmother's house with thoughts of him talking to Fella at Slim's funeral. He wondered if Fella would have called him to ride on Chris would he be in cuffs this evening too. Thoughts of his sick grandmother and his baby brother being left alone ran through his mind. Brandy's voice brought him back to reality as she screamed his name through the phone. Mills conversed with her as he entered the house and climbed the steps leading to his room. As he passed his grandmother's room he noticed her laid on the floor next to her bed. "momma!" Mills yelled as he ran to her aid. Her body was pale, and she fought for her life with each short breath she took. Mills quickly dialed 911.

Pimp was in his first heroin spot with Sonny when he received the call about his grandmother. In thirty days time Sonny helped Pimp make his first fifteen thousand dollars, which was almost as much as he'd stacked from hustling crack in three years. It didn't take Pimp long to make the switch, that Sonny promised would one day make him rich. Mills wanted to pick up his little brother, but Pimp quickly told him he would meet him at the hospital. When Pimp arrived, Mills was seated in the waiting area. Pimp rarely seen his brother cry, but today he just couldn't hold it back. Mills wrapped his arms around his brother, as he apologized for not paying closer attention to him and their grandmother. Being the man of the house he blamed himself for his grandmother's health. The dope game had separated him from his only blood family. The game had separated his mother and father from him and his baby brother. Now it was doin the same thing to him, his younger brother and grandmother. He now understood what it meant to be in too deep. Though Buck and Neesh both talked to him about leaving the game, he still hadn't given it much thought. It seemed like the deeper he got in the game, the harder it became for him to leave. It was like a person trying to kick an old cigarette habit.

He had reached a status where quitting had to be agreed on, and planned ahead of time. He could not just give hundreds of thousands of dollars worth of dope away, and say he was finished. Mills knew he had to have a talk with Chico, his connect, and it had to be done sooner than later, because he didn't want his baby brother falling victim to the game. He was walking in his mothers and father's footsteps, and he refused to let Jimmy walk in his. Little did Mills know he was three years too late.

Shortly after Mills and Jimmy had a seat, the doctor arrived. He didn't know how to explain to the young boys that their grandmother was dying, but they had to know. The doctor was subtle but that didn't stop the tears. Their grandmother had no longer than a month to live, and there was nothing they could say or do to change that. When they entered their grandmother's room, she was wide awake. They both stood in the middle of the floor, trying to controll the tears that ran down their faces.

"Come on over here, and wipe those tears from ya'll faces unless they are tears of joy." Grandma Mills said. The boys took baby steps as they gravitated towards her. "I raised you boys to be strong, don't be coming in here acting weak. I've lived my life and served my purpose which is walking in the name of the Lord I'm going to heaven and that's my utopia. So be happy and praise the lord for choosing your grandmother as a houseguest." Grandma Mills let out as much laughter as she could without coughing up her insides, but the boys were hurt, even if they wanted to, they couldn't laugh with her. They both spent the night at their grandmother's bedside. Mills mind raced the whole night. He wondered why God always chose the best people to die, while allowing the worst people to live. Here D-Roc and lil Walt was killing people every day with no remorse, and God allowed them to live and keep taking lives. His grandmother was pure, and non-judgmental, she served the Lord every day of her life and God took her over all the evil doers. Unlike Grandma Mills, Mills was non-religious, but he wondered if the Lord was trying to send him a message by taking all the people he loved. For the first time since he was a child, Mills conversed with the "almighty one" before dozing off into a light sleep.

-CHAPTER TWENTY-

It didn't take Black and Brandy long to decide they were made for one another. They were everything the other wanted in a mate. Their relationship became serious quick. Brandy was slowly but shortly pulling away from the game, while Black was cutting deeper into it. Lil Walt was his protégé before he got locked down and he thought he'd be able to get his young killer back on his team, but Lil Walt made it clear that he was a jackboy for life, which Black wasn't getting back into. It wasn't that Black needed Walt, because once he showed his face on Mound & Gilbert the block was his, he just felt that it would be good to have his day one nigga by his side, Walt was like a little brother to him, Black had taught him everything he knew, but Lil Walt was all grown up now, and black had to respect it. He hoped the rift between Mills, Walt, and D-Roc didn't escalate into gunplay because no matter how tight he and Walt were, his loyalty resided with Mills. Black pushed his new Intrepid up Mound Street headed for his number one money machine, that he had his new protégé operating out of. Lil Mark was a baby when

Black went down, but now he was a buck wild teen, with all the potential in the world. All he lacked was guidance, which Black was now providing for him. Black wasn't the flashy type. He wore no jewelry, and his car had no rims or beat in the trunk. Beside the tint on the windows, the car was exactly the way it looked when he copped it. As he pulled in front of the row of apartments, he spotted two men with pistols running out of his spot. It was dark, so he didn't recognize their faces, but he got their attention as he let his .40 caliber chase them down. "Pokka! Pokka! Pokka!" the jackers ducked and zig zagged, but quickly returned fire.

Black continued dumping off shots as the robbers aimlessly fired back. He knew he hit one of his targets when he saw the guy's body spin and fall to the ground. Black took off after the robbers as lil Mark came running out the front door with his pistol in hand. The robber that wasn't hit let off a few shots to slow Black down, then helped his partner up and dragged his body around the corner. Black licked off a few more shots while in pursuit, but his chase was to no avail, the robbers were peeling away from the scene by the time he rounded the corner.

Black angrily marched back to where Mark stood. "What the fuck happened?" Black asked. "That was them scandalous ass niggas Pook and Duke they wanted some work, I let um in, then turn my back for a second to lock the door, and they upped on me." Lil Mark explained. "Where the fuck was ya' gun at?" Black screamed. "The niggas come buy work all the time so I put my pistol in my back pocket while I was locking the door and that's how they got the jump on me." Lil Mark said embarrassingly. "Damn Mark, what I tell you about slipping like that, you don't trust nobody but me, never put yo strap down, I don't give a fuck who you serving. Is anything left in the house?" Black asked.

"Nah big bro, they took everything." Lil Mark answered shamefully. Black's jaws tightened as he shook his head in disgust. "How much is everything." Black asked. "Like ten grand and half a slab." Lil Mark answered. He looked at the ground because he couldn't stand the look of disappointment on Black's face. "My mistake my loss, I'll work without pay until I make every dime back." Lil Mark said. Hoping he could make this right. Lil Mark was only fifteen years young, so Black knew he had alot more mistakes to make. If one didn't grow up fast in this game, the game would chew that person up and spit him or her out.

Black wanted to be sure that he got his point across to Mark without bruising his ego, so he chose his words wisely. "It's not about the money Mark, we can always get more money, but you only have one life and aint no getting that back. When it's gone, its gone, game over nah mean? This is a thinking man's game, start using your head before one of these thirsty ass niggas knock it off. Lock that door and let's go before the rollers get here. Black ordered.

After hitting an easy lick for a brick of cain, ten pounds of hydro, and fifteen thousand cash, D-Roc and Walt kicked back over one of Walt's loyal freak's house. They were semi keeping a low profile after learning of Fella's arrest. They weren't sure if Fella could handle a murder beef with his mouth closed, so they only came out to hit licks, and they never stayed at the same place longer than two or three days.

Fella on the other hand sat in the county jail without a helping hand. After all the robberies he'd committed, he had only ten thousand dollars to his name. He had a couple cars, and plenty jewelry but no one to sell his belongings to. He thought he'd be able to count on D-Roc and Walt for some help with his lawyer fees or at least to handle the selling of his belongings, so he could cash his lawyer out with that money but every time he had his mother reach out to them they fed her some B.S. It only took a couple weeks for them to change their numbers completely,. As the old saying goes, "There is no honor among thieves."

Fella had his mother give the most reputable attorney in Columbus the ten grand he had in his stash, and after a few short weeks he was receiving his second visit from the infamous attorney Clyde "the glide" Slaytor. His nickname came from the way he seemed to glide through all his cases.

Clyde "the glide" was known throughout the system as a shark. He could make any case disappear for the right amount of cash, but Fella knew that his ten grand wasn't nearly enough for his case, and "the glide" wasn't the type of attorney that showed any remorse for a client who was short on paper.

Fella walked into the small room assigned for him and Clyde's visit. He sat in a chair across the table from Clyde who was talking to another one of his clients on his cell phone. He quickly ended the call and reached across the table to give Fella a firm handshake while saying, "Mr. Stargell, how are you feeling today?" "I'm aight Mr. Slaytor, tell me something good." Fella replied. "Please just call me Clyde, and I do have some good news for you, but I also have some bad news. Which would you like to hear first?" Clyde asked. "I've heard enough bad news for one lifetime, give me the good." Fella answered.

"Well the good news is, I've found out who the prosecution's only witness is, and without her testimony they have no case. Have you ever heard the saying a case is only as strong as the prosecutor's witness? A case can only barely exist without a snitch I.E Witness." Clyde said while making a quote unquote gesture with his fingers. "That's a true statement by the way." Clyde continued. "Now for the bad news. The ten grand you gave me isn't going to be enough for my representation. I'm going to need at least twenty more thousand. This is a double homicide case, so I'm gonna have to work my ass off to get you some rhythm. Those numbers you gave me to contact your buddies for some more cash have been cut off. I talked to the guys once, they said they didn't know you. Our first court hearing is in February, so that gives you ninety days to come up with some more cash." Clyde shuffled through some folders while Fella sat in silence. He watched Fella squint his eyes and furrow his brows out of anger. Fella's jaw's tightened and he clasped his hands together to stop them from balling into fists. "I can't believe them niggas playing me like this." Fella thought. "Do you smoke?" Clyde asked, breaking Fella from his trance. "Yeah why?" Fella said with a hint of attitude. "Here you go, stuff these." Clyde said while secretly sliding Fella a pack of Newports across the table. "Well Mr. Stargell you have my number, you can call me collect if you have any questions, requests or new information." Clyde shook Fella's hand before heading for the door. "aye Clyde, you never told me that witnesses name." Fella said before Clyde made his exit. "Lisa Pittman." Clyde said on his way out the door.

The name echoed in Fella's head. Now he knew why Lisa hadn't been accepting his calls. She had turned on him. He never spoke about Chris around Lisa, but after Chris and India's death Lisa had started acting funny. Unbeknownst to Fella, India had told Lisa that she was going to kick it with Fella and his boys, and the next morning she was found dead. Lisa had been involved with Slim long enough to know how he and Fella got down. She knew they were jack boys and crazy, to say the least, so it didn't take her long to put the pieces of the puzzle together. As the guards escorted Fella back to his tank, the only thing on his mind was getting rid of Lisa. Clyde told him without a witness, his case barely existed and the only way to get her out the way now was by death. Soon as he reached his tank, he got on the phone. D-Roc and Walt were the only ones who could help him out now. He'd kept it gee, when the detectives interrogated him. The least his supposed to be homeboys could do was get rid of the witness for him. He may not have been able to count on them for cash, but he knew he could count on them for a 187, or so he thought.

Roc and Walt sat on the couch getting high off the weed and coke they just jacked for. Walt's mom screamed down in the basement telling him to pick up the phone. When he heard the voice on the phone he instantly became paranoid. "What the fuck I tell you about calling my phone nigga!" Walt yelled. "Slow the fuck down bro, ya'll been playing me real fucked up, changing ya'll numbers and shit. I thought we was family, now I need ya'll niggas help, it's fuck me huh?" Fella yelled back. "Who the fuck is that!" D-Roc asked Walt. "Listen my nigga, I aint gone tell you again, don't call me or Roc's phone, my momma's phone either. Nigga you said you a gee, now gee the fuck up, do yo time nigga, and remember yo momma healthy out here bro, keep it that way." Walt said with authority before hanging up.

Mills had been spending more time with his little brother these last few weeks. Jimmy didn't mind spending time with Mills. In fact he loved it, Mills was his idol. The shopping and kicking it was beyond cool, but he didn't want to chance being spotted by someone who knew him by the name that was ringing so loudly in the streets. Mills was being over protective of his baby brother, and between being with Mills and spending a few hours out of the day with his grandmother, Pimp's business was being neglected. Mills hadn't talked to Chico, but he knew by the year 2000, he wanted to be out the game, assisting Buck with enriching the black community, putting his baby brother through college, and starting a family with Neesh. 1999 was less than forty days away, so Mills knew he had to talk to Chico soon. He'd give Chico another year of hard grinding, then plug him in with Peko, who could move just as much product as him. Neesh was more than happy to hear Mills speak of leaving the game. She worried herself to death when he was out in the streets. She wanted to have a much needed talk with him but he always seemed to have a lot on his mind, and she didn't want to aggravate him. With his grandmother's health, him neglecting his little brother, and worrying about D-Roc and Walt, he stayed in a small state of despondency.

Mills, Neesh and Jimmy were now pulling into Grant hospital for their daily visit with grandma Mills. Last week the doctor informed Mills that her condition was getting worse, and it would probably be best for her if he agreed to let them pull the plug. Mills refused. When they strolled into the hospital they received horrifying news. Grandma Mills had passed away twenty minutes before they arrived.

The boys broke down in the hospital hallway then charged into their grandmother's room. they pushed past the nurses surrounding her bed and covered her body with their own. It took numerous doctors and nurses to remove Mills and Jimmy from their grandmother's corpse. They knew it was coming but there was no way to prepare for such a loss.

Mills did what he knew his grandmother would've wanted. He put it all in God's hands and silently said a prayer while watching her body be carried away. As Mills felt the warmth of the omnipresent lord and savior, his baby brother felt his own heart going cold. Everyone he loved was being taken from him, and for that, everyone would feel his pain.

Their grandmother's funeral came quickly. Mills kept it simple, because he knew that was how his g-ma would've wanted it. Mills spent the next few weeks in the house. He even attended Sunday services at his grandmother's church. She had raised him and Jimmy at the Shiloh Baptist church, and he knew going there on Sunday would make him feel closer to his g-ma, and help him find the closure he needed to move forward with his life.

He thought a lot about his baby brother during his solitude. He didn't know much about how Jimmy spent his time outside of school. He always knew that where he slipped with his little brother, his g-ma would pick up the slack. Now she was gone, and Jimmy's guidance was solely his responsibility.

-CHAPTER TWENTY ONE-

The new year was closing in fast and Mills hadn't done much kicking it since being released from juvy. He had even missed Brandy's birthday celebration, so when she spoke of bringing in the new year with a new year's eve party at one of the hottest clubs in the city, he didn't refuse. The red Zone was one of Columbus's main attractions. It was the club that all the rappers and professional athletes hung out at when visiting the city. It was also the club of choice for all of the athletes and students of OSU's campus. Everyone had decided to go, including Buck and Ta'Meka. The year had been rough on them all, so they were all in need of a good time. Peko stopped by Deedrah's apartment to check on her and his son before he got dressed for the new year's eve bash. As always, his visit turned sexual, and he now sat in Dee's parking lot smoking on a fat blunt while thinking about how beautiful it was to have two good looking baby mothers. Several doors down, he noticed a couple standing in the doorway making out. He groped himself and thought about going back in Dee's apartment for round two, but what he saw next caused him to nearly burn hisself with the fire on the tip of his blunt. "Oh shit!" he said as the view of the couple became clear.

He watched Butter shove his tongue down Mek's throat while grabbing a handful of her ass. Peko wasn't sure if he was seeing things clearly until he watched Mek pull out the apartment complex in the brand new Mercedes truck that Buck had copped her last Christmas.

He dialed Mills number immediately. The phone rang several times but he got no answer. "T-money this is Pee, call me as soon as you get this message it's an emergency." Peko said while pulling into traffic.

Meanwhile Brandy stood in front of her mirror, with nothing on besides a pink lace bra and some matching boy shorts. Black's manhood rose in his boxers, as he watched Brandy groom herself in the mirror. "Stop Black." Brandy whispered seductively as he pressed his half excited pole between her cheeks, while sucking on her neck. "C'mon Bee, we gone make it quick." Black persuaded. "Baby no, cause we gone be late for the party, and we aint been out since you came home." Brandy pleaded. "I don't ever have to go out, as long as I got you bae." Black said as he grinded on her from behind. She broke loose and ran around the room while Black chased her with his pole now at full attention. While they played hide and go get it in their bedroom, Buck sat in his game room while watching the Buckeyes play the Iowa Hawkeyes. When Tameka walked through the door, Buck was screaming at the television "C'mon man tighten up that defense, watch the back door." "what's up baby." Mek said as she sat on Buck's lap and rubbed on his bald head. "My stomach bae, I'm starved." He responded while planting a bit one on her lips. "Baby I don't have time to cook, we gotta get dressed for the bash tonight." Mek replied. "I can't go nowhere on an empty stomach, now go in that huge kitchen of yours and throw ya man something together." Buck ordered. Tameka playfully smacked her lips as she headed for the kitchen.

A short while later, Buck walked into the kitchen talking loudly on the phone to Butter. He joked with him about the money he had just won from his Buckeyes second half blowout. Mek was preparing his plate of fried chicken, mashed potatoes, mixed vegetables, and his favorite side, baked beans. "Aye bae me and Butter gone ride together, you can take the Benz out tonight, Ima tell Mills you gone pick Neesh up so she can ride wit you." Buck said after ending his call. "No Buck we said we was rolling together tonight, why that nigga always got to tag along wit his trick ass." Mek said with attitude. "Bae I'm not going through this Butter shit wit you tonight. That's my only homeboy and he's like a brother to me, and ya'll gone start this year off getting along with one another, and that's the end of this conversation. Now come on over here and enjoy some of this dinner with yo man, and that face aint gone got you yo way tonight." Buck said. Mek stomped over to the large table where Buck sat. He grabbed her by the waist, pulled her to him and said, "Give me a kiss and quit pouting, you too beautiful to be making such an ugly face."

Mills phone was filled with messages as he and Neesh finished their third round of sex. Neesh slid up and down his pole, bringing both of them to their fifth climax of the day. She collapsed on top of him as his manhood shrunk inside her. Both of them were worn out. They had two hours until they were to meet everybody at the club, and they decided to spend one of those hours sleeping. Neesh set the alarm clock on the phone and decided to check their messages. The only message on the phone was Tameka, informing Neesh of the change of plans. Mills noticed the light on his cell phone blinking, informing him of his messages. He disregarded the messages for now, Neesh curled up against him and he rolled over with nothing on his mind but his queen.

Except for Mills not returning his call, Peko's night was going perfectly. He got to enjoy the inside of both his baby mother's caves. Then he and Shy had the talk he had been waiting for. She agreed to give him another chance. Although she said they would take things slow, Peko was happy to be back home. As he pulled away from their condo, he knew tonight had to be memorable, because it would be his last night as a single man. Shy was everything he wanted and needed in a woman. Tomorrow was their starting over point, and he refused to fuck up his happy home again. He let Too Short's Freaky Tails blast from his speakers as he took the highway all the way to his brother's apartment. He puffed on the finest dro, as he admired his expensive attire, and bobbed his head to the music.

He wore a purple waist-length mink, over his crispy white tee, which coordinated with his white Murray sneakers with a purple gator toe. His dark blue denim jeans were fresh off the rack. His grill was on gleam, his neck and wrist were on freeze, and both his pinky fingers were on bling. His eyes were covered with Christian Dior shades, while an all white Yankees fitted cap sat lightly on his head. He rapped along with Too Short, until he pulled in behind Shawn's car. Shawn's' girlfriend Reese answered the door after a few knocks. Reese was cold blooded, at 5, 2" she was 130 pounds of pure stallion, and her stomach was flat as an ironing board. While her breasts and badonka donk stood out like a red t-shirt at a Crip gathering. Her hips rolled off her body in perfect harmony with her legs and apple bottom. Her complexion was golden brown almost matching her hazel brown eyes identically. Her hair was reddish brown, and it hung to the middle of her back. Peko shook his head as Reese sashayed back to the couch where she sat Indian style watching TV. Peko's nephew came running out of nowhere. He wrapped himself around Peko's leg, while slobbering on his pants. "Boy where yo clothes at." Peko said as he lifted him into the air. He had nothing but Spiderman draws on, as he stole Peko's hat and took off running. "lil nigga give me my hat." Peko said. "Shawn Jr. give yo uncle his hat back and tell yo daddy to put some pajamas on you." Reese yelled. Shawn Jr. Ran right into his sire. Shawn gave his brother his hat back, and carried his son to his mother. He kissed both of them and told Reese he'd be back kind of late, then walked out with his brother. Shawn wore a tan waist length mink over his navy blue Sean John sweater. His navy blue Sean John jeans had tan stitching, coordinating with his sweater, jacket and tan Timberland boots. His eyes hid behind a pair of Gucci frames and his grill was on chill. His iced out Cuban link hung down to his belly button, with an iced out cross hanging from it. On his wrist was a matching bracelet, and Malvado time piece. Shawn and Reese had a fairy tale relationship, they broke each other's virginity, and neither one has been with anyone else since. He's been taking car of Reese since they were thirteen, and she trusted him with her life. Shawn could bed multiple women like his older brother but he was committed to Reese and she knew it, that's why she never gave him any problems about going out, or coming home late.

D-Roc and Walt sat outside the club macking on honeys, snorting coke and stalking victims. They knew all the ballers would be at the New Years Eve bash, and they had dollar signs in their eyes. Keisha and Iesha didn't know who D-Roc and Walt were, but when they walked up to the car the bling satisfied them. After exchanging numbers the girls disappeared. D-Roc and Walt looked at one another with sinister grins as the money green Lexus pulled into VIP's parking area. The Lex was nasty, and they couldn't wait to see who was driving it. When Mills stepped out the Lex with Rio, both D-Roc and Walt's jaws tightened. Mills blessed Rio with some cash and heavy weight when he got home, and just like Mills knew he would, Rio quickly locked his neighborhood down with the same math that took Mills to the top.

The gold flakes sparkled as Mills leaned up against his car while Rio flagged down some honeys. Mills wore a money green waist length mink over top of his thick white tee, with some faded blue denims, and white Murray sneakers. His presidential Rolex lit up the parking lot, while his ears were on freeze with two karats of flawless VVS diamonds. His gold Cartier frames had summer tint, and they complimented his gold grill and five karat pinky ring nicely.

Rio wore a royal blue quarter length mink, a matching blue tee, some regular blue denims, and matching Murray sneakers. Rio wasn't actually a gang member, but he was affiliated with the Crips by way of his neighborhood so he sported his True Blue in honor of his hood. His grill was blinding passers by as well, as the princess cut diamonds in his fangs entertained the females he flagged down.

"Look at this bitch ass nigga, who the fuck he think he is?" D-Roc said as Mills and Rio strolled through the parking lot headed for the club's entrance. Walt was listening but his attention was elsewhere. "Aye Roc aint that the nigga Deuce's lil brother right there?" Walt said while pointing at a midnight blue Lexus on chrome Lorenzo's. D-Roc watched the Lexus pull into the parking lot. "Yeah that's the lil niggas ride. I hope his fat ass brother is wit em." D-Roc said.

"Looks like yo wish came true dawg." Walt said as Mike and his big brother Deuce stepped out the Lex looking like rappers. Their diamonds seemed to glow in the dark as they turned the parking lot into a light show.

D-Roc and Walt silently slid out the car and crept through the parking lot. Mike was talking to a female while deuce yelled at someone through his cell phone. They both exuded a confidence that showed no worries, which made them totally oblivious to their adversaries ambush.

Walt shoved the girl Mike was talking to out of his way and greeted Mike with the barrel of his Desert Eagle. "You know the procedure, hands on the hood, and spread them legs boy!" Walt said calmly. Deuce thought he was hearing things, but when he looked over his shoulder and saw Walt, he knew he had been caught slipping. He thought about going for his pistol, but the feel of D-Roc's Taurus pressed up against his temple killed that thought. "Yo fat ass try anything stupid and I'm uh blow ya noodles all over the hood of this Lex. Now both ya'll pussies come up off that shine." D-Roc demanded. Walt smacked Mike across the mouth with his Desert Eagle, dropping Mike to his knees. "Bitch ass nigga strip before I put something hot in yo lil chubby ass." Walt ordered. Mike and Deuce did as they were told. They placed all their valuables and cash on the hood and trunk of the car. Walt knew the girl that he mugged to the ground was probably informing some of Mike and Deuces homeboys of what was taking place, so he rushed D-Roc as he repeatedly beat Deuce in the head with his pistol.

D-Roc and Walt filled their pockets with the goods, then Walt shoved Mike on top of his brother. "Ya'll bitch ass niggas better enjoy that lil shit while ya'll can, cause I be to see ya'll niggas ASAP." Deuce growled. "What the fuck you say?" Walt asked with authority. "You heard me nigga, ya'll clowns gone die for this shit." Deuce answered as blood leaked from his head and mouth. "BLOWL! BLOWL! BLOWL! BLOWL! BLOWL! Walt fired off several shots hitting both of his targets in their upper body. Everyone in the lot dove for cover as Walt fired off a few more rounds into the air to distract the onlookers. He and D-Roc quickly ran to their g-ride and sped out the lot. Some of Deuces homeboys pulled up as he and Mike laid in a puddle of blood on the side of Mike's Lexus. Peanut told Kiesha and Iesha to inform T-Bone and Fresh of what happened as he and the rest of the goons loaded Deuce and Mike's bodies into their car. Inside the club, Mills and Rio climbed the stairs that led to the VIP section. Buckshot and the rest of the entourage already had two tables occupied. Bottles of Moet and Henessey filled the table, while clouds of hydro chronic smoke filled the air.

Across the room T-Bone and his crew occupied a table, which was also filled with green bottles. "Look at Buckshot's hoe ass over there slipping. We been sitting here for over a half hour and he still aint noticed us. All that money done went to his head, that's why niggas like him don't last, they get so rich that they get relaxed, they lose that animalistic instinct, they senses get weak, they can't even sense when danger is near, they don't even realize that they been stalked until ah nigga breathing on they neck and by that time, it's too late, game over." T-Bone said. "Yeah, it would be real fucked up if we crash they lil party while they out with they lil wifey's and shit." Fresh added. The thought of actually crashing their party caused T-Bone and his crew to burst into laughter.

Kiesha and Iesha stopped their laughter as they hurried across the floor with the bad news. T-bone didn't even let the girls finish before he was on his feet and rushing out of the club. Fresh and the rest of his crew were quickly on his heels with Kiesha and Iesha tight on their tail.

Mills and Rio joined the rest of the crew, quickly ordering a few bottles of Moet, and Hennessey. Mills finally caught the secret looks Peko was giving him, so he followed Peko over to the bar. "What's up bro?" Mills said. "Damn bro, why you aint call me back I been leaving you messages all day. This shit I gotta tell you is ill man." Peko said while shaking his head at the thought of what he was about to disclose, Mills could see the seriousness in Peko's face, so he didn't waste any time with small talk. "What's going on bro, talk to me." Mills said. "Listen bro, this shit about to sound stupid, but it's real as a hundred dollar bill, that nigga Butter and Mek is fucking, no lie." Peko said. "What! Get the fuck out of here bro, you wiggin out." Mills said. "Nigga I aint wiggin, I said real as a hundred dollar bill, I was at Dee's earlier today visiting her and my baby, and I saw Butter slobbing Mek down in the doorway of his apartment… I thought I was wiggin out then but I watched her get into the Mercedes Buck bought her, just watch the looks they keep giving each other. I know when cheating is going on c'mon bro, I'm like the poster boy for it." Peko said. They both started laughing. "I'm laughing bro but I'm serious, look at um." Peko continued. Mills ordered a drink for him and Peko, while they watched the affair. Mek and Butter exchanged a variety of looks. When no one was looking Butter would tease her with his tongue, and she'd roll her eyes. By the end of his second drink,

Mills had seen enough. He was furious because he knew how Buck felt about Butter.

That was his only homeboy. He trusted the dude almost as much as he trusted Mills. They

came up together, from being knee high to a Cadillac bumper. Mills watched Butter and

Buck toast with bottles of Moet. Over the table Buck was telling Butter how he loved him

so much and how this was their year to change the game. As they embraced, Mills

walked up and pulled Buck to the side.

Meanwhile T-Bone and Fresh were at the hospital. Mike and Deuce were in bad shape,

but expected to live. Keisha and Iesha walked through the doors as T-bone flipped on

everyone who couldn't tell him who the shooters were. After the girls told him of their

encounter with the guys in the Bonneville named D-Roc and Walt, the descriptions they

had received of the robbers fit them perfectly. T-Bone thought of Buck and his crew back

at the club. "Touch two of mines, I kill all of yours!" he thought as he rounded his boys

up and headed back to the club.

--

Mills and Buck sat at the bar secretly watching Mek and Butter as Mills told Buck about

their secret love affair. Buck was at a loss for words. He treated Mek like a queen, and

loved her unconditionally. He never cheated on her, or put his hands on her. As far as he

knew their sex life was beyond fine. He had a thick eight inch pole, and he knew he

worked it like a fifteen, and the dish between her legs was his favorite meal, so there

wasn't anything he could think of that she had to cheat for. Butter was his main man,

from grade school on up. They were like brothers, and he and Mek couldn't stand one another. Mills and Buck watched the table from a distance as Peko had him do. It didn't take Buck long to notice the signs. His blood boiled as Butter rubbed Mek's hand. And he watched Mek kick him under the table. Tears took over his face as he stormed across the room. Without saying a word he grabbed Butter by his sweater, and drug him across the table. He slammed Butter's liquor soaked body to the floor and smashed his face repeatedly with his fist. "You disloyal mutha fucka, I should kill you, ya'll been playing me like a fool! I trusted you! Buck said as he beat blood out of Butter's face. Everyone jumped out of their seats, as Moet and liquor poured from the table top. Mek couldn't believe what she was seeing. Buck was onto her and Butter, and his rage was evident. Butter was finished but Buck snatched him off the ground, and threw him on the table, then grabbed Mek by her throat and held her over Butter's bloody body. "You two disloyal mutha fuckas deserve each other. I treat you like a queen bitch, and this is the thanks I get?" Buck screamed. Neesh wanted to help her sister but she was frozen by the thought of her sister cheating on Buck with his best friend. She had never seen Buck so enraged as she watched him backhand her sister across her face. "You disloyal bitch!" Buck said then drew his hand back for another smack, only to have it grabbed in mid swing. He yanked away from Neesh with full force, but after seeing who it was he gathered enough self restraint to let Mek go and back away from the table.

Bouncers came from everywhere, sending Buck right back into his rage. One of the bouncers grabbed Buck by his shoulder and caught a right to his chin. The bouncer hit the pavement hard and the rumble began. Bouncer number two hit Buck from behind, and Mills went in on him with a flurry of punches. Bouncer number three and four were being molly whopped by Peko, Shawn and Rio. Bouncer number five picked the wrong one,

Black had him in the air and sent him crashing down on the table. Bouncer number six took a bottle of Moet to the head from Brandy as he rushed Black from his blind side. As the bouncers filled VIP with mace, Mills told Brandy to get Neesh and take her outside. Black grabbed lil Mark off of bouncer number four and told him to watch out for brandy. When the mace became too strong, and began to tear through the fellas eye's and, skin they dashed for the steps. Once outside, Buck and Mek went back at it. Peko and Shawn sat in Peko's 'lac with the doors open letting the air cool their skin off from the mace. While Black did the same thing in Brandy's Benz, as lil Mark stood guard with his gloc. Mills vision was blurry as he and Rio headed for the car. But he could hear Mek and Buck screaming at one another. Mek was begging for Buck's forgiveness, while Buck called her every dirty name in the book. Buck was pissy drunk, and could barely stand still. He swayed back and forth, as he spit out all kinds of disloyal bitches and hoes. Mills couldn't see very clearly but he caught two gunmen walking across the parking lot with their pistols drawn. They were headed right for Buck and the rest of his crew. Mills grabbed his twenty one shot top of the line nine, and took off running across the lot while screaming Buck's name. By the time Buck heard Mills, it was too late. T-Bone and Fresh were firing off shots. Buck could of dove for cover but instead he shielded Mek, and caught three of T-Bone's slugs to the chest. Lil Mark spotted the gunmen and opened fire on them with his gloc. Lil Flip, and a few more gunmen came out of nowhere covering T-Bone and Fresh.

Mills let his gun cut loose. Peko hit his stash box and rose wit his four fifth. T-Bone and his crew retreated, but Mills chased them down dumping with his nine. Mills watched his slug rip through T-Bone's shoulder, knocking him to the ground, but Fresh backed Mills up with a few shots, then helped T-bone to his feet. Flip and Cat Man began firing off rounds as Mills shielded himself with a car.

T-bone and his boys loaded in their vehicles and sped off. Mills opened fire on the car before turning around and jogging to Buck's aid. Mek and Neesh were over his bloody body. Both of them were crying and screaming as Mek held Buck's head on her lap. She cried out to God for help. "Oh Lord, please no, not him take me, it's all my fault." She cried. "Buck please don't leave me baby, I'm sorry I love you please no!!" Mek continued to scream but her cries were to no avail. Buck was gone.

-CHAPTER TWENTY TWO-

Buck's death affected more than just Mek and his daughter's life. He protected, provided for, and guided everyone up and down Main Street for a twenty to thirty block radius. His death affected the masses, but no one was more affected by Buckshot's death than Mills.

Buckshot was more than his older brother. He was the father figure to Mills that Mills own father never got a chance to be. Everything that Mills knew, he had learned it from Buck.

On the surface Mills blamed Mek for Buck's death, but deep down inside he put all the blame on himself. It was his duty to watch Buck's back but he let his brother die on his watch, so naturally he took the blame.

The identity of the shooters had yet to be disclosed, so he had no one other than Mek to take out his frustrations on. Mills couldn't stand the sight of her. Just hearing her name infuriated him.

After trying to hunt Butter down for the last two weeks, only to realize that he's disappeared, Mills began to blame Mek for that as well. He believed that she warned Butter to leave the city, informing him that he was a dead man if he didn't. He thought about taking Mek's life, but he knew Buck wouldn't have wanted it that way. He loved her too much, so much that even after learning of her betrayal, he shielded her body with his own, taking three slugs that he could've dodged.

Mills knew he couldn't kill her. Not only for Buck's sake, but for his niece's as well. He wouldn't kill her, but he would never forgive her, nor forget what she had done and what it cost him. To him Ta'meka was dead.

As Mills descended the steps, he froze at the sight of Mek sitting on his couch. He gritted his teeth and shot Mek the look of death. Then he cut his eyes and Neesh. "I can't believe she got this bitch over here after I told her I didn't want that whore around me" Mills said to himself. His jaws tightened as he watched Neesh console her sister. He made it clear that Mek was the enemy and Neesh was not to go around her, "Yet here she is holding her and rocking her like a baby" Mills thought.

Mills thought back to the moment during Buck's funeral, when Mek tried apologizing to him, no matter how much she cried, and begged and pleaded he showed her no love. He cursed her out and told her she was the enemy, then spit on the ground in front of her. Mek was such an emotional wreck that she was numb to Mills's feelings and ill treatment towards her. Like him, she blamed herself for Buck's death, and frequently talked of taking her own life.

Neesh knew Mills didn't want her to be involved with her sister but she was worried about Mek, she knew Mek was in no condition to be left alone, so when she showed up at her door this morning, Neesh welcomed her inside, knowing that Mills would lose his lid when he woke up, but willing to face that music for her sister and niece's safety.

"I thought I told you I didn't want that disloyal whore over here." Mills growled. "Mills not right now." Neesh answered. "That's what I say, not now, not ever, either she goes or I go, it's your choice." Mills said stoically.

"Mills she's in no condition to be left alone, look at her, what about your niece?"

"Mek's condition is of no importance, she doesn't exist to me, DayDay can stay, but Mek has to go.... NOOOOWW!" Mills screamed.

Tears streamed down Neesh's face. She had never seen Mills be so evil. Buck has been dead for two weeks, and Mills attitude and condition was no better today than it was the night of Buck's death. She was beginning to think that Mills may never come back from this loss.

"Mills I understand how you feel, but I won't kick my sister out. She did a terrible thing, she betrayed the only man who ever loved us. I'm upset at her too, but she needs me and

I have to be here for her." Neesh said while sniffing up her tears and attempting to wipe them from her face. "'Nough said" Mills growled.

He headed back up the steps only to return fully clothed with his car keys in hand. He looked at Neesh one last time. She rocked her sister back and forth while they both cried a river. "Mills I need you, your niece needs you, what am I supposed to tell Jimmy when he comes here?" Neesh whined.

"Jimmy knows where to find me, and you choose your side." Mills stormed out the door. Mek was responsible for Buck's death. She was disloyal, and for that she didn't deserve anyone's loyalty. Not even her own sisters. Mills wanted nothing to do with Mek, nor anyone who had anything to do with her. So when Neesh chose to console her sister, Mills perceived it as betrayal. His mind started playing tricks on him. He started feeling like he didn't know who he could trust. He cut off contact with the outside world, Neesh included. He barricaded himself inside his grandmother's house. He refused to leave until he found out who Buck's killers were. And when he did, he vowed to make them pay with their lives.

While Mills mourned Buck in solitude, his little brother became more drawn to the streets.

With Sonny's connect and assistance, Pimp's heroin house was doing numbers. This month alone his spot was doing three thousand dollars a day. And this was only his second month in business. But money bred envy so with his bank roll came more problems.

"Aye homeboy, let me take a look at you for a second!" Eazy yelled as he and his two soldiers jogged across the street. Pimp knew this day was coming. Sonny had warned him about Eazy, who at the time was Long Street's most feared hustler.

Pimp didn't say anything, he stood his ground while clutching the pistol he had in his coat pocket. "You the guy with the heroin spot on 18th with that old head Sonny right?" Eazy asked, while sizing up Pimp. "Yeah that's me, what's happenin?" Pimp replied. "What's happenin is that you fuckin up my money. Slowin down my traffic. You in the wrong lane homie, my name Eazy and this is my strip." Eazy explained. Pimp bit down on his teeth. Not only did he have a temper like his father, but with his grandmother passing and Buckshot's death, he was itching to lay his murder game down. "Check it out Eazy. If this is yo turf, you gonna have to step yo game up to keep it, cause I'm here and I aint goin nowhere!" Pimp said while staring into Eazy's eyes. Eazy could tell Pimp was packing and he nor his solders had their iron handy, so he backed off.

"Aight big dawg, I thought we would be able to handle this the easy way, but I see we won't be coming to an agreement. Tell Sonny Eazy said hey…later Homeboy." Eazy said before he and his soldiers walked away. Pimp wanted to wax Eazy but it was too many witnesses out for his comfort. When Pimp made it back to his spot, Sonny was in his favorite chair. For once he wasn't high, and Pimp was glad because he needed to talk to him about Eazy. Once Sonny heard of Pimp's run in with Eazy, he wanted to handle the situation himself. Pimp didn't know it but Sonny was an old school killer. He had taken plenty of lives with his blade, and just as many with his revolver. Mostly everyone from the old school knew of Sonny and made it clear to all the young hustlers that he was not to be taken lightly. Pimp told Sonny he didn't want him to do anything to Eazy. He made it clear to Sonny, "If Eazy wanna go to war he got the right one."

It only took Eazy a few days to make his move. He marched around to the 18th Street with a chopper, and three of his goons. They unloaded over a hundred rounds into Pimp's spot. Pimp was gone but Sonny was lucky he stood in the kitchen, because his favorite chair got riddled with holes. Sonny hit the deck as bullets tore through the house, but his buddy Paul was too high to react with enough speed. The chopper shells tore through his skull and midsection. The gunshots seemed to never end, but when they finally did Sonny didn't waste any time dashing out the back door headed for Liley's house two streets over.

After spending close to a month in solitude, confined in his grandmother's house, Mills was finally ready to come from underground. After taking a shower, and throwing on some clothes, Mills checked the messages on his cell phone. He had plenty from Neesh. Now that he had his thoughts together he knew he was being inconsiderate and unfair. He missed Neesh, and the sound of her tears cut him deep. He had messages from

Brandy, Black, Shawn, Rio, Chico, B-Nut, H.T. and Peko as well. All of them were worried but Black and Peko's messages seemed the most urgent. As soon as Mills turned his ringer on, his phone was ringing. "T-Money what the fuck man, why aint you been answerin yo phone. I know you heard us banging on the door too. That girl Neesh been callin me like I'm fucking her or something." Peko yelled. "My bad Pee, I just needed some time to pull myself together, emotionally I was all over the place, you dig." Mills said. "Like a shovel. But I got some news that will brighten ya day." Peko said. "Oh yeah, try me." Mills replied. "Black's lil cousin got word to us about who smoked Buck, he know where da niggas be at and all. We been tryna hit you up, Black's lil cousin fuck with the niggas, he was out there in the parking lot that night. You would never believe who all this shit is over." Peko explained. "Who?" Mills asked impatiently. "Listen bro, don't move I'm bout to call Black and we bout to be on our way over there."

A half hour later the fellas were all in Mills grandmother's living room. When Peko told Mills the whole story, it only made him feel worse. He blamed himself and Tameka for Buck's death when it was actually D-Roc and Walt's fault. He couldn't believe he slipped so much that night. Not only did he not notice D-Roc and Walt's g-ride in the lot, but he never noticed T-bone and his crew in the VIP section that night. Mills thought of how cold he had been acting towards Neesh for consoling her sister. He knew he owed her an apology, but it would have to wait. Right now nothing was more important than avenging the death of of his Brother / Father.

Later that night Black got all the information they needed from his little cousin. T-Bone and Deuce had an after hour spot on Cleveland Avenue. The after hour was also one of their top Drug houses. Not a night went by when they weren't there. Mills called H.T. for a throw away van, and some artillery. "Tonight vengeance would be his."

෧෧ ෧෧ ⑧ ⑧ ⑧ ⑧ ⑧ ෧෧ ෧෧

D-Roc and Walt pulled in front of Keisha's house in their newest ride. The Navigator was chocolate brown, on gold hundred spokes. The paint was dripping, with three wet coats of candy, while tinted windows hid them perfectly. The slap in the trunk rattled the house, as D-Roc called Keisha to inform the girls they were outside. Keisha and Iesha stepped out on the porch looking gorgeous. D-Roc killed the engine and the girls escorted them in the house.

෧෧ ෧෧ ⑧ ⑧ ⑧ ⑧ ⑧ ෧෧ ෧෧

Black sat behind the wheel of the van. Mills road shotgun, Shawn, Peko, and Lil Mark rode in the back. They were all dressed in black, resembling a team of ninjas. The only difference would be the choice of weaponry. Ninja's weapons of choice were swords and Chinese stars, Mills and his crew came equipped with heavy artillery. The place was packed, and the vehicle Black's cousin said that T-Bone and his homeboys would be riding in, was parked out front. The only thing left to do was wait.

⮎ ⮎ ⑧ ⑧ ⑧ ⑧ ⑧ ⮎ ⮎

Meanwhile Pimp had already had enough of Eazy. Eazy made it clear that someone had

to go, and Pimp refused to let it be him. After riding around for two hours looking for

Eazy, Pimp and Sonny had finally caught a break. Sonny caught an addict by the name of

Wiz coming out of Eazy's heroin house. The addict's money was short, and Eazy's

worker refused to serve him, which worked in their favor. Pimp gave wiz a few packs of

his fire heroin and Sonny drained him of all the info he needed. Eazy was at the club on

Champion and Mt. Vernon while his homie ran the spot by himself. Sonny wanted to run

in the spot, take Eazy's money, and kill his homeboy, but Pimp didn't want his homeboy,

he wanted Eazy's life.

They now sat across the street from the club, ducked off in the parking lot. Pimp

was so furious and the wait was so long, he decided to smoke his first blunt. The weed

had him tripping, it made him paranoid and impatient. Some females came walking out

the club talking loudly. One of them held pieces of her weave in her hand, while

another's shirt was almost torn off her. It was clear they were drunk and had been in a cat

fight.

Shortly after the females came out; Eazy came out the club leaning on one of his

homeboy's shoulders. They were lit and talking loudly about the way they sprayed

Pimp's spot. They staggered to the car parked a couple of vehicles in front of Pimp and

Sonny. Pimp pulled his ski mask on, and checked his gun. It was ready for action. Eazy

stood outside the car taking a piss, while his homeboy enjoyed the night's air. Pimp popped out of nowhere. "Eazy look out!" His homeboy yelled as Pimp slid down on him. "Die mutha fucka." Pimp said as he delivered a few shots to Eazy's upper body. His partner spun around and met Sonny's problem solver. His head exploded as his body hit the concrete. His other homeboy ran towards the females as they dove for cover. Bullets from Pimp's Ruger chased him down, a bullet to his back spun him around into a parked vehicle, while another went through his neck knocking him to the ground. His eyes were open, and he could see feet running but his body couldn't move.

Back at Keisha's, blunts were being lit, and Walt was setting the mood as he rubbed on Iesha's sweet spot. Keisha managed to sneak away from D-Roc long enough to phone T-Bone. She held the refrigerator door open while hiding behind it as she whispered through the phone. "Bone hurry up cause these niggas is getting horny. "Well give them some pussy, give em sum head, I don't give a fuck, do what you gotta do to keep them there we on our way!" T-Bone said before disconnecting. T-Bone and his crew came walking out the after hour. Deuce was walking slowly still hunched over from the staples in his chest and stomach. He was supposed to be on bed rest but he refused to not be a part of killing D-Roc and Walt. Mills spotted the five walking out towards T-Bone's car. "There go them niggas right there." He said while pulling his ski mask down, and his gloves on tight. Everyone in the van did the same. Fresh helped Deuce in the front of the car, while T-Bone unlocked the driver's door. Mills slid out the truck followed by Peko. He didn't waste any time, as soon as he hopped out the van he started blasting. He let the Tommy rip through T-Bone's body. Peko unloaded on the truck filling Deuces body with holes. Mills walked over top of T-Bone's dead body, plugged him a few more times then joined Peko with rearranging the Lexus truck. Fresh blasted off shots in return as he made a run for the after hours front door. Fresh never saw Black coming as he turned right into the barrel of his shotty. "BLOWL!!!"

One shot exploded Fresh's head, slumping his body immediately. The rest of T-Bone's crew dumped off a few rounds while taking off up the street. Shawn and Lil Mark gunned them down dropping them a few yards from the truck. Black was already back in the van, he whipped it on the side of the Lexus, and yelled for Mills and Peko to get in. Shawn and Mark were already sliding in the back. Mills and Peko hurried into the van, and Black put the pedal to the metal.

D-Roc and Walt had wrecked Keisha and Iesha's sheets. The girls let them have their way with no limits, as they tried their best to keep the guys there until T-Bone arrived. After a couple hours of banging headboards, D-Roc and Walt were in the wind. Keisha couldn't believe T-Bone and his crew missed an opportunity. She called his phone repetitiously, angry that she had just gave her goodies away for free. Little did she know

T-Bone wouldn't be answering his phone ever again.

⌘ ⌘ ⑧ ⑧ ⑧ ⑧ ⑧ ⌘ ⌘

The M was one of Columbus's five star restaurants, and one of Chico's favorite places to have lunch. The ambiance was nice and peaceful. The customers were primarily upper level of society. On any day you could bump into the mayor, professional athletes, high priced attorneys and such. Chico had his own table where he and Mills now sat enjoying lunch and shots of Patròn. Chico's goons occupied the tables to his left and right.

It has been two weeks since Mills got vengeance for Buck's death. He still wanted Butters head, but the blood of Deuce, T-Bone and their goons lifted an enormous amount of weight from Mills shoulders. He was now level headed and a lot of the things his mentor had told him was starting to make sense. It had been a rough couple of months. After losing buckshot he nearly lost his sanity. During these couple of months when he shut down, he had hurt and shut out the people he cared about most. Now that he had things back in order with his squad and his woman, the only thing left for him to do was have this sit-down with Chico.

"So…Comrade, is thees a habit of yours, starting sunthing and no fineesh it?" Chico asked. "No Chico, it's not a habit, and a quitter is something I've never been. It hurts me to be asking you for this favor but if there's one thing I learned from Buck, its that a player must know when to play and when to step away. I've lost my grandmother, I've lost Buckshot who was probably the single most important person to me in this world, but before losing Buck and my G-ma, I lost my mother, my father and every aunt and uncle I ever knew. I promised myself and Buck that I wouldn't let my baby brother fall victim to this lifestyle… Chico I don't even know where my baby brother is half the time. And to be truthful Chico, I don't even know if this is a permanent decision. I'm not even sure if this is what I want to do, but I know that it has to be done. I need some time to get my priorities in order, clear my head, nah mean. Its like I've gained so much from this lifestyle, but compared to what I've lost, the gain is non existent." Mills passionately explained.

Chico just nodded his head. He stared into Mills eyes. The youngster reminded him so much of Buckshot, whom he loved like a son. "Comrade, I want you to understand sunthing… there's rules to thees game that we all must abide by. Including me. You can't just put thee game on pause and come back to it later like thees is jus sun video game. Thees is real life Mills, thees is no fucking game…" He paused for a moment, still holding his stare into Mills's eyes. "Listen Comrade, under normal circumstances, I would be telling you no, but because of the love, loyalty and respect I have for Buckshot, along with the fact that you're giving me someone whose equally qualified to take your place, I'm gonna make an exception… you step away from this lifestyle, but only if you can move 50 kilos a month for the next twelve months. That's twenty more kilos than what you're currently moving, along with that you have to pay me a fee of 1.5 mill. Can you handle thees?"

"Si" Mills answered. Chico smiled. He liked when Mills used Spanish. It showed respect.

"Mills understand sunthing. I do thees for you because you're familia. There is no love lost, but thees friend of yours, Peko, before you bring him to me, please understand that you will be held accountable for any and all of his foul ups. You bring him into the fold, you are held accountable for him, comprendae?"

"Comprendae." Mills answered.

"Peaceful journey familia, but sun words from the wise. Never trust Peace, peace is like a gorgeous woman, its beautiful but its not to be trusted!" They rose to their feet, embracing one another, then gave each other a head nod before departing.

Mills couldn't believe how fast his life had changed. It seemed like yesterday that Buck was taking care of him and his little brother, and he was sneaking around smoking on blunts. Now he was nearly a millionaire, but the man who helped him reach his status and taught him everything he knew was dead. His grandmother was dead, Slim was dead, and his once best friend was behind bars facing the death penalty. What he gained from the game seemed so little compared to what he had lost. His grandmother had once told him "The Lord giveth, and the Lord taketh away". He now understood the mighty quote.

As the rain fell on his window pane he heard Buck's voice as if he were riding shotgun. "Mills drugs didn't just end up in the black community; they were delivered there, as a secret weapon to aid the white man's genocide on the black race. This shit is bigger than petty hustlers, if it wasn't the government would have been ridded our country of drugs. We sell this shit to make those mother fuckers more money than we could imagine. And what do they do? Make laws against the shit to send us to the modern day plantation called prison. Don't let money blind you T-Money, cause we lose more than we can ever gain. And if you survive through the losses, you'll one day ask yourself, was it all worth it." Mills thought of his mother, father, aunts, uncles, grandmother, Buck and his friends. He now knew the answer to that question. "Black on black crime is at an all time high, don't you see the white man's plan working. We killing one another over this shit. Give us blacks the guns and drugs and let us do their work for them. We just got to open our third eye. And we'll recognize the design."

Tears fell from Mills's eyes as he thought about the only father figure he knew. It hurt Mills to know that Buckshot had to die for him to really understand his words. The brother was deep and he never had the chance to shine his light on the world.

-CHAPTER TWENTY THREE-

Detective White and Brown sat behind their desk piecing together the vast amount of murders that had taken place in the last couple of years. Detective Brown was furious behind the trail of bodies, but White could care less. White puffed on a Kools Long, while his young partner shuffled through files on his desk. "I'm telling you Whitey, a lot of these murders are linked together, and we're just missing something." Brown said as the cases started to overwhelm him. " I'd love to lock the mutha fuckers up and throw away the key Browny, but I'm not gonna wreck my fuckin brain, behind the deaths of a bunch of low life, gang banging drug dealers. They can kill each other off, for all I care." White pulled hard on his cigarette before continuing. "Do nothing but make our jobs a lot easier, fucking pieces of shit!" Brown searched through one file, while another sat in front of him wide open. "Check this out Whitey, Fella Stargell is behind bars for the deaths for Chris Palmer and India Cypress. The key witness on the case is India Cypress friend Lisa Longley. She informed us that Fella and his cousin Anton "Slim" Stargell, along with some of his buddies robbed Chris Palmer about a year or so prior to Palmers death." "And she knows this how?" White asked. "She knows this because her friend India was present when the robbery took place, India was also involved with one of the robbers, which is Anton "Slim" Stargell." Detective Brown said. "So this India whatshername may have been in on the robbery." White inquired. "Maybe but that's not my point, here's my point… About a year after palmer was robbed, Anton "Slim" Stargell was gunned down, while at a store in Palmer's neighborhood." "So Palmer was a part of Stargell's death." White said. "Exactly! And further proof of that is a month later Anton Stargell's cousin and some of his buddies, probably the same ones from the robberies, went to Palmer's apartment and killed him and the once again present India Cypress. All three murders are linked together like one big chain. But listen to this, the missing pieces to the puzzle are the Stargell boys buddies, which we now know without a shadow of a doubt is their all time running buddies." … White finished the sentence for Brown. "Derrick 'D-Roc' Sanders and Walt 'Lil Walt Burns." "Exactly!" Brown yelled. "Okay, so how do we prove that Sanders and Burns were involved and how does these murders link to Daylon 'Buckshot' Draggs's murder, and the whole situation at the night club." White asked. "Well I'm getting to that, listen to this, Sanders, Burns and the Stargell Boys, and Check this out, Tony Mills are all a part of Draggs gang. Mills and a few others were present the night of Draggs death. As usual they claim to know nothing. But after questioning the girl Keisha Smith, we know Mills and the rest of the crew are lying." "Keisha Smith, who the fuck is she?" White asked. "She's the girl whose phone number we found in Tydus 'T-Bone' Carter's phone on the night of his death. We questioned her a few days ago." Brown reminded his partner. "Oh okay, I remember, keep going." White said. "Well Keisha Smith told us that Sanders and Burns robbed and shot T-Bones homeboys, Dustin 'Big Deuce' Driver and his brother Michael 'Lil Mike' Driver in the club's parking lot the same night of Draggs's death. With T-Bone being dead, she had no problem telling us that he was the shooter that killed Draggs that same night. They were killed in retaliation for his buddies, the Driver boys." White added. "Exactly!" Brown yelled again. "She also stated the night of T-Bone's death she was a part of a scheme to set up D-Roc Sanders and Walt burns. She was calling T-Bone's phone because he was supposed to be on his way to her house, to catch Sanders and Burns, but never made it." "Let me guess, because someone killed him and his buddies before they could get there." White said. "Exactly!" Brown yelled. "Sounds like a double set up to me." White said. "My point exactly. That's where Mills and his buddies come in at." Detective Brown explained. "I don't get it." White said. "While Ms. Smith, and Mr. Carter thought they were setting Saunders up, Saunders and Burns had some men camped outside." Brown said. "And that's why Carter, Driver, and those other guys never made it to Smith's house. "So where does Mills come in at?" White asked. "With both of the Stargell boys being out the picture, Carter and Burns had to team up with Mills and his crew" Brown explained. "And how do we prove all this?" White asked. "Well the Stargell boys and the Palmer and Mr. Cypress case is easy, but the thing with Buckshot, Draggs, T-Bone Carter, Mr. Mills and the rest of the guys are going to be tricky, we have two witnesses in Ms. Smith and her friend, but we need a few more to put the puzzle all the way together." Brown said while rubbing his chin. "Good luck finding them, everybody's dead!" White said, clearly becoming irritated by the young detective's logic… "Tell me something Brown, since you've put all that together, what ya got on the Detroit boys homicides?" White asked in an irritated tone. "I haven't got much on them, but what I do know is that the Detroit boys on Oak Street are affiliated with the Detroit boys in Linwood, so the two cases could probably be connected. Word in the streets is some youngster by the name of Pimp and L's may be involved. Brown answered.

While the detectives wrecked their brains about piecing together the various homicide cases. Fella's lawyer was busy getting his first court haring continued.

Fella felt the walls closing in on him. He was running out of options to come up with Clyde's money. And Clyde had made it very clear, no money, no motivation.

Unknowingly to Fella, Mills had a meeting with Clyde for later that evening.

After thinking of all his losses, Mills thought of Fella's mother, who he had been neglecting throughout him and Fella's fallout. One evening Mills stopped by to check up on her, and apologize for his absence. She cried her heart out to him about Fella's situation. Telling him of how D-Roc and Walt had been acting towards her and Fella and how the lawyer needed twenty thousand dollars to defend her son. Mills peeled back a few dollars to help her out with her bills then he took the lawyer's information assuring her that Fella would be okay. Mills asked Clyde to continue the case, and assured him that he'd be to see him after court hours. Mills took Clyde ten grand and promised him the other ten grand in a few days. Clyde agreed and in return told Mills the specifics about Fella's case. He let Mills know about the one and only key witness in the case, and Mills promised to have a talk with her. After promising Lisa twenty thousand she agreed to lie on the stand for Fella. Mills gave her part of the money and promised her the rest when the job was done. Money moves everybody. Buck once told Mills, and he was now seeing it happen. Mills couldn't understand why he was helping Fella, after the way he failed to watch over his grandmother and baby brother while he was on lockdown, not to mention him after choosing D-Roc and Walt over him. Mills thought of the argument they had in front of his grandmother's when he told him he couldn't trust D-Roc and Walt, and Fella defended them. Mills knew the average man would have let Fella fry, but he was taught that two wrongs didn't make a right. Real niggas did real things, and loyalty was more than just a word, it was a way of life, and he lived by those lessons. No matter what he and Fella went through, Fella was family, and he knew now more than ever, that nothing is more important than family.

Peko sat in his weight house clocking major dollars. It was the first of March and all the young hustlers where running through his packs faster than a New York minute. D-Roc and Walt were parked a couple of apartments down from Peko's, contemplating their next move. They'd been planning to rob Peko for over a month now, Only problem was getting inside his apartment. They surely couldn't knock on the door, Peko would either not answer or open the door with his gun in his hand ready for action. They couldn't kick in the door because that meant they would have to go in shooting, and they really didn't want to kill him, they just wanted to take him through the ringer, to show him and Mills they could be touched. As young Clarence got out his car and gravitated towards Peko's back door the solution fell in their laps. By the time Clarence knocked on the door, Walt had his Desert Eagle to his temple. "Don't say a word, or I'm a knock ya noodles loose." Walt threatened. D-Roc pressed his glock 40 to the other side of Clarence's head, "Who is it?" Peko yelled from inside. "Tell em who the fuck it is." D-Roc whispered. "It's Clarence." Clarence mumbled. "Who?" Peko said while pressing his 9mm against the door. Walt pressed his gun into Clarence's temple with force. Reminding him that his noodles were at stake. "Young Cee Clarence!" Clarence yelled. Peko lowered his weapon after hearing Clarence's voice, and name. He was waiting for Clarence to come and pick up his usual four and a half ounces. He yanked the door open with his gun held to his side. The site of D-Roc's gloc 40 in his face, and Walt's Desert Eagle at Clarence's head froze him immediately. "Don't be stupid nigga, drop the pistol on the floor and back the fuck up. Keep yo hands at yo side too nigga." D-Roc said while smiling a bedazzling smile. They pushed their way inside, backing Peko into the kitchen counter. Walt kicked the door closed and made Clarence and Peko empty their pockets. Walt took Clarence's money, shoved him to the ground and told him not to move. He shot through the house while D-Roc handled Peko. "You got any more guns in here lil nigga?" D-Roc asked Peko while pressing his gun to his head. Peko didn't answer; he stared at D-Roc with a look of a killer. D-Roc cracked Peko upside his head, causing blood to leak instantly. "When I ask you a fucking question you better answer me nigga, and fix that look on ya face, you aint no mutha fucking killer now where the shit at?" D-Roc asked again. Peko wanted to go for D-Roc's gun, while he had him alone, but D-Roc quickly changed his mind with another smack upside his head from his gloc 40. He shoved Peko to the floor. "Ima ask you one more time, where the fuck is the dope?" D-Roc said while hovering over top of him and aiming his gun. "It's in the drawer man." Peko replied. "That's more like it, now get the fuck up and get it." D-Roc ordered. Peko did as he was told. Walt returned with a tech nine and several thousand dollars in a bag. D-Roc shoved Peko back down to the floor, and ordered him not to move. Peko did as he was told but the look he gave them bothered Walt. Walt delivered a forceful kick busting Peko's mouth open. "who the fuck you looking at bitch! I'll blow yo shit loose, and by the way tell ya boy Mills he's next." Walt said before following D-Roc out the door. Peko jumped to his feet, and called Mills immediately. Walt found his other gun so he didn't bother trying to impede their getaway. Young Clarence was shaking like drug store dice. Clarence aint want Peko thinking he had anything to do with the robbery, so instead of running off, he begged for Peko's forgiveness. Peko knew Clarence was a victim of circumstance, and robbery wasn't in his jacket. Clarence was a school boy trying to be a hustler. Peko helped him reach the level he was on, and he knew Clarence looked up to him. He told Clarence not to worry about anything. He promised to put him back on his feet, but told him he needed to leave right now. Peko was beyond mad, his pride was hurt, he was robbed while holding a gun. His head and mouth both leaked blood, and when Mills arrived with his artillery he was going to make sure his blood wasn't the only blood shed. Mills arrived quickly. He didn't know what to say, his ace Boone had been violated. Peko's blood stained the floor, and his clothing. Mills tossed him a vest, and an AR-15. He decided to let his actions speak for him. All he could say was "Let's ride." D-Roc and Walt could be anywhere. The only place Mills could think of was their mother's houses. Mills pulled by D-Roc's mother's house first. A few of D-Roc's cars were parked out front, but no sign of him. "Fuck that T-Money, pull back by that bitch I'm lighting it up!"

Peko ordered. Mills busted a U-Turn at the end of the block. When he neared D-Roc's mother's house, Peko hung out the window and let off multiple rounds into the home and vehicles. Peko's response wasn't over, Mills headed for Walt's mother's house where Peko laid down an identical demonstration. Peko didn't know it but one of those bullets almost hit D-Roc's baby sister, had D-Roc's mother not of been so quick on her toes, the AR-15 slug would have done more than grazed her.

The next day, Peko's mother came home to a vandalized house, Her front door had been kicked in, and the house was trashed. D-Roc and Walt riddled the inside of the house with A.K holes, as a message for Peko. Had his mother been home, she would have died. D-Roc knew Peko and Mills would retaliate for the robbery, but he didn't think they had it in them to bring it to his front porch. They almost killed his baby sister, and for that the life of anyone in their family was at risk. The only rules that applied in this war was kill or be killed! Peko and Shawn had secretly purchased their mother a new two hundred and fifty thousand dollar home. They wanted it to be a surprise but with the street war it was clear their mother had to be out of her old house as soon as possible. While Mills was helping Peko and Shawn with their mother's transition, Walt and D-Roc were ransacking his grandmother's home. Mills didn't find out about his house until the following day. When he pulled up to the hose the next morning, he instantly noticed his front door laying on the floor. He held his 9mm by his side as he crept in the house. He didn't keep any money or drugs in the house, because that was his grandmother's demand. Even with her resting in peace, he still honored and respected her home. To his knowledge nothing was missing, but when he called his little brother to inform him of what had taken place, the first thing on Jimmy's mind was the half a key of heroin, and the thirty thousand cash he had stashed in his room. Mills knew things had gone beyond hood beef, and it was best if he and Jimmy moved in he and Neesh's condo for a while. He had the door fixed, then headed for Peko and Shy's condo. When Jimmy arrived after school, his thoughts were confirmed, his stash was gone. He knew of his brother's beef with D-Roc and Walt. At that moment he promised himself if the opportunity presented itself, he'd put a bullet through D-Roc and Walt's head. The money and drugs taken weren't a big problem. Although the loss hurt, more was secretly stashed in Leslie's bedroom, and L's mother's house. He had Long Street on lockdown, and his name was both respected and feared.

After a month of non-stop shootouts, Mills had to get back to his money. He had a goal to meet, and he couldn't let D-Roc and Walt's jealousy interfere with his mission. He knew he would catch them slipping sooner or later, and when he did, he would cook the beef.

Peko and Shawn on the other hand, they couldn't let the beef simmer. It was twelve o'clock in the afternoon, and they were out lurking. Little did they knew, D-Roc and Walt had the same agenda. Peko pushed the Altima up Oak Street, after checking for D-Roc and Walt at one of D-Roc's girlfriend's houses. As he reached the stop sign at the corner of Oak and Kelton, he couldn't believe his eyes, D-Roc and Walt were coming his way. He knew their Bonneville from anywhere, D-Roc and Walt weren't aware that Peko had switched his rental car up so when they neared it, Peko caught them off guard. He stuck his hand out the window and blasted shots off at the Bonneville as it passed. D-Roc hit the brakes as glass shattered in his face. Walt came out his window, unloading on the car as Peko made the U-Turn. Walt fired his twin Desert Eagles, but they were no match for the chopper Shawn swung out the window. The rapid fire sent Walt sliding back in the window and D-Roc smashing the gas. Peko was on their trail and Shawn never stopped shooting. The chopper was tearing the car to smithereens, but the Bonneville's 350 turbo was too much for the Altima's small engine. D-Roc eventually left Peko in his rearview, but it was now clear to him and Walt that this war wasn't one to be taken lightly. Peko, Mills and the rest of their crew had to go, ASAP!

-CHAPTER TWENTY FOUR-

Pimp sat in his all white Bubble Lexus, on chrome eighteen inch Lorenzo's. The dark tinted windows hid him perfectly, as he watched the King of New York on the flat screen television that rested on his dashboard. Leslie called him on his car phone and told him L's was calling back shortly and wanted to talk to him, so he rushed from his new spot to his partners call. When he entered the house Sonny was nodding as usual. Pimp had helped Liley shake her jones but Sonny was a harder task.

He hated seeing Sonny with such a bad jones. He respected and cared for Sonny like a father figure. The sight of Sonny nearly falling off the couch was all Pimp could take. "Get the fuck up Sonny, c'mon man you gotta go to rehab and get some help." Pimp said while saving him from falling on the floor. "C'mon Pimp, my life is over, you cant' help a person that don't want help. I'm gone." Sonny whispered as his head nearly rolled off his neck. "I aint tryna hear that shit Sonny, you like a dad to me man, I can't watch you go out like this." Pimp's words cut him deep, he had grown to love the young gangster like he was his own. "Don't waste your time youngin, I'm gone, just let me fade away." "Naw fuck that, I tried this boy game out for you, now I'm asking you to try this rehab out for me, just give it ninety days, if you get out and cop I'll leave you alone, but you have to at least try man. I did it for you, now do it for me… Tip for Tap Sonny." "Why are you doing this Pimp? I'm not worth it." Sonny replied. "To me you are, now we got a deal or what?" Pimp was adamant, and Sonny had no response. It hurt him to let the youngster down, all he could do is drop his head in defeat. "Pimp! L's is on the phone" Leslie yelled. "This is an important call Sonny, but since you aint say no, I'm taking that as a yes." He ran up the steps and grabbed the phone. "What's up bro?" "Shid you the one with it, I'm tryna get it." L's responded. Pimp laughed. "I hear you talking slick, did you get them flicks?" Pimp asked "Yes sir, that Lexus looking good, I know you copped me one too." L's replied. "Nah I aint do that, but ya bro got it on lock, and whatever you want when you get out, it's yours. Half of everything I own is you my nigga, I can't wait to show you this new game, its beautiful bro." Pimp explained. "Well you gone be showing me sooner than later cause I come home next month!" L's said enthusiastically. "Get the fuck out of here." Pimp yelled. "real shit bro, I get out three months early for good behavior, so tell all them niggas the real Frank White is coming home, and if a nickel bag get sold in the park I want in!" L's said reciting the words of an actor from their favorite gangster flick. They both burst into laughter. "Yeah its on bro, I love you man!" Pimp said. "I love you too bro, but I gotta go my time is up, you be careful." L's said before ending the call. Pimp was pumped, he would have his partner back in a month, and it couldn't be sooner. He was going to see his connect about giving him more weight. He recently started copping half a kilo of heroin and got fronted the other half, but now he had enough cash to cop his own kilo, and he wanted to be fronted another on consignment. He'd have to be a little late for his appointment with his connect, because right now his mind was on Sonny. He told Leslie to bag up eighty thousand dollars and he'd be back to get it in an hour. He left with Sonny and headed for the nearest rehab. Sonny signed himself over to the facility for ninety days. He was placed in the detox tank, where he'd clean himself up cold turkey, for two weeks. They told Pimp everything he'd need for his stay, and he immediately returned with sweat suits, under clothing, and hygiene. He had to give his name for the visitor's list, and provider of clothing. When they dropped Sonny's clothing off, he thought his mind deceived him as he looked at the name on his property sheet. He was higher than a kite, but he knew the name with clarity. James Keys stood out like a stop sign. The only Keys he knew was his old friend, the notorious Tony Keys. He thought Pimp had a familiar face, but he couldn't pinpoint the identity. He thought of the youngsters temper, and the way he handled Eazy, and knew right then and there, whose child Pimp was.

Jimmy stood on the porch talking on his cell phone, while waiting on his cab. Mills pulled up with Rio in Rio's new car. Rio was only a few streets over from Long Street. He had Mt. Vernon on lock with crack and powdered cocaine. As close as he was to Pimp, he'd never seen the notorious youngster, though he's heard his name plenty of times. The youngsters name held weight in the streets, and his unseen hand made him more of a legend. As Mills and Rio stepped on the porch, Jimmy quickly ended his call. "What's up bro." Mills said while wrapping his arms around his little brother. "Nothing much" Jimmy replied. "Rio this is my little bro. Jim this is my homie Rio, real good dude." Mills said while winking at Rio. "This the genius slash football star?" Rio asked while giving Mills a playful elbow. "The one and only." Mills said proudly. "What's up lil bro, Mills talks about you all the time." Rio said. "Sup" Jimmy returned with a smile. "Rio entered the apartment to the sound of Neesh's voice yelling for Mills to come upstairs. Mills left Rio in the living room alone. When he walked in the room the first thing he noticed was Tameka sitting on the bed. Although he no longer blamed her for Buck's death, he still had not forgiven her for cheating on him. In his book Tameka couldn't be trusted. The sight of Daylana going crazy to get in his arms, made him overlook Tameka. "C'mere my baby." Mills said as he grabbed her out of Neesh's hands. Neesh loved the sight of Mills with Daylana. Her niece loved Mills and he loved her. "What's up bae? Why you screaming like somebody attacking you?" Mills said after kissing her soft lips. Neesh looked at Tameka. "Well sis, it's about time for me and Day-Day to get going, I love you." Tameka said. "I love you too, call me." Neesh replied. "Mills gave Daylana a big kiss before handing her over to her mother. "Bye Mills take care." Tameka said. Mills was caught off guard, they hadn't spoken in months. Mills gave Neesh a look that asked where did that come from. "Boy aint nobody mad no more but you." Neesh said while playfully rolling her eyes. "I know that's right…" Mills said playfully. "What's up bae, I got company downstairs." Neesh didn't know how to say it so she just spit it out. "Mills I'm pregnant." "Damn bae, as much as I want us to have children, right now.. it's real fucked up timing." Mills replied. For a moment Neesh couldn't believe what she was hearing. "I know he's not saying what I think he's saying." Neesh thought. "Mills I know you're not asking me to kill our baby?" Neesh said with attitude, while pulling back from his hold. "c'mon bae, I love you too much to ever ask a thing like that of you, I want us to have our baby, I'm just saying the timing was off. I'm stuck in these streets moving this shit for about eight more months, which means I won't be able to go through the stages of pregnancy with you like I always imagined, then I'm in the middle of a fucking war with Roc, and Walt, its on sight gunplay, and I don't want you and my baby in the middle of my bullshit you know." Mills explained. Neesh was once again speechless. Mills made some valid points, and the last one he made frightened her. She was well aware of D-Roc and Walt's craziness. Mills could see the worry in her face, so he pulled her closer to him, and assured her that everything would be alright.

"Don't worry bae, I'll die before I let anything happen to you and our baby. As soon as I finish my business with Chico, we leaving this crazy ass city."

He owed Chico eight more months of the game before he could leave the game. Peko would take his position, and Shawn would take over Peko's wieght house. Chico was happy to be dealing with apples from the same tree, because he knew what to expect. Buckshot gave Chico ten years of his life, and Chico just needed another hustler like Buck who was in the game for the long haul. Mills knew Peko could possibly be that guy, and for that reason he introduced him to Chico. Although Mills brought Peko and Shawn into the game, they were born to hustle, and Mills couldn't think of anyone who actually hustled harder than those two. Mills was in the middle of explaining their new positions when he spotted D-Roc a couple cars ahead of them, riding shotgun with his girlfriend Tasha. "Pee, that's D-Roc a couple cars in front of us, keep it cool, but stay on his heels." Mills said from the backseat of Peko's low key Ford Countour. One of the cars between them had turned off leaving one car between them. Tasha whizzed through the light as it turned red. Peko swerved around the car in front of him, and thrust out into traffic behind her. D-Roc spotted them as Peko closed the gap. Tasha smashed the gas, she swerved around a few cars, then made a quick turn. Peko was on her trail, but the quick turn put a little distance between them. When Peko made the sharp turn, D-Roc and Tasha were hurrying out the car. "Stop! Stop!" Mills yelled. Peko hit the brakes directly behind Tasha's Honda. Mills hopped out of the car, and beat D-Roc to the punch. Mills squeezed off the first shots. D-Roc shielded himself behind Tasha's car, while snatching her to the ground. He took a bullet to the hip, and the hot one burned as he squatted for cover. D-

Roc stuck his hand over the trunk of the car, and squeezed off a few rounds. When he popped up he took another one of Mills 40 caliber slugs. His arm felt like it was on fire as the bullet entered his bicep. Lucky for him, Mills ran out of bullets. D-Roc took advantage of that, and continued squeezing off shots from his gloc nine. Mills dove in the car, as Peko covered him, emptying the eleven shot clip from his Smith and Wesson. D-Roc ran behind another car for cover, and Shawn raised out the window splashing with his Ruger as Peko pulled away. D-Roc popped off a few times as Peko bent the corner. "get the fuck up and take me to the hospital." D-Roc yelled at Tasha, who was still on the ground covering her head. D-Roc hadn't crossed paths with Mills in over a month. He couldn't believe he was caught slipping, but the argument he was in with Tasha distracted him. If he wasn't checking to see if there were any police in sight, before he popped her in the mouth, he would have never seen the car zipping through the red light behind them. Mills, Peko and Shawn Shawn had the last shot today, but D-Roc promised himself that the next time they traded shots, he'd be the opener and the closer.

Summer was finally here, and at seventy five degrees, the weather couldn't have been better for L's return to the real world. L's loved all the respect Pimp had gained in his absence. Pimp was serving weight, and bundles of boys. And every corner he and L's bent his name was being screamed. Pimp gave L's the low down on the boy game, and caught him up on all the beefs he buried in the last nine months. By the time they reached 18th Street, L's was up to date, and ready to play his position. "So how we gone handle things now Pimp?" L's asked while enjoying his first time passing his ace a blunt. "Like we always do it… together, We family. All I got is you and my big bro, it aint nothing we can't accomplish together. We bout to get rich bro." Pimp said as he inhaled the hydro smoke. While Pimp and L's walked up 18th Street, Rio and his young homie Tiger were rolling in Rio's low key mobile. Rio did all his hustling out of the old school Cutlass. He named it brown bomber, after its ugly brown paint job. Tiger was a youngster who sold heroin and crack. He copped his boy from Pimp, and his crack from Rio. Tiger was where Rio heard most of the stories of the notorious Pimp, and as they rolled through the streets now, Tiger was at it again. "I'm telling you big homie, he done took Long Street over, if a mutha fucka selling boy they getting it from Pimp and he a young nigga like my age getting that one kind of paper." Tiger said as he puffed on the blunt. "Yeah I been hearing about him a lot in the streets, but I aint never seen the lil nigga, it's like he ghost or something." Rio said "Yeah he be ducked off in those boy spots, he got like three of them shits, he here one day, there the next, and over there the next." Tiger said while using his hands to point all over the place. Rio burst into laughter as he hit 18th Street. Tiger was surely fascinated with this Pimp guy. Tiger spotted Pimp and L's leaning up against Pimp's Lexus. "There go Pimp right there Tiger said. Rio stared through the tint as Tiger pointed Pimp out. Rio almost hit a parked car as he stared at Mills little brother Jimmy. Rio fumbled with his cell phone as he quickly called Mills.

ঌ৽ঌ ঌ৽ঌ ⑧ ⑧ ⑧ ⑧ ⑧ ঌ৽ঌ ঌ৽ঌ

Meanwhile, Mills sat in a booth staring at Fella through the glass as the guards escorted him to an unexpected visit. When Fella reached the booth, he couldn't believe his eyes. His mother and lawyer told him everything Mills was doing for him, but Mills also told his mother not to give him his number. Mills wasn't being nasty, he just didn't want to talk to Fella over the phone, because he knew Fella's calls were being monitored. He knew he'd visit him one day, but he just didn't know when. Mills and Fella grabbed the phone at the same time. "What's up bro." they said in unison. It was a moment of silence then Mills spoke. "Man aint nothing changed still grinding, and tryna stay away from the law." "I can dig it." Fella said. "So how things looking in the court room?" Mills asked. "A lot better thanks to you." Fella explained. "Don't worry about it bro, I told you if you ever needed me, I'd be there for you, a lot has changed between us, and I don't know if things will ever go back to the way they used to be, but It'll take more than what happened between us, for my loyalty to you to die. I got cha back like I'm following you bro." Mills said. His words caused Fella to drop his head. Fella allowed his greed for street fame to cost him everything. His one true friend, and possibly his life. He and Mills conversed for another fifteen minutes. He caught Mills up on the ups and downs of his case, and Mills caught him up on the streets, including the rift with D-Roc and Walt. When Mills spoke of his baby brother, Fella's mind went straight to the scene of Jimmy shooting at the robbers on Oak Street. "Mills listen bro, first I apologize for not telling you sooner, but ya little bro in them streets deep." Fella explained. "What you mean

Fells, not my lil bro, my lil bro in school handling his biz." Mills said with authority. "T-Money listen man, I know you've been hearing about them lil niggas L's and Pimp?" "Yeah, but what that got to do with Jimmy?" Mills said. "Just think of the nick name we gave Jimmy when he was a youngin." Fella said. "J-Pimp!" Mills blurted out. "We named him J-Pimp, cause he was a chic magnet, I seen it with my own two eyes bro, D-Roc's lil freaks cousin was hooking us up with the low down on Pimp and L's, cause we was gone rob them niggas, but when I seen who it was, I cut that lick short ASAP. But then the wildest thing happened, as Jimmy and his dude came walking out the store, some guys was robbing they spot and Jimmy and his partner got to blazing on them boys, shit wig me out. Get yo lil bro before he fall too deep into the trap."

Mills couldn't believe his ears. He was angry at Fella for not telling him sooner. He thought of all the murders Pimp and L's name was on. Then his mind shot to the massacre on Linwood and Fulton. He rose from his seat without saying a word, and rushed out the county's visiting booth. He ran to his car, he was right on time too, the minutes meter had just ran out. He slid between the tint, removed his t-shirt, and pulled his vest over the top of his tank top, then pulled his t-shirt back on. Mills was in a rush but he couldn't forget about D-Roc and Walt. They'd take his life on sight, so he had to vest up, and stay strapped. As he pulled his 500 Benz into traffic, he reached for his cell, which sat on the passenger seat. Before he could dial his little bother's number, a call chimed in. "Yeah who dis?" Mills asked. "This Rio, where you at bro?" Rio said. "I can't talk right now, I'll get wit you later." Mills clicked Rio off before giving him a chance to say another word. He dialed Jimmy's number and Jimmy quickly answered. "What up?" "Where you at lil bro, I'm coming to get you, it's important." Mills replied. Jimmy couldn't let Mills come and get him. He and L's were sitting in one of his boy's spots, and Mills coming to pick him up anywhere around Long Street was a bad idea. He had to think quickly because he could hear the urgency in his brother's voice. "What's going on Mills, why you sound so serious?" Jimmy asked. "Cause this is a serious situation, now where you at?" Mills replied. "I'm with Leon and his mom, can she drop me off somewhere?" Jimmy was lying to his brother and Mills knew he was being lied to but he didn't have time to argue. "Meet me and Neesh's right now Jim." Jimmy didn't get a chance to respond, Mills hung up immediately after his demand. "what's up bro?" L's asked. "I don't know I think my bro is in some trouble." Pimp responded. "What kind of trouble?" "I don't know man, but c'mon you gotta drop me off at his girl's apartment, he wants me to meet him there, something aint right bro." Pimp said as they headed for his Lexus.

Mills was a wreck, he couldn't' believe he let his little brother fall victim to the streets. He neglected his responsibilities as an older brother, and as a guardian. If his brother is who he thinks he is, he had to get out of Columbus ASAP. Pimp's name ran through the streets, for over five murders. He couldn't imagine his little brother being a stone cold killer, but if he really was a spitting image of their father, then maybe he'd inherited his rage, temper and need for power. Mills thought of detective White and Detective Brown who had been harassing him and his crew since they were young. The detectives were persistent and lately they had been back on the prowl. They've been working hard to piece Buck's murder together, and the murder of the Detroit boys. If he knew the detectives as good as he did, they've already been informed of the names Pimp and L's that had been floating through the streets. He grabbed a screw driver from his night stand as he rammed through his dresser drawers. Mills was paranoid, and he easily broke a sweat, as he held a Mack Eleven in one hand and unscrewed the wall in his closet with the other. He laid the Mack by his feet, and removed his shirt, and vest. His tank top was drenched with sweat. He removed a duffle bag from the hole in the wall. He opened it up and glanced at the 50 kilos he'd got from Chico yesterday. He threw the bag on the bed. The sight of three million dollars and fifty kilos of pure cane made him more paranoid. He paced the floor with his Mack in his hand until he figured out what to put all the cash in. He ran downstairs and returned with some large trash bags. He piled the cash into the heavy duty garbage bags, and carried them along with a duffle bag of cane downstairs. Mills knew he owed Chico six more months, but he needed to get his brother, his woman, and their child on safe ground first. He'd give Chico his money and explain to him what was going on in his life, and ask him to let Peko take over for him. He was sure Peko would do his last six months for him. He'd leave Peko his clientele, and let him profit the 250,000 a month.

D-Roc and Walt sat in Walt's girlfriend complex bobbing their heads to Ja'rule, while smoking on a fat blunt, and taking a hit of coke before hitting the road. Neesh was driving up the street in her new Infiniti. She drove right by the Navigator, never noticing D-Roc and Walt behind the tint. "Look at that." D-Roc said as Neesh drove by. "That's

Mills little bitch aint it?" Walt asked. "Yes sir." D-Roc replied. "Follow that bitch Roc, I bet she going to her and Mills crib… lets go dawg." Walt said as he rushed D-Roc to pull off. D-Roc quickly caught up to her, as she pulled into her and Mills complex. D-Roc and Walt watched her park next to Mills Benz. "Looks like Mills got him some new wheels." D-Roc said. Neesh grabbed her backpack out the backseat, and hurried into the condo. "Pull over there." Walt said while pointing to a spot a few spaces down from Neesh's Infiniti. "We about to go get this one while we got it. I knew we would catch this nigga sooner or later." "That nigga got money and dope in there for sure." Walt said while checking his twin Desert Eagles.

When Neesh walked in the door, Mills was pacing the living room floor while taking strong puffs from his hydro filled blunt. Neesh looked at Mills in his sweaty wife beater, then she looked at the duffle bags full of drugs, and three heavy duty garbage bags filled with money. Mills held one Mack eleven in his hand, and another sat on the couch. "Mills what's wrong with you?" Neesh asked as she froze in the middle of the floor. "Bae shit fucked up right now, my lil bro may be in big trouble, he's on his way here, we got to leave town bae." Mills explained. Neesh was getting scared, and paranoid, but she tried to stay calm. "Okay baby, just calm down, and put the gun down, do you want Jimmy to see you like this, do you want him to see all this money and drugs? C'mere baby." Neesh said. She grabbed Mills in her arms, and removed the gun from his hands. "Let's sit down Mills, talk to me until your brother gets here, what's the problem?"

The front door hit the floor after two hard kicks. The fist one startled Mills and Neesh, but the second caused Mills to grab his gun off the couch. By the time he raised his weapon, D-Roc was coming through the front door. He spotted Mills and blasted shots immediately. The first bullet struck Mills in his shoulder knocking him backwards. Mills still sprayed off rapid shots from his Mack Eleven. D-Roc took a few shells in his midsection but continued to shoot back, hitting Mills in his gun hand. Walt burst through the door clapping with his twin Desert Eagles. He hit Mills in his stomach causing him to drop his weapon. From there Walt took control over the battle, he hit Mills a few more times knocking him to the floor. Mills hit the carpet hard, he couldn't move. He glanced to his left and noticed Neesh laying in a puddle of blood. He tried reaching for her hand as it rested on her protruding belly, but his arm wouldn't comply.

Outside, Pimp stopped his Lex at the entrance, he didn't want Mills to see how he arrived. When he exited the car, he noticed the condo door wide open. He couldn't tell, but a body appeared to be laid out in the doorway. He spotted Walt coming out of the house with two duffle bags in his hand. He took off running towards the condo with his browning nine in his hand. The closer he got the more he saw. Walt threw the bags in the back of the Navigator and then headed back to the condo for the final bag. Pimp let his nine roar from a distance. Hot ones tore through Walt's body dropping him immediately. One of his Desert Eagles flew from his hand. L's was right behind him, he didn't have a pistol, but that didn't stop him. As Pimp ran for the condo, L's spotted Walt reaching for his waist. L's picked up the Desert Eagle and finished him off before he could get off a shot. Pimp heard the shots and turned to see his partner standing over Walt's body with a forty four in hand. He knew L's had just saved his life. As he ran into the apartment, he stepped over D-Roc's dead body and ran to his brother's aid. Mills was leaking. "Fuck no, not my brother!" Pimp said to himself. L's came running in. He looked at three bodies laid out, and then he noticed the bag of cash next to the couch. "That nigga outside had two trash bags full of money, and a duffle bag full of coke in the backseat, I loaded that shit into the Lex." L's said. "That was my bro's shit L's, they was robbing my brother." Pimp said as tears ran down his cheek. "Jim…Jim…Jimmy." Neesh whispered. "Oh shit Neesh you still alive baby, don't worry we bout to get you and my brother out of here, don't' talk." Pimp said. L's come grab her, I'm a get my bro, we gotta get them to the hospital." L's scooped Neesh up with ease and said, "Bro, c'mon we gotta hurry up, the cops will be here in a minute." Pimp grabbed Mills car keys off the table, scooped his brother up, and rushed out the door behind L's. Put her in the front seat of my brother's Benz" Pimp yelled. L's put Neesh in the front seat and helped Mills in the back. Pimp watched Mills move his fingers as he laid across the backseat. "He moving his fingers L's my bro still got some fight in him. Grab those guns and that bag of money in the condo, put em in the Lex with the rest of that shit and let's bang out." Pimp ordered. L's rushed in the apartment and quickly returned with the guns and the bag of cash. "Keep fighting bro, don't you leave me now." Pimp said, as he looked down at his brother in the backseat. He pulled the Benz out, and sped out the complex with L's right behind him in the Lexus.

TO BE CONTINUED …